INTRODUCTION

Tumbling Blocks by Andrea Boeshaar
Elsa Fritch's dreams tumble from their heights when Shane Gerhard comes to town to fulfill the contract between their parents. Could God expect her to endure an arranged marriage with a man who antagonizes her and disregards Him?

Old Maid's Choice by Cathy Marie Hake
Betsy Larkin thinks she must choose between the siblings she is rearing and a man who loves her. Blacksmith Tyson Walker is used to bending iron, but can love, patience, and acceptance bend the iron will of a woman who is sure she is destined to be an old maid?

Jacob's Ladder by Pamela Kaye Tracy
Samantha Thomasohn dreams of riches and of escaping her mundane life, clerking for her father's store. One man holds the riches while another holds her heart. How is true love to be defined, and where will Samantha place her priorities?

Four Hearts by Sally Laity
Diana Montclair covers her loneliness with an arrogant exterior and a drive for perfection that keeps friends at bay. She reluctantly endures the weekly sewing circle. Can Mrs. T's words of truth and a newfound friend help her realize she has been seeking the needs of her heart in the wrong places?

the Sewing Circle

*One Woman's Mentoring Shapes Lives
in Four Stories of Love*

Andrea Boeshaar
Cathy Marie Hake
Sally Laity
Pamela Kaye Tracy

BARBOUR
PUBLISHING, INC.
Uhrichsville, Ohio

Tumbling Blocks ©2001 by Andrea Boeshaar.
Old Maid's Choice ©2001 by Cathy Marie Hake.
Jacob's Ladder ©2001 by Pamela Kaye Tracy.
Four Hearts ©2001 by Sally Laity.

Illustrations by Mari Goering.

ISBN 1-58660-135-0

All Scripture quotations, unless otherwise noted, are taken from the King James Version of the Bible.

Published by Barbour Publishing, Inc., P.O. Box 719, Uhrichsville, Ohio 44683 http://www.barbourbooks.com

 Member of the
Evangelical Christian
Publishers Association

Printed in the United States of America.

the Sewing Circle

Tumbling Blocks

by Andrea Boeshaar

Dedication

To Margaret Been—A Titus 2 woman.

———

Chapter 1

Early March, 1837

Feeling aggravated after his journey, but extremely grateful to have survived it, Shane Gerhard lifted his valise and stepped off the stern-wheeler. What a ride. He'd never experienced one like it in all his twenty-four years. Springtime meant high waters on the Mississippi and Ohio Rivers, high waters and swift currents. But Captain Butch Robertson hadn't seemed to mind either, and the crotchety old man had navigated his mail packet at full throttle in order to beat his competition's time—which wasn't anything to speak of, as far as Shane was concerned. Why, he could have walked to Hickory Corners from St. Louis in the time it had taken the steamboat to arrive.

Well, at least he was finally here. Sort of. He'd been told it was another mile into town. Shane chose to stretch his legs and make the trek on foot. Within ten minutes he passed a rustic-looking sign which read: WELCOME TO HICKORY CORNERS. He supposed this was it.

Looking around, he took in the modest, if not primitive sights of the small, Ohio village. It wasn't anything like the cosmopolitan city of St. Louis, with its paved, tree-lined avenues and majestic mansions, such as the one in which he'd been raised. Walking up a street, which ran perpendicular to the river, Shane decided his parents' home was bigger than Hickory Corners' boardinghouse, dress shop, and bank put together.

What am I doing? he asked himself for the umpteenth time as he stood across from the boardinghouse. This entire undertaking seemed incredible, if not downright absurd. But, of course, he knew all too well that if he didn't find and marry Elsa Fritch, a resident of this sorry excuse for a town, he'd never get his inheritance.

"And she's probably some homely spinster with a long, pointy nose and buck teeth," he grumbled, crossing the dirt road. But a moment later, he reminded himself that a long, pointy nose and buck teeth were nothing compared to a half a million dollars. For that amount of money, he'd marry his next door neighbor's hound dog. Of course, it wouldn't be a real marriage; he'd have to pay Miss Fritch a tidy sum for her trouble. Then, after the wedding, he didn't care where she resided. Here in Hickory Corners or Paris, France, it mattered little to him. All Shane wanted was the wealth rightfully due him, and he didn't think he would ever forgive his deceased parents for including this most unfair stipulation in their will.

Shane pushed aside his tumultuous thoughts and entered the boardinghouse. One sweeping glance of the place told him this was no palace. To his right, several rough-hewn tables and benches stood in the midst of what was obviously the dining common. Not much in the way of art to admire on the unfinished, plank walls.

"*Guten Morgen,*" greeted an elderly, gray-haired man, perched behind a long counter to Shane's left. His face was wrinkled, etched by time, and his blue eyes resembled dull marbles. "Nice vetter ve are having, *ja?*"

"Yes, Sir. Nice weather." Shane immediately recognized the man's dialect, since his own parents had emigrated from Germany years before his birth. While he didn't speak the language fluently, he understood enough to get by. He removed his hat. "Can I get a room?"

"*Ja,* sure. How long vill you stay?"

"Not long. . .hopefully."

The man, dressed in an ivory homespun linen shirt and brown pants supported by suspenders, pulled out a ledger. When he quoted the price for a night's stay, including meals, Shane almost laughed aloud. It was a mere pittance compared to the hotels he'd grown accustomed to in the bigger cities, like New Orleans, Chicago, and New York.

Shane penned his name and paid for a week's lodging.

"Gerhard. . .from St. Louis," the old guy read from the ledger. Next he eyed Shane curiously. "Related to Georg Gerhard, *ja?*"

"Yes." Shane brought his chin back, surprised. "I am his son."

The man's lined face brightened. "I am Arne Fritch!" He shook his head in disbelief. "*Gueter!* Dis is amazing! Do you know me?" He thumped his chest in question. "I know you. I know your vater. Ve ver gute friends. Elsa! Elsa!" he called up the narrow stairwell. "*Kommen sie her!*"

Shane stood there, feeling stunned by the series of events. So, this was Arne Fritch, Elsa's father. Elsa Fritch, the woman he had to marry in order to receive his inheritance. Shane rubbed a hand over his stubbled jaw. He hadn't meant to present himself to the Fritches, looking like some vagabond. And after days on the steamboat without a bath and a close shave, Shane felt even more unkempt than he appeared.

"Elsa! Elsa!"

"I'm coming, Papa."

Shane heard her footfalls on the steps before he ever saw the young woman. When she appeared at the base of the staircase, Shane sucked in a breath, then grinned. *Not bad. Not bad at all. . .*

Elsa Fritch wasn't anything like he'd imagined. She had walnut-colored hair and he bet it felt as soft and smelled as clean as it looked. Her sparkling, indigo eyes were like none he'd ever seen on a woman. They reminded him of untouched pools of deep, deep blue, like the hue of a quiet lake on a cloudless summer day. Her full lips were perfectly shaped and watermelon-pink, just waiting to be kissed, and even her plain brown dress with its starched white apron couldn't hide her buxom figure.

Shane swallowed hard.

"What is it, Papa?" she asked, looking concerned. She glanced at Shane and gave him a perfunctory smile before turning back to her father again.

"Dis is Shane Gerhard," the old man said excitedly. "Gerhard. From St. Louis."

Elsa's expression changed to one of interest. "You mean the same Gerhards who sponsored us?"

"Ja, ja! Dey sponsored our journey to America."

"Oh. . ." The young lady stepped forward. "Pleased to meet you, Mr. Gerhard," she stated in a honey-sounding voice that coated his insides. "I've heard much about your family."

"The pleasure is mine, Miss Fritch," he replied with a smile. Moments later, he frowned. "It is Miss, isn't it?" The notion suddenly struck Shane that perhaps she had already married someone else. Of course, that would be in violation of the contract the Fritches had made with his folks some sixteen years ago.

But to his relief, she blushed and shook her head. "No, it's Miss."

Shane grinned.

"But not for long. I'm betrothed."

He felt his smile fade. "Is that right?"

Elsa nodded while Shane glanced at Arne. He wondered why the older man had consented to his daughter's engagement when he'd signed a legal document, stating she was to wed Shane as a settlement for his family's passage to this country. Had Arne Fritch forgotten his pact? He better not have. Shane's fortune depended on his marrying Elsa.

"Will you be staying with us here at our boardinghouse, Mr. Gerhard?"

He swung his gaze back to hers. "Ah, yes. . .yes, I will."

"We're honored, aren't we, Papa?"

"Ja. It vill be gute to visit." Arne grinned broadly.

"Did you arrive by stage?" Elsa further inquired.

"Packet."

"I see. Well, you must be very tired. May I show you to your room?"

"That'd be great."

"Papa, can I have the key to Mr. Gerhard's room?"

"Key?" The old man looked confused. "Vhat is. . .key?"

"Schluessel, Papa. Key. . .to unlock the door to Mr. Gerhard's room."

"Oh, *ja, ja*. . .da key."

Elsa gave Shane an embarrassed smile. "Papa is often forgetful these days."

"*Ja*, sometimes my memory fails me," the older man agreed.

Shane nodded his understanding, then followed the comely young woman to the second floor and down a narrow, but carpeted hallway. The walls were whitewashed and, after Elsa opened up the bedroom, Shane decided things seemed clean and orderly, from the simple, pearly cotton spread on the bed, to the wooden shutters, opened now to allow the sunshine in.

"Thank you, Miss Fritch. I'm sure I'll be quite comfortable here."

"Please let me know if I can be of further assistance."

Shane set down his valise, pivoted, and grinned. "I will."

She turned to go, then paused just outside the doorway. "Um. . .if you don't mind me asking. . .what brings you to Hickory Corners? We're not really on the way to anywhere."

Shane chuckled. "True enough. The fact is, I have business with you and your parents."

"Oh. . ." Elsa looked troubled. "My mother's in Glory—"

"Excuse me?"

"Heaven."

"Ah, she's dead. I'm sorry to hear that."

"Don't be," Elsa said with a gentle smile. "As I said, she's with the Lord in heaven."

Shane rubbed the back of his neck. He never enjoyed discussing religion.

"And Papa, well. . ." Elsa peered to her right, down the hallway. "Papa's mind hasn't been quite right ever since Mama died. Perhaps you could state your business and I could help you."

"That suits me fine. It's really you I'm concerned with."

"Me?" Elsa's dark brows knitted together in consternation.

Shane reached into his overcoat and produced the document he'd been handed by his parents' attorney. "Can you read?"

"Yes, and quite well, thank you."

With a wry grin, he handed her the contract. "This explains my, um, dilemma. You see, Miss Fritch, you are its resolution."

Opening the document, Elsa began to read while Shane watched her expression closely. Though she did her best to conceal her shock at its content, he saw Elsa's chin quiver ever so slightly.

"Mr. Gerhard, I don't know what to say."

"That's easy. Say you agree to the two of us getting hitched."

"But, I'm betrothed."

"Yeah, to me. Ever since you were four years old and I was eight."

Elsa took a step back at his harsh tone, and Shane immediately regretted losing his temper.

"Forgive me," he said. "It's been a long trip, and I'm not exactly thrilled with this setup myself. I never knew a contract between our parents existed until my folks' untimely deaths eight months ago."

"I see."

Shane didn't think she really did. "I cannot acquire my inheritance until the contract is fulfilled, and Miss Fritch, I have every intention of claiming what's mine. . .including you."

She gasped, then paled. "There must be some mistake."

"Yes, I had hoped so too. But, unfortunately, that contract

in your hands is legal and binding and must be executed in order for me to get my money. Lady," he said, inching closer to her, "I want my money. It's all my parents left to me, but it'll see me through life quite nicely. And there's some for you too."

"I don't want your money. I cannot marry you."

"Yes, you can. And you will."

"I won't."

"You will, or—"

"Or what? You'll shoot me?"

Shane saw her glance at the sleek pistol he habitually wore at his hip. He'd bought the weapon after getting robbed in a gambling den in New Orleans a few years ago.

Elsa shook her head. "I'm not afraid to die, so go ahead and shoot."

Little imp, he thought as aggravation coursed through his veins. "Look, Miss Fritch, the contract," he said, pulling it from her grasp, "is a binding, legal document."

"You said that already."

He ignored the remark. "It means you and I do not have a choice in the matter. We have to get married."

"Then I will go to jail."

Shane rolled his eyes. How could he make her understand? "It's not that simple."

"All right, all right. I will speak to my father about this matter, and if I must, I will ask our sheriff here in Hickory Corners about it. . .this contract," she all but spat.

Her cheeks were flushed, and Shane thought he could relate to her indignation.

"I understand your anger and upset, Miss Fritch," Shane stated, fighting to keep his voice calm. "I felt angry too. But I hired attorneys in St. Louis to check and recheck this document, and they couldn't find a loophole. I doubt your small-town sheriff will know what to do about it."

Elsa looked like she was about to burst into tears. "But I don't want to marry you."

"I don't want to marry you, either."

"Then let's pretend we never saw this document."

Shane chuckled at her ignorance. "Honey, I'd love to, but there's half a million bucks waiting for me as soon as you and I say, 'I do.' Now, look, I've got a plan. I'll give you ten thousand dollars, and you can go your merry way and forget all about me after the ceremony. How's that?"

Elsa shook her head. "No."

"Well, all right," Shane drawled, "how's twenty thousand?"

"Mr. Gerhard, you could not persuade me to marry you for two million dollars."

"Well, three is out of my price range," he quipped.

Else gave him a look of utter disgust. "You insolent man! No amount of money will do. Don't you know marriage is sacred before God? He created it and designed it to be a beautiful thing between two people who love each other. It's not something you can buy."

Shane shrugged. "Guess I'll die tryin', then."

"Elsa! Elsa!" Arne's voice was filled with concern as he called to her. "Elsa, vhat is happening up dere dat you are shouting like a fishmonger?"

"I'm not shouting, Papa!" she shouted.

Shane laughed at the irony, and Elsa's cheeks flamed when she realized it herself.

"We'll talk later," he said with a wink. "*Schatz.*"

She inhaled sharply. "I am not your. . .sweetheart. How dare you call me that!"

"Elsa. . . ?"

"Coming, Papa," she said, softening her voice. Then, after tossing Shane a scathing look, she made haste down the hallway.

Shane closed the door, leaning against it, grinning. *This might be fun,* he thought.

But one thing was sure—he meant to marry Elsa Fritch, and he would not leave this little hole-in-the-wall town until he succeeded.

Chapter 2

*N*ein, *nein,*" Arne said, shaking his head. "I paid Georg Gerhard."

"Are you sure? You paid him?" Suddenly the hysteria that had been brewing inside Elsa all afternoon began to dissipate. "So there's no outstanding debt and I don't have to marry Shane Gerhard?"

"Ja, das right."

Elsa blew out a breath of relief and continued kneading the bread dough in the kitchen while her father sat at the small table and sipped coffee. He'd just awakened from his afternoon nap and this was the first time Elsa had been able to discuss the matter with him. "Well, it sounds like a misunderstanding," she said. "You and Mama made a contract with the Gerhards after they sponsored us, but later you discovered they made strong drink—beer."

"Ja, und I paid Georg und told him no daughter uf mine marries into a family makin' sinful beer."

Elsa worked her lower lip between her teeth, trying to put all the pieces into place. "The Gerhards had been good friends of yours in Germany, is that right, Papa?"

He nodded. "But Vanda und I," he said, referring to his

deceased wife, "never knew about da strong drink—und da Gerhards got rich makin' it."

"Despicable." Elsa didn't like Shane Gerhard, and this latest discovery only intensified her negative feelings. Of all the nerve. The man should have made sure of his facts before storming into a person's life and demanding she marry him.

Dividing the dough, Elsa shaped it and put it into two pans, then slipped them on to the iron rack in the hearth. Now to finish supper. Henry Peabody, her fiancé, was coming, and as always, she wanted to display her culinary skills. They would marry next month and live here at the boardinghouse so Elsa could continue to look after her father. Henry disliked the idea, but what else could she do? Her father needed her. With each passing day, he became more and more forgetful.

"I cannot believe da Gerhards are dead," Arne said mournfully, staring into his cup. "Such a shame."

"Yes, I'm sure it is."

"Georg und Lise ver younger dan me. Dey ver your mutter's age. I vas an old man vhen I married Vanda, und yet I outlived her. . .und da Gerhards."

"Don't despair. Mama's in heaven, and I'm glad I have you still around." She glanced over her shoulder at her aging father who looked so forlorn, she felt tears stinging her own eyes. "Were the Gerhards believers?"

"Oh, *ja*. But dey still made da beer."

"I don't think their son is a Christian."

"Nein?"

"No. He said rude things to me, Papa."

"Vhat did he say?"

Elsa swallowed down the last of her indignation. "He called me. . .*schatz*."

Her father's guffaw filled the warm, steamy room.

"It's not funny, Papa." Elsa gave him a stern look and he managed to wipe the smirk off his face. "I think you should speak to him about his manners."

"*Nein.* Young Shane is, like your brother Herrick, teasing you."

Elsa sighed and gave up the cause. All her life she'd felt like there was no one in the world to protect her. Why should things change now that she was twenty years old? In school, if the boys goaded her, Mama used to cluck her tongue and tell Elsa to ignore the jeering. She said the boys were "sweet" on her, and that's why they harassed her so. Papa always chuckled and told her to be proud of her ample bosom, causing Elsa to feel even more self-conscious about her full figure. Why couldn't God have made her tiny and slender like Betsy Larkin, one of the young ladies at Mrs. Tidewell's Tuesday afternoon sewing circle? Betsy, with her golden-blond hair, brown eyes, and petite frame was everything Elsa wished for in her own physical appearance. Instead, Elsa stood five feet and six inches—as tall as Henry!

"Anybody home?"

Elsa cringed. He'd only been in Hickory Corners four hours and already she'd grown to recognize and despise the sound of Shane Gerhard's deep voice. To further her animosity, the man walked into her kitchen uninvited, and if there was one thing Elsa couldn't abide, it was a man in her kitchen. She tolerated her papa's presence, but only because the Bible instructed her to "honor thy father. . ."

"Sure smells good in here."

"Hungry, young Shane?" Arne asked with a wry grin.

"Sure am. I haven't had a decent meal in over a week."

"Vell, Elsa is da best cook in town."

Stirring her pot of stew over the open hearth, she refused to look in Shane's direction.

"From what my nose is telling me," he said, "I'm inclined to believe it."

"Sit. Sit," Arne invited. "Elsa, make our guest something to eat."

"The stew will be done in an hour," she replied curtly.

"*Nein*, make him something now."

"Aw, that's all right, Mr. Fritch, I can wait."

Without even so much as a glance, Elsa knew her father was frowning at her disobedience. But she couldn't seem to help it.

"I imagine your daughter told you why I came to town," Shane said.

"*Ja*, und I told her dat I paid your vater da money he put up to bring us to America."

"You paid him?" There was a note of incredulity in Shane's voice.

"*Ja*, dere is no contract. Your vater made strong drink, und I vould not allow my Elsa to be a part of such sin."

Slowly, she turned from the large, bubbling, black kettle to glimpse Shane's reaction.

"My father owned a brewery."

"*Ja*, das right."

"What do you mean to call it sin? I don't understand."

"Da Bible says woe upon dem who is givin' der neighbor strong drink. Breweries make und sell it, und da people get drunk. Drunk is a sin too. It hurts people, makes dem sick."

Shane shifted, appearing uncomfortable. Then he glanced at Elsa who nodded.

"Well, before you condemn me," he said on a harsh note, "let me just put things into perspective for you. I wasn't the one who started the business. My father did—and I didn't even inherit it. My oldest brother, Edwin, is now president of Gerhard and Sons Brewery. My second oldest brother, Frederick, was awarded my parents' estate. Being the youngest of three boys, I got a handsome sum of money, except I can't get my hands on it until this contract is satisfied." Shane pulled out the same folded piece of paper Elsa had read earlier. "I don't suppose you'd have receipts, Mr. Fritch, or something showing that you paid my father."

"Receipts? *Ja*, I got 'em."

Shane smiled broadly, revealing strong white, even teeth, and Elsa had to admit he was a handsome man, but in a rugged sort of way. He certainly wasn't her kind of man and, goodness, but his dark-blond hair could use a good trimming. The tendrils hanging past his collar and over his ears gave Shane a reckless appearance.

Suddenly, he glanced her way, his hazel eyes alight with gladness, and Elsa returned a tiny smile.

"I am as relieved as you are, Mr. Gerhard," she assured him.

"Well, now, I meant no offense," he explained. "I'm just not a marrying man, but if I were, I'm sure—"

"I am already betrothed."

"Oh, right. . ."

Papa rose from the wooden chair. "I go to find da letters uf payment from Georg."

Elsa watched her father saunter into their family's quarters off the kitchen before she turned and resumed supper preparations.

Shane cleared his throat. "Um, I guess I was a bit brash this afternoon."

"A bit?" Elsa replied, keeping her back to him. "I would say you behaved like a rogue."

Shane laughed. "I've been called worse."

His mocking tone grated on her nerves, and Elsa deliberated on what name she would really like to call him—none being very Christian-like.

"I'll tell you what, Miss Elsa Fritch. How 'bout I apologize for my knavish conduct, and we begin anew?"

Cautiously, she turned around.

"Don't look so suspicious." With a charming smile, Shane stood and bowed. "I am sincerely sorry for offending you this afternoon. I was just having a bit of fun. Of course, I did want my inheritance—still do—but I reckon I wasn't thinking clearly. Now that I've rested up some, I can see the error of my ways. Please forgive me."

"I think you have rehearsed that speech one too many times, Mr. Gerhard."

He replied with a wounded expression. "I'm quite serious, I assure you."

Elsa didn't believe him, and she certainly didn't want to accept his apology. However, she knew it was her Christian duty. "All right, I forgive you."

"Why, thank you."

It was then that Papa appeared at the doorway. "Elsa, vhere is da box uf important papers I keep by my desk?"

"I don't know. It should be there, Papa."

"I don't know. . ." He shook his head, frowning heavily. "I cannot find it."

"May I help you locate it, Mr. Fritch? Elsa says there's

time before supper." Shane swung his gaze around and winked. "I believe she said we have an hour before we eat."

"Yes, that's right," Elsa replied, feeling somewhat flustered all of a sudden.

"*Ja*, come und help me, young Shane."

"My pleasure," he said, crossing the kitchen. Then he paused in mid-stride and glanced at Elsa. "Now, I don't mean that personally."

She stifled a grin. "I will be praying you find those receipts. . .very soon."

Sixty-five minutes later, the table was set, the stew and bread were done, and now Elsa was watching out the window for Henry, her arms folded in front of her. Papa and Shane were still scouring his bedroom for any letter of release that might prove the contract was no longer in effect. But the longer they turned up nothing, the more Elsa began to fret.

"Oh, Papa, what did you do with those papers?" she muttered just as Henry came walking up to the front door. Henry, a clerk at Montclair's Shipping Office just up the street, wore round, wire spectacles, and kept his light-brown hair neatly parted and combed.

Elsa ran to the door to greet him. "I'm so glad to see you," she said, helping her fiancé off with his overcoat.

He cleared his throat. "I'm glad to see you too. Do you think you could rub the back of my neck? It's been bothering me since I woke up this morning."

"Of course. Come and sit down."

"And my head is throbbing."

"You poor man," Elsa cooed. Once Henry was seated on the wooden benches, she kneaded his neck and shoulders.

"Not so rough, Elsa."

"I'm so sorry," she replied, lightening up her touch.

"Why are there four places set tonight?" Henry asked.

"We have a guest."

At that very moment, Shane and her father ambled through the kitchen.

"Did you find what you were looking for?" she asked hopefully.

"Nein," Papa replied, looking disappointed. "But I know I have dose receipts somevhere."

"What receipts?"

"Oh, nothing, Henry dear," Elsa said quickly. She looked at Shane and silently pleaded with him not to divulge the circumstances. She saw his head dip in subtle acquiescence. "I'll fetch supper. Papa, why don't you introduce the two men."

"Ja, I can do dat."

In the kitchen, Elsa ladled the stew into thick, wooden bowls, then sliced the fresh bread and put in on a platter. Next she filled a pitcher with fresh milk before placing everything on a large tray. Hoisting it above her right shoulder, she carried their meal into the dining room.

Seeing her approach, Shane jumped up from his seat and rushed to her aid, taking the tray from her.

"I can manage," she assured him even though he had already set it down on the table.

Shane gave her a quizzical glance. "Women should not carry anything heavy."

Elsa laughed softly. "I carry heavy things all the time. Please, Mr. Gerhard, make yourself comfortable and enjoy your meal."

"I plan to. It looks wonderful."

Feeling oddly pleased by the compliment, Elsa took her

place beside Henry. She felt more at ease, probably because her fiancé was here to force Shane Gerhard into behaving himself for a change.

"Papa, will you ask the blessing?"

Shane listened to the old man pray, thanking God for the food and for Elsa's capable hands that prepared it. Shane remembered as a young boy hearing his parents pray. They were Christians, like Elsa and her father. But over the years, his parents' faith seemed to wane, and Shane figured religion wasn't all that important. They had never talked to him about God. He was Someone who had an omnipresence—similar to the portrait of Shane's grand-father that hung on the wall by the stairwell in his folks' mansion. The painting was there in the background, but no one really paid much attention to it, and that's how Shane viewed God—just sort of there and everywhere, but who needed Him?

"Would you care for some bread, Mr. Gerhard?"

Shane snapped from his reverie. "Don't mind if I do, Miss Fritch. Thank you." He took a slice off the plate she held out to him.

As he ate, enjoying every savory bite, he glanced from her to Henry Peabody and wondered what Elsa saw in the man. He resembled a scrawny little weasel and didn't talk. . .he whined.

"I think I'm getting another cold. My throat is sore again."

"You poor thing," Elsa murmured in a motherly tone. "Must be your quinsy acting up."

"Quinsy?" Shane sure hoped it wasn't contagious.

"Severe tonsillitis," Henry informed him. "Doc calls it quinsy."

"Oh. . ." Shane chanced a look at Arne, who seemed oblivious to everything around him as he spooned his dinner into his mouth.

Several seconds of uncomfortable silence ticked by.

"So, Mr. Peabody," Shane began, attempting small talk, "did I understand Mr. Fritch to say you're employed at a shipping company?"

"Yes, and I hate my job. My eyes get so tired looking at numbers all day long. From sunup to sundown."

Elsa gave her fiancé a sympathetic smile, while Shane wagged his head at the pitiful scene.

They don't even look good together, he thought, harboring an amused grin. *Elsa has larger biceps.*

The meal proceeded, and Shane couldn't help feeling things were all wrong between the couple. Of course, he was no expert, but he had a good set of eyes. Why didn't Arne see it? Was he really going to allow his daughter to marry a dandy like Henry Peabody? Elsa needed a real man.

Well, it wasn't any of his business. What did he care? All Shane wanted was his inheritance and as soon as he finished supper, he planned to help old Arne find those letters of receipt. After that, Shane would hop on the next packet leaving Hickory Corners, and he'd never look back.

Chapter 3

S hane didn't enjoy getting up early. Since his college days, he'd grown accustomed to parties until the wee hours of the morning, then sleeping until at least noon. But here he was, up with the sun, no doubt because he'd gone to bed shortly after supper last night. Did all of Hickory Corners close after dark? Why, Arne said there wasn't even a saloon in town!

Walking across the room, Shane grasped the white, porcelain pitcher and poured water into the matching basin on his bureau. He washed quickly, shaved, splashed on some musky-smelling tonic, and ran a comb through his hair. After dressing, he ambled downstairs where he found the dining common vacant, but delicious aromas wafted to his nostrils from the kitchen. His stomach rumbled at the smell of fried ham, biscuits, and brewing coffee, and Shane began heading in that direction before he could give the matter a second thought.

Entering the kitchen, he found Elsa standing precariously on the service counter and peering into the uppermost part of the ceiling-high cupboard.

He stepped closer. "G'morning."

She gasped, turning. As she did so, she lost her balance

and fell backward. Shane rushed forward and caught her easily enough.

"Oh, *mein Schreck!*" she exclaimed with wide, startled blue eyes. "I felt so scared."

"I've got you." He grinned. "Must be my lucky day."

"Lucky day?"

"Sure. It's not every day a lovely lady falls right into my arms."

Elsa gave him a look of reproof. "Put me down at once."

More than a little amused, Shane complied with her wishes and set her feet on the plank floor.

With crimson cheeks, Elsa smoothed down the skirt of her brown dress. She'd worn the same outfit yesterday, causing Shane to wonder if she ever changed clothes. Where he came from, women had morning gowns, afternoon gowns, traveling gowns, evening gowns, and ball gowns. But for the second day in a row, Elsa had worn her simple brown frock with its white apron.

"Thank you for breaking my fall," she muttered.

"My pleasure." Shane leaned against the adjacent service counter and folded his arms. Despite her rudimentary attire, he decided he enjoyed watching Elsa and he took to wondering what her hair would look like if she freed it from its pinning.

"Breakfast will be ready shortly."

"Great. I'm starved." Shane paused while Elsa busied herself with slicing more ham. "So what were you looking for up there? Maybe I can help you."

"I was searching for the receipts from your father," she said over one shoulder. "I thought, perhaps Papa had put them up in the cupboard for safekeeping."

"I see. Would you like me to check?"

Elsa shook her head. "The shelf is empty. I was able to see that much before you walked into my kitchen unannounced and scared me half to death."

Shane chuckled. "My humble apologies."

Elsa glared at him, her expression incredulous.

"And don't worry," he continued, "I reckon those receipts will turn up. . .if they really exist."

"Of course they really exist. Papa wouldn't lie."

"I wasn't implying he would. After spending time with your papa yesterday afternoon, I'm confident he speaks the truth. Of course, the question still remains as to why my father never changed his will if the debt had been paid."

"Yes, I thought of that myself."

"I probably won't ever learn the answer to that one," Shane mumbled remorsefully. Now that his parents were dead, there were suddenly so many questions he wanted to ask them, about their faith—and about this contemptible contract!

Returning his gaze to Elsa, Shane thought she appeared fretful herself, and he suddenly longed to change the subject. He preferred to see a little fire in Elsa's eyes, rather than distress.

"Let me ask you something," he began mischievously.

"Yes?"

"Say I was Mr. Quinsy a few minutes ago. . ."

"Who?"

"Your fiancé—the guy with the quinsy."

Elsa huffed with indignation and set her hands on her rounded hips.

"Well, I was just trying to imagine him catching you falling from the service counter."

"And?" she asked with an annoyed expression.

"And I think you'd squish him like a bug." Shane grinned broadly as her gaze sparked, and he thought she looked so pretty, all pink-cheeked and furious.

"Get out of my kitchen before I squish you like a bug!"

Shane chuckled. "Well, now, Honey, you're sure welcome to try—squishing me, that is."

"Get out!"

"I don't suppose I could get a cup of coffee first."

Elsa reached for the closest thing to her, which happened to be an earthenware bowl, and hurled it at Shane. Having anticipated her reaction, he ducked just in time. The bowl hit the doorjamb with a thud before crashing to the floor in pieces.

"Whoo-wee, you've got some temper there, little lady," Shane remarked with a laugh.

"What's going on? Elsa? What's all the racket?"

Her eyes grew wide with horror. "It's Henry," she whispered. "I don't want him to know how angry I got."

Shane quickly scooped up the sections of earthenware from the floor and handed them to Elsa. When Henry arrived at the doorway, Shane donned a well-practiced look of innocence.

"Miss Fritch just, um, dropped her mixing bowl, and I was just about to help myself to a cup of coffee. How 'bout you? Coffee?"

"Yes, but Elsa always pours it," the smaller man whined. He glanced from her to Shane, wearing a curious frown. "Elsa doesn't approve of men in her kitchen."

"Aw, that's just an ugly rumor," Shane quipped, giving her a little wink.

She ignored him. "Why don't you both have a seat in the dining room and I'll take care of the coffee." Walking to the open hearth in the corner of the kitchen, she added, "Papa should return from his morning walk momentarily. When he does, I'll serve breakfast."

Shane figured he'd tried Elsa's patience enough for the time being, and without another word, he followed Henry into the dining common.

Elsa's hands trembled as she pulled the pan of biscuits from the iron rack in the hearth. She felt angry, afraid, and humiliated all at once. Angry at Shane Gerhard's insufferable remarks about her and Henry, afraid because he was right about squishing poor Henry like a bug, and humiliated that Shane could antagonize her to the point where she lost her self-control.

Lord, I'm not much of a witness for You this morning, am I? she thought. But in the next moment, she remembered that today was Tuesday and she'd see her friends at Mrs. Tidewell's house for their weekly sewing circle. Elsa decided the meeting would surely put her in a right spirit, and perhaps Mrs. T would offer a piece of advice. Being the pastor's wife, the older woman was good for suggesting godly remedies from the Bible.

Feeling heartened by the idea of escaping the boarding-house and Shane Gerhard, Elsa gloved one hand with a thick, quilted pad, took hold of the hot coffee pot, grabbed two cups with her other, and strode into the dining room. She found both men reading the newspaper. With-out a single glance at Shane, Elsa poured the dark, steaming brew. Afterward, she walked several feet to the box stove, placing the pot on its top to keep warm.

Back in the kitchen, she fried six fresh eggs in the same skillet as the ham, and when she finally heard her father's voice, she served up the meal.

"Won't you be joining us, Miss Fritch?" Shane asked lightly.

Elsa marveled at the man's audacity. "No, I'm not. . . hungry," she stated, looking at the tips of her worn, brown leather shoes. Then she made haste back into the sanctity of the kitchen.

Minutes later, as she sipped a cup of tea at the small, scarred, wooden table, Elsa wondered over the events of the morning. Shane had called her "little." He'd said, ". . .you've got some temper there, little lady." Elsa hadn't been described as "little" since. . .well, she couldn't recall the last time that word and her name had appeared in the same sentence. Always, Elsa had been bigger than her girlfriends and most boys, until later in her teenage years when almost all the young men in her class had grown taller than she. Still, Elsa had never felt "little" around them.

Oddly, however, in Shane's presence she could nearly imagine herself as such. He'd caught her when she'd fallen and his arms under her knees and around her waist had been strong—strong enough to hold her. Shane hadn't even appeared strained, and Elsa clearly remembered how nice he smelled and how muscular his shoulders felt beneath her palm as she'd clung to him. His hazel-eyed gaze seemed to penetrate her own, and that rakish smile of his. . .

Elsa gave herself a mental shake, and reined in her wayward musings. She was engaged and ought not think of any other man but Henry in such an intimate way.

She sighed, steering her thoughts toward today's sewing circle. She was in desperate need of the spiritual uplifting she'd find there. But poor Mrs. Tidewell certainly had her work cut out for her!

Chapter 4

A nd he says the most outrageous things to me," Elsa lamented as she continued to enlighten her sewing circle of this latest travesty in the form of Shane Gerhard. While she spoke, her needle went in and out of the pieced-together fabric beneath her fingertips. The quilt pattern on which all five young ladies around her worked was called Tumbling Blocks, and Elsa couldn't help but think how the intricate design described her life right now. Tumbling. And all because of one arrogant, highfalutin man from St. Louis who wanted to kick her dreams of marrying Henry right out from under her for his own selfish purposes.

"Elsa, my dear, I don't think you should have thrown the bowl at him," Clara Bucey remarked from her corner of the quilt. She was Charlotte Warner's niece, and everyone in town admired the Widow Warner's commitment to charity. A slim gal with light-brown hair and brown eyes, Clara was following in her aunt's footsteps. "Losing one's temper just isn't ladylike, nor is it Christian."

"I'm sure you're right," Elsa replied, "and I have already asked the Lord's forgiveness."

"I wouldn't have stooped so low as to throw anything,"

Diana Montclair drawled, sipping her tea and watching the others stitch. The attractive blond rarely attended the sewing circle with the other town girls. Having attended various elite boarding schools, Diana had grown accustomed to more elevated entertainments, and she had been quite vocal about her distaste for such mundane endeavors as needlework. But for some reason, she had graced the group with her presence today. "Of course, I would not have been performing menial kitchen duties," she added with a haughty tilt of her chin, "and, therefore, I wouldn't have had access to an earthenware bowl in the first place."

"You know, Diana," Elsa retorted, "you would make a perfect match for our self-important guest, Shane Gerhard."

Diana glared back, her silver-gray eyes sparkling with resentment.

"Girls, girls," Mrs. Tidewell said, "the wrath of man does not produce the righteousness of God. We must remember that before losing our tempers."

Elsa felt herself blush with conviction. She knew the older woman was right. And she wasn't exactly a Christian role model for Diana Montclair.

Elsa glanced first at Mrs. Tidewell, then Diana. "Please forgive me for my lack of self-restraint."

Diana replied with a bored expression, but Mrs. T readily accepted the apology.

"Of course, Dear," she said, patting her downy-white hair that was pulled back into a prim little bun. "No one is perfect. Now then, let's get on with our prayer requests."

Mrs. T sat down opposite Diana at a small, polished side table in the parlor, while Betsy Larkin cleared her throat.

"I have a request," she said. "I have several requests, actually."

Elsa turned to her immediate left. She had known Betsy most of her life. They'd gone to school together and played at each other's homes. But then Betsy's mother died in childbirth three years ago, leaving her with the responsibility of caring for her four siblings who ranged in age from newborn to five years old. Betsy had been forced to grow up awfully fast in order to fill her mother's shoes.

"Please pray for Karl," Betsy said, her blond hair slightly mussed. "He turned eight on Saturday and suddenly decided he knows everything. And Will is easily influenced by his older brother, so the two of 'em are double trouble."

Everyone laughed softly, except Diana who appeared infinitely bored with the entire conversation.

"And please pray that I can nurture Marie and Greta," Betsy continued, looking down at the squares on which she stitched, "like Mama would have."

A rueful moment hung in the air.

"Of course, we'll pray for your brothers and sisters," Mrs. T said in a comforting tone. "And we'll pray for you too, for a nice young man to come into your life and sweep you off your feet."

Betsy brought her chin back while Elsa chuckled softly at her friend's startled expression.

"I'll never get married, Mrs. T," Betsy said. "Who'd have me, what with all my responsibilities at home?"

"A very special man, that's who," the older woman replied with an easy smile. "Now, anyone else have a prayer request? Samantha? What about you?"

"For my mama," she said. Like Betsy, Samantha Thomasohn had been a friend since elementary school. Her father ran the mercantile right across from the boardinghouse.

"Your mother's no better?" Clara asked with a pained expression.

Samantha shook her head, her blond ringlets swinging from side to side. "No, there's been little or no improvement. She's still so sick."

Elsa's heart constricted painfully. She knew what it was like to have an ailing mother. . .and to lose her.

"We'll be sure to pray, Samantha," Mrs. T said with a determined look in her green eyes.

A few other prayer requests were mentioned, then Mrs. Tidewell asked the girls to stop their sewing and bow their heads. As the older woman prayed, Elsa felt a deep, abiding sense of communing with the Savior, and a verse from the Book of Matthew came to mind: *"For where two or three are gathered together in my name, there am I in the midst of them."*

How awesome, Elsa thought, that a holy God heard their prayers and cared about their welfare!

When Mrs. T ended her petitions with a hearty, "Amen!" Elsa felt renewed, refreshed.

"Now, how about more tea, girls?" Mrs. T asked, looking rejuvenated herself. "Afterward, we'll see if we can finish this quilt."

Midafternoon, Shane ambled down the dusty street of Hickory Corners. He passed a dress shop on his left and the tinsmith to his right, across the road. Both businesses were housed in single-story, rough-hewn buildings, albeit the dress shop had whitewashed shutters adorning its two glass windows. Next came the bank, a red-brick building. After that was Montclair's Shipping Office, another wooden structure, and

Shane remembered it was Mr. Quinsy's place of employment. He shook his head. What did Elsa see in that guy—and why did Shane even care?

Standing on the corner, he spied a barbershop and decided on a haircut. He crossed the street, nodding politely to a man who was loading supplies into his wagon, and entered the shop. Immediately, Shane saw a feeble-looking, gray-haired man, sitting in a chair, reading the morning newspaper.

The old man peered up over the top. "What can I do for you, Son?"

"I'd like a haircut." Shane's gaze roamed over the sparsely decorated shop. He spotted a few shelves of barber bottles that most likely contained scented hair tonic. A few wooden chairs lined the wall near the doorway and above them were several hooks. Shane hung his black, wide-brimmed hat on one of them.

"Haircut? Why, sure." The old man stood on rickety legs, dusted off the red leather seat on which he'd been perched, and held his hand out, indicating Shane should take his place. "Make yourself comfortable."

Shane strode across the plank floor and sat down.

"You're new in town."

"Not 'new.' Just here on business. . .temporarily."

"I see." The old man fastened a cape around Shane's neck, then took his scissors in one hand a comb in the other. "Folks call me Doc."

"Nice to meet you. I'm Shane Gerhard." Peering through the mirror at the man who stood behind him, Shane saw him tremble with age. "Why are you called 'Doc'? Do people need medical attention when you get done with them?"

Doc laughed until he sputtered and coughed. "Mercy, no!

It's against my practice to administer a blood-letting and a haircut at the same time." He cackled again. "I'll have you know, young man, that I have a steady hand once I get going. And, I'm 'Doc' because I'm the physician in these parts."

"You are?" Shane grinned. "No fooling?"

"I wouldn't josh about a thing like that." He began snipping around Shane's ear.

"Well, in that case, I reckon you can sew back on whatever you accidentally cut off."

"Never cut off anything that didn't need cutting off," the old man retorted.

Shane decided he'd best hold real still. . .just in case.

"You staying at the Fritches' place?"

"Yep."

Doc pushed Shane's head forward and snipped around his collar. "Elsa Fritch is one fine cook."

"Found that out already."

"What did you say, Son?"

Shane spoke louder. "I said, yes, she is. . .a fine cook."

"Fine cook," Doc repeated. "And she's grown into a fine-looking young woman too. Why, I remember when Elsa was just a schoolgirl in braids, playing in the road with her brother, Herrick and their little sister, Heidi." Doc *snip, snip, snipped* around Shane's other ear. "Heidi got married a year ago, and I think poor Elsa felt badly that it wasn't her having a wedding, since Heidi is younger."

"Mm. . . ," Shane replied, fighting his curiosity.

"Then Henry Peabody came to town. He's from Boston, you know. Works for Mr. Montclair, who's the richest man in southwestern Ohio."

"Is that right?"

"Sure is."

"I haven't met Montclair, but I met Mr. Peabody." Shane closed his eyes as Doc commenced trimming the front of his hair. "He says he's got something called quinsy."

"That he does. Probably should have those tonsils removed."

Shane grinned. "Sharpen up them scissors, Doc."

The old man chuckled. "Oh, no, I don't do surgeries anymore. Henry would have to go to Fort Washington for that. And I suspect he will some time in the future. It's no fun having a sore throat prett' near every day. Perhaps once he and Elsa are married, she'll be able to convince him not to be afraid of having the operation. Although, I wish. . .oh, never mind."

"You wish what?" Shane opened his eyes and glanced at Doc.

"Aw, nothing. I spoke out of turn, Son."

Shane thought it over, told himself it was none of his concern, but still couldn't squelch his curiosity. "Might help if you spoke your mind, Doc, since my business has to do with Miss Fritch. . .and her engagement to Peabody."

Doc paused, his bony hands suspended in midair. "Maybe if you explain your, um, business—"

"Sure." Sensing the elderly man was trustworthy enough, he relayed the predicament and his reason for coming to Hickory Corners—leaving out the sum of his inheritance.

"If that don't beat all," Doc said, wagging his gray head. "What if Arne doesn't find those receipts?"

"Then I plan to marry Miss Fritch as soon as I can find a willing preacher to perform the ceremony."

Doc let out a long, slow whistle. "And does Elsa know this?"

"Yes, Sir, she does."

"I don't imagine she's too pleased about it."

"Let's just say she's as pleased about it as I am."

"I see." Doc sprinkled some tonic water onto Shane's head and proceeded to rub vigorously. "Does Henry know?"

"I don't believe so."

"Hm. . ." Doc combed Shane's hair into place.

"Now, what were you going to say? What is it you wish?"

The old guy produced a wheezing laugh. "I was going to say that I wish Elsa were marrying someone else, not that I don't think Henry is a good man. But he's. . .well. . ."

"Not the man for her."

"That's it," Doc agreed. "Furthermore, my instincts tell me Elsa pities Henry more than she loves him, but she wants to get married and he's the one asking, so. . ."

"So she might as well marry him."

"Uh-huh."

"Look, Doc, just to set things straight, I'm not exactly husband material, got that?" Shane yanked off the striped cape and stood, brushing the loose hair from his clothing. "Elsa would be better off with Mr. Quinsy Peabody than with me."

"You'd know best."

Shane nodded, then paid for the haircut.

"But just the same, I'll keep the matter in my prayers."

"Sure. You do that, Doc."

Donning his hat, Shane left the barbershop, feeling oddly unsettled. He didn't want to get married. He wanted his money. That's it.

He paused, staring across the street. Then why did his gut just tighten upon seeing Elsa heading for the boardinghouse on the arm of Henry Peabody?

Chapter 5

Elsa glimpsed Shane Gerhard from out of the corner of her eye, and chose to ignore him. But she quickly reminded herself that she had to be courteous at all costs. The Lord would not approve of treating Mr. Gerhard with anything less than her Christian best. Even so, Elsa tightened her hold around Henry's elbow.

"Ouch! Why are you squeezing my arm?"

"I didn't squeeze it, Henry."

"Yes, you did."

Elsa clenched her jaw, feeling irked with her fiancé for the first time ever. *Why couldn't he act like more of a man?* Oh, she didn't mean that! Poor, dear Henry didn't feel good again today. He couldn't help being so. . .so sensitive.

Elsa released her hold on his arm, and to her chagrin, Henry rubbed it as if she'd just socked him. At that precise moment, Shane crossed the street, all long legs and broad shoulders, and stood in their way, looking like a bully. Wearing dark trousers, a crisp white shirt under a black, tweed vest and matching jacket, he looked the part.

He removed his hat, nodded politely, and Elsa noticed the haircut. She glanced at the barbershop where Doc stood in the doorway and waved. Forcing a smile, she waved back, then fixed her eyes on Shane again.

"Lovely day for a stroll," he said.

"Yes, I suppose it is," Elsa replied, doing her best to be friendly.

"Will you be joining us for an early supper, Mr. Gerhard?" Henry asked in a hoarse voice. He cleared his throat. "We're on our way to the boardinghouse."

Shane's lips curved into a rather wolfish-looking grin. "I'd be delighted to join you," he said, staring pointedly at Elsa.

"Actually, I do the cooking, not the eating," she stated with an uneasy glance at Henry who seemed oblivious to Shane's flirtations. "And I really must get back to the kitchen. Excuse me."

Elsa skirted around Shane and made for the boardinghouse. Inside, she removed her bonnet and quickly strode through the dining room. It was then she noticed Zeb and Horace Bunk, sitting patiently at one of the long tables and awaiting their meal.

"Thought you'd never git back," Zeb said with a toothy smile. His wide face was unshaven, as usual, and his brown hair was matted. Even from her distance, Elsa could smell that the brothers were in need of a hot, soapy bath.

The Bunks were what the Hickory Corners called "river rats." They made their living by trading up and down the Ohio River, and Zeb and Horace were quite successful. And, while they were friendly enough fellows, they were a young lady's nightmare for a potential suitor—which was another reason Elsa was glad to finally be betrothed.

"We're starving, Miss Elsa," Horace declared. "Whatcha serving up today?"

"Leftover stew."

"That's my favorite." Zeb's smile broadened. "Yours too, eh, Horace?"

"Yep." He didn't look much different from his brother, same stocky build and short legs, except Horace had rusty-colored hair. Like his brother's, however, it was in need of a good scrubbing. "Say, Miss Elsa, you got some of them biscuits to go with it?"

She nodded. "Coming right up."

Behind her, she heard Shane and Henry enter the boardinghouse. She quickened her step and headed into the kitchen.

"Papa, what are you doing?" she cried, seeing the disarray on the table and service counters.

"I have been searching for Georg's receipts."

Elsa grimaced. "You haven't found them yet?"

"Nein."

Feeling discouragement creeping in, Elsa tried in vain to will it away. She prayed while sliding the biscuits onto the iron rack in the hearth to warm and ladling the stew into four bowls. *Father in Heaven, please allow my Papa to find what he needs to prove the debt was paid so Shane Gerhard can be on his way and out of my life forever!*

Elsa loaded up her round serving tray, waiting a few more minutes on the biscuits before pulling them from the hearth. Setting them onto a platter, she placed that too onto the tray. But before she could carry it into the dining room, the object of her troubled thoughts sauntered into the kitchen.

"I thought you might need some help."

"Thank you, but no. And I'll thank you to stay out of my kitchen."

Arne chuckled under his breath.

"Whoa, little lady, I'm just trying to be useful," Shane

said, palms up as if in self-defense.

Elsa inhaled deeply, remembering one of the fruits of the Spirit was temperance, although she didn't miss the fact he'd referred to her as "little" again.

She softened her tone. "Thank you for asking, but I can manage."

"Miss Fritch, you are going to hurt yourself if you continue to carry that heavy tray."

"I won't hurt myself, and I only dropped it once and that was when I was thirteen."

Shane looked at Arne. "Talk some sense into your daughter, Uncle Arne."

Uncle Arne? Elsa swung her gaze to her father who chuckled.

"You remember, young Shane."

"Yes, I remember. . ."

"What? What are you two talking about?" Elsa wanted to know.

"Back in Germany, your parents and mine were as close as siblings," Shane explained, "and I called your father 'uncle' and your mother 'aunt.' You did likewise with my folks, although I suspect you were too young to recall."

"I remember too," Arne said with a faraway gleam in his eyes. "My Elsa followed young Shane around like a puppy."

"I did no such thing!" Elsa exclaimed, feeling her cheeks flame.

"Ah, but you did. Und young Shane put up vith it, quite a marvel for an eight-year-old boy."

"If my memory serves me correctly, I believe I gave you, Miss Fritch, horsey-back rides."

Elsa felt so embarrassed, she wished the floor would open

up and swallow her. But, no such luck.

With a rakish wink in her direction, Shane picked up the tray and carried it into the dining area.

"Papa," Elsa whispered, "please find those receipts. . . fast!"

"*Acht!* I am trying, but I cannot think uf vhere to search next." He stood from where he'd been sitting at the table, sifting through various documents and articles of importance. Pausing before Elsa, he patted her cheek affectionately. "Meanvhile, ve can enjoy young Shane's visit. He reminds me of Georg, und I miss my friend. I vish your mama und I vould not have burned bridges betveen da Gerhards und us. Ve might not have agreed vith der vocation, but dey ver still our friends. Now it is too late to reconcile."

"Papa—"

"But maybe not," he added, the lines on his face deepening with an emotion Elsa could not discern. "Maybe not."

With that, he walked into the dining room.

Flustered, Elsa followed him and finished serving the meal from the tray Shane had carried in for her. When the Bunk brothers grabbed more than their share of biscuits, Elsa smacked both their hands. "Half a dozen each is plenty. There are other mouths to feed here besides yours."

"My apologies, Miss Elsa," Zeb said with a lopsided grin, "It's jest that your biscuits are the best we've ever tasted."

"They're nothing special," she contended. "Why, they're not even fresh. I made them this morning."

"Pardon me, Miss Elsa, but they're a far sight better than the hardtack we've been gnawin' on," Horace said with his mouth full of stew. Gravy dribbled from the corner of his mouth, down his chin, and into his scraggly beard.

Appalled by the Bunks' table manners, Elsa quickly set the platter down in the middle of the table and retreated to the kitchen. She smoothed down her apron and took a deep, calming breath. In that moment, she wasn't sure who disturbed her more, Shane Gerhard or Zeb and Horace.

A knock sounded, and Elsa strode to the back door at the far side of the kitchen and opened it. Mrs. Tidewell's pleasingly plump form stood in the threshold, her beaming face framed by her snowy-white hair. She held out an apple pie.

"I thought perhaps you could make use of this."

"Why, thank you, Mrs. T, I certainly could. I didn't do any baking this morning."

"I figured, what with the sewing circle and all."

The pastor's wife stepped inside and Elsa closed the door.

"There are five men in my dining room as we speak who will be happy to see this pie."

Mrs. Tidewell chuckled. "Yes, I heard the Bunk brothers were back in town, so I thought they would show up at your dinner table soon enough. You're the closest thing this town has to a public eatery."

"I try my best."

"I know you do, Dear, and I can tell you are feeling overwhelmed."

Unexpected tears filled Elsa's eyes, and she nodded.

"But do you think any of this is a surprise to God? Of course it isn't. No matter what is occurring here on earth, God is still on His throne. He is still in charge."

"Everything would be just fine if Shane Gerhard would go back to St. Louis where he came from," Elsa whispered as she began to slice the pie.

"He's that much of a nuisance, is he?"

"That much and more!"

"Hm. . .well, I have an idea," Mrs. T said as she took plates from the cupboard. "It goes along with what we talked about this afternoon."

"Yes?"

"You need to kill him, Elsa."

"Mrs. Tidewell! How could you even suggest such a thing? You're a pastor's wife."

She laughed. "No, no, I don't mean really kill him. I mean, kill Mr. Gerhard's badgering with kindness. Do what the Bible says in Proverbs 25: 21–22. 'If thine enemy be hungry, give him bread to eat; and if he be thirsty, give him water to drink: For thou shalt heap coals of fire upon his head, and the LORD shall reward thee.' "

"I'm not sure I understand."

"Be courteous to Mr. Gerhard, Elsa. My husband and I have run up against his kind before. He thinks it's fun to tease you because you react, but if you're not rankled and instead you're sweet-spirited, he won't be quite so amused."

"Really?"

"Try it and see."

Elsa liked the idea of heaping coals of fire on Shane Gerhard's conceited head. In her opinion, it was the least he deserved. "I'll do it, Mrs. T."

"Good girl. Now, don't forget about our planning meeting on Thursday, and we'll do our baking the following Friday night at my house. Our Spring Fling is going to be so much fun this year. The unmarrieds in this town need a bit of prodding, I'd say."

Elsa grinned, and for the second time that day, she felt God's peace that passes all understanding fill her being. She wrapped her arms around the older woman, thinking Mrs. Tidewell was as motherly as her own mother might have been, were she still alive. "Thank you, Mrs. T Thank you for coming over this afternoon."

"You're quite welcome." She returned Elsa's hug with a small squeeze of her own.

Moments later, she was on her way out the door, leaving Elsa to wonder if she'd squish Henry like a bug if she embraced him as heartily as she'd embraced the good pastor's wife.

To her dismay, she presumed she probably would!

The next morning, Shane sat on the outside stoop and watched Elsa hang clothes on the line. The sun's rays felt warm against his face on this March morning, and the breeze felt tepid, comfortable. Arne said it'd been an early spring this year. But Shane didn't give a whit about the weather. He was growing restless in this sleepy little town. He wanted to get back to St. Louis and its nightlife. He wanted his money, just sitting there waiting for him in that trust account. He envisioned the extravagant parties he could throw with that kind of loot lining his pockets.

"You know, I think you're going to have to marry me," he told Elsa. Then he grinned, anticipating a tart reply.

To his disappointment, she sighed. . .and agreed. "If Papa doesn't find those receipts, I'll have no other choice but to fulfill our part of the contract."

"Well, look at it this way, as soon as I get my money you can divorce me and marry your precious Henry."

"I could never divorce you."

Shane frowned. "Why not?"

"Because the Bible says God hates divorce. I could never do something God hates."

"All right, then I'll divorce you."

"Suit yourself."

Shane felt suddenly perturbed. Standing, he walked toward her. "Look, I don't know what you're thinking, but all I want is my inheritance. I have no intentions of getting saddled with a wife."

To his shock and delight, Elsa smiled at him, the prettiest smile he'd ever seen on a woman. A smile that produced dimples in both her cheeks. A smile that caused his heart to flip.

"I completely understand your frustration, Mr. Gerhard."

"Um, sure you do." He swallowed hard, but recovered quickly. "I think it's high time you called me by my given name, don't you?"

She looked a bit taken aback. "Well, I don't know. . ."

"Aw, c'mon," he teased her, "Mr. Quinsy won't mind. He scarcely pays any attention to you unless he wants to whine and complain about his many ailments."

Elsa's cheeks flushed slightly, but not a spark of indignation reached her blue eyes. "If you insist. . .Shane. Then you must call me Elsa."

"It'd be my pleasure."

She bent and picked up one of her father's shirts from the large wicker basket.

"So, what do you do for fun around here, Elsa?"

"There's church tonight."

"Oh, I can hardly wait," Shane quipped.

She gave him an amused glance while pinning the shirt on the line. "There's the Spring Fling coming up in a week from Saturday."

"What's a Spring Fling?"

"A gathering of all the young people in town and some older ones too. Mr. Stahl plays his fiddle, and—"

"Don't tell me you all dance."

"Oh, no!"

Elsa looked aghast, and Shane hung his head back and hooted.

"Somehow, I didn't think so," he said.

She reached for several linens and hung them over the line to dry. "This year, we're having a big surprise for all the unattached fellas. We girls are making big, round cookies and baking a slip of paper with our names inside of them. Who-ever gets that particular young lady's cookie, has to eat supper with her."

Shane grinned. "You'd best hope and pray Zeb or Horace Bunk don't get your cookie."

Elsa paled visibly.

"Well, now, don't worry," he assured her with practiced charm, "you just tell me what your cookie looks like, and I'll make sure it falls into the right hands."

She gave him a skeptical look. "I appreciate your kind offer, but I'm sure you'll be back in St. Louis by the time the Spring Fling comes around."

"And miss this grand event? Not a chance."

"You can't mean that. I—"

Elsa seemed to catch herself before a sharp retort could pass though her berry-pink lips. They were ripe for kissing, as far as Shane was concerned.

"You're more than welcome to attend, of course," she began again, "although I don't imagine you'll find our simplistic form of entertainment to your liking."

"Guess we'll see about that, won't we?"

After a shrug, she picked up her now-empty basket and headed for the boardinghouse. Shane watched her enter through the back door, thinking he might indeed find the Spring Fling to his liking. . .especially if he chose Miss Elsa Fritch's cookie.

Chapter 6

The man was making her crazy. For a full week, Shane had followed Elsa around like a veritable shadow, albeit a talking, teasing, cajoling shadow! Elsa was at her wits' end.

She sighed as she slipped the blue calico dress over her head in preparation for the midweek prayer meeting. Shane hadn't gone last week, nor had he attended the Sunday service. Then, as now, she looked forward to some reprieve from Shane's company. However, if she were completely honest with herself, she'd have to confess to enjoying the attention somewhat. He paid her compliments and he offered to help with her chores. They had interesting conversations about their relatives in Germany, and on that account, she and Shane had much in common. They'd grown friendly toward one another, the very thing that disturbed her greatly. Shane Gerhard possessed a charming manner which affected Elsa more than she cared to admit. Furthermore, she found herself wishing Henry would act more like him.

Then, of course, there was the perplexing question as to why Shane behaved as though he were romantically interested in her, and at times, Elsa couldn't discern his intentions. Were they merely friends? Just acquaintances? She did suspect he was trifling with her out of sheer boredom, and she prayed without ceasing that Papa would find those receipts and send Shane back to St. Louis. Her heart couldn't endure much more of that man's flirtations. Unfortunately, Papa liked him and wasn't in any hurry to see him go. Still, her father spent his every waking hour searching for the vouchers from Georg Gerhard, and many times, Shane aided in the hunt.

"Acht!" Elsa muttered in frustration as she brushed out her dark-brown hair. If only her mother were alive and could advise her. . .or if Heidi were home. Oh, what was the use of wishing things were different? Wishing couldn't change her situation. She still had Papa to care for and the boarding-house to manage. Soon, she could add Henry to the list.

Giving herself a mental shake, Elsa considered her appearance in the oblong, mahogany-framed looking glass. She decided to wear her hair down tonight, save for the combs she wore on either side of her head, above her ears. She wanted to look her best for Henry. . .or was it a reaction from Shane that she secretly coveted?

"You must stop thinking like that," she scolded her reflection. "It's the Lord's opinion you need to care about, and He sees the heart, not physical beauty. And a good thing too!"

Elsa considered her full figure. Even in Mama's best dress, she didn't feel the least bit pretty. She was tall and big-boned, hardly a delicate, feminine little thing, and surely not the type of woman Shane Gerhard would be drawn to. And even if she was, he'd said he wasn't a marrying man, and if it came down to the contract being fulfilled, he would divorce her once he got his money. Elsa couldn't impress Shane if she tried. In fact, she couldn't impress any man with her physical attributes. . .except for Henry, although she wasn't certain that quality had initially attracted him either.

Elsa often wondered why Henry wanted to marry her. He never said he loved her, not even on the afternoon he proposed. And he never once tried to kiss her, much to Elsa's disappointment. But she sensed he needed her, just like Papa. Poor Henry, chronically ill; however, Elsa had two very capable hands, not to mention a strong back. Perhaps she'd even be the one who would nurse Henry back to health, and maybe God would bless the two of them with children.

She allowed her gaze to wander around the small bedroom she once shared with Heidi. Soon she would share it with Henry. On the double bed lay a multi-colored patchwork quilt Elsa and her sister had made two years ago at Mrs. Tidewell's sewing circle. In one corner, there stood a wooden wardrobe Papa had built and beside it was a small chest of drawers. Elsa had inherited her mother's looking glass which she placed near the tiny dressing area, and she never ceased to marvel at the fact it had survived the trip from Germany.

In a month's time, I'll share this room with my husband, Elsa mused. She prayed that she would be a good wife.

On that thought, Elsa left the bedroom and walked down the narrow hallway toward the kitchen. Dinner had been served at five o'clock sharp this evening to afford her ample time to prepare for the midweek church service. When she'd left the dining room to change clothes over thirty minutes ago, there were several guests still lingering over their coffee, including Papa, Shane, Henry, and Doc. However, it sounded quiet, as though all the men had gone.

Would Papa have left for church without me? Elsa wondered.

Making her way through the kitchen, she peered into the

dining room, seeing Shane and Henry. Shane was gazing out the front window, one hand in the pocket of his dark trousers, and Henry was writing on a ledger of some sort at a table.

Elsa took two steps into the room. "Did Papa leave?"

Both men glanced her way, and she watched as Shane's expression brightened with interest. From the sparkle in his hazel eyes to the wry grin curving his mouth, Elsa could tell he appreciated that she'd fussed with her toilette this evening. His next words confirmed it.

"Well, now, don't you look pretty."

"Thank you," Elsa said, feeling herself blush. However, she inwardly acknowledged it was the exact response she had hoped for. Furthermore, she felt amazed she'd accomplished such a feat.

"As for your papa," Shane added, "he went on ahead to church with Doc."

"Oh. . ." She looked at Henry, disappointed that his countenance registered nothing but a pained frown. "Well, we can walk together."

"I'm not feeling well enough to sit through church tonight," he complained. "I think I'll go home." He tossed a glance at Shane. "Mr. Gerhard offered to escort you."

Elsa's heart sank. "But, Henry, it isn't right. . .that is, I'm your fiancée. Shane shouldn't have to escort me."

"He offered. It would be rude to refuse him." Henry cleared his throat and winced, clutching his neck with pale, lanky fingers. "When I get home, I'll make myself some of that tea Doc gave me."

He stood, picked up his ledger, then strode toward the front door of the boardinghouse. No hug or kiss good-bye, no affection whatsoever, not even in his expression. He never once said she looked pretty, or gave her some minuscule promise to hang onto. And he never gave it a second thought that she'd be in another man's company this evening. To sum it up, Henry seemed not to care.

Shane walked slowly toward her, and Elsa blinked back her tears of dejection. She looked his way, and Shane narrowed his gaze.

"You getting the picture here?" he asked, pointing to his temple. "Is it beginning to sink in?"

Elsa swallowed convulsively. "What are you talking about?"

"Mr. Quinsy." Shane shook his head. "He either doesn't love you, Elsa, or he's the biggest fool that ever walked the earth."

"Don't say that. Henry's not a fool. He's just ill."

"More like self-absorbed. Why, I'd have to be dead or dying before I turned my fiancée over to another man's care—especially if he was a man like me."

Elsa had to grin at the irony of his statement.

"There, that's better," he said with a charming smile. "You're far too lovely to be frowning so hard." He held his arm out to her. "Shall we go?"

On a sigh of resignation, Elsa stepped forward and slipped her hand around his elbow. "You're really coming to church?"

Shane shrugged his broad shoulders. "Sure. I reckon it can't hurt."

Arm in arm, they walked down Main Street, heading for Birch Street. As they passed the shipping office, Elsa looked for any signs of Henry, but saw none.

"Who's got the fancy house over yonder?"

At the corner, Elsa glanced to her right. "The one painted

dove gray? That's the Montclairs' home."

"Seems out of place, what with all the log buildings around here except for the bank and the church."

"Yes, I suppose it does. But Mr. Montclair is one of Hickory Corners' founders, and perhaps, for that reason he maintains a lovely home, even though he and his wife are rarely there to enjoy it."

"So the house is a monument of sorts."

"Something like that."

Despite Shane's attempt at a light conversation, Elsa felt heavy-hearted. She gazed up at him, and in spite of herself, couldn't help admiring his predominant jawline covered with a hint of a shadow. "Do you really think Henry doesn't love me?"

Shane looked at her and Elsa saw the sympathy in his eyes. "He's a fool."

Elsa shook her head in disagreement. "He doesn't love me."

"Well, look at it this way—at least you found that out before you married him."

"But I thought I could make him love me by taking care of him."

"Darlin', he is supposed to take care of you."

"But—"

"All right, all right," he said as if to forestall any debate, "I imagine marriage is something of a give-and-take arrangement. Wives take care of their husbands by cooking and cleaning and such. Except in your case, life with Mr. Quinsy would be you doing all the giving and you'd end up one unhappy woman."

Elsa thought of several retorts; however, the truth of

Shane's words kept her from verbalizing any of them.

Reaching the church, Elsa and Shane climbed the steps and met a small group of friends chatting in the tiny vestibule. She introduced Shane, and hearing he was from St. Louis, several of the older Stahl boys—no longer "boys" but married men now—engaged him in conversation.

Elsa had to grin. The husky, dark-haired Stahls would keep Shane occupied for awhile. They hailed from a large family whose farm resided on the acreage behind the church.

"Where's Henry?" Betsy Larkin asked.

"He's ill tonight."

"The poor man. Is it his throat again?"

Elsa nodded.

"Are you and Mr. Gerhard getting along better now?" Samantha Thomasohn wanted to know, her brown eyes sparkling with mischief. "It would seem the two of you are quite friendly."

Elsa didn't feel up to the teasing or giving explanations, and merely nodded.

"Does Henry know you and Mr. Gerhard are 'quite friendly'?" Clara Bucey asked, looking alarmed.

"Yes, and it's all his fault too!"

The girls were wide-eyed with curiosity.

Elsa glanced around the small group. "You're my best friends. You've known me practically my whole life."

They nodded.

"Then you'll understand when I say I'm having serious doubts about marrying Henry. Of course, I haven't breathed a word of this to anyone else yet."

"We'd never repeat a thing," Samantha promised, and Elsa knew it was true. Her friends were not gossips. When they heard of a trial or tragedy, they prayed.

"Mantha and I warned you 'bout Henry," Betsy said earnestly. "We just had a funny feeling concerning the two of you." She suddenly grinned impishly. "Now, you and Mr. Gerhard, on the other hand—"

"Oh, hush," Elsa said, cutting off further reply.

A man cleared his throat, and Elsa turned to see one of the Stahl brothers motioning them into the sanctuary. Bidding her friends a hasty farewell, Elsa walked up the aisle. Shane followed and joined her and Papa in the fourth pew from the front—their usual place.

"I am pleased dat you came tonight," Papa said, leaning toward their guest.

Shane shrugged. "Haven't seen any bolts from out of the blue yet. I reckon that's a good sign."

Elsa smiled at the quip, then sent up a silent prayer that Pastor Tidewell's message tonight would somehow touch Shane in a special way.

Chapter 7

S hane ambled out of the quaint, clapboard church and walked alongside Elsa and Arne back to the boarding-house. He wondered at what he'd heard tonight from Pastor Tidewell's pulpit. Was it true? Was there really a place called heaven and a place called hell? Sure, he knew that's what Christians believed, but was it true? The question continued to play over and over in his mind.

"I'll make some tea," Elsa said, once they entered the boardinghouse. She headed for the kitchen, leaving Shane and her father in the dining common.

"So, Uncle Arne, tell me," he began, "do you think the Bible is truly God's Word?"

Ja. The old man nodded vigorously.

"I always wondered. . ."

"Your parents did not teach you da Bible?"

Shane shrugged. "I have had some Sunday school lessons. That is, when I didn't get tossed out of class for misbehaving."

Arne chuckled softly just as Elsa reentered the room.

"I set the kettle on to boil."

Shane grinned in reply. He didn't give a whit about tea,

but he'd sit and sip it politely just to be in Elsa's company. He watched her take a seat at one of the long tables and marveled that in the course of a little better than one week, he'd begun behaving like some lovesick swain. What in the world was wrong with him, anyway?

"Your vater vas a troublemaker in his younger days too," Arne said, still grinning broadly. "But after he met your mutter, he settled down. Could be das vhat you need—da love uf a gute voman."

"You think so, eh?" Shane had to keep from glancing at Elsa. He forced himself to walk toward the small window at the front of the dining room. Moving the curtain aside, he gazed out onto the darkened dirt road. Across the way, the mercantile had already closed for the evening. The entire town seemed to close up after sunset. No theaters. No race tracks or gaming tables. No dance halls. "I rather enjoy my life. Carefree, no responsibilities. I don't have to answer to anyone except me. I can stay out all night if I want to. I come and go as I please."

Who am I trying to convince, he wondered, *the Fritches or myself?*

When no reply came from his hosts, he turned to face them. "Getting back to our original topic, I've got another question for you."

Arne nodded as he sat down by the hearth. "Ask, young Shane."

"If what the Bible says is true, and there really is a heaven and a hell, and my folks knew it. . .then why didn't they sit me down, look me in the eyes, and tell me that I was a sinner destined for a godless eternity? My parents loved me, cared about me." He paused, searching his own mind for an answer. "Why didn't they tell me?"

Elsa looked at her father.

"Perhaps, young Shane," Arne began, "your parents did not think you vould listen."

"Maybe. And maybe they would have been right too, but they still could have said. . .something."

Arne appeared momentarily thoughtful, then said, *"Ja,* dey could have said something. But das no longer an excuse, is it? Tonight, you have heard da truth, dat Jesus Christ is God, sent by God da Vater, and salvation is through Him."

Shane nodded out a reply. "Sure, I heard. I just don't know if I believe it."

"That's the decision we all encounter at one time or another," Elsa said.

The warmth in her voice touched Shane's heart in an odd way. He crossed the room and straddled the bench opposite her, the scarred tabletop between them. "So you didn't believe all this Bible stuff at first either, is that what you're telling me?"

"I was twelve years old when I accepted the Lord," Elsa explained. "Papa tried to tell me about Jesus. Mama tried to tell me too. But I thought I was a good girl, because I always tried to obey at school and at home, and I couldn't understand that I was just as much a sinner in need of salvation as anyone else."

"Hm. . ." Shane thought it over. "Well, I don't have trouble with the sin aspect. Contrary to your childhood disposition, I was always the 'bad' one, the rabble-rouser. In fact, my grandfather often called me a 'ne'er-do-well'."

"It's never to late to change," Elsa stated with a hint of a smile.

Shane folded his arms and grinned back at her. "Are you insinuating that I haven't changed?"

Her cheeks turned a pretty shade of pink. "I think I hear the water boiling for our tea," she said, hastily rising from the wooden bench.

She fled to the kitchen, leaving Shane chuckling in her wake.

The next morning, Elsa finished dressing two chickens for the noon meal, then impaled them on a spit which she placed over the fire in the hearth. The Bunk brothers had announced at breakfast that another packet arrived in town. They told Elsa to expect some hungry river men at noontime—themselves included, of course.

Elsa fretted over her lower lip. Perhaps she should roast three chickens. . .no, she'd just double up on the biscuits instead.

"Papa," she called into the back hallway. "Papa, are there more canned beets in the cellar?"

"Ja, I think so." He walked slowly out of his room and headed her way. "I vill get you a jar."

"Fetch two please, Papa. We might have several guests today."

He nodded, and Elsa's heart went out to him. Her father had been searching relentlessly for those receipts since awakening this morning. Finding nothing, he looked so defeated. It almost seemed as though he felt his honor was now at stake, although Shane appeared to believe Papa when he said he paid the debt in full.

A disturbance in the dining area suddenly caught Elsa's

attention. Wiping her hands on her apron, she strode into the other room where she found Shane pushing a two-tiered, wooden tea cart on wheels in the front door with Samantha Thomasohn trailing behind.

"What's all this?" Elsa asked.

"Look what Mr. Gerhard purchased for you!" Samantha exclaimed, her cheeks reddening with enthusiasm. "Nathaniel Harmon made it in his carpentry shop."

"For me?"

Shane nodded. "So you won't have to carry that heavy tray anymore."

"First, Mr. Gerhard came to our mercantile," Samantha explained, "but we don't sell what he had in mind, so he ordered it special from Mr. Harmon. I just had to come over and see the look on your face."

"Well, I'm certainly surprised, but I do not need a cart."

"Yes, you do too need it," Shane said. "Now, look here. . ."

Leaving the tea cart in the middle of the dining room, he sauntered into the kitchen, and Samantha gasped.

"He's in your kitchen, Elsa. He just walked right in!"

"He does it all the time," she muttered.

Samantha brought her fingers to her lips in effort to stifle her giggles, while Elsa shook her head as Shane returned with the offensive serving tray.

"See, Elsa? You simply place your tray on top of the cart, load it up, and voila! You push it into the dining room instead of carrying it. Much easier. Underneath the cart, you've got some shelf space for water pitchers and the like." He grinned. "What do you think?"

She opened her mouth to reiterate how unnecessary a tea cart was; however, Shane looked as excited as a little boy on

Christmas morning. How could she break his heart?

"I think. . ." She glanced at Samantha who gave her an encouraging smile. "I think this is the nicest thing anyone has ever done for me. Thank you, Shane. I'm ever so grateful."

"I knew you'd like it." His grin broadened and an amused twinkle entered his hazel eyes. "Besides, you can always wheel Henry around on it when you're not serving food. This cart seems sturdy enough."

Elsa narrowed a warning gaze at him, and Shane laughed.

"I think I should be getting back," Samantha said, looking curiously from one to the other. She turned toward the door and her dark blue skirt swirled at her ankles. "Mama probably needs me. She's still so sick."

"Of course," Elsa replied, walking her friend to the door. "Is there anything we can do to hasten your mother's recovery?"

"Pray." Samantha's blond brows furrowed with concern. "Please keep praying."

"We shall."

Elsa gave her friend a quick embrace, then Samantha raced back to the mercantile across the road.

Spinning on her heel, Elsa placed her hands on her hips and faced Shane.

"I know what you're going to say," he blurted before she could utter a single word. "You're going to tell me I shouldn't have poked fun at Mr. Quinsy, and I reckon you're right. I apologize."

He gave Elsa a humble-looking bow, and she rolled her eyes. "Always the charmer, aren't you? I'll bet you got yourself out of plenty of whippin's when you were a lad."

"Why, Miss Elsa," he said with a wounded expression,

"are you suggesting that I'm being insincere?"

"Yes!" With that, she walked past him into the kitchen. As she suspected, Shane followed.

Papa had returned from the cellar with two jars of beets and a small crate. "Look, Elsa. Look vhat I found." He set his burdens on the kitchen table.

"Do you think the receipts are in the crate?" she asked.

"*Ja*, dey could be."

Shane rubbed his palms together in anticipation. "Want me to help you, Uncle Arne?"

"*Ja*, sure."

The two men pulled out their chairs and began to sit down when Elsa halted them.

"Out of my kitchen," she ordered. "I've got biscuits to bake. You two can do your sorting at a table in the dining room, and Papa, please remember to charge guests who come for lunch today. We forgot yesterday. It's just a good thing our guests were honest."

Standing, her father nodded his head and scooped up the crate with both hands.

"Is she always so bossy, Uncle Arne?" Shane asked with a teasing grin.

"*Ja*. But she keeps me in line."

"Who keeps her in line?" He winked at Elsa.

"Das a gute question, young Shane. Gute question."

The men chuckled together on their way out, and Elsa decided to let them have their fun. She couldn't out-quip Shane Gerhard if she tried. Returning to the service counter, she mixed together the ingredients for her famous baking soda biscuits.

It was shortly after the noon hour when the Bunks and six other scraggly-looking men clamored into the boardinghouse. Their deep voices and laughter seemed to fill every nook and cranny.

Knowing the men were hungry, Elsa quickly placed the tray onto the tea cart and set several plates of food on it. Next she wheeled it into the dining room, deciding it was much easier to push than to carry.

"Well, well, what do we have here?" a scruffy-bearded man asked.

"Chicken, biscuits and gravy, and canned beets," Elsa replied politely.

"Forget the supper, you're quite a dish yourself, Honey."

Chuckles went up and down the table and Elsa tried to ignore them as she continued to set a plate in front of each guest.

"What's your name?" the man persisted.

"This is Miss Elsa Fritch," Zeb Bunk answered. "Miss Elsa, that there is Weaver."

"My full name is John Adams Weaver."

Unimpressed, Elsa gave him a perfunctory smile, then glanced over the men's heads to where Shane sat at a nearby table, watching the goings-on with a critical eye. She looked to her far left and saw her papa, sitting behind the greeting counter, busying himself with the funds he'd collected. Elsa quelled her uneasiness by telling herself she was safe with Shane and Papa in the room. Then she wondered why she felt so flustered. She had managed bold men by herself in the past.

The river men began to eat and Elsa noted only a few bowed their heads and thanked the Lord before digging in. Back in the kitchen, she prepared two plates for Shane and her father.

"Thank you for being patient and waiting," she murmured to Shane as she set the meal before him.

"Aw, Elsa, I'm not that much of a guest."

She replied with a grateful smile, then served her papa.

"Looks gute," he said.

She kissed the balding crown of her father's head before returning to the kitchen.

At the service counter, Elsa sliced the cinnamon spice cake she had baked earlier, and lay each piece on a dessert plate. Next she served the river men, taking away their empty dinnerware and stacking it onto her new tea cart.

"You sure are a purty thing," Weaver said. His hair and beard were the color of the brown mud along the banks of the Ohio. His deep-set eyes seemed spaced too far apart on his wide face, and Elsa thought he resembled a reptile. "How 'bout a little kiss for dessert instead of this here cake?"

"I think you'll have your cake," she retorted.

Several guffaws emanated from Weaver's cronies.

"I think I won't." He stood, a determined gleam in his eyes.

Elsa swallowed her sudden fear and tried to back away, but Weaver caught her shoulders. She pushed on his chest, turning her head to escape his eager lips.

In the next moment, Weaver abruptly freed her, and Elsa staggered backward. A strong arm caught her around the waist. Before she even saw him, she knew it was Shane. But then Elsa glimpsed the shiny pistol in his hand, pointed directly at Weaver.

"Don't you ever touch this woman again," Shane said, in slow, menacing intervals.

"Das right!" Papa hollered from across the room. "Und you can leave my boardinghouse dis minute!"

Weaver held up his hands as if in surrender. "Now, look, I was just having a bit of fun."

"Get out," Shane demanded.

The river man nodded, and grabbed his battered hat from off the bench on which he'd been sitting.

"Me and Zeb'll see to it he leaves for good," Horace Bunk announced.

He took one of Weaver's arms, and Zeb took the other. Ignoring his protests and arguments, they escorted their unruly pal to the front door of the boardinghouse. Then, taking Weaver by the seat of his pants, the Bunk brothers tossed him out onto the road. Elsa winced at the resounding thud of humanity hitting hard dirt.

"Anyone else have a mind to try my patience?" Shane asked, waving his pistol at the other men at the table.

"Nope."

"Uh-uh."

Another man shook his shaggy, blond head and continued to eat his cake.

"Good." Shane tucked away his gun and peered down at Elsa. "You all right?"

"Yes," she stated, feeling embarrassed and grateful all at once. She stared up into his hazel eyes, and in that moment, she determined Shane was something of a hero.

As if divining her thoughts, he suddenly appeared chagrined. Releasing Elsa, he stepped away, nodded politely, and walked off in Arne's direction. When he returned to his place at the table, Arne gave him a congratulatory clap on the shoulder. Shane looked over at Elsa and she smiled.

My hero, she thought, making her way into the kitchen. *He special orders a tea cart to ease my workload, and he defends my virtue.*

Conversely, she wondered what she'd ever do when he left to go back to St. Louis!

Chapter 8

U ncle Arne, think," Shane beseeched the old man. "Where would you have put those receipts? What about in a safe deposit box at the bank?"

"Nein, nein," Arne despaired. Sitting at one of the long tables, he put his graying head in his hands.

Shane sighed and paced the dining common. He had to get out of Hickory Corners. If he didn't leave soon, he might never get away. There was something strange about this tiny community, and it was drawing him in with its powerful clutches.

This morning, for instance, Doc had come over and he, Arne, and Shane had chattered on like long-lost friends. Next, he'd met Oskar Bedloe, the wiry-framed tinsmith. Bedloe's place was located between the mercantile and Doc's barbershop. Shane got along well with all three men, as they discussed politics and America's new president, Martin Van Buren. And for the first time ever, Shane felt like he belonged. Doc and Bedloe didn't know about the Gerhards' fortune, so they weren't befriending him thinking they had something to gain. Furthermore, they hadn't an inkling about his past, so they weren't looking down pious noses at him. They accepted him at face value.

Then there was Arne, who behaved like the proud uncle. He introduced Shane to everyone who passed by on the street.

Of course, Elsa didn't help matters. Since noontime yesterday, she had regarded him as if he walked on water. Him! A rake among rakes. Rogue among rogues. Worse, Shane couldn't seem to keep his distance. When she looked up at him and smiled, he felt twelve feet tall. As for marrying Elsa so he could claim his inheritance. . .well, he wouldn't mind that a bit. Only problem was, he didn't think he could marry her, then leave her behind. He'd want to take her with him, but what kind of life could he possibly provide for a decent woman? And he sure wasn't about to stay here. What sort of vocation could he pursue?

The only viable option was to find those receipts and sail out of this town as quickly as he could!

"All right, all right, Uncle Arne, let's put our heads together. Is there an attic in this place?"

"*Ja*, but I have searched it."

"Let's search it again."

The old man nodded. "First thing tomorrow vhen da light is better."

Shane expelled an impatient breath and glanced at the windows. Beyond them, he could see the evening dusk rapidly descending.

"Papa, I'm leaving."

Shane swung around, hearing Elsa's voice. She'd removed her apron and had donned a pretty lace collar over her brown linen dress.

She smiled at Shane.

In spite of himself, he smiled back.

"Vhere are you going?" Arne asked.

"To bake cookies with Mrs. Tidewell and a few other ladies. Remember, I told you, Papa?"

"*Ja, ja,* I remember now."

"Tomorrow is the Spring Fling."

"Oh, that's right," Shane drawled, snapping his fingers. "I plumb forgot. Why, I imagine this is the biggest event of the whole year."

Elsa gave him one of her quelling looks, and he laughed.

She turned to her father. "Henry will be here in a few minutes. He said he had to work late tonight. Papa, are you still going to talk to him for me?"

"*Nein,* Elsa. Talk to him yourself. I am a tired old man."

"But, Papa—"

"Do not argue," he warned her, rising from the bench. "It is best Henry hears your feelings from you, not me."

With that, Arne shuffled over to his daughter and kissed her cheek. "*Aufwiedersehen, bis Morgen,*" he said, patting her shoulder affectionately.

"Yes, see you in the morning, Papa."

"Young Shane. . .*Gute Nacht.*"

"G'night, Uncle Arne."

He watched the aging man head for his bedroom, via the kitchen. Returning his gaze to Elsa, he encountered her perturbed expression.

"May I be so bold as to inquire over what it is you wanted your father to say to Mr. Quinsy?"

Elsa puffed out an exasperated breath, but shook her head.

"Aw, c'mon. You can tell me," Shane cajoled. He strode slowly toward her. "Maybe I can help."

"You can't." Elsa folded her arms in front of her and dropped her gaze to the tips of her leather ankle boots.

"Let me guess. You changed your mind about marrying Henry. Someone else came along and. . .and swept you off the service counter."

Elsa let her arms fall to her sides. "You are the most vain man I have ever met."

Shane laughed. "I reckon you're right about that." He took another step forward. "Elsa," he said in all seriousness, "don't fall in love with me. I'll only break your heart."

She sort of rolled her eyes and looked away, so Shane took hold of her chin, urging her gaze to his own.

"Look at me, Elsa."

She did and Shane's heart splintered seeing fat tears fill her eyes.

"Honey, I'm a no-account gambler. Why do you think my father didn't leave me his company or the family estate? He knew I'd probably lose everything in some high stakes card game. I've been known for drinking and carousing until dawn. I haven't held a job for more than a few months at a time. That's the kind of man I really am, Elsa. I'm not husband material for a fine, Christian woman like yourself."

"I know what kind of man you are," Elsa said staring back at him with misty eyes that held such tenderness it took Shane's breath away.

He caressed her cheek with the backs of his fingers, fighting the urge to kiss her. He had a hunch she wanted to be kissed too.

At that precise moment, however, Henry burst through the front door. "Elsa?" he called in his habitual, whiny voice. "Elsa?"

"Over here, Henry."

Shane lowered his hand, and stepped backward. "Well,

good evening Mr. Qu—I mean, Peabody."

His near blunder earned Shane a rap in the arm. He grinned.

"Come in, Henry," Elsa invited. "Papa has already retired for the night, and I'm on my way to the Tidewells' house, but I'm certain Mr. Gerhard will keep you in plenty of company. He likes to play cards." She made for the door and grabbed her shawl and bonnet. "Good night."

"Whoa, Elsa, just a minute here," Shane called.

But the door slammed shut, signaling her hasty departure.

"Little imp," Shane muttered. He strode to the windows and saw her walking up the street in the company of the blond gal from the mercantile.

Behind him, Shane heard Henry clear his throat. "Imp? Is that what you called Elsa?"

"Ah, yes, it is." Shane pivoted, considering the small man standing several feet away. "You know, if you're not careful, Mr. Peabody, some blackguard is liable to steal your woman."

With the cookies baked, frosted, and decorated, Elsa and Samantha bid farewell to Mrs. Tidewell and headed for home.

"Won't Betsy be pleased with the cookie we made for her?" Samantha said.

"Yes, it's perfect," Elsa replied, wondering who would choose their friend's treat tomorrow. Betsy's pa deemed it unsafe for her to drive the wagon into town from her family's farm after dark. Besides, she had her siblings to care for and tuck into bed.

"I wonder who'll get my cookie," Samantha mused. "I hope it's Martin Crabtree. He just got home from law school today. He'll be in town through Easter Sunday, so he'll attend the Spring Fling tomorrow."

"Make sure you give him a hint about your cookie before one of the Bunk brothers gobbles it up."

The girls shared a little laugh as they turned onto Main Street.

"What about you? Will you give Henry a hint?"

Elsa shook her head, glad it was too dark for Samantha to see her. "I know I'm betrothed to Henry, but. . .well. . ."

"It's that Mr. Gerhard, isn't it?"

"Yes," Elsa whispered. The admission seemed to float on the breeze and carry through the budding treetops.

"I thought maybe you had developed feelings for him."

"It's worse than that, Samantha. I'm in love with him."

"Oh, dear. . ."

Elsa could faintly see her friend's face peeping out from beneath her bonnet as they paused in front of the boardinghouse.

"Don't worry about me," Elsa said as they prepared to part for the night. "God knows my heart and He is in control. He knows the situation, and He has already planned for it in His throne room. This turn of events is no surprise to God."

"Very true."

"How's your mother?" Elsa asked, changing the subject.

"She's not faring well. I overheard Doc telling my father that. . .that it's likely she'll. . .die. We should be prepared."

Samantha sniffed audibly, and Elsa pulled her friend into an embrace. "There, there, don't cry." She wished she could say something profound to ease Samantha's sorrow.

"Oh, I'll be all right," she said, giving Elsa a bit of a squeeze before pulling away. "I know God is in charge of my situation too. But trusting Him is easier said than done. Mama and I are very close."

"Yes, I know. . ."

A solemn moment hung between them.

"I should get home," Samantha said.

Elsa nodded. "Good night, my dear friend."

"Good night."

With sadness filling her being, Elsa walked the rest of the way to the boardinghouse—and nearly tripped over Shane's form perched on the stoop by the front door.

" 'Bout time you got home."

"And who might you be, my guardian?" Elsa asked tartly.

"Guardian angel, maybe."

In spite of herself, she laughed.

"What did I hear about your friend's mother?"

Elsa sobered. "She's sick. . .possibly dying."

"That's a shame."

"Yes, it is. Mrs. Thomasohn is a fine woman, caring in every way. When my mama was ill, Mrs. Thomasohn checked in on Heidi, Herrick, and me, and she made sure things were running smoothly. After Mama died, Mrs. Thomasohn proved such a comfort to us." Elsa paused thoughtfully. "I just wish there was something I could do in return, but it seems Samantha is managing."

"How long since your mother passed away?"

"Almost five years."

"Guess everyone has to go sometime, hm?"

"True. Tomorrow isn't promised to any of us." She tipped her head, straining to see Shane's features in the darkness. Only a small light flickered behind him from inside the boardinghouse. "Do you miss your parents?"

"Some. But if the Bible is true, they're walking the streets of gold in heaven right now. Their enthusiasm for God may have dwindled, but I know they were true believers."

"How did you know about that. . .about the streets of gold in heaven?"

Shane chuckled. "Seems I'm remembering some old Sunday school lessons. I've had a lot of time to think since coming to Hickory Corners. Not much else to do around here after sundown."

Elsa sat beside him. "Did you and Henry get along all right tonight?"

"Did we get along. . . ? I ought to take you over my knee for pulling that prank."

Elsa grinned.

"Oh, I suppose Henry and I had a friendly conversation," Shane finally admitted. "I did my best to make him see that he sorely neglects you, but ol' Henry just wanted to complain about his throat. By the way, he feels better today. I thought you'd want to know."

"Yes, thank you. That is good news."

"I told him he should go back to Boston where he wants to have that operation—a tonsillectomy. I believe Henry is seriously considering the idea."

"Really?"

"Uh-huh." There was a smile in his voice when he added, "I hope you'll enjoy living in Boston."

"I'm sure I'll never know. I don't plan to leave my papa and Hickory Corners. Henry knows that. Besides, I've changed my mind about marrying him."

"Is that what you wanted your papa to talk to Henry about?"

"Yes."

"Well, I'm glad you've finally come to your senses, although I hope it's not on account of me."

"Of course it is. You spared me from a loveless marriage. I'm forever grateful."

"Grateful? To me?" He chuckled lightly. "All right, just so long as you're not in love with me."

Elsa chose not to directly reply to the latter. "I have decided something else too," she announced.

"What's that?"

"I've decided that if Papa cannot find those receipts, I will marry you so you can collect your money, even though I know you'll divorce me soon afterward."

Elsa was fully aware that God's Word warned Christians against marrying unbelievers; however, she rather thought her predicament was similar to Queen Esther's. Surely God would honor Elsa's arranged marriage the way He blessed Esther's marriage to a heathen king. Besides, it wasn't like hers and Shane's would be a "real" marriage.

"You're willing to marry me?" Shane asked incredulously. "You know full well I'm not the husband type."

"I know that, yes," Elsa began. "But in these past two weeks, you have cared more about me than Henry has in all the months we courted. Of course, I understand you didn't mean to show me any special affection," she put in quickly. "You were simply being the brave champion you always are."

"Brave champion?" He chuckled once more.

"You're my hero, Shane," Elsa whispered, leaning closer to him. "You're a regular knight in shining armor in my eyes."

At that, Shane hung his head back and hooted. "Elsa, you've got things all inside out and backward. Didn't you hear anything I told you earlier? I'm no champion, no hero—"

"You are to me." She placed her hand on his arm. "But, I don't expect anything from you. If we're forced to marry, you're free to return to your life in St. Louis while I live mine in Hickory Corners, knowing I spared my father's honor just the way Queen Esther spared the lives of the Jewish people."

"Queen Esther?"

"In the Bible." She suspected her rationale was weak, yet she longed to believe it.

"Ah, yes. . ."

The cool, springtime air caused Elsa to shiver. Standing, she smoothed down the skirt of her brown dress, then pulled her shawl a little tighter around her shoulders. "I guess I'll go in for the night. I think I've caught a chill. See you in the morning."

"G'night, Elsa."

With a parting smile, she walked into the boardinghouse. She had peace about her decisions, but she had to wonder how God would use it all together for His good.

Chapter 9

*S*he *thinks I'm a hero,* Shane thought, pacing his room the next morning. *A knight in shining armor.* He shook his head. *She sure is mistaken! Why, if Gramps was still alive, he'd laugh till his sides ached. Brave Champion, his "ne'er-do-well" grandson? Ha!*

Pausing, he glanced out the window at the sunshine beating down on the building next door. He had to admit, part of him longed to live up to Elsa's expectations, but the other part wondered if it were even possible. A guy like him?

A knock on the door interrupted his musings. Crossing the room, Shane answered it.

"Young Shane, vill you come up to da attic vis me und help me find dose receipts?"

"Um. . .sure." He gave the older man a quick once-over glance, and decided he looked weary—even more than weary. He looked like he hadn't had a decent night's sleep since Shane arrived. "On second thought, Uncle Arne, why don't we take a little break from our searching?"

"But I thought you ver growing restless und vanted to find da vouchers from your vater."

"I am, but. . ." Shane smiled easily. "Look, tomorrow is

Easter Sunday. Why don't we just wait until Monday to continue our search? We'll give ourselves a couple of days of rest and, who knows, maybe if you're not thinking so hard on this matter, you'll remember where you put those miserable things."

"*Ja, ja.* . .maybe if I don't think so hard. . ."

"Give your mind a bit of relaxation."

"*Ja,* I think you are right, young Shane." The old man's lined face split into a grin. "How about some breakfast?"

"Now there's an offer I won't pass up."

Grabbing his hat, Shane followed Arne down the narrow stairwell and into the dining common. Several men, riverfaring men, judging from their unkempt appearances, were on their way out. Shane nodded politely, then a wave of anxiety got the best of him, and he made a beeline straight for the kitchen.

"Elsa, are you all right?" he asked, both hands on either side of the doorjamb. His heart suddenly thundered in his chest.

She turned, a pot in her hands, a dishtowel slung over her shoulder. "I'm fine," she answered, wearing a curious frown. "Why wouldn't I be?"

"I just saw those men leaving. . ."

"Ah," she replied with a knowing look in her blue eyes. "Not to worry, Shane. I don't think the men from the docks will be getting fresh with me any time soon. I believe word of what took place last Thursday has made the rounds."

"Glad to hear it," Shane said, although he wasn't completely assuaged.

"Vhat is going on?" Arne asked, sauntering to the kitchen doorway.

Shane pivoted to face the elderly man. "Uncle Arne, you

just can't leave Elsa unattended when there's a pack of men in the dining common. It isn't safe."

"Oh, Elsa can handle herself," Arne stated confidently. "She vill take her cast-iron frying pan und go. . .bonk! right over der heads."

"Carrying those pots she's going to have arms like a man!" Shane placed one hand on Arne's shoulder and gave it a mild shake. "Look, Uncle Arne, she's a woman and you need to protect her."

"I do protect her like any gute vater!" Arne said, his voice raised in self-defense. "But you, young Shane, have over-stepped your bounds. How I care for my family is none uf your business."

"Papa—"

"No, Elsa, he's right," Shane replied, staring down into Arne's faded blue eyes. "I overstepped my bounds. My apologies, Sir."

With that, he donned his hat and left the boardinghouse. Outside, the sunshine felt warm against his face, and Shane decided if he had even a lick of common sense, he'd set sail on the next packet going anywhere. By staying in Hickory Corners, he was getting involved in all sorts of messes, none of them having to do with his sole purpose for being here— claiming his inheritance.

Strolling up Main Street, Shane had just passed the dress shop when he glimpsed none other than Mr. Quinsy leaving the shipping office. The small-framed, thin man started in his direction, and Shane felt sure Henry was on his way to the boardinghouse to see Elsa.

And it's none of my business, he told himself. As Henry neared, Shane inclined his head politely.

"Good morning, Mr. Gerhard. It's a lovely day, isn't it?"

"Sure is."

"My throat is so much better. . .did you notice how clear my voice sounds?"

"Uh. . .yes. Sounds infinitely clearer."

"I no longer croak like a frog." Henry laughed.

Shane forced a perfunctory smile.

"Say, did you recently come from the boardinghouse?"

"Yes, I did."

"Was Elsa there?"

"Sure was."

"Good. I hope she'll be ready to leave on time. I just hate being late for social functions."

"Oh?" Shane arched an inquiring brow. "What social function are you referring to?"

"Why, the Spring Fling, of course. I promised Elsa I'd take her if I felt well enough. Seeing as I do, I thought I might walk up now and break the good news to her ahead of time. The Spring Fling doesn't officially begin until one o'clock."

"Glad you're on the mend," Shane replied, wondering if Elsa would be the one doing the "breaking"—breaking off their betrothal, that is. After all, she had said she'd decided against marrying poor ol' Mr. Quinsy.

"Have a good day," Henry said, continuing on with his trek to the boardinghouse.

"And it's none of my business," Shane muttered, ambling off in the opposite direction. However, the farther away he got, the more uneasy he became. What if Elsa couldn't get herself to relay her decision to Henry? Naw, that wouldn't happen. Elsa possessed a lot of gumption. Of course, she had a soft side to her also—the side that put up with the likes of

Shane Gerhard. The side that thought he was a hero.

Against his better judgment, Shane turned around and walked back to the boardinghouse. Entering, he found Arne sitting at the greeting counter.

"Young Shane, I am sorry I lost my temper," he stated, looking sincere.

"Quite all right. Now I know where Elsa gets it!"

"Vhat?" The old man frowned, looking confused.

"Never mind." Shane chuckled. "Apology accepted. But, if you'll excuse me. . ." He glanced around the dining common. "Where did Elsa and Henry go?"

"Out in da back, I think. But, young Shane, dey are having a private talk just da two uf dem."

"Right. I'm aware of that. I just thought maybe Elsa might like some support, you know? Encouragement."

Arne grinned, causing the wrinkles on his face to multiply. "You are fond uf my Elsa, *ja?*"

"Ja," Shane admitted, although he wished it wasn't true. The feelings he'd developed for Elsa only complicated matters.

"She is fond uf you too," Arne said.

"So I've gathered."

Just then, booted footfalls sounded from the kitchen, through the dining room, and Shane turned in time to see Henry marching for the front door. The man's overall expression registered nothing, although Shane saw the grim slant of his thin lips.

Without a single word, Mr. Quinsy left.

"See," Arne said, "my Elsa alvays knows vhat to say."

Sitting outside the kitchen door on the back stoop, Elsa felt horrid. She'd crushed poor Henry by stating she had changed her mind, she couldn't marry him. He'd looked so forlorn and disappointed. Nevertheless, he didn't try to talk her out of her decision. In fact, he never even said he loved her. In her heart, Elsa knew she'd done the right thing. . .for the both of them.

Suddenly, she sensed the presence of someone standing behind her. Tipping her head back, she stared up at Shane who appeared as tall as an elm from her present viewpoint.

He grinned down at her. "Want some company?"

She righted her bearing, nodded, and scooted over to make room for him on the stoop.

"I saw Mr. Quinsy on his way out," he said, taking a seat beside her. "I take it you broke off your engagement."

Elsa nodded.

"Are you sorry?"

"No, only that I'm sorry I hurt Henry."

"He'll get over it."

Elsa had to grin at the piquant reply.

"So, um. . .would you care to attend the Spring Fling with me this afternoon?"

She turned and gazed into his face, expecting to see a sparkle of mischief in his hazel eyes; however, all she saw was the light of sincerity.

"You really want to go?"

"Only if I can take you."

Elsa smiled and lowered her gaze to the skirt of her brown dress. "I would be honored to accompany you, but just make sure you're the one who gets my cookie." Glancing back at him, she added, "You can't miss it, Shane. It has the initials S. A. G. swirled into the frosting."

"S. A. G.? Hm, those sound like my initials."

"They are," Elsa said, leaning a little bit closer and slipping her hand around his elbow. "I peeked at your signature in our guest book."

He stared at her for a good half a minute, searching her face as if her countenance held the answer to some mysterious, universal question.

At last, he grinned and looked out over the yard. "Why do I suddenly feel like I'm sinking in quicksand?"

"What?"

Shane shook his head. "Never mind." He stood, drawing Elsa to her feet. "You just go on and get all pretty for the Spring Fling."

Smiling, she nodded and reentered the boardinghouse.

Hickory Corners' annual Spring Fling took place in the one-room schoolhouse across the street from the church on Birch Street. Inside, fabric flowers of all colors decorated the little building, and desserts were lined up on a table, sitting off to one side, enough to satisfy even the Bunk brothers. Shane noticed the Fling drew primarily the unmarried townsfolk. In fact, it seemed to him, that this was Mrs. Tidewell's subtle attempt at matchmaking.

"I'm so glad you decided join us," the pleasingly plump, downy-haired woman stated upon meeting him for the second time. The first had been at church last Wednesday evening.

"Yes, well, I'm happy to be here."

It wasn't a fib either. Truth to tell, Shane couldn't think of a place he'd rather be at the moment than here with Elsa. In his eyes, she was the belle of the ball with her walnut-colored hair unpinned and cascading to her waist in silky waves. She wore a fitted, lilac blouse and full black skirt which, she said, once belonged to her mother. Elsa added that she only wore it on special occasions. He figured the Fling was as "special" as it got in this town, but he decided to quit fighting the inevitable and enjoy himself.

The afternoon began with casual socializing. Shane and Elsa chatted first with Samantha Thomasohn. Her mother wasn't any better, so Samantha didn't plan to stay at the Spring Fling for long. Next, they conversed with Betsy Larkin whose siblings were playing outside in the adjacent school yard, all except the youngest, that is. Three-year-old Greta with her feathery, blond hair and enormous cocoa-brown eyes seemed permanently attached to her older sister's hip. Awhile later, Shane was introduced to Brady Forbes, the Tidewells' nephew, and Lars Douglas, an employee at the grist mill up the road. Shane had to admit, the more folks he met in Hickory Corners, the more he liked the place.

After the mingling, they engaged in an organized game of musical chairs, which the men played a second time blindfolded. The young ladies giggled and watched from the back of the schoolhouse as the gents tripped over each other and missed chairs completely, only to land on their backsides on the hard wooden floor. Shane decided he'd be stiff until Tuesday after that little escapade.

Finally, the event everyone had been waiting for—the cookie caper. Shane managed to acquire Elsa's baked treat, even though he almost had to wrangle it out of Horace Bunk's meaty paw. As the winner, his reward was sharing Elsa's boxed supper out on a grassy knoll in the school yard.

As they strolled back to the boardinghouse that evening, Shane had to admit he'd had a fine time. Good clean fun proved surprisingly enjoyable. Turning onto Birch Street, Elsa's arm looped around his elbow, Shane realized this sleepy, little town offered him more than his inheritance could ever buy. Love. Friendship. Respect. Dignity.

They passed the shipping office, and he saw the fretful mar above Elsa's brow which her bonnet failed to shadow.

"I warned Henry a blackguard might steal his woman if he wasn't careful."

"I take it you're referring to yourself," Elsa said with a demure, little smile. "But I hardly think of you as a black-guard. . .and neither does anyone else in Hickory Corners."

"Just shows how little you all know me."

" 'There is none righteous,' Shane, 'no not one.' Every man alive has made his share of mistakes."

Shane wagged his head and chuckled. "Well, Lady, you can't say I didn't warn you."

They paused in front of the boardinghouse, and Elsa peered up at him with questions pooling in her blue eyes. "What does that mean?"

"It means, Miss Elsa Fritch, you're going to marry me whether your father finds those receipts or not. You see, it just so happens that in two weeks' time, I've fallen in love with you."

Chapter 10

As Elsa dressed for church the next morning, Shane's words whirled around in her head. "I've fallen in love with you. . ."

Hearing them last night was like a dream come true, and Elsa felt tempted to pinch herself to make sure it was truly reality. Shane defended her, protected her. . .everything she'd asked God for in a husband. But she had mistakenly thought she would have to forgo those attributes because of her own capabilities.

The only problem remaining was Shane's unbelief, and if they were to have a real marriage, as opposed to one procreated by their parents' contract, then his lack of faith was an issue. But Elsa felt certain his conversion to Christ would occur in the near future. He had agreed to attend this morning's Resurrection Sunday service, and Elsa claimed the victory beforehand, knowing it was God's will that none should perish but that all should come to repentance.

Wearing her Sunday best, a raspberry-colored, linen frock with white lace adorning the neckline and sleeves, Elsa left her bedroom and walked down the hallway to the kitchen. Breakfast had been a simple fare this morning of porridge and canned peaches, so as to allow Elsa time to prepare for church, and she'd thought all the guests had left. But in the dining room, she heard male voices. They sounded somber. Curious, Elsa slipped into the adjoining area just in time to hear Doc tell Shane and Papa that Mrs. Thomasohn died last night.

"I did everything I could. So did the family."

"Ja, I am sure das true," Papa replied.

"Well, I thought, being neighbors, you would want to know."

Tears filled Elsa's eyes and she bit her bottom lip in effort to thwart them. Poor Samantha. . .

"Was Mrs. Thomasohn a. . .a Christian?" Shane asked hesitantly.

"Oh, *ja,* she loved da Lord," Papa replied.

He nodded. "Guess that's something to be thankful for, huh?"

"Yes, you're right, Son," Doc said, clapping Shane on the back with one arthritic hand. "We don't have to mourn like the heathen do, because as Christians, we know there's life ever-lasting once we leave this world. In heaven, there'll be no more pain, no more sorrow. . .and God will wipe away all tears from our eyes."

Recognizing the heartfelt promise from the Book of Revelation, Elsa choked on a sob. A moment later, Shane's strong arm was draped around her shoulders, hugging her to him.

"There, there, now, don't cry, Elsa. I know you're sad, but think of it this way—we're all on a journey, and Mrs. Thomasohn's just gone on ahead of us. You'll see her again."

"Amen!" said Doc. "The Good Book says to be absent from the body is to be present with the Lord. I s'pose this is like resurrection day for that dear lady. We call it Easter Sunday when we celebrate our Lord's ascension from the grave and in many respects, we could celebrate for Mrs. Thomasohn in the same manner."

Doc's analogy lessened Elsa's sorrow, although she knew it would take time for God to heal Samantha's heart, and the hearts of her father, brothers, and sisters-in-law. It had taken a long while before Elsa didn't mourn for her mama and even now she missed her sometimes.

Shane reached into the inside pocket of his vest and produced a white handkerchief. "Here you go, Darlin'. Dry your eyes. That's right. Now, blow."

Elsa complied, feeling like a little girl. But, finally, her embarrassment overtook her and she snatched the linen wipe out of Shane's hand. "I can blow my own nose, Shane Gerhard, thank you very much."

Grinning, he allowed her the courtesy, after which time Elsa absently passed back his handkerchief. Shane pocketed it once more.

"See that, Arne?" Doc asked with a chuckle. "Looks to me like true love."

"*Ja*, only true love vill compel a man to return a soiled handkerchief to his pocket."

Elsa winced and looked over at Shane, an apology on her heart. For the first time ever, she saw an expression of chagrin creep across his features.

Standing up in front of the church, Elsa sang a solo and Shane decided she had the most beautiful voice of any woman he'd ever heard. A deep second soprano, she serenaded the congregation with a stirring number. After she returned to the pew and her place between Shane and Arne, Pastor Tidewell delivered his sermon.

On the whole, the Sunday service had a somber feeling to it, Shane thought. Not only were the parishioners grieving for their friend and neighbor, but Pastor Tidewell chose to speak on a very weighty subject: the Crucifixion. He said in order to rejoice on Easter Sunday, one had to understand what transpired the few days before.

Shane tried not to wince when Pastor Tidewell described how the Roman soldiers nailed the Lord Jesus to a rugged cross, leaving Him there to suffer in bitter agony.

"And do you know who Jesus Christ saw while He hung on that tree? He saw you, and you, and you, and me." Pastor Tidewell pointed at various individuals and Shane felt sure it was no accident that his gnarly finger included him. "Christ died for all, and if you don't believe me, look here what the Bible says in Romans chapter ten, verse thirteen. 'For whosoever shall call upon the name of the Lord shall be saved.' Whosoever means anyone who has a mind to accept God's free gift of salvation. And how do we know it's a gift? Well, look with me, if you will, at John chapter three, verse sixteen. Let's all read that passage together, shall we?"

Shane looked on with Elsa and read along with her. " 'For God so loved the world, that he gave his only begotten Son, that whosoever believeth in him should not perish, but have everlasting life.' "

"Did you see that word 'gave'? That's right, God gave us His Son to suffer in our stead. Now, I want you to read that verse once more, but silently this time," Pastor Tidewell said, "and I want you to substitute your own name where the passage says 'the world'. All right, go ahead. Read it."

Shane did so, swallowing hard. *For God so loved Shane Gerhard, that he gave his only begotten Son. . .*

He sat there and stared at the words now swimming before his eyes. Christ died for him? Shane Gerhard, a no-account, "ne'er-do-well" fellow that didn't deserve anything less than hellfire? Yet, Shane believed it, although he might not have had Elsa not deemed him her "hero." She'd started turning his thinking around. Furthermore, he couldn't explain why, but he suddenly believed the Bible too. It was like the times when his gut instincts took over during a card game and he called the right deal. This morning, his gut instincts were calling him to choose a different way.

"Did you feel it?" Pastor Tidewell asked, smiling broadly, his gaze roving over his congregation. "Did you feel that little tug on your heartstrings? Why, that's the Holy Spirit. He's trying to get your attention."

All right, Lord, Shane prayed silently, unable to help a small grin. *You got my attention. It's taken You twenty-four years, but I'm listening now.*

During the week following, Elsa noted a change in Shane. He seemed more. . .mature, and she wasn't sure what caused it. But instead of pestering her in the kitchen, teasing and talking her ear off, he took to helping Papa around the boardinghouse. He even tilled the plot out back for the vegetable garden and fixed the outer stairwell which had grown rickety from neglect.

"Uncle Arne," Shane said after supper one evening, "have you ever thought of making this place into a hotel?"

"*Nein,* too much vork, und I am an old man."

"Well, I'm a young man, and I'd be willing to put forth the funds and some of the labor."

Coffeepot in hand, Elsa slowly turned from the box stove in the dining room and stared at Shane.

"*Nein,* I do not vant to run a hotel."

"I do. I've given the matter plenty of thought."

Elsa set down the coffee pot, and wiped her hands on her apron. "What kind of hotel?" she couldn't keep from asking.

Shane smiled. "A very respectable one. No gaming tables. No strong drink, and I'd like to renovate this boardinghouse and stay in Hickory Corners."

"You would? Why, that's wonderful." Elsa caught Shane's enthusiasm and glanced at her father.

"Vith you und your hotel, den vhat is to become uf Elsa und me?" Arne asked, looking concerned.

"I've got that all figured out. See, as part of the reconstruction, I would erect special quarters for you and I'd build an apartment above the hotel rooms for myself and. . ." He bestowed Elsa with a meaningful look and her knees weakened.

Shane cleared his throat and began again. "Uncle Arne, I want to marry Elsa and live here in Hickory Corners."

Arne gave him a suspicious frown. "Marry my Elsa?"

"That's right." He glanced at her again, before adding, "If she'll have me."

"Oh, I will!" she declared, stepping forward.

Shane grinned.

"Now, vait a minute, here. . ." Arne held up a forestalling hand. "Young Shane, I cannot allow my Elsa to marry a man who does not share our faith. Da Bible says so."

"I share your faith, Uncle Arne. I believe."

Arne narrowed his gaze. "I thought you had questions

about God und salvation."

"I did, but the Lord answered them."

"Vhen ver you born again?"

"Excuse me?" Shane frowned.

"Born again. . .da change dat happens vhen you believe."

"Ah, let's see. . ." He rubbed his shadowed jaw as he contemplated the question. "I would have to say it happened on Easter Sunday."

Watching the exchange, Elsa sensed Shane's earnestness. His reply didn't sound anything like those practiced apologies he had delivered during the first days after his arrival.

"I'm a Christian, Uncle Arne. It's just like that song we sang on Wednesday night—'Amazing Grace.' I once was lost, but now I'm found. That's me. Found."

"Hmpf!" Arne stood. "Ve vill see about dat."

He shuffled passed Elsa and headed into their back rooms. She frowned in his wake, then turned back to Shane. "What do you suppose has gotten into him?"

With a shrug, he rose from the bench and walked toward her. "Will you really marry me?" he asked, taking her hands in his.

"I really will. You're my hero, remember?"

"Sure, I do."

Her father reentered the dining room all too soon as far as Elsa was concerned. In his hands, he carried a leather portfolio. "Look vhat I found just dis afternoon. It vas in my bureau. In da bottom drawer."

Elsa felt the blood drain from her face. "The receipts?"

"*Ja.*"

"Why didn't you say something, Uncle Arne?" Shane asked, releasing Elsa's hands and striding over to the table.

He opened the leather packet.

"Elsa called us to supper, und I forgot. But now you don't have to get married. You can go back to St. Louis und collect your inheritance."

Elsa opened her mouth to rebuke her father for trying to dissuade Shane, but suddenly she saw the situation for what it really was—a test of Shane's love for her. She willed herself not to cry while she watched Shane inspect the vouchers. He had a choice to make.

"Looks like everything is in order. The debt's paid." He pivoted and faced Elsa. "Do you see this?"

She nodded weakly and forced a little smile.

Receipts in hand, he stepped toward her. She met his gaze, holding her breath, waiting, wondering. . .hoping. Then in one, two, three smooth moves, Shane tore the documents into shreds. Arne began to chuckle, while Elsa stood by and watched as Shane tossed the pieces into the air. They floated to the ground like fat snowflakes.

Elsa began to half laugh and half cry.

"I no longer care about those receipts," Shane told her. "I don't even care about my inheritance. I've discovered something more valuable than gold right here in this sleepy little town. Now, all I want is to marry you, Elsa. . .because I love you. Because I'm your knight in shining armor, and you need me."

"Oh, Shane. . ." Elsa practically threw herself into his arms. "Papa, say I can marry him. Please."

"*Ja*, go ahead. You have my blessing."

"Can I kiss her, Uncle Arne?" Shane asked, wearing a desirous expression that caused Elsa to tremble in his arms with anticipation.

"Ja, but only one kiss. You are not married yet, und do not forget it."

"Yes, Sir." A rakish gleam entered Shane's eyes. "Reckon I'd better make this one count."

He pulled Elsa close, then his mouth captured hers in the sweetest of all kisses.

And she immediately knew this man who had first made her life tumble like a child's blocks had just set it aright again.

ANDREA BOESHAAR

Andrea was born and raised in Milwaukee, Wisconsin. Married for almost twenty-five years, she and her husband, Daniel, have three grown sons. Andrea has been writing practically all her life, but writing exclusively for the Christian market since 1994. To date, she has authored eleven **Heartsong Presents** titles of inspirational romance.

As far as her writing success is concerned, Andrea gives the glory to the Lord Jesus Christ. Her writing, she feels, is a gift from God in that He has provided an outlet for her imagination and her desire to share biblical truth, whether it's presented in an evangelical light or subtly implied. In either case, Andrea ultimately wants her stories to fill her readers' hearts with hope and happiness.

Visit her web page at: www.andreaboeshaar.com.

Old Maid's Choice

By Cathy Marie Hake

Dedication

To my sister, Carolyn,
and my critique partner, Debi Boone—
Faith, constancy, and love are the fabric of your lives.
The Word of God is your pattern,
and regardless of the circumstances of life,
you've stitched straight and true.
The quilt of your Christianity is beautiful
and warms my soul.

Chapter 1

K arl, stop your sniveling and hold fast to Will. Will, you'd best quit wiggling, else Marie is going to tumble." Betsy Larkin hoisted little Greta higher onto her hip and held the reins in her other hand. All four of her younger siblings wouldn't fit on their plow horse, so she held the youngest. The other three perched precariously atop the mare and hung on to one another.

"I wanna walk, Sis," Karl whined again. "*You're* walking."

"Only because Jenny came up lame. I'd be riding, otherwise." Betsy hitched Greta again and hoped her petticoat wasn't peeping out from beneath her hem. "If I let you boys get down, you'll be muddy as piglets by the time we get to church."

"Little bitta mud never hurt a body," Karl grumbled.

Betsy ignored his observation. She made it a point to try to enter God's house in a good mood. Scolding her youngers could be the ruination of a glad heart, and she refused to let that happen. Mud sucked at her too-big boots, making each step an effort. She knew the bottom six inches of her dress were spattered beyond redemption, but there was no helping that. Cleanliness might well be next to godliness on most days, but after last night's fierce gully washer, she knew a muddy worshipper would please God more than a vain slacker who didn't make it to church.

They got to the hitching post just outside Hickory Corners Bible Church as the steeple bell pealed. "Here. I'll take Greta," her friend, Elsa, offered from the steps.

"Oh, thank you!" Betsy handed over her youngest sister and carefully pulled Marie from the nag. Once she did, both brothers flung themselves earthward. "Mind that mud puddle!"

"Aw, Sis!"

She quickly set Marie on the church steps beside Elsa and tied the mare to the hitching post. A bit of grit speckled her chapped hands, so Betsy conscientiously wiped her palms off on her skirt. Satisfied she'd gotten them fairly clean, she took a pair of mended cotton gloves she'd tucked into her sash and pulled them on.

"My, you and Shane are aglow with happiness. Marriage agrees with both of you," Betsy said as she smiled at Elsa and her handsome bridegroom. It was their first Sunday back after their extended honeymoon, and Elsa wore the pale blue wedding gown the sewing circle had helped her make.

Shane gave Elsa an affectionate squeeze. "Someday, you'll make a man as happy as my Elsa has made me."

Betsy manufactured a smile for him and didn't bother to correct his misconception. She knew better. Because of her family obligations, she was destined for spinsterhood. Men disappeared quickly once they realized her brothers and sisters claimed her time and devotion. One beau actually pretended he'd be happy to farm alongside Pa in the fields, but as soon as he learned the farm was to go to her brothers—not her husband—that one hiked on down the road. Before he left, he listed her liabilities and made her painfully aware there'd be no husband in her future.

Betsy herded her flock on into the chapel and toward the second to the last pew on the left. Once they were seated, she pulled a handkerchief from her sleeve, surreptitiously moistened it a bit with her tongue, and tried to rub a trace of dirt from behind Will's ear. He jerked away. She gave him a stern look, and he made a face as she diligently rid him of the flaw. After gently tucking one of Greta's little blond curls behind her ear, Betsy settled in. She was ready to worship.

Tyson Walker followed the tiny woman into the church. He stood in the back and watched her fuss like a hen over her brood. Her moves were quick, economical, and gentle. A wide-brimmed, flower-bedecked straw hat that had seen better days hid the color of her hair and eyes. Oddly enough, that piqued his curiosity. He waited until everyone took a place in the polished oak pews and looked for an empty spot.

"Howdy!" An old man in a black suit hobbled up. His sparse gray hair looked freshly slicked down. "Josiah Gardner. Folks call me Doc."

Ty accepted his gnarled hand and shook it carefully. His own hands were suited to holding a hammer, and he conscientiously monitored his strength so his grip stayed gentle enough to keep from harming the bony palm, yet firm enough to preserve Doc's dignity. "Tyson Walker. I just bought the smithy."

Doc let out a rusty laugh. "Glad to have you here in God's house and over at the smithy. You'll have plenty of work to keep you out of trouble."

"I was hoping that would be the case." He smiled. "I'd be honored to be your friend, but I hope I don't need your services."

The old gent chuckled. "Just as well that you're healthy. I'm getting too old to make nighttime house calls."

Ty didn't want to make the old man feel self-conscious about his frailty, so he diplomatically changed the subject. "Looks like you have a full house this morning."

"Now that's a fact. We're near to busting out the seams here." Doc looked around and nodded toward the woman Ty had been watching. "Yonder is a seat. You can sit with Miz Miz Betsy and her little brood. Mr. Larkin doesn't come, so you'll have plenty of room."

"Thank you." Ty walked over and slipped into the pew. Miz Betsy turned and tilted her head back a bit to face him. He'd expected a weathered, slightly careworn housewife. Instead, compassionate, big brown eyes glanced back at him. A generous set of freckles sprinkled across her nose. She was young! How young, he couldn't quite say. Her mouth seemed a tad big for a tiny woman, but when a hesitant smile lifted her lips, she radiated kindness. One thing for sure—a pretty face like hers could steal a man's breath away. Even in the dim interior of the clapboard church, she glowed. Ty scarcely remembered his manners enough to nod a silent greeting to her.

Her smile widened. As soon as she'd paid him that polite attention, she scooted a bit to the side and rested her hand on the older boy's leg to stop him from swinging it. "Sit still," she whispered.

As the service went on, Ty watched her manage her brood. The youngest two kids were too short to get back up on the pew after they stood for singing. She lifted them back into place, seated herself, and tucked her skirt a mite closer to her sides without any fuss or nonsense. When the older girl got restless, Miz Betsy deftly folded her handkerchief diagonally, rolled the sides inward, and then flipped back the tiptops to form a hammock with "babies" for her to use as quiet entertainment. The youngest fell asleep during the sermon, so Miz Betsy cradled her in her lap. No matter what attention her children required, she paid it; but he watched her from the corner of his eye, and Ty felt certain she'd not missed a single word the preacher said.

He thoroughly enjoyed the sermon, but he also fought a strong streak of curiosity that never managed to thin, no matter how hard he tried to tame it. Miz Betsy surely couldn't have borne these children. Simply put, she was far too young to claim them as her own. Had she married their father and taken them as part of the package? She certainly disciplined them with ease. The older of the little girls favored Miz Betsy as far as her wide, brown eyes and delicately rounded chin went. Could they be sisters? Ty wanted to know if Miz Betsy Larkin was already bound in matrimony or if she might be free for a bit of courting.

He wasn't a man to act hastily. The fact that he'd set to wondering about courting her this early on was completely out of character. Mere looks didn't hold his attention—though hers, alone, were sufficient to captivate any man in five counties. She seemed tenderhearted with the wee ones, yet she kept complete control of them. A woman with a level head, soft heart, and hardworking hands was a prize well worth pursuing.

Ty didn't understand how other men said God spoke to

them directly and told them to do something. It never happened to him. Still, he'd been praying about his future. The smithy just happened to be listed for sale in a gazette he read, and the price suited his budget. He'd saved up every last little coin he could for years until this opportunity came up and felt maybe the hand of God swept him here. A man couldn't hope to meet a woman at a better place than church—though that wasn't why he'd come to worship. If the Lord had set him in this town, could it be He also set him on this pew, next to this woman, for a reason?

Chapter 2

When everyone else rose for the benediction, Miz Betsy stayed seated. Other folks started to leave, but still, she sat there. Towering over her felt rude. Ty couldn't very well shove his way into the stream of folks ambling down the aisle, though. Big as he was, he worried about bumping into someone. He barely heard Miz Betsy's whisper, "Karl, my boot needs tying."

Karl bobbed his towhead and knelt at her feet. A second later, he held up a bedraggled length of string. "It broke, Sis. I'm sorry."

She sighed softly. "These things happen. We'd best be on our way. Pa will be hungry."

Sis. Pa. That answered that question. Ty felt a surge of delight. She wasn't taken. . .yet.

The church was close to empty. A few folks stayed to visit here and there. Ty left the woman and her kids behind. As he met the preacher at the doorway, he heard an uneven footstep. The slight clump and drag bothered him. Betsy would likely rub a blister on her heel if she didn't knot the ends of the lacing string back together and tie up her shoe.

He and the preacher both turned toward her at the same

time. When she'd walked up to the church with the smaller girl perched on her hip, Ty hadn't given it a thought—but now that the little one lay draped across Betsy's arms, he realized she was a fair burden for a petite woman to carry.

When he reached out for her toddler, Betsy gave him a startled look. "I'll tote her for you, Miss."

"Now isn't that nice," Pastor Tidewell said. "Betsy, this is Tyson Walker. He's the blacksmith we've all been waiting for. Mr. Walker, this is Betsy Larkin. You'll be seeing a fair bit of her and her kin. Their farm is the first one on the edge of town, so that makes you neighbors. Being here all on your own, you're fortunate to have friendly folk so close by."

Betsy clung to her sister and dipped her head as she murmured, "Nice to meet you, Mr. Walker."

"Likewise, Miss Larkin. Here. Let me help you." He gently took the child from her arms.

Miss Larkin's smile could light a forest at midnight. "If you could hold her just a moment, I'd dearly appreciate it." She turned her attention back to the parson. "Pastor Tidewell, that message touched me deeply. I surely do appreciate your Bible learnin'."

"Thank you, Betsy."

Ty watched her take off her gloves. She'd bleached them white as could be. Compared to the red, dry skin on her hands, they looked whiter still. Unaware of his scrutiny, she tucked the gloves into her sash, stooped, and modestly lifted her mud-splattered hem just enough to tend to matters. She started to mess with the string she used to lace up what was obviously a man's boot. A boot far too big for someone her size.

His eyes narrowed. Her gown wasn't supposed to be slate blue. Time, sun, and daily wear and tear faded the fabric. . .

but they hadn't managed to leech a single dab of this woman's zest for life. He tried to be subtle as he studied the children. They were all clean. Hair combed, slicked, and faces scrubbed pink as could be. They stayed in a huddle beside her, and he reckoned all of them probably felt cowed by his hulking size. To his dismay, kids often feared him.

Miss Larkin didn't quite manage to quell her sigh. She straightened a tad, took off her hat, and pulled a washed-out looking blue ribbon from it. As she used the ribbon to bind the ankle of her boot tight, Ty stared at her. The thick, golden braids she'd looped around her head looked like ripened wheat sheaves.

"If a woman have long hair, it is a glory to her." First Corinthians 11:15 sang in his mind. Indeed, the verse applied more to this woman than to any he'd ever seen. He wanted to reach out, touch her plaits, and test their softness. Certainly, a woman who had such a tender heart and gentle voice would have hair soft as spring rain. Instead, he disciplined himself to divert his attention to the tiny girl in his arms. "How old is this little dumpling?"

"She's three," said the other girl. "I'm Marie. I'm five. Karl is eight and Will is six and a half." Without even blinking, she continued, "Betsy is nineteen. She's the oldest."

Ty winked at her. "Thank you, Marie. It's a pleasure to make your acquaintance. I'm afraid if I bow to you as I ought, I'll drop your baby sister."

Giggles spilled out of the little girl. Her big sister rose and smiled at him. She gently reminded Marie, "Thank the gentleman for his respects."

Marie dipped a surprisingly dainty curtsey. "Thank you, Sir."

"And thank you for holding Greta." Betsy closed the distance between them and made a basket with her arms to receive her youngest sibling.

Ty eased little Greta a bit closer to his heart. He liked holding her. She was soft and sweet-smelling, and the way she nestled close to him in her sleep made him feel glad for his strength instead of clumsy from his size. He tried to keep his voice soft to allow her to slumber on. "You lead the way, Miss Larkin. I'll tote her to your wagon."

"We rode the mare," Karl griped. "Betsy didn't want us to get muddy."

"Washing muddy clothes is hard work," Ty said in a man-to-man whisper out of the side of his mouth. "She and your mama already—"

"We don't got a ma."

"We don't have a mother," Betsy corrected her brother in an even tone. "But we'll see her at the banqueting table in heaven some day."

"Speaking of food," Karl said, "I'm powerful hungry, Betsy. What're you fixin' to have for supper?"

"She put a roast in a pot over the fire before we left," Marie reported, "and there's peach cobbler for dessert."

Ty's mouth watered. He'd not eaten breakfast, so the mention of food caught his attention.

Miss Larkin looked at him, then at the minister. "Pastor, you and your wife and Mr. Walker are welcome to our table. There's gracious plenty."

The pastor chuckled. "Edna ordered me to come home for Sunday supper today. She doesn't want the trout I caught yesterday smelling up the place. Mr. Walker looks like a man who appreciates a good meal." The pastor smiled at the blacksmith. "You're in for a mighty fine treat. Betsy can cook like a dream."

Before Ty could say a word, Karl yanked on his brother's brown, woolen, broadfall pants. "C'mon, Will. If we don't drag Sis outta here, she's going to start jabbering with everyone 'bout quilts and sewing again, and I'm too powerful hungry to last through that."

A fetching blush tinted Miss Larkin's cheeks. She let out a self-conscious laugh. "You don't look like you're languishing, Karl."

Karl tilted his face toward Ty. "Sir, I spent all mornin' smelling something good baking. Matter of fact, that was 'bout all I could set my mind on for most of the service."

"Karl!"

Karl ignored his big sister's chide. "So if you'd take pity on me and head toward our farm, Betsy would race right after you. She keeps an eagle eye on our Greta."

Ty watched as embarrassment and resignation warred over Miss Larkin's pretty face, then shot her a bolstering grin. "Would you rather I ignore him, or shall I threaten to eat his slice of dessert for not attending to the pastor's words?"

Karl let out an outraged yelp as his sisters and brother laughed. Betsy turned to lead her tribe outside. Ty stepped alongside her. Most women shied away when he came close. They'd let their heads drop back and stare way up at him like he was evil old Goliath, come back to life. Miss Larkin didn't. She busied herself hanging onto Will's shirtsleeve and calling to Karl not to step into the mud.

Karl climbed atop a stone and flung himself over the horse's back, then sat up. His independent spirit was fun to behold, but Ty wondered if Betsy sometimes got a bit weary, trying to keep up with him. She cupped her hands around Will's middle and got ready to heft him upward.

"Whoa there." Ty frowned at her. "You're not aiming to hoist a strapping young man like Will, are you?" He temporarily passed little Greta over, lifted Will onto the mare, and then looked down at Marie. "Come here, Smidgen," he said as he peeled off his blue, store-bought suit coat.

"Smidgen?"

"Yes, Smidgen. You're just a little dab of a gal. I think you're just the right size for a piggyback ride." He draped the coat over the hitching post, effortlessly slung Marie onto his back, and settled her hands on his suspenders so she couldn't choke him. He picked up his coat again and reached over to rob Betsy of little Greta.

"Oh, my! They're too much for you to carry!"

He ignored her protest. As he enveloped the toddler in the folds of his coat and smoothly stole her away, he said, "I don't think you have any call to fret, Miss."

"Nope, you don't need to worry none," Karl agreed as he eyed Ty with undisguised interest. "He's pert' near big enough to drag a plow himself, Betsy."

"Karl! Mr. Walker is not a horse!" She looked at Ty with apology shimmering in the brown depths of her eyes. "Please forgive him. He's liable to let any half-baked thought flee from his lips."

Marie shimmied up his back a bit more, peered over his shoulder, and rubbed her soft cheek against his. The action held a catlike affection that warmed his heart. "Karl's wrong. You're not big as a horse; you're big as a mountain! I can see forever and a mile from up here!"

"Oh, mercy," Miss Larkin moaned.

Ty chuckled. "You needn't worry, Miss Larkin. It's no secret I'm a big fellow."

"Which Miss Larkin are you talkin' to?" Marie asked with all of the gravity a self-important child could muster.

"Now that is a knotty problem." Ty craned his head a bit so he could wink at her. "There are three of you."

"Greta's a baby still. Nobody calls her Miss Larkin yet."

"Nobody calls you Miss Larkin, either," Will tattled from horseback.

Betsy unhitched the mare and started to walk. "Nobody's going to eat supper if we listen to your silliness."

Ty paced along slowly, careful to keep his stride short to measure hers. "You might be a smidgen, Marie, but you're still a young lady. What say I call you Miss Marie and call your big sister Miss Larkin?"

"Don't think you ought to do that," Will said. A frown twisted his face. "Makes Sis sound like an old maid."

Ty studied Betsy for a long moment. Until now, she'd been modest enough not to stare at him, but she'd met his eyes. Suddenly, her lashes dropped and she looked as if she'd rather be dancing barefoot on hot ingots than subjected to his scrutiny. He softened his voice, "No one would ever believe she's an old maid. There must be a dozen bucks coming to your door, wanting to court such a fine-looking, God-fearing young woman."

"Nope." Karl shook his head and had to shove a lock of white-blond hair off his forehead. "Sis feeds 'em and sends 'em packing."

Marie clutched his suspenders tighter. "She's feeding you, but you don't have to go packin'. We like you."

Ty chuckled. "I surely do think I'm going to like being

your neighbor. Since I'm the blacksmith, you can bet I'm not going to pack up and leave. The anvil is too heavy to move!"

Though he teased lightheartedly with the children, Ty noticed how Betsy kept silent. Her reserve intrigued him. Why had she sent other men packing? She didn't seem angry or standoffish. Maybe she was a tad on the shy side. With her sister and brothers acting like chatterboxes, she probably didn't get much privacy or peace.

The mare knew her way home. Once they reached the yard, the boys rode her into the barn. Betsy led Ty to the freshly chinked log cabin. He took care to scrape the mud off his boots before he ducked under the lintel and inside.

She watched as he knelt on the blue rag rug between the hearth and trestle table, then coaxed Marie to slide off his back. Not many men were this tolerant of her rambunctious siblings, yet he'd handled them as if they were his favorite little cousins. For such a giant of a man, he managed to keep his bass voice at a quiet rumble. The sound of his deep, soft words made Betsy feel strangely warm inside. So did the way he tenderly looked down at Greta.

"Do you want this little snippet to wake up for supper, or shall I put her to bed?"

"She'll nap awhile longer. I'll take her—"

He shook his head. "No, Miss Larkin. You just tell me where to lay her down."

His dark, wavy hair looked like it needed a trim. Betsy silently scolded herself for thinking anything so personal about a stranger and led him over to the far side of the cabin. She pulled back the thick, green wool blanket that partitioned off the small bedroom she shared with her sisters. For a moment, she wondered what he thought of her home. Though bigger than most log cabins, it wasn't fancy in the least. Farming and frills didn't go together.

A smile broke across his face. "Karl mentioned something about you and quilting. I can see why. That piece you have on the bed is handsome as can be."

"Thank you." She glanced at the Star of Bethlehem she'd pieced out of several shades of blue and green in hopes it would brighten the dim space. "I just finished it last May."

He carefully lowered Greta into the center of the bed the three sisters shared, then smoothed a few curls away from her forehead before he stepped back.

Betsy's heart melted. His gentleness disarmed her. He might be big, but a softness in his hazel eyes and something about the way he took care to leash his strength left Betsy feeling she could rely on him. She silently unhooked Greta's little shoes, gave them each a small twist to help them come off more easily, then took away his coat and covered her with a well-worn, pink-and-white striped, flannel blanket. Greta wiggled onto her side and popped her thumb into her mouth.

"She's darling," the blacksmith murmured as he slipped the coat back up to cover his brawny shoulders. "All of them are. You take mighty good care of them. Someday, your husband will be glad of all of your experience with children."

Straightening up and ignoring the twinge in her heart, Betsy shook her head. "There won't be a husband, Mr. Walker. My family needs me."

Chapter 3

The next morning, Ty stoked the fire and couldn't get Betsy's words out of his head. *There won't be a husband. . . .* What a terrible thing for her to believe. Shouldn't a young woman with a heart as sweet as hers dream of falling in love? *My family needs me.* She'd said the words so simply, so calmly—as if it were a fact no one ought to question; but there'd been something in her eyes that made him wonder if she'd been hurt by a foolish local buck who told her he didn't need her. A woman deserved to be needed and loved. . .*and Betsy Larkin is some woman.*

Ty turned back to his anvil to examine the horseshoe. He planned to shape the next one just a shade wider. He'd slipped into the Larkin's barn last night and pried the shoe off their mare. He'd noticed she was nodding down—a sure sign something was wrong with one of her hind legs. He suspected the problem lay with the mare's shoe. The least he could do was make a new one—especially after he'd spent all Sunday afternoon at the Larkin table, eating the finest, most flavorful roast he'd ever tasted.

"Excuse me."

Ty set down the shoe as he pivoted around. His pulse

sped up. "Miss Larkin! How nice to see you this morning."

Morning sun slanted in through the wide-open, double doors and bathed her in a golden glow. The heightened color in her cheeks made her freckles disappear, and the nut brown color of her homespun dress made her eyes look even more enchanting. She stared at the anvil. "Excuse me, Mr. Walker, but I need to ask if. . .that," she jutted her chin toward the horseshoe, "belongs to me."

"Of course it doesn't." He leaned casually against a rough wood workbench and grinned. "You're a lady. That shoe belongs on a horse."

Her eyes widened, and she gave him a disbelieving laugh. "I see you're a clever man with words. Does that shoe belong to Jenny?"

He lifted a shoulder negligently. "Used to. It was loose and a tad on the small side. I figured since I was just starting up the fire in here today to get a feel for things, we'd do each other a favor—I'd fix up Jenny, and it would allow me a simple task so I could become accustomed to my shop."

"I'll tell Pa so he—"

"No need for that." He waved a hand at the cobwebs and scattered tools left in disarray by the untimely death of the previous blacksmith. "You can see I need to put things in order, and the morning's chilly. I'd have fired up the forge, anyway."

"I'll send Karl over after school to help you clean a bit. He might be on the small side, but he's a good worker. I'll expect you tonight for supper too."

Ty adjusted his leather apron. "Miss Larkin, am I to figure you and I are starting a habit of swapping howdies and favors?"

"Pa and I have a rule. We won't be beholden to anyone."

"I live by the same standard. Wonderful as Sunday supper tasted yesterday, I'd best put you on notice: I'm going to search for things to do for your farm every now and then since you counter my labors with meals." He waggled his brows playfully. "In fact, lovely Miss Larkin, I have a confession to make."

"Oh?"

"I'm all thumbs when it comes to fixin' vittles, so I just might start making everything from doorknobs to shutter dogs to earn me a place at your supper table."

Her eyes twinkled. "Mr. Walker, you're getting the short end of the deal on that—especially since we also have a policy that there's always an open place at our table."

Karl and Mr. Walker arrived about a half hour sooner than Betsy anticipated. She had a length of wool laid across the table and was trying to figure out how to get dresses for both girls and a skirt for herself out of it. No matter which way she worked it, she lacked fabric.

"Hey, Sunshine," her new neighbor said, "why are you wearing clouds?"

Sunshine? No one ever called her anything other than Betsy or Sis. The way he rumbled the sobriquet coaxed a smile from her. "I'm a bit short on the measure." She felt her smile fade when she caught sight of Karl's dirt-and-soot-covered clothes.

"We got his shop all put to rights, Sis," Karl boasted. Like the new blacksmith, his hair was wet, and his face and hands looked freshly scrubbed.

Mr. Walker rested his palm on Karl's head. "Aye, he's a

hardworkin' lad." He rumpled Karl's hair and ordered, "Now remember what I said. Go grab something else to wear. Your sister doesn't need you smudging her tidy home. Best if you change outside, then shake these out. When's laundry day?"

"Wednesday," Betsy said. She tried not to show her dismay. She seriously doubted Karl's clothes would ever come clean. She let out a small sigh and resigned herself to cutting britches for him from the wool. She could make do without a skirt for awhile yet.

Pa came through the door. "Tomorrow's Tuesday. You getting ready to go to Miz T's again, Betsy?"

"Yes." She hastily folded the cloth and set it aside. She could cut the dresses out after supper. Hungry men shouldn't have to wait. She put biscuits in the large, shallow kettle and hung it high above the fire so they'd bake without burning. Next, she knelt on the flagstone hearth. The rich aroma of venison stew filled the house as she stirred the pot. "Ruthie Schmidt said she'll mind Greta for me again."

Pa pulled out a bench and sat at the table. He gave her a rueful look. "I ripped the elbow of my shirt."

"It happens," she said. "I'll try to get to it after supper. Will, the wood box is nigh onto empty."

"I'll help you fill it." Mr. Walker walked out the door with her little brother. A minute later, the ring of the ax sounded. There wasn't an immediate need for wood to be chopped. Pa already had seven cords done. Clearly, Mr. Walker wasn't a slacker.

"He's a good man, Betsy," Pa said softly.

"He'll make a fine neighbor."

"A man like that would likely make a good husband too." She opened the kettle and pretended to check the biscuits, even though she knew they weren't anywhere near done. She didn't want Pa to see the longing in her eyes. "We'll have to introduce him around, then."

"So Betsy, tell us about your new blacksmith." Samantha brushed a speck of lint from her black dress the next day as they sat and sewed in Mrs. T's pristine parlor.

Betsy concentrated on mending the rip in Pa's shirt. "He's not mine. His name is Tyson Walker, and I'd be happy to introduce you."

"What is he like?" Samantha pressed.

"I just met him at church two days ago." Betsy wished her cousin wouldn't be so curious or perceptive. She bit the thread and knotted it. "I could scarcely have anything more than a weak first impression of Mr. Walker."

"Weak?" Elsa laughed merrily. "Oh, he's anything but weak. Shane said Mr. Walker shot a five-point buck early this morning and carried it from the woods to his place over his shoulders without a bit of help!"

"Then we can assume he's not going to go hungry this winter," Mrs. T said matter-of-factly. She used her porcelain thimble to push the needle through several layers of wool. "Though with Betsy's good cooking and the Larkins' hospitality, I didn't worry for a moment that he'd starve."

"Speaking of food," Betsy said in an attempt to change the subject, "Samantha, I still want your recipe for that scrumptious squash casserole."

"I'll write it down for you. Mama made that one up. She loved it too." Samantha blinked back tears.

Betsy set aside her needle and squeezed Mantha's hand.

Mantha gave her the "be brave for me" look, so Betsy forced a lighthearted tone, "As much squash as I grew this year, we'll probably eat that casserole for the next month!"

Mrs. T took the cue, laughed, and picked up the Bible from the side table. "The reading I chose for today is about how God abundantly supplies all of our needs."

Betsy carried the big willow basket full of freshly mended clothes on her hip. Underneath them, a wool dress she'd begun for Greta lay stuffed in a clean sugar sack. Betsy would work on it late at night and use the daytime hours when Marie was at school to stitch on Marie's. Christmas was coming up fast, and she wanted to have something to give each of them. She'd spent much of the summer sitting out on the porch in the evening, spinning while Marie carded the wool.

Pa had planted a full acre of flax. Less than half that would have been gracious plenty to weave the linen they'd need for the year, but Betsy held her silence. Some days, his anger toward God was a fearsome thing. When he grew restless or bitter, she was just as happy for him to be out plowing a field or spending his wrath on the earth. Though he'd come in worn out those nights, he never looked at peace.

He still refused to go to church. He sat in stony silence as Betsy led the children in prayers. Most evenings, when she read to them from the Bible, he'd go out to tend the beasts in the barn. It burdened her terribly to know he'd turned his anger toward God. Still, Pa allowed her to worship under his roof and take her youngers to church. For now, that had to suffice.

Maybe she could squeeze in more time at her loom. With

all that extra flax, the extra cloth—no, she shook her head. As it was, she barely seemed to get everything done. Aunt Rachel used to help now and then when the mercantile was slow, but since she'd died, even that little bit of help was gone. With winter coming on, Betsy knew she'd spend more time indoors, but she'd learned to use the cold months to do other things.

Marie and Greta were five steps ahead. Marie had just learned to skip. Greta fancied that she could, too, so she galloped alongside her sister and giggled with glee. Karl and Will dawdled behind her until the smithy came in sight. They both sped up. "Let's go see Mr. Walker!"

"Boys! Don't bother him. He's at work!" Even as she called to them, Betsy knew it was a lost cause. Part of her wanted to hasten, too; but that would be unseemly, and she didn't want to look like she was interested in the handsome, strong, new man in town.

Mr. Walker showing up for church of his own accord spoke volumes. The noontime conversation on Sunday made it clear he honored the Lord and loved reading the Bible as much as she did. Betsy admired a man who lived his relationship with God so naturally. There was something about having a man say grace or mention the Lord that made a house feel safe and her heart feel warm. Especially with Pa at odds with the Almighty, it would be wonderful to have a Christian brother so close by.

Long before she reached the wide opened doors of the smithy, Betsy could smell the smoke and hear the clang of hammer on metal. The blows carried a rhythm and music the previous smith never attained. It reminded her of the joyful peal of the church bells. Betsy felt her heartbeat change to match the hammer's cadence, and she felt a shiver of delight at stopping by to see Mr. Walker. She stood behind the children, but their chatter had already garnered attention.

"Hello, my new little friends! It's so nice of you to stop to see me when school is over for the day." He looked past them, and his smile widened as he spied Betsy. "I pounded together a small fence there, just inside the door. That way, the children can come watch when they have your permission, but you won't need to worry that sparks or slivers of metal will hit them."

"You're very thoughtful, Mr. Walker. You needn't feel obligated to entertain my little brothers and sisters."

He chuckled. "I have a feeling they'll entertain me far more. You're always welcome, Miss Larkin—you, and the kids. Did you have fun, visiting with your friends as you sewed?"

The tilt of his smile made the welcome personal. She felt her cheeks grow warm and tried to hide her reaction. "Yes, the sewing circle is special. Mrs. T—that is, Mrs. Tidewell—is a lovely woman. She took to heart the verse in the Book of Titus that exhorts the older women of the church to guide and instruct the younger ones. She invites us over each Tuesday for tea, sewing, and Christian fellowship."

His head tilted to the side a bit. He glanced down at the children, then back at her. A flash of understanding glinted in his eyes. "Must be nice to talk things over with womenfolk and have a chance to sit down for a few minutes."

"I confess, I do look forward to Tuesdays almost as much as I anticipate Sundays. The reverend has a way of making the Bible come alive."

"I noticed." He shoved back an errant lock of hair. "If the ground is wet again this Sunday, I'll stop by with my horse so we can all ride."

"Oh, but you shod Jenny." Though Betsy demurred, something deep inside dared to hope he'd insist.

Concern furrowed his brow. "Even if you and little Greta ride Jenny, these other kids are getting so big, it's precarious for all of them to share a horse."

"I could ride with him, Sis." Marie's awestruck look and tone made it clear she'd be delighted to do so.

"Hey! Me!" Will pounded his chest. "He's a boy. Boys stick together."

"I'll take turns giving all of you rides," Mr. Walker said diplomatically.

"Even Betsy?" Greta asked.

The blacksmith looked at Betsy with twinkling eyes. Her cheeks felt scorched by heat, but he simply chortled and shrugged. "Told you they'd entertain me. Tell you what, kids, I hope to repair the sleigh over on the side of the smithy. When it snows, we'll ride to church in style. That's how your big sister will ride with me."

The children chattered excitedly. "Misser Wakka, can I go too?" Greta asked.

He leaned over the spanking new fence and hoisted Greta high. Rolled up shirtsleeves left his ropy forearms bare, accentuating his strength and making it clear he took pains to be extra gentle as he playfully bounced her up and down. "Hmmm. I suppose you don't weigh too much. We'll tuck you in." He stood her on the fence and kept his huge hands clasped around her. "If we're going to be friends, 'Misser Wakka' sounds like a big mouthful for a half pint like you. Why don't you call me Ty?"

"Sometimes I tie Betsy's apron," Marie said as if the name and the verb were all the same.

To Betsy's amazement, Ty took Marie's childish reasoning in stride and looked down at his sooty leather apron. "Her apron doesn't look anything like mine." He carefully set Greta back down beside Betsy. "Can't say I end up looking very respectable once I set to work."

"Pa gets sweaty and muddy all of the time," Karl declared. "Betsy says that a man who comes home clean didn't mind his work. Course, she makes sure Pa washes up on the porch and scrapes his boots 'fore he comes inside."

"I'll remember that tonight. Your pa invited me to supper. I hope you don't mind, Miss Larkin. He and I were making some neighborly arrangements, and he told me to be there just past sunset."

Glory, what will I fix? I was just going to sliver ham bits in some noodles. . . .

"I brought down a buck this morning," he continued, completely unaware of the panic he'd set her into. "We stuffed a roast in the pan, if that sounds all right to you. Your pa is sowing the winter wheat today, so I figure he's going to have a fair appetite too."

"Yes. Yes, he will," Betsy stammered. How could one man upset the balance of her day with just a few sentences? "I'd best go slide it on the spit right away. It was very generous of you to share it with us. Come, children."

"Bye-bye, Misser Ty," Greta said. The others echoed her—including Betsy. Once she caught herself being familiar, she felt the telltale tingle of another blush.

"I'll see you later—all of you." He lifted his hammer. "I'm looking forward to your delicious cooking, Miss Betsy."

Chapter 4

They left, and Ty turned back to his forge. He used the bellows to fan the fire and grinned at the collection of implements waiting for repair. Hickory Corners had been without a blacksmith for months, and essential things had fallen into disrepair. Most of the men within a whole day's ride had dropped by with items that needed urgent attention.

They needed him there. Aye, they did—and he'd been a bit of a rascal, inserting himself into the Larkins' life and even daring to address Betsy so familiarly. She had better get used to it. He was here to stay, and he wanted *her* to need him too.

A steady work pace soon resulted in several sound repairs. Ty set the items on a shelf and carefully kept them with the tags he made to remind him of the owners' names. In a week or so, he'd know them all by name and recall what belonged to whom, but for now, the paper helped him remember names and faces.

The tiny cabin next to the smithy left much to be desired. He'd slept on a pallet of pine needles the past three nights because the iron bedstead needed joint work and the mattress had boasted a nest of field mice. Though he'd gotten rid of the creatures and knocked down the cobwebs, the place clearly hadn't been inhabited for a long while. He'd lived in far worse. Having slept in the woodshed until his stepfather sold him into his apprenticeship, he still shuddered at being in small, dark places.

Thanks to Betsy's fine cooking, he hadn't had to fix a real meal for himself. Just as well too. He still needed to visit the mercantile to lay in essential supplies. With the bartered goods or money he'd collect from the men who would claim their repaired goods, he'd be able to fill his larder and pick up staples on Friday. In the meantime, the loaf of bread, wheel of cheese, and apples he'd bought would take care of him. . .but he surely did long for sunset so he could go to Betsy's big, happy home and sit at her table.

"Oh, for goodness' sake!" Betsy stood in the doorway with a quilt wrapped around herself for warmth and modesty. She gaped at Ty. His boyishly handsome, lopsided smile could melt a weaker woman's heart, but she'd just about had enough of him and his early morning wake-up calls. In the past week, he'd arrived with the cock's crow five times. Each time, he brought something he'd managed to hunt. To his credit, he diligently skinned and dressed everything. In addition to the buck, his tally rated as more than impressive: another deer, a full dozen snared rabbits, seven late-migrating ducks, and now, a sizable string of fish.

"You've gotten enough meat to see yourself well through winter," she said as she tried not to let her teeth chatter.

"Not at all, Sunshine. I'm just getting started. Besides, when we butchered your pa's sow so you could make the sausage, we agreed to share."

She gave him a weak smile. Venison sausage tasted too gamy on its own. They'd had a two-day long commitment where Leonard Melvin and his son closed the livery and harness shop and came over to help Pa and Ty slaughter a sow and butcher the second deer.

Betsy called upon Virginia Alexander and Elsa to come help her grind the scraps of pork along with venison to flavor the sausage. They'd spent long, hot hours chopping, grinding, and seasoning meat, washing the tripe, and filling it before they hung the sausages in the smokehouse. Five households— four, if she didn't count Tyson's since Pa invited him to dine with them regularly—all came away with a generous supply. Part of her felt elated they'd have delicious food for the months to come; part of her was too tired to be glad about much of anything. She stared at the fish and compressed her lips.

"Your pa was already going out to milk the cows. He told me to bring these to you. We could have some for supper, and I'll hang the rest in the smokehouse." Ty glanced down and frowned.

She curled her cold, cold toes beneath the hem of her nightgown. It was hard to be gracious when he kept seeing her at her worst. "Go on to the smokehouse and bring the rest back in a pail of water so they stay fresh for supper. I'll get breakfast started."

"You don't need to feed me breakfast, Betsy. You're already making supper every night."

"You're hunting it!"

"It's the least I can do. My smokehouse is rotted clean through, so your pa is letting me use yours, and he's loaned me wood 'til I can catch up on the repairs everyone needs.

You folks take neighboring and hospitality far beyond the commonplace."

Betsy clutched the quilt closer and shook her head. She glanced back at the far side of the cabin toward the boys' bed when Will muttered in his sleep. She found it too hard to look Ty in the eye. "You don't know the difference you're making," she whispered. "Pa's so tired. You sharing your meat takes some of the burden off of him, and the way you shod Jenny and fixed the barn hinges—those things are easing his lot. It's good, too, for Karl and Will to hear a man pray at the table again. Pa stopped praying the day my stepmama died. Bad enough he lost my mother, but losing Frieda when he had a whole passel of children hardened his heart."

She bit her lip. *Why am I babbling? This is so awkward. He didn't need to know that about Pa.*

"Betsy," Ty said softly, "your pa's a good man."

"I know! Yes, I know this!"

He nodded. "Prayer and time. We'll pray and give God time to work. Your pa will let go of the hurt and stop blaming God. In the meantime, I'll come each Sunday so the boys will have a man to accompany them to church."

"Then you must stay for Sunday supper."

He winked. "I was hoping you'd say that."

Something in the way he smiled and winked sent the telltale tingle of a blush straight to her cheeks. *And he thinks we're acting more than neighborly?* "I'll. . .um, we'll see you for supper, then." She took the pail from him.

"That thought's enough to make me wish the day away." Ty nodded and left.

As he paced off, Betsy realized the warmth in her heart had made her forget about her cold toes. She hastily shut the door and choked back a sob. She couldn't allow herself these feelings. She needed to mind her obligations instead of day-dreaming about what could never be. Her brothers and sisters needed her. Pa did too. Ty Walker would have to warm some other woman's heart and feet.

Chapter 5

The first half of autumn blew past so quickly, Ty scarcely could keep track of the days. He cut coal straight out of a four-foot vein in the earth just east of the edge of the township and filled the sledge twice to bring it all back. In the past, he'd done the same chore and thought nothing of it; this time, he'd come back just as filthy as always. He groaned as he caught sight of Betsy taking down her snow white laundry. Manners demanded he stop.

"Pa said you were going after coal." She unclipped another daintily embroidered pillowslip. "I overheard the sheriff and Mr. Schmidt talking about what a hardworking man you are. It's plain to see they're right." Her smile was honest and sweet as a first spring rain.

"Yeah." He looked down at his black hands and clothes. "I'm well past dirty, going on to squalid."

"It'll wash. After you dump that load, rinse your clothes and bring them over. I left the lye pot for you and banked the fire. If you do them right away and hang them in front of your fireplace tonight, they'll dry just fine."

He cocked his head to the side. She never ceased to

astonish him. The wife of the man to whom he'd been apprenticed constantly harped about the black smudges. "You really don't mind the coal dust mess, do you?"

Her brows rose in surprise. "You need coal to earn your living. I'll make a deal with you. I won't notice you're coal black if you ignore how I get covered in wheat chaff, come harvest."

He smiled. "I'm afraid I can't agree, Miss Betsy. It'll just make you look like the golden angel you are." The shocked look on her face made him chuckle. "I'd best get going. Thanks for saving the wash water for me."

In addition to getting the coal, Ty used the next weeks to chop over twenty cords of wood. He repaid the Larkins with four for the one he'd borrowed and knew the satisfaction of being sure he had enough fuel to heat his cabin and fire his forge for the winter. He'd also been careful to buy sufficient lamp oil, wicks, and candles over at Thomasohn's Mercantile to keep from living in the dark. Karl and Will dropped by and helped him chink his cabin.

One day that first week, someone had slipped into his place while he worked and cleaned up the inside. The canning jar with flowers and fresh, flour sack curtains made a difference. Those touches let him think someone cared and reminded him he wasn't a burden to be suffered any longer.

Betsy was too shy to have done the task alone. He suspected she'd pulled along a friend or two from her sewing circle. That sewing circle surely did put a gleam in her smile and gave her a bit of a break. He never once heard her complain about how much work her brothers and sisters created. She set herself to tasks and seemed to keep a glad heart, even though he sometimes wondered if she didn't long to marry and have children and a man of her own instead of tending to her siblings. Anyone who reared kids who weren't their responsibility and treated them well rated high in his estimation. Betsy not only did that—she went well beyond duty and cherished her little brothers and sisters.

The cabin still felt cramped as could be. It wouldn't take much to heat, but a man could go daft in a cabin he couldn't sneeze in without bumping into the wall or hiccup without hitting his head on the roof. At night, when the fire burned down low, he recited Bible verses from memory to push back the bad memories of childhood. Even now, years later, he loathed dark, small places. When they were cold, that made them even worse. If he didn't want to make a fool of himself by crawling to the Larkins' by midwinter and begging to live in their big house, he'd best do something quick about the situation before bad weather made it impossible to build.

Word was the Thomasohn brothers were hard workers. Ty sought out Zack and asked him for a bit of help felling trees for logs. The next day, six work-hardened men showed up. By that evening, they had it all chopped and ready for a cabin raising. Their neighborliness pleased Ty.

Ty originally planned to simply add on to his existing cabin. To his surprise, Samantha Thomasohn grabbed him by the arm, yanked her biggest brother to the side, and gave them her opinion. She emphatically insisted on leaving the cabin ten feet away. "You can use it to house an apprentice or your wife can use it as a summer cookhouse. You have plenty of logs. Fix it up right. . .like the Larkins' or the Schmidts' place."

Though he'd love to have a plank floor, Ty knew he didn't have time to make one. A space not far from the cabin was already fairly even and free of stumps—he presumed it had once been a vegetable patch. He chained a log behind his horses, stood on it, and had them drag back and forth over it to compact and level the ground. As foundations went, it was rugged, but recent rains actually made the ground soft enough to shape, but had compacted the earth enough to let him know he'd not have any nasty dips or sinking spots later. He hoped to buy planks and add in a floor come spring.

The next sunrise, even more men appeared and set to work. Soon, women brought baskets of food. It humbled Ty, knowing his neighbors had ceased their own labors without any advance planning and done this to welcome him. The whole church family set to work, and by the day's end, Pastor Tidewell dedicated Ty's home to the Lord's service.

Samantha Thomasohn was among the last to leave. Ty felt a bit awkward. Though a nice gal, she simply didn't strike a spark in him like Betsy did. Nope—he'd already set his heart on the pretty, little farm gal across from his smithy. He watched Samantha put a crock of colorful autumn leaves on the table. As she walked past him, she said quietly, "Those were Betsy's idea. She's not just my cousin, Mr. Walker. I count her as my dearest friend, and I do hope you keep in mind a heart as big as hers can be shattered easily."

He smiled. "Miss Thomasohn, Miss Betsy's a woman worthy of a man's highest regard. Her tender heart and her love for the Lord are wondrous qualities. I can promise you, I'll do my utmost to be considerate and mindful of her."

Samantha nodded, drew an inky shawl about her shoulders, and slipped out the door. Ty grabbed a lantern and stretched his legs to fall into pace alongside her. "It wouldn't do for you to find your way home alone after sunset."

"Do you need any sugar?" Uncle Silas asked Betsy the next afternoon as she dropped off her eggs at the store. "I'm not sure I'll get more in before Christmas."

Betsy thought for a moment and tried to project how much sugar she needed. Most of the time, she used sorghum molasses, honey, or maple syrup for sweetening. The money in her egg account would cover a little real sugar, though. She chewed her lip and thought of how much Ty ate and how partial he was to sweets. "Yes, I'd better get two pounds."

"Fine." As he turned to fetch the sugar, he said over his shoulder, "That new blacksmith seems to be a fine man."

"Handsome as sin too," Olivia Crabtree interjected. She looked down her nose and waggled her finger at Samantha's father. Her widow's weeds rustled about her thin frame as she stepped closer. "You'd better be sure of him, Silas Thomasohn. He's working fast—mighty fast, if you ask me. I saw him with your daughter last night, strolling down the street, close to her side."

Betsy felt her heart drop into her boots. Her ugly, too-big boots. Her suspicions were true. Ty and Samantha were fond of each other, and they were starting to court.

"You're making a barn out of a berry box, Olivia." Samantha's father shook his head, "I will say, he's a hard-working man. What do you think, Betsy?"

Betsy forced herself to agree, "Hickory Corners is fortunate. We've needed a blacksmith for a long while now." She barely managed to keep a smile on her face until the store-keeper gave her the sugar. She carried it out the door and down the street. The whole time, she wanted to cry. It was silly. She ought to be happy her dearest cousin and a godly man were interested in one another. It wasn't as if she had anything to offer him.

No, she truly was no bargain. She wrapped her braids up in a simple style instead of taking time to curl her hair. Her drab brown homespun gown looked dull as could be, and she never managed to save up quite enough for all of them to have new shoes. What with her youngers growing so fast, she couldn't very well fritter away good coins on a cobbler's services for herself when Karl and Marie could both get good wear out of shoes and still pass them down to Will and Greta. It never bothered her before, but now, she was acutely aware of the fact that she clomped around in ill-fitting boots a hired hand left behind two years ago.

As if her appearance wasn't enough to put a man off, Pa's sour attitude and her four rambunctious siblings would make any sane man look for a wife elsewhere. She loved them all— but she knew she couldn't expect a man to share her with her family. No bride saddled her groom with such a heavy burden. She didn't think of them that way, but the men who had come around made no bones about their opinions once they learned she'd never walk off and leave Pa alone with the kids. The apostle Paul talked about how being unmarried allowed him to be a servant of the Lord. He'd been content; she'd have to learn to be content being an old maid.

But deep in her heart, Betsy wept. She wanted to serve God, and she loved her family. Still, seeing how happy Elsa and Shane Gerhard were left her aching with a loneliness she couldn't put into words. Betsy knew in her head Ty Walker would never be hers, but somehow, somewhere, she'd forgotten to keep that fact straight in her heart. He was a wonderful man, and he'd make some woman—probably her very own cousin—a happy bride. Some things in life just happened. This was one of them, and it hurt something fierce. For the first time, Betsy caught a glimpse of the anguish Pa felt in being widowed.

Chapter 6

Ty concentrated on turning the metal strip over the end of the anvil to get the right angle to the twist. He'd messed up on this the first time, and Ed Stahl would be back by sundown to pick up the hoe. If Ty had his way, he'd close his doors and work on fittings for his own place. It needed shutter dogs and a swing arm for the fireplace so he could heat water. Every other house in Hickory Corners needed a fire for cooking, but Betsy fixed his meals as a matter of course.

Betsy. He surely hoped she approved of the house. In fact, he hoped someday he'd carry her over the threshold. The buck's antlers hung over the hearth and held his rifle and powder horn. Each day, he added a shelf or a hook to the cabin to make it feel homey, like hers. He'd built it so it looked much like Betsy's, but he'd planned to do something different. He wanted to put in a real glass window instead of clarified hide. For now, the clarified hide would suffice—especially since he'd taken the cheery, yellow striped curtains Betsy made for his old cabin and hung them there.

From the first time he sat at the Larkins' table, he'd been made to feel welcome. Mr. Larkin spoke to him, man-to-man in a way that let Ty know he'd been judged and approved. Mr. Larkin made it clear he didn't want to listen to Ty talking about God, but he'd jaw about anything else, and they'd forged a fair friendship. It saddened Ty to see the pain in Mr. Larkin's eyes and the angry lines around his mouth whenever Betsy and the kids bowed theirs heads for grace—but at least he didn't stop them from praying.

Most evenings after supper, Ty and Betsy traded turns at reading the Scriptures to the kids before she served dessert. Her love for the Lord and the Word were sweeter than anything she baked—and nobody baked like Betsy. To Ty's joy, she made him feel as if she didn't merely set a place at the table for him out of charity—she welcomed him to join them. In fact, she'd even taken to making gingerbread once a week when he'd confessed he had a powerful weakness for the treat.

Mr. Larkin and Betsy wouldn't take money for the meals. They always pointed out that Ty had hunted most of the meat that now filled the smokehouse. He'd chopped cords of wood for them too. Still, he didn't reckon a man with his hearty appetite was paying his fair way—not for the vittles, and not for Betsy's extra work. Because of that, he made it a game to do chores and make essentials for them.

Nails or pegs used to hold things in the Larkin home. Ty made hooks for the dishcloths and aprons, devised a holder with parallel bars a few inches apart for the towels that held four of them neatly in a small space. Betsy's pretty brown eyes glittered with delight over that invention. He'd made three decorative shelves with porcelain knobbed hooks for Betsy and her little sisters to use for their clothes. From the joy they showed, Ty might have thought he'd built them a bridge straight into heaven.

Thrice now, he'd taken Karl and Will fishing. When they returned, he told Betsy with absolute sincerity, "I had more fun than the boys!" He'd reinforced a weak spot on the plow for Mr. Larkin too. A replaced hinge here, a cowbell there. . . all little things Ty hoped would show his appreciation—not just for the food, but for the way the Larkins gave him what he'd not yet had: a place to belong, a family. He knew, too, that Betsy was definitely the heart of that family.

Ty struck one last blow, then plunged the hoe blade into a barrel of water to cool. It took a few minutes to affix it to an elm stick. With that done, Ty picked up the first piece he'd ruined. If he played with it a bit, he could still salvage the metal—Betsy needed a hoe.

Round about a half hour later, Will peeped over the rail. "Whatcha doing, Mr. Ty?"

Ty looked at him and Karl. "Where's Marie?"

Karl jerked his thumb toward the street. "Mary Abner has a new doll. Marie stopped by to see her, and her ma said she can stay for supper."

A smile lit Ty's face. "Shut the door, boys. Christmas is coming, and we have work to do."

The winter wheat looked like green stubbly grass all over the field. The snows so far hadn't stayed, but they'd moistened the ground. Pa went off with Mr. Melvin and the Bunk brothers to cut lumber. The sawmill paid a bit for logs, and the men made a habit of using a few winter weeks when the fields needed no tending to go saw down trees, take them downriver to the mill, and get some cash money. Since Greta was born and Stepmama died, Betsy dreaded these excursions.

She worried about Pa and fretted she'd not be equal to the task if anything went wrong while she carried on alone with her youngers.

She stood on the porch and waved them off to school. Karl carried their McGuffey's primers and readers. A pail dangling from Marie's fingers banged against her knees in a noisy announcement to Ty that his dinner was on the way. Betsy had started packing his dinner pail along with the kids'. It took but a moment more, and it was only fair. Ty did so much for her, she wanted to return his favors and reward his good deeds.

The smoke curling from his forge smelled good. All day long, it served as a reminder to her that she wasn't alone. Greta napped while Betsy went out to bring in the wash. It hadn't dried completely, but most of the water had dripped off, so they'd finish steaming inside without mildewing. She needed to hurry—the sky was getting dark, fast. Betsy cast a look down the road and wished Master Jarrod would let school out a bit early today. It looked like a mighty storm was blowing in.

Indeed, less than an hour later, the wind howled and snow flurries filled the sky. The kids hadn't gotten home from school, and she hoped they weren't lost outside. Betsy cried out, "Protect my youngers, Lord. They're so helpless, and the storm's so bad. . . ."

Loud thumping sounded on the porch. Betsy flew to the door. As soon as she opened it, Ty pushed his way in, swiveled, and shoved his weight against the door to shut out the cold. He opened his coat, and Marie's arms and legs unwound from his neck and waist. She slid to the floor, and Will slowly released his death grip on Ty's left thigh.

Ty gave Betsy a grin. "I knew you'd be worried, so I fetched the kids and I'll fill your wood box. I had to be sure you'd be all right. Karl is back at my place, warm as can be. Storm's getting worse, so I'll keep him there."

Tears of gratitude filled her eyes. Betsy gathered her sister and brother close and whispered, "Thank you, oh, thank you. God bless you, Tyson."

"He does." Ty shot her a quick smile, then made three swift trips to bring in a generous supply of firewood. He made one last trip, dumped those logs by the front door, and nodded his satisfaction. Before she could say a word, he hiked to the smokehouse and brought back a big bag for her and another for himself. "That's enough to keep you warm and full for a good long while. Do you need anything else?"

Betsy stood on tiptoe and wound a gray-and-blue striped wool muffler around his neck. "This was supposed to be for Christmas, but you're too cold to do without. Thank you, Ty. Thank you for looking out for us."

He smiled and ran icy fingers down her cheek in a tender caress. "I'd do anything for you and yours, Betsy."

They stared at each other, and heat scorched her cheeks. She inched away. Ty tightened the muffler and smiled. "This was a wonderful surprise. I've never had finer. You're quite a woman, Betsy Larkin. There's not a woman on the face of the earth with a bigger heart than yours. Your family is blessed to have you, and God surely must be pleased to call you His daughter. I'd stand here singing your praises all afternoon, but I need to get back to Karl."

She picked up a thick quilt. "Wrap up in this. When you get home, Karl can use it. Hang onto this corner here. I tied a flour sack to it with dry clothes for him."

There wasn't time to waste. The wind howled a warning. As Ty pulled the quilt tight around his shoulders and readjusted his hold on the meat and sugar sacks, he said, "I'm keeping my eye on you. If you have any trouble at all or want my help, tie a red scarf to the west post of the front porch. You can be sure I'll be watching, so don't you hesitate for a single moment. The second you need me, I'll come running. I'll stop by the barn and water and feed the animals, so you won't need to trouble yourself for a few days."

He left, and when he disappeared into the swirling snow, Betsy wasn't sure what to think. Should she be elated that he'd been so good to her and God had answered her prayers to keep her siblings safe, or should she feel bereft that she could never know the joy of marrying such a wonderful man?

It wasn't as if she got to make a choice, anyway. He'd already walked Samantha home. He'd set his heart on a woman who could devote her every waking moment to his happiness. Samantha and Ty were her two favorite people—but Betsy couldn't bring herself to find joy in their romance. She felt guilty for coveting what simply wasn't ever to be in her grasp. . .but that guilt and all of her fervent prayers didn't erase the ache in her heart.

Four days later, the storm ended. Ty and Karl rode over. Betsy opened the door, and Ty filled his eyes with the sight of her. "You look wonderful," he decided.

"Yeah!" Karl threw his arms around Betsy while Ty gladly hugged the children. He would have happily lifted Betsy up and swung her around, too, but the way she went bashful over his compliment held him back.

After they ate bubble and squeak for lunch, Will and Marie started to squabble. Betsy shrugged apologetically. "The kids are pretty rowdy from being stuck inside."

"That's understandable. It's still bitterly cold outside, but they could probably go to the barn to frolic."

"That's a fair notion. You kids bundle up warmly and tend to the animals while I put Greta down for a nap." The kids obeyed with alacrity. As she came back to the main room, Betsy caught Ty eating the last few bites from Marie's plate. Her delicate brows rose.

"Now don't make fun of me. Smidgen left that for me." A woeful shake of his head accompanied his outrageous claim. "Karl and I were pitiful bachelors. We managed, but nothing we took from the hearth tasted anything like what you make. Truth be told, I could probably knock the center out of my dumplings and sell them as horseshoes."

She stacked the dishes and laughed.

"You have a lovely laugh. I wish you'd do it more often," he said. "It's like a rare gift, seeing you lighthearted." He walked over to her and took her hand in his. "Speaking of gifts, I feel like God gave me the sweetest present in the world the day we met. First time I saw you in church, you nearly stole my breath away. I didn't know at that time, you'd steal my heart too—but you have."

"No, Ty. Please don't do this." Betsy tugged her hand from his. "Your friendship means so very much. I don't want this to come betwixt us."

He stared at the just-swept plank floor. "It's because I'm so big and clumsy, isn't it? I scare you."

"No!" She didn't hesitate for a single second, and that fact made her response ring with truth. "I always figured a man's strength was a gift God gave him so he could provide for his wife and protect her."

He looked back at her. "Then what's the problem?"

Betsy bowed her head and knotted her hands in her apron pockets. Tension sang in the stiff lines of her stance, yet sadness radiated from her words, "You deserve a bride who pampers you, Ty. A woman who can devote her whole heart to you—someone like Samantha. I can't."

Just then, Marie, Will, and Karl ran in. Will and Marie were both crying. Karl tattled, "They were climbing up to the hayloft and got splinters in their hands."

Ty watched as Betsy gathered them close, soothed, sympathized, and sent Karl to fetch a needle from her sewing box so she could pick out the splinters. As he leaned against the table, the truth finally dawned. Betsy thought he expected her to abandon the children! After years of caring for them, she'd become more of a mother than a sister; and fool that he'd been, he hadn't considered the fact that she didn't know he'd gladly take them all into his home. He'd already opened his heart to them.

Words came cheaply. Actions would have to be his tool. He'd show her over and over again. Yes, that's what he'd do. He'd let her think he'd accepted her refusal and simply be her friend. . .and with time and patience, he'd prove his love.

She could take her silly notions about Samantha Thomasohn and cast them to the wind. In his whole life, no one had ever touched his heart like Betsy Larkin, and she was silly if she thought he was going to give up on her and plug anyone else in just because she'd taken a crazy notion in her head. Her family wasn't a burden; it was an utter joy. Far as he could see, it wouldn't take long for him to prove his feelings. He might not have gotten her pledge of heart and hand today—but Ty felt certain that would come. God wouldn't have brought them together if He didn't intend for this to work out.

Ty left, and Betsy felt like he'd taken her heart along with him. She tried to be cheerful for her siblings, but the fact was, Ty hadn't refuted her assertion at all. He hadn't even offered a token denial that the kids weren't a burden. Just as telling, he'd not contradicted a word she'd said about Samantha. It hurt. It hurt really bad.

She kept busy. That ought to help. She'd been through this four times before. By now, she should be used to it—men simply didn't want a bride who brought a dowry of nothing more than hungry, noisy children. Oh, when the shoe was on the other foot, it was a different matter. Widowers with children regularly remarried and expected their new wife to take on the responsibilities of caring for children. Pa had done that. Frieda married him and had been good about taking Betsy under her maternal wing and shepherded her from being a gawky eight year old into early womanhood.

Greta plopped down in the middle of the floor and awkwardly wrapped her dolly in a little baby blanket. She picked it up, cradled it, and crooned. Betsy turned away and tried to blink back her tears. She'd never have a babe of her very own to cuddle. That blanket had been one she'd made to go in her own hope chest, but when Frieda died and the baby things were so worn-out, Betsy had taken it out and used it for Greta.

After she tucked her youngers in for the night and stoked the fire, Betsy sat at the hearth and held her Bible. She had always loved the Word, and she treasured the fact that Ty did too. Because the Good Book was a link they shared, she couldn't bear to even open it tonight. Hands tightly clenched around the battered black leather, she clutched it to her bosom and silently prayed, *God, I'm so thankful for my youngers. Please give me the love and patience I need to rear them. Forgive me for my selfish wishes, and renew my heart. You set me in this family, and Pa and the kids truly need me. Help me to continue to serve them in Your name and with a willing heart. Don't let foolish dreams tempt me, I pray—*

"Sis?"

She hastily wiped away her tears and didn't turn around. "Yes, Karl?"

"Mr. Ty uses tongs so he doesn't get burned, but he's taken to wearing cotton gloves under leather ones now. Funny thing: He said leather lets the heat come straight through, but cotton doesn't. He didn't used to wear 'em, but he started to once he moved here so's his hands don't stay coal black all the time. Old Mr. Willon's gloves were still there, but they're falling apart. I sneaked one and traced 'round it. Since you already gave Mr. Ty the scarf, I thought maybe you and Marie could stitch him some new gloves for Christmas. It wouldn't take long, would it? That way, he'd still have a Christmas surprise."

"That's a fine idea."

"Know what? He's been doin' hunting and not telling folks. Since Mr. Alexander got hurt, he can't bring in food. Ty's been taking meat over to them. After he brought Marie and Will home to you, he went back to the Alexanders' just to be sure they had wood and meat for the blizzard."

"He's a good man," Betsy whispered hoarsely.

Karl padded over and hunkered down. He rested his head on her arm. "I had fun with him. We did some neat stuff, and he taught me some things; but Sis?" his voice dropped to a whisper, "I missed you. Don't tell Will, though."

Betsy pressed a kiss to his rumpled hair. "I missed you too, and I'll keep it a secret."

"I'm keeping lots of secrets these days."

"Oh?"

The firelight painted her brother's face and made his smile gleam. He nodded. "Can't tell. Christmas is going to be extra fun, though."

"It's only nine days away. I reckon Pa ought to be home in about three more days. I want to finish sewing his shirt for Christmas before he gets back."

"Tomorrow's Tuesday, isn't it? You go to Mrs. T's."

Betsy shrugged. "I might not go. The storm set me behind a bit." She didn't add on the biggest truth: She didn't think she could go and pretend to be happy for Samantha. Best she just stay home and tend to family matters.

Late Wednesday morning, Mrs. Tidewell stopped in for a visit. "We missed you yesterday. Karl dropped by on the way to school to say you wouldn't come, but since you're here alone with the kids, I wanted to be sure you were all right."

As Betsy concentrated on pouring steaming tea into their cups, she said, "The storm caught me by surprise."

"It caught us all by surprise. Noah said the Almanac didn't even predict it. Ty was wonderful. It would have warmed your heart to see how he hurried out to the schoolhouse with a rope. The storm came up so fast, he didn't even take time to put on his own coat. He already knows which kids are related to whoever is in town and made them cling to the rope until he reached that building. He dropped them off until he reached his own place."

Honey. Betsy added more honey to her tea. She stirred it around and around and tried to sound casual, "I'm very thankful. I'd been worried and just finished praying, and he appeared at the door with Marie and Will."

"He's become quite devoted to you, my dear." Mrs. T smiled softly. "The girls spoke of little else yesterday at the sewing circle."

Betsy shook her head. "No. It's just a friendship. We're good neighbors."

"Good friends and neighbors are a gift from the Lord." Mrs. T sipped her tea and reached for a small bundle she'd brought. "We decided on a pattern for our next group quilt. I brought you some squares to work on. Since you've begun to teach Marie to sew, I put in a few extras. She could make a little crib quilt."

"Thank you," Betsy said as she opened the bundle and looked at the cream, blue, and rose fabric. "These colors look wonderful together. What pattern are we making?"

"Old Maid's Choice."

The fabric fell from Betsy's hands.

Mrs. T rose and came around the table. She stood behind Betsy and enveloped her in loving arms. "Ah, Betsy. I'm sorry. Please don't feel that was a reflection on you. It wasn't. You've always loved the four and nine patch quilts. Every quilt the group has made went to someone else—you never asked for one, never suggested it was your turn to have us make one for you. We voted that it's well past your turn and started this yesterday because we love you. Samantha chose the colors because she knew they were your favorites, and Elsa suggested quilting it with hearts and lines because your love radiates to everyone."

Tears slipped down Betsy's cheeks. Though her shoulders shuddered with her weeping, Mrs. T held her tightly. That made it even more bittersweet. No one ever held her. Pa didn't, and the kids gave her hurried hugs, but she hadn't had the luxury of being consoled, comforted, and cosseted by anyone for years. The only hugs she'd ever have would be old maid hugs—ones from other women, or from nieces and nephews. . .and that knowledge broke her heart.

Chapter 7

Christmas morning, Ty could hardly wait to get to Betsy's. He'd seen the candle burning in the window at the Larkins' to guide the Christ child to their home. Just as surely, it had beckoned him. He hastily washed with cold water, shaved so he'd look respectable, and quickly hitched the horse to the sleigh. He'd already put the bags of gifts in the sleigh last night, excited to have a family he could celebrate Christmas with. It would be the first time since he was a small boy that Christmas would be filled with love.

The horses pulled the sleigh across the short distance. Bells jingled merrily, proclaiming the joy of Christ's birth. The first rays of sun sparkled on the snow and made the whole world look full of promise.

Karl opened the door and ran out to greet him. "Mr. Ty! It's Christmas! Can we show our secret now?"

Will danced from one foot to the other. "Betsy kept peering out the window, looking for you to come. She even made you gingerbread for *breakfast.*"

"That was 'posed to be a su'prise," Marie chided.

All three kids stared wide-eyed as Ty set both bags down on the porch. He felt a spurt of delight at hearing Betsy had anticipated his arrival. Clearly, she wasn't indifferent to him. Patience. He'd just wait, and she'd finally figure out that they were meant to marry. In the meantime, he chuckled as the kids tried to hide their curiosity and greed. "From that first Christmas, when God gave us His Son, Christmas has been about giving."

Dressed in her faded blue Sunday gown, Betsy came to the doorway. Greta straddled her hip. "The sleigh bells sounded beautiful, Tyson. We've been looking forward to riding with you. Kids, hurry, or we'll be late for church."

"Aww," Karl whined, "I want that gingerbread!"

Ty chortled at Betsy's look of dismay. "I do too," he admitted. "Nothing on earth compares to your scrumptious gingerbread, hot from the fire. Betsy, would you mind if we all ate a chunk in the sleigh, on the way to church?"

His compliment made her whole face glow. Ty relished the way little things pleased her. He hoped the gift he had for her would bring her joy. Virginia Alexander refused to take any more food unless she could sew for him, so he'd bartered her sewing for his hunting. She'd been good about helping him keep things quiet so Betsy would be surprised.

"Gingerbread and children are a messy combination," Betsy reminded him. "I suppose it's all right, if you don't mind sticky fingers in your sleigh."

"If you pass Greta to me, I'll wrap her in her cape. Boys, no fair peeking—you carry those bags inside."

Betsy passed Greta to him, and he quickly slipped her into her blue woolen cape. She giggled when he gave her a playful squeeze. Marie scrambled in, and he soon had her tucked beneath a big, bear fur to keep both girls warm. Once they dragged the heavy, clanging bags into the house, the boys joined their little sisters.

Ty got down and waited for Betsy. He shifted from one foot to the other, eager to have her beside him. She came out and put a fragrant basket into his hands. "Merry Christmas."

"Mmmm." He inhaled deeply. "Merry Christmas to you too." He passed the gingerbread up to Karl, then turned back to Betsy. "Your pa's not coming?" he murmured softly so the children wouldn't hear.

Betsy shook her head.

He cupped her waist and squeezed gently. "I'm sorry, Sunshine. Maybe soon. We'll keep praying." For just an instant, she dipped her head and rested against his chest. Ty slipped his arms around her and held her tight for a sweet moment. She filled his arms just as perfectly as she filled his heart. All too quickly, she straightened up and pulled away.

She stammered, "We don't want to be late."

He lifted her into the sleigh and climbed up to sit next to her. Once he settled a lap blanket over their legs, he slipped an arm around Betsy and drew her close. It made sense to him that God used Adam's rib to create Eve. With Betsy by his side, he finally felt complete.

Her eyes went wide.

"Huddle close, little lady. It's cold as can be today." He took up the reins and set off. The way she stayed next to him and fed him bites of gingerbread made his heart soar.

After church, they went home and had roast duck. Betsy gave Pa and the boys their new shirts and pants, then gave the girls their new dresses and aprons. She shyly put the cotton gloves in Ty's hands. *I hope he likes them. . . .*

"Will you look at these?" Ty beamed. "How did you know I needed these?"

"Karl told me. He traced around your old ones."

"Your stitching is just as clever as his thinking." Ty tried one on. "It's an exact fit!"

Marie proudly gave Betsy and all of the men—including Ty—a handkerchief she'd hemmed. For Greta, she'd sewn a dolly blanket. Pa gave each of the little ones a shiny penny, an orange, and a tin whistle. For Betsy, he'd used a bit of his lumber money and gotten her a paper of sewing pins and a length of green wool, "So you can make yourself a skirt."

It already seemed like the best Christmas ever, then Ty dragged over the sacks. "Karl and Will have been busy," he said. The boys' scrawny chests puffed out with pride as the set of gardening tools appeared. "They made and painted the handles on these, themselves."

"You spent a lot of time with them," Betsy looked into Ty's eyes and marveled softly. "Thank you. Thank you so much!"

"You're welcome!" Will said, oblivious to the fact that his sister had expressed appreciation for the mentor as much as for the tools.

Ty's warm smile let Betsy know he understood her intent. He gave each boy a hammer and a bag of nails. "Young men with your talent need to have tools of their own. This is a start. I'm sure your pa can help you make toolboxes."

"Can you, Pa?"

"Sure enough." Pa smiled. Betsy couldn't remember the last time she'd seen Pa grin. That, alone, made the day.

"I thought we needed something pretty for the little princesses," Ty said as he reached into his other sack. He set rabbit fur muffs in the girls' laps. While they squealed with joy, he stood and carried the still-bulging sack behind Betsy. She sat still and didn't dare turn around to see what he was doing. His deep voice dipped lower and made her shiver, "For the queen of the home."

Something heavy descended on her shoulders and enveloped her—a cape of thick, soft, butternut wool. Betsy gasped as he stepped to her side and gently lifted the hood over her hair. Lined and edged with mink, it was the softest thing she'd ever felt. "Oh, Tyson! It's beautiful."

Ty drew her to her feet, and as he fastened the toggled buttons at the throat, he murmured, "Not half as beautiful as the woman it graces. I chose this," his fingertip brushed the fur, "because it's the same rich color as your eyes."

He didn't ask. He simply nodded to her pa, then escorted Betsy out the door. They went to the barn, and he quickly hitched the horses to the sleigh. "Come on, Sunshine. Let's go for a ride."

Betsy hesitated.

"I have a sled John Altmann had me make for his children that I need to drop off."

Did she want people to see the two of them—just the two of them—together? Betsy didn't know what to do. She wanted to be with Ty, but it was unfair to make him think they were courting. Just as bad, they'd travel straight through the length of town to reach the miller's house. Goodness only knew how many tongues that would set wagging! She averted her gaze. "Tyson, I've told you we can't be more than friends."

He cupped his hands around her waist. "I asked you to ride with me to deliver a sled. I won't try to sneak a kiss or propose again. Come along as my friend. You can help distract the kids so John and I can unload the sled without them seeing it."

His hands stayed at her waist. She could feel their strength all of the way through her new cape and clothes. They could be no more than friends, but she'd learn to accept and enjoy that. So far, she had—and it was good. Betsy nodded.

"There's my girl." His deep, soft tone held approval.

Once Ty lifted her into the sleigh, he put on his jacket and slipped the muffler she'd made for him around his neck. After he climbed up, she turned and carefully pulled it higher, over his ears. "Your ears will get too cold. If you still have some fur, I could sew you a cap."

"I'd be obliged, Betsy." He flicked the reins, and the sleigh pulled out into the snow.

"I'm obliged, Tyson. You were far too generous for Christmas. We're all overwhelmed."

He tilted his head and studied her for a moment. "Betsy, my pa died when I was Marie's age. Ma married up again. The day she had his son, he sent me out to the shed. I thought it was for a whuppin', but I hadn't done anything wrong. Fact is, it wasn't for a whuppin' at all. I lived in the shed. He had no room in his home or heart for me. Ma couldn't do much, else he'd take away her new babe. Almost four years later, they apprenticed me out to a blacksmith."

Tears filled her eyes. "How awful for you!"

"It wasn't good. I'm not telling you this for pity; I'm telling you so you can understand what a gift it is to me, that you and yours open your door and welcome me in. The little things I do and bring are tokens of my gratitude. I couldn't ever begin to match what you've given me. The Christian love you share makes every day feel like Christmas to me."

Chapter 8

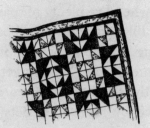

The weeks after Christmas, Betsy kept busy with sewing on the quilt and doing her winter chores. Ty came over each morning and evening—not just for meals, but for Bible reading. It felt right to have him there—natural. Greta and Marie demanded good night kisses from him, and though the boys didn't ask, they clearly loved it when Ty tucked them in bed. Ty pulled the blanket closed so the boys would drift off, then looked at Betsy. "What're you doing, Sunshine?"

She nudged the table over a bit more. "Making room for the loom. I need to start weaving."

Ty gently set her aside and pulled the table back to its usual spot, then looked at her pa. "If you don't mind, we could go set up the loom in my old cabin. It'll be out of the way, but close by. No use in you being so cramped here."

"That seems like a right fine notion."

"Are you sure you won't mind?" Betsy chewed on her lip. Did he really want her near him all day long? She'd finally admitted to herself that Ty wasn't carrying a torch for her cousin, and Mantha nearly laughed herself silly at the notion that the blacksmith and she might ever be more than friends.

Still, Betsy couldn't allow herself to believe...

"It'd be a pure pleasure to look out my forge door and see you weaving," Ty said. "There's no reason for you to give up precious room when I've plenty of spare space. Soon as I rise of a morning, I'll start a fire so it'll be cozy for you and little Greta. Having my Sunshine and Sunbeam there will chase away the winter gloom. You just get things ready—I'll tote them over in the sleigh tomorrow afternoon."

Secretly pleased by his words, Betsy murmured, "I'm obliged."

Two days later, Betsy sat in the sewing circle, making another square for the quilt top. Ten to the inch, the stitches marched up her needle before she pushed it through and rocked the needle back and forth again to gather the next inch of fabric.

Diana Montclair was visiting. She didn't work on the quilt with everyone else, but instead embroidered pansies on the yoke of a fine lawn nightgown. "I hear you're at that blacksmith's cabin every day, weaving and cooking for him," she said in a tone as airy as the fine fabric she stitched.

"She's weaving for her family," Samantha said at once.

"The way I see it, her father and the children are there for all of the meals. It's fine for her to cook," Elsa added on. "None of the rest of us would expect Mr. Walker to eat alone—especially since he hunted so much!"

Betsy felt glad of her friends' loyalty. She'd worried about gossip.

Diana arched her brow and stared pointedly at Betsy. "Are you telling me the two of you aren't courting?"

Betsy shook her head. She swallowed hard, and tears filled her eyes and voice, "I've told him we cannot be more than friends. Pa and my youngers need me."

"Well," Diana sniffed, "if you're silly enough to let them use you as a slave so you sacrifice your future, that's your own fault, and I think it's a mistake."

Betsy stuck her finger and quickly pulled back so she wouldn't bleed on the quilt. She looked at Diana and shook her head. "Life isn't always about what you want; it's about others you love and what they need. Most of the time, I'm very happy with my life. Yes, I have days when I start to wallow in self-pity, but then I remember God doesn't glory in a daughter who's being a martyr."

"What verses do you think Betsy can claim for this?" Mrs. T asked quietly.

" 'Seek ye first the kingdom of God, and His righteousness; and all these things shall be added unto you.' " Elsa smiled brightly. "I claimed that one during the days when Shane arrived and turned my world upside down."

"How about Psalm 37:4?" Clara Bucey's beautiful brown eyes sparkled as she quoted, " 'Delight thyself also in the LORD; and he shall give thee the desires of thine heart.' "

"And Psalm 40:8," Samantha added. " 'I delight to do thy will, O my God: yea, thy law is within my heart.' "

"Yes," Mrs. T nodded. "Our covenant with God isn't written on stone anymore; it is written in our hearts by the Grace of Christ. Our focus is to desire to do God's will, to love the things our Father loves. Because He is our Heavenly Father, He wants the very best for us. By trusting in His will, we live in the faith that though we go through trials and are tested, God will bless us in His own way and time."

As she walked home, Betsy paused under a tree and stared ahead at the smoke rising from Ty's forge. *Father, I do want to do Your will, to please and glorify You. Give me discernment and courage to walk the path you put before me. Through Jesus I pray, Amen.*

She continued on toward home with a restored sense of peace.

Ty stood in the door and smiled at the sight of Betsy sending the shuttle back and forth with a sweeping rhythm. She'd made several yards of linen from the flax in the past few days. She sang a nonsense song with Greta as she worked, and the small cabin still held the sweet aroma of honeyed corn bread and fried ham steaks she'd made at midday. Her Pa dropped by Ty's new cabin earlier in the day, and all of them ate together before he left to cut more lumber.

As she waved good-bye, Ty noticed how Betsy held little Greta a shade closer than usual. *She's scared.* "He'll be fine, Betsy. If you're worried, I can hurry and join him."

"Don't you dare go off! I couldn't bear having you and Pa both gone at the same time."

Pleased at the depth and speed of her reaction, he still knew better than to play it up. Instead, he pasted on a roguish grin and needled, "Is that your way of saying having me underfoot isn't too big a burden?"

She hitched Greta higher on her hip and got the sassy gleam in her eye he loved so much. "Go back to your forge, Tyson Walker. I have work to do, even if you don't."

He'd tickled Greta's neck, then sauntered off to the forge. Now, he listened to Betsy repeat the tune as she wove. "Sunshine?"

She looked up, startled. A fetching blush stole across her

164

cheeks. "Oh! How long have you been standing there?"

"Long enough to wonder why the pig in your song likes to wear a hat." He chuckled, "I've always thought pigs looked better in shirts."

"No, Misser Ty. The horse wears the shirt," Greta informed him somberly.

He leaned forward and rested his hands on his knees so he'd be closer to eye level with her. "Well, imagine that! What does the turkey wear?"

"Dunno. Sis? What does—"

"A feather duster," Betsy ventured with a playful shrug. "Did you need something?"

"Actually, I do." Ty straightened up and tilted his head toward the smithy. "Reverend Tidewell came to me with a toothache. The molar is rotten and needs to be pulled. I've gotten my tools ready, but I was wondering if you might have a bit of laudanum and cloves."

"Yes. I try to keep a good supply of things on hand. I'll be right back." She took Greta's tiny cape off the hook.

"Greta can stay with me," Ty offered. "She's my littlest sweetheart."

Betsy set the cloak back and started to wrap the one he'd given her for Christmas around her shoulders when Greta tugged on his pant leg. "Who's your biggest sweetheart?"

He carefully lifted the hood and smiled at Betsy. Silly woman still couldn't understand he loved her. "The lady of my heart hasn't figured out the answer to that puzzle. I'll have to wait and let her work on it a bit."

Betsy wouldn't meet his eyes, so he let her go. She brushed past him and murmured, "I'll be back in a jiffy."

Ty didn't like pulling teeth. Somehow, somewhere,

someone had determined it was part of a blacksmith's job. He kept a few small pliers and a tiny bullet mold he'd altered a bit to use to accomplish the dreaded task. Betsy set Greta on a workbench out of the way, gave Pastor Tidewell a dose of laudanum, and put three cloves in a little scrap of cheesecloth muslin.

Reverend Tidewell removed his coat. "I expect I'll not feel much like preaching this Sunday. I've asked Brady to fill in for me. You can pass the word we'll still worship."

"Your nephew handled the church hayride just fine," Betsy said softly. "God did a mighty work in Brady's life, and it's a blessing to see him serving his Master."

The pastor nodded, sat on a bench, and Betsy held his head. Greta started to sing about the hat-wearing pig—a strange accompaniment for the event, no doubt. As soon as the task was over, Betsy slipped the cloves in place to help stop the pain and bleeding. By the time Ty got back from walking the pastor home, she'd already washed off his instruments and put them away.

"Betsy, you are like the Proverbs 31 woman—a priceless ruby."

She let out a self-conscious laugh. "Not at all. I'm just a sow with a hat and a feather duster. I'd best better get back to my weaving. Since you've helped Pa with so many of my farm chores, it freed some of my time. I got overambitious and am weaving almost twice my usual amount of linen. I want to have it done by tomorrow."

Ty watched her go back to the cabin. Through the open door, he saw her pick up the shuttle. *She weaves cloth.* . . . Oh, yes, Betsy was a woman who fulfilled all the Scriptures said. One of these days—hopefully soon—the woman he loved would finally realize she was meant to be his wife and pledge her heart in return. She was already his helpmeet in the truest sense of the word.

The next morning, Ty walked out into new drifts of snow and went to the stable. He watered and fed his horse, mucked the stall, and headed for the smithy. To his dismay, the glass pane he'd sent for was broken when it arrived. He'd thought on it all evening and just about the time he'd decided to accept it as a loss, he'd had his devotions and read about how the Stone that was rejected became the Cornerstone. It spurred his thinking. Maybe something beautiful could come from this brokenness.

All morning long, Ty worked on his plan. He kept the door to the smithy almost shut—an unusual thing because of the forge's heat, but he wanted what he was doing to be a surprise for Betsy. By midmorning, he realized he'd lost track of time because he'd gotten so involved with this new project. His stomach growled, making him even more aware of the fact it was almost noon. It seemed odd the children hadn't dropped by on their way to school. Betsy had said she was going to come finish her weaving today too. Concern furrowed his brow. Ty took off his apron, quickly plunged his hands into the wash barrel, then headed outside. As soon as he looked to the north, his heart leapt to his throat.

Tied to the Larkins' porch post, fluttering in the wind, was a red scarf.

Chapter 9

"B etsy!"

She wearily petted Marie's sweat-dampened hair and raised her voice so she'd be heard over the peculiar coughs that filled their home, "Don't come in here!"

"Wild horses couldn't keep me away." The door swung open. "I came as soon as I saw the scarf—who's sick?"

"Will and Marie. I suspect Greta is too. She's not herself." Betsy looked up at him and warned, "If you've not had whooping cough, you'd best back straight out the door."

To her relief, he came on in and firmly shut it behind himself. "I'm safe. What about you and Karl?"

"We had it while my stepmama was carrying Will."

Marie started to go into another paroxysm of coughs, so Betsy pulled her upright. The loud, whooping bark had gotten worse since sunrise.

"I've given them pine tar and elderberry cough syrup. It's not helping."

"How much wild cherry bark do you have?"

"Nowhere near enough for this," she confessed.

Ty paced over to Will's bed, gently lifted the boy and cradled him to his chest and shoulder as if he were nothing more

168

than a wee babe. "How much have you gotten them to drink?"

"I made broth. They don't keep it down very well."

"I don't suspect they will." He sat next to her and calmly ironed his big, capable hand up and down Will's shuddering spine as the little boy coughed. He waited until the brace of whoops was over, then said very matter-of-factly, "We'll just have to be diligent to keep them drinking. What say we give them both some apple cider, maybe make a poultice, then I'll go get some more cherry bark. We'll need it. What else do we need?"

She strained to think. "Honey. It'll be impossible to get a lemon. I'm trying to remember what else is good for coughs. Linden, and anise, and—oh!" Frustration had her nearly in tears. "I don't remember!"

"It's going to be all right," he soothed. "After we get the kids settled, I'll go ask Doc what he recommends."

"Doc Gardner's ailing from his rheumatism. He's not been to church for nigh unto a month now. Samantha's father said the cold troubles Doc so badly, he can't go out on calls. I don't think he'll come help."

"I'll get his advice. We can make it through, Betsy. We need to send word to your pa, though."

Her arms tightened around Marie. "You don't think—"

"No, of course not," he cut in quickly. "Everyone's going to get well, but no one's going to get much done or chalk up any sleep around here for almost a month. It'll be good to have his help." He petted Will's head and murmured, "I need you to drink for me, little man. Sips. Loads and loads of sips. No runnin' around. I want you actin' lazy as a 'possum until your cough's all gone."

"Yes, Misser Ty." Even those three words sent Will into

spasms of coughs again.

Ty was heartbreakingly gentle with her brother, and that meant the world to her. Betsy wanted to wrap her arms around the two of them.

Ty brushed a subtle kiss on her temple and murmured, "It's going to be fine." Betsy blinked at him in surprise, but he acted as if he'd done nothing out of the ordinary. He calmly reached for Marie and settled her on his other knee. "Come here, Smidgen. Your sis is getting you some cider. It'll make your throat feel better."

A little more than an hour later, Marie and Will stayed side by side in Pa's bed. Karl piled pillows and a rolled quilt up behind them to prop up their shoulders and heads to make them breathe better. Betsy started making cherry bark tea, and Ty brought in firewood and three big buckets of snow to melt on the hearth for water.

"I'll go into town and talk to Doc Gardner." He came close and gently pushed a strand of hair back from her forehead. "I'll be back as soon as I can. Do you need anything from the mercantile?"

"I have plenty of willow bark to bring down their fever. Karl can give you the egg basket. If you trade the eggs for some cherry bark, I'd appreciate it."

He nodded. "Karl, you're going to have to fill in and shoulder a man's place here," Ty said. "You be mindful to slop the hog, milk the cow, and do your stable chores. I want you to fix up the spare stalls in the stable. I'll be bringing over my horses."

"Why?" Karl asked.

Ty cupped Betsy's jaw and tenderly arced his rough thumb across her cheek. "I'm going to stay here until your pa gets home. We're going to see this through together."

Betsy leaned into his gentle caress. Ever since Frieda had died, she'd carried on pretty much alone. For the first time, she couldn't handle matters; but Ty was here, and together, they could manage. This man was a gift from God, and she needed him—not just for the kids, but for herself.

Betsy knew she probably ought to object; it wasn't proper for an unmarried man and woman to stay beneath the same roof. Doubtlessly, Olivia Crabtree would stir up a whole scandal over the arrangement. Then again, with four children as chaperones and three of them sick as could be, necessity seemed more important than propriety. God's mercy counted more than Mrs. Crabtree's pettiness. She covered his hand with hers. "I'm thankful, Ty. Truly, I am."

He could hear the terrible racket fifty yards from the cabin—loud, barking coughs in long, ugly strings. Ty winced. He'd had whooping cough and still remembered how sore the coughing made him and how sick he'd been. Greta seemed far too small to suffer such a malady, and talkative Marie had been alarmingly silent this morning. Normally a wiggle worm, Will's listlessness seemed all that much more alarming. Ty resolved to make them comfortable. . .and to make sure Betsy didn't wear herself to a frazzle.

"I'll take your horses to the stable, Sir," Karl said somberly as soon as Ty nudged his horse toward the porch.

Ty dipped his head once in approval. "Son, I'm not sure just who is more proud of you 'bout now: me, Betsy, or Almighty God."

Karl beamed as he took the reins and led the horses off. "I'll take good care of them."

Ty hefted the sacks with essentials he'd brought and went on into the cabin. The place smelled sour. Betsy was holding Greta's head, and the little girl was coughing so hard, she'd ended up emptying her stomach. At night, they'd have to shut the door for warmth, but if he could leave the door open for snatches of time in the day, it'd be wise. Ty used one sack as a doorstop.

"What did Doc say?" she asked without even looking over at him.

"He gave me two recipes for cough syrup. Said to keep their feet and chests warm and their faces cold. Make 'em drink as much as we can. I brought back a dozen of the eggs too, Betsy. Doc said the kids'll do well if you feed them scrambled eggs and custard."

"Oh, but what about getting more cherry bark?"

"Samantha's father has plenty in the mercantile. Mrs. Stahl was there too. She's already made a cough elixir from cider vinegar and a bunch of other stuff she rattled off that escapes me at the moment. She promised to bring over a pint of it."

"Thank you, Ty. You'll never know how much I appreciate your help." Betsy wiped Greta's mouth, settled her back onto the pillows, and carried the slop jar toward the door.

Ty reached over and took the foul-smelling thing. "I'll get that."

Over the next two days, he and Betsy worked side by side to tend to her little siblings. By the third day, Marie's and Will's fevers broke. Greta's stayed high, though.

"I brought honey," Samantha said from the doorstep. "It'll help soothe their cough. Elsa sent over some bread so you wouldn't have to bake. Is there anything you need?"

Betsy sat on the bench and wearily rested her back against

the edge of the table. Greta cuddled close, and her tiny body started to jar with a wracking brace of coughs. Betsy waited until they were over, then said, "Karl gathered the eggs. Can you take them back to the store?"

"Sure." Samantha came on in, calmly straightened up a bit, and started a stew over the fire. "Mary Abner has the cough too. Her mama is making pancake poultices, of all things. She makes a pancake, puts it on Mary's chest 'til it goes cold, then has her eat it!"

A weary smile tugged at Betsy's lips. "That's better than what Zeb Bunk swears by. He came by with three big, black, ugly beetles and said if I wrap them in a cloth and have the children wear them against their chests, soon as the beetles die, the cough will be gone. Horace came with him. He said the part about the beetle dying was true, but it worked better if I'd keep them in tiny boxes, so he'd carved—"

Samantha went into gales of laughter. "Beetles in boxes! Oh, Betsy! What did you do?"

"Tyson took care of it. He thanked them. You would have thought those beetles were diamonds and pearls to hear him talk. When he took them in his hand, I nearly swooned. Zeb and Horace left, and Ty sat out on the porch like he didn't have a care in the world until they were out of sight—then he hightailed out to the field and got rid of them!"

"Ty's been a godsend, Betsy." Samantha coaxed Marie to have a sip of water. "I think the two of you—"

"Could you please dip this cloth?" Betsy interrupted as she thrust out a soggy rag. It hurt too much to have Samantha play matchmaker. No matter how much she cared for Ty, she couldn't abandon her siblings. "Greta's so hot, Mantha. Her fever still hasn't broken."

Heavy footsteps on the porch warned Ty was back. He'd gone out to see to the animals. Now he filled the doorway and held her big washtub.

"I thought maybe our little Greta would like to cool down in her very own bath," he rumbled gently. He crossed the floor and set the washtub down by the hearth. Betsy couldn't imagine how he'd carried it so easily—it was half full of water! Unaware of her astonishment, he dunked several cloths into the fresh water, wrung them out, then handed two to Samantha. As she tended Marie and Will, Ty came toward Betsy. "Here, Betsy."

Betsy gratefully accepted the cloth, but before she could start to gently wipe Greta, Ty sat down and pulled the toddler into his own lap. He bowed his head and tenderly kissed her sweat-dampened curls. "God bless you, Dumplin'."

Betsy folded the wet rag around her hand and started to cool Greta's sizzling brow. To Betsy's astonishment, Ty lifted his hand and gently ran the last moist cloth over her cheek! She gave him a startled look.

"It's all right," he soothed. "I'll sit with her awhile until the water warms up. Why don't you go nap a bit?"

Betsy moistened her lips. "No, I'm fine." She fought the urge to lean against him. The way he trailed the cloth over her cheeks and forehead felt heavenly. Her eyes fluttered shut with bliss, then flew open as Greta began to cough again. Over on the bed, Marie started hacking too.

Betsy automatically started to rise, but Samantha called over, "I have her." Indeed, she did, so Betsy slumped back down.

Ty slipped his arm around her and tucked her close to his side. She sagged against his strength and rested her cheek on his suspender. Greta stopped coughing and didn't even have enough strength to lift her thumb to her mouth. That fact nearly tore Betsy's heart in two.

"O worship the King," Ty started to sing softly.

Betsy barely managed to keep her composure until he hit the last verse. "Frail children of dust, and feeble as frail. . ." Tears ran down her face and wet his shirt. He still cradled Greta to himself, but his other hand cupped Betsy's head and slowly stroked through her mussed hair.

"Here. I'll take her."

Samantha's quiet bidding let Ty know he'd lost track of time while praying over Greta and trying to comfort Betsy. Was it sheer exhaustion that finally dragged Betsy to sleep, or had she found some comfort in his arms? He loosened his hold, and Samantha claimed the limp toddler.

"The water's tepid. I'll bathe her—it'll cool down her fever. I folded back the covers on Betsy's bed."

Ty nodded and turned his attention toward Betsy again. In all his years, he'd never once seen a woman this bone weary. She nestled into his side as if that was where she belonged, and her words echoed in his mind. *I always figured a man's strength was a gift God gave him so he could provide for his wife and protect her.* Ty would gladly have her as his wife, provide for and protect her—but regardless of their wishes, only God ruled over life and death, and Ty felt every bit as helpless as Betsy did in face of the children's illness.

Silently, he found the strings to her apron and untied them. As he eased the apron straps over her head, a loose hairpin caught and halted the progress. Soon, he had half a dozen hairpins in his hands and Betsy's breathtakingly soft plaits tumbled down. He'd known her hair to be long—but the sight of her thick, golden plaits reaching her waist made him wish he could see it hanging loose and free. Even with the kids as sick as they were, she'd been careful to slip behind the blanket partition to tend her hair each day.

The soft plop of water and Samantha's sweet singsong reassured him Greta was in good hands. Ty carefully scooped his arm beneath Betsy's knees and twisted so his other arm cradled her shoulders. As he stood, she slipped neatly into his possession. Her head lolled over his heart as he carried her to the bed Samantha had prepared. Ty stood at the bedside, whispered a prayer as he snuggled Betsy close, then brushed a kiss on her brow.

Once he slipped her onto the thick feather bed, he winced at the high neck on her dress. Certain she'd never sleep well with it constricting her throat, he carefully slipped the uppermost button free, then trailed his fingers down her soft, sweet cheek. She might be a slightly built woman, but her backbone was forged steel and her soul was pure gold. "Betsy Larkin," he whispered, "you're worth waiting for. I reckon if that fellow in the Bible waited for fourteen years for Rachel, I can be patient for you."

Ty quietly unlaced her boots and took them off. He loathed them. Pretty little Betsy wearing dreadful, heavy, men's boots—it was a shame. He'd given serious consideration to getting her dainty kid boots for Christmas, but decided not to because he feared he'd embarrass her by doing so. Her feelings were far more important than her looks. Satisfied she looked comfortable, Ty drew up the beautiful quilts he knew she'd made and left her to slumber.

Chapter 10

Betsy pushed back the blanket divider and stopped. Still a bit disoriented from her nap, she couldn't quite believe her eyes. Karl sat at the table, slurping soup. Marie sat on the edge of the boys' bed, absently swinging her stockinged feet as she drew on her slate. She set it aside to cough, then, calm as you please, picked it up and continued to draw afterward.

Ty sat in a chair across from the fire. Will sat on one of his thighs and leaned against his chest; Greta slumped on his other leg. Ty's massive arms wrapped securely round both—and all three were fast asleep. Will's body started to quake with his heavy coughs, and Ty's huge hand automatically ironed up and down on his back to brace and comfort him. When Greta started in, Ty simply drew her a tad closer so his forearm would support her.

"Mr. Ty said you're 'posed to eat when you woke up." Marie's voice was croaky from all of the coughing. She probably needed another dose of elixir.

Betsy tiptoed over to the dish shelf. They didn't own a timepiece and simply depended on the church and school bells. The Montclair's housekeeper, Millie Sanderson, graciously lent her a mantle clock to determine when to give the children their medicines. Afraid the rising heat from the hearth might damage the beautiful timepiece, Betsy had placed it on the dish shelf. She looked at the clock and gaped in astonishment. Eight thirty! She'd slept the whole afternoon away!

"Mr. Ty gave them their cherry cough stuff at sunset. Greta got willow bark then too," Karl reported dutifully. "Mr. Ty made me promise you'd eat straightaway. He already ate two bowls of Miz Samantha's stew."

Betsy debated whether to eat or take her siblings from Ty's arms so he could sleep better. He didn't seem troubled in the least to be holding them. Then again, he never acted as if they were a bother at all. She'd just eat quickly and have a little bowl. . . .

As she ladled the aromatic stew into her earthenware bowl, Betsy marveled at Samantha's strength. It hadn't been easy for Mantha to come help. She'd spent the spring caring for her own mother. Even with Mantha's fine nursing, Aunt Rachel slipped to the hereafter. Being here, seeing the children sick, had to stir up Samantha's grief—yet she'd come. Betsy whispered a prayer of thanks.

All three kids started coughing again. At the same time, a cold blast shot through the cabin. Betsy wheeled around. "Pa! We didn't hear you over the racket!"

"I came right away." He shut the door and peeled off his coat. Deep lines etched his pale face. "How are they?"

"Noisy," Ty rumbled with a tinge of humor. He gave Betsy a sleepy wink.

Marie sidled up to Pa and clamped hold of his leg. He immediately picked her up and crossed over to see Will and Greta. "Has Doc been by? What does he say?"

"Doc's not up to traveling out here," Betsy said. "Will and Marie are weary from barking all of the time, but they're doing well enough—"

"And my Greta?" Anguish filled Pa's voice as he knelt. His hand shook a bit as he reached over to touch her cheek.

"She's still feverish," Ty said softly. "It's harder on her."

"Here, Pa." Betsy shoved her bowl into his hand. "Eat and warm up a bit. Elsa sent bread. I'll slice you some."

Though he probably should have gone home, Ty spent the night. He didn't offer to leave, and no one suggested it. Just past midnight, Greta's fever climbed higher still. Betsy put her in the washtub again. The door slammed shut, and she could hear Pa out in the yard, yelling, "Why, God? Why? You took Hilda. Then You took Frieda. Two wives. Two! Wasn't that enough? Not my Greta too!"

Betsy bowed her head and started to cry. Ty dipped down, kissed her temple, and walked outside.

Ty whispered a prayer for wisdom and stepped off the porch. Matthew Larkin stood out by the pump, his hands fisted and his head thrown back as he continued to rail at heaven. A man with that much anger and pain deserved comfort.

Betsy's pa spun around and growled, "So you came out here to give me all the answers, did you?"

Ty shook his head. "No, I came to be with you—to share your grief and be with you so you didn't have to stand alone."

"Stand close, and God might well strike you dead by mistake," Matthew sneered.

"God makes no mistakes." Ty closed the distance between them. "Things happen. I can't understand them. I don't know His reasons why, but still, I trust. He sent His Son and watched Him die. He understands your anguish. He's big enough to listen to you bellow."

"He sent His Son. He got Him back again."

"True," Ty agreed promptly.

"I didn't get Hilda back. I didn't get Frieda back. If He takes my little Greta—" Matthew's voice cracked.

Ty stood next to him and simply reached around and cupped his shoulder. He didn't have the right words. He didn't have a perfect answer, so he stayed silent.

A horse whinnied and the cow lowed. They could hear the kids coughing inside the house. An icy wind clawed at them.

"Why did you come out here?" Matthew finally asked in a defeated tone.

"I came to stand alongside you so you wouldn't be alone. There've been times in my own life when I needed such a person. Sometimes, it's been a friend. Other times, there was no one—but in those times, I learned to lean on Christ. He was with me. If you feel you don't have the comfort of the Lord, you at least deserve to have someone to help you shoulder this pain so you aren't crushed by it."

"Why would I want anything to do with a God who might take my baby daughter, my Greta, away?"

Ty thought for a moment. "Because He made her and lent her to you. She brought love and laughter to you. I pray she stays to fill our days with joy. Still, if God calls Greta home, He would hold her on His lap until the day you go to join her and Him in heaven."

"God would hold my child? Mine? I'm the man who hates Him!"

"God is bigger than your hatred, Matthew. He already

conquered it on the cross."

"I wouldn't know what to say to Him."

Ty slowly exhaled, then ventured, "Maybe it's time you stopped shouting at Him and started listening. Wait a moment. Tell me what you hear."

"My sick children."

"And Betsy's sweet voice, soothing them."

"The wind."

"Sweeping away the snow clouds so tomorrow will be warmer."

Matthew shot him a grim smile. "You're trying to show me how I look at the wrong things. I'm a contrary man."

"You're a man who hurts. Maybe it's time you're a man who healed. Just be sure you seek God because you want to be right with Him—not to make a bargain for Greta. Even if He spares Greta, life will demand other sacrifices later. Faith doesn't mean we walk a smooth path—it means we don't walk the path alone."

"I'm so tired of being alone," Matthew confessed in a hushed tone.

"You don't have to be alone any longer. Can I pray with you?"

Chapter 11

Betsy carried her mending into Mrs. T's house. "Hello!"

"After being cooped up for over two weeks, I imagine it feels good to get out," Mrs. T said as she hugged her.

"Yes, it does." Betsy turned and gave Clara and Elsa quick hugs. "Pa's staying home today. Marie and Will are springing back nicely. Doc said since they're strong, the cough will run its course in about three weeks."

"How's Greta?" Samantha asked as she joined them.

"Still puny, but she kept broth and cider down for the past three days." Betsy smiled. "She'll just take a mite longer, but God was merciful."

Everyone sat down and started to sew. Betsy popped her thimble on her finger and deftly let down the hem in Marie's dress. Her needle stopped midair when Samantha blithely announced, "Betsy, we were talking about you last week when you weren't here. We all agree—you and Ty ought to get married."

She felt the tingle of a blush start at her bosom and climb straight up to her forehead. Bad enough Mrs. Crabtree scurried all over town, whispering tales. Now, her own friends were imagining things! "Mr. Walker and I are good friends—nothing more."

"There's a pity," Elsa muttered.

Mrs. T patted her hand. "Things have changed since you refused his suit. Your father went to church this past week. He's finally shedding his anger at the Lord. He'll be sure to tend to the children's spiritual lives."

"I know, but—"

"Your other concern was that the children needed daily care," Mrs. Tidewell continued.

"Oh, for goodness' sake!" Samantha impatiently shoved her sewing aside. "You live right next door. The kids already practically live at the smithy. You did all of your weaving there this past winter. They can spend the daytime with you and the nighttime with your father."

"We have it all planned out." Clara grinned at her.

"And don't you dare try to convince any of us that Tyson won't welcome your little brothers and sisters. He's crazy about them." Samantha paused. "When Greta's fever was so high, he called her 'our Greta' and his love for all of them is plain as can be."

Mrs. Tidewell picked up her Bible and started to read 1 Corinthians 13. " 'Charity suffereth long, and is kind; charity envieth not; charity vaunteth not itself, is not puffed up. . . Beareth all things, believeth all things, hopeth all things, endureth all things.' "

She looked up at Betsy. "Charity is love—love freely given. You've been so busy loving others, you've been blind to how much someone loves you. Ty Walker's a fine man. He's been patient and gentle, trying to earn your heart. Think on how he hasn't envied your time with the children, how he's prayed and believed alongside you 'til your father returned to the Lord, how he's still hoped to capture your heart without asking you to sacrifice anything that was dear to you. For years, you put everyone's needs ahead of your own. Ty's come to town and done that for you."

She let out a small laugh. "Betsy, you're two peas in a pod. Surely God fashioned you to be together. Don't you think it's time both of you were free to receive love, too? The man adores you. You love him, don't you?"

"I do love him," Betsy confessed quietly. "He's everything I ever dreamed of as a young girl. I lost my heart to him weeks ago, but I couldn't ask him to take on my family." She smiled. "I guess I've been pretty silly—he's already done that from the day we met, but I lived by fret instead of by faith."

"That settles that! I'll bake the wedding cake," Elsa planned.

"We'll all finish that quilt for you," Clara agreed.

Samantha rubbed her hands gleefully. "I just got new fabric in. You can choose something pretty, and we'll make a dress for you too!"

"I don't think I can go to him. It's so—so. . .bold!"

"Nonsense," Mrs. T said. "Ruth went to Boaz. That was way back in the Bible days when women were far more reserved. She did it; you can too!"

"Oh, what will I say to him?" Betsy fretted.

Mrs. Tidewell drew her out of her chair and nudged her to the door. "Love will find a way."

Betsy started down the street. Her heart beat twice as fast as normal, and her boots scuffled the clumps of snow. Did she dare go speak her heart? The air was redolent with smoke from chimneys. As she drew closer to the smithy, she could hear Ty's mighty hammer at work. Her nerves jangled with every strike. *What do I say?* Moments later, it wasn't the metallic clang of hammer and anvil, but the solid sound of a mallet on wood.

The moment he spied her, Ty set down his mallet and hastened to her. "Betsy! What is it? Is our Greta all right?"

Our Greta. Samantha was right—at some point, Ty had already wormed his way right into the family. "She's fine."

He wrapped his hands around her arms. "What is it, then? Where is your cape? You're cold!" He pulled her close to the forge and briskly rubbed her arms. "Do you need something?"

I need you. The words sounded too stark, too forward. Betsy hitched a shoulder and shivered as he took her chilly hands in his, gently blew on them and rubbed them until they warmed. *How could I have doubted that this man loves me?*

"I was working on something special. Want to see it?"

She nodded.

Ty turned and lifted a big, wooden frame. As he swiveled, her jaw dropped open. A beaming smile lit his face. "The glass was broken in several places. I asked Mrs. Tidewell for a few patterns. This is the one she said would work best. What do you think?"

He'd taken the broken pane of glass and cut it into more pieces, then added in a few pieces of colored glass. He'd connected them with leaded cames into his own version of a stained glass window. "I got the pieces of blue and green glass from the peddler who came through last week. Elsa and Shane were by the other day. She said her grandma called this quilt pattern Old Maid's Puzzle."

She choked out, "Mrs. T calls it Old Maid's Choice."

"Don't you think it'll look wonderful in the cabin?"

Betsy reached out and tentatively ran her fingers over the

edge of the frame. She whispered a quick prayer for courage, then asked, "Would you be willing to let me share this window with my youngers during the daytime if they still slept at Pa's each night?"

Ty stared at her, set down the window, and gathered her in his arms. "Sunshine, I'd share that window with them day and night if it meant you were mine."

"So this old maid doesn't have to make a choice between her family and the man she loves?"

"You're a beautiful young woman, not an old maid. Love, my sweet Betsy, isn't something that draws lines and shoves others out. Love is a bond that draws others in. You already took my heart. Are you ready to take my name?"

"Yes," she whispered before his lips met hers.

Two weeks later, as soon as the kids' coughs settled, everyone in Hickory Corners met at the church. Betsy wore the pretty yellow dress her friends helped her make. She wiggled her toes in the soft kid boots Ty had given her and brushed one last kiss on Pa's cheek before he walked her down the aisle.

The wedding ceremony was sacred and beautiful until Pastor Tidewell asked, "Do you, Tyson, take Elizabeth to be your wife—"

"No!" Greta cried. "No!" She stood up on the pew and burst into tears.

Betsy's heart flipped for a moment, but she squeezed Ty's hands and promised, "Give me a minute. I'll be right back."

Greta wasn't about to wait. She planted her little hands on her hips and piped out, "You marry our Betsy. Not 'Lizbeth. You're ours!"

Folks in the church muffled their laughter.

Ty kept hold of Betsy's hand. He led her over to Greta, and said very evenly, "Betsy is a little name. Your sister's whole, big name is Elizabeth—just like my name is Tyson, but you call me Ty."

Greta wound her arms around his neck and gave him a weak hug. "I didn't want nobody else to get you. You b'long to us!"

"Yes, I do," he agreed. "Now if you let go and sit back down with Smidgen, Betsy and I will finish here so you can have some yummy cake."

Later that afternoon, Ty carried Betsy over the threshold of their cabin. He kicked the door shut, and afternoon light flooded through his beautiful window and spilled across the quilt the sewing circle had finished just days before.

He kissed his bride long and deep, then set her down and held her close. "Welcome home, Sunshine."

Betsy beamed up at him. She knew she'd made the right choice.

CATHY MARIE HAKE

Cathy Marie is a Southern California native who loves her work as a nurse and Lamaze teacher. She and her husband have a daughter, a son, and a dog, so life is never dull or quiet. Cathy considers herself a sentimental packrat, collecting antiques and Hummel figurines. She otherwise keeps busy with reading, writing, baking, and being a prayer warrior. "I am easily distracted during prayer, so I devote certain tasks and chores to specific requests or persons so I can keep faithful in my prayer life." Cathy Marie's first book was published by **Heartsong Presents** in 2000 and earned her a spot as one of the readers' favorite new authors.

Jacob's Ladder

Pamela Kaye Tracy

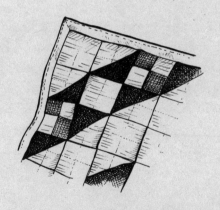

Chapter 1

Samantha Thomasohn loved weddings. . .until this one. A footprint of melted snow glimmered on the wooden floor of the crowded church. Samantha snuck a look up and down the family pew, lifted her blue skirt, and placed her black leather boot over the wet spot. With the tip, she wrote "No." Then, carefully, she enlarged the word. She'd been eighteen for a week and so far nothing good had happened. She wanted seventeen back, and her mother. What if this melancholy feeling never went away? An itch developed under her white stocking, near her ankle. One more annoyance to add to her memories of 1838.

"Samantha, stop fidgeting." Zack's blond eyebrows pinched together in a frown. Only two years older, this brother —who looked so much like her, right down to the light blond hair and slight build—always managed to make her feel amiss.

Samantha sighed. It was more than Zack making her feel out of sorts. This morning, at her father's insistence, she'd shed the black mourning dress she'd worn for *only* five months.

Zack elbowed her. Oh, it was fine for him to sit there all pious. He did not have to share quarters with the soon-to-be new Mrs. Thomasohn, a woman unknown to the family a mere two months prior. No, Zack would leave the wedding celebration, take his bride home to their farm, and the burden of dealing with a new stepmother would fall to Samantha. Thank goodness her papa hadn't indulged in a three-day wedding celebration like Zack. Of course, marrying in blustery, late February took some of the punch out of the fifty-year-old man.

The population of Hickory Corners stood. Zack took her elbow. Did he worry she wouldn't stand? Dare he think she might faint! Samantha clenched her teeth tightly and tried to breathe. Today couldn't be happening. It was all a dream, except there really was a woman walking up the aisle and a silly grin on a groom's face.

Across the aisle Betsy Larkin—er, Betsy Walker—leaned against her new husband. The sweet voice of Elsa Gerhard sounded from behind. Any other service, Samantha would listen and enjoy, but now the perfect harmony didn't belong. Today wasn't perfect, didn't deserve perfection, and Samantha wanted to scream. Elsa chirped on. Looking behind her, Samantha tried to send a warning glance to her friend. Instead, she caught the gaze of Jacob Stahl, and *he* winked.

How dare he! Fresh! Quickly Samantha turned to face the front, hoping he'd not noticed her face redden. This day couldn't get any worse. What if somebody had seen?

The bride stepped to the altar wearing the white silk that had arrived at the store months ago and been deemed too fancy by most of the female clientele. Cecilia hadn't batted an eye at the price tag or color. Samantha had refused the offer of a new dress. There'd be whispers as to why she wore her old blue linen. There'd be more whispers speculating why she'd shed the black.

Love? Could it happen in two months as her father claimed?

Looking over at Betsy and Ty, Samantha knew it could. And, if anything, Elsa sang even better since becoming Mrs. Gerhard.

The congregation sat, and Samantha stared at Cecilia's back. Brown hair coiled under a white veil. She looked so different from the woman who had been ushered into town a few months ago by river men. Then, grieving her husband, Cecilia's long hair hung in a tangled mess over garments too thin for the Ohio cold. Two hundred miles to the east and Cecilia might have called Fort Harmar home. One hundred miles to the west and Fort Washington would have been the lucky spot. Cecilia James settled in Hickory Corners, took a room at Elsa's boardinghouse, and started helping out Virginia Alexander, the dress shop owner.

Samantha's father, Silas Thomasohn, took a shirt over. At the time, Samantha puzzled over the fact. Her mother, Rachel, had patched his sleeves until last year. After her death, Samantha took over the job. The basket, the needles, the worn thimble all belonged to her mother. Touching them inspired beloved memories.

It took her father five shirts to woo the widow. The day after the wedding announcement, Samantha tucked the last of her mother's personal belongings into the old cedar chest and tried to hide the fact that with every fiber of her being she didn't want a stepmother.

The ceremony began. "No" dried into nothingness on the church floor. A silent cry unheeded by all. Samantha's brothers stared forward, unperturbed. Even Raymond, who'd hurried home from Ohio's Willoughby Medical University, seemed calm about the nuptials.

If only Mama had lived.

Up front, Noah Tidewell, the minister, looked to be enjoying himself. A tuft of white hair nodded in agreement to every word he said. He acted like it was every day a local businessman married a woman twenty-two years his junior. *Only nine years older than me,* Samantha thought, closing her eyes. Cecilia James—*oh, and with the minister's words it became Thomasohn*—claimed the same birth year as Samantha's oldest brother, Trevor.

Samantha tried to sneak a glance back at Jacob. He stared at her instead of straight ahead. The nerve of the man. Her stomach tightened. He'd traveled home with Raymond, intent on helping Doc. It had been a year since she'd last seen Jacob. Her memory had him patting the top of her head, *as if she were a child,* and going off with her brother. Just one scant year later, his chestnut hair was a bit longer; his shoulders a shade wider; and his manner a whole lot brasher.

Raymond intended to finish school and switch places with Jacob. Both men agreed that Doc's eyesight impaired him more than the crippling arthritis. Samantha suspicioned that Jacob was out of money, thus his college days were over. The Stahls thought little of education. They were of the land. Samantha often heard Gunther Stahl question Jacob's choice of professions. When the Stahl men came into the store, they seemed to think that she heard nothing as they jawed about prices, crops, and Jacob.

Doc certainly never winked at women during church. Jacob must have learned a few things at college besides how to mend bones. His mother would be none too pleased. The Stahl family always set the perfect example of how one should behave during church services. Samantha shifted uncomfortably. Why was Jacob behind her instead of in front of her? Had the Stahls finally overflowed their favorite bench? Zack said if many more Stahls were born, they'd need to change the name of the town to Stahls' Corners.

"I do."

It was over. Done. Samantha had a stepmother.

"And you're seventeen, Dear?" Cecilia asked the first time they'd met. *"Why aren't you married?"*

Because I won't marry the first person who asks, Samantha had thought, *and because I'm happy where I am.*

Never mind that no one had asked. It hadn't mattered until today, when suddenly Samantha wasn't happy.

The minister called for a prayer. Samantha bowed her head. She'd been continually praying Cecilia would disappear. Instead, today, the woman would be moving into the upstairs of the mercantile. Obviously God wasn't listening to Samantha Ann Thomasohn.

Zack cleared his throat. A sound designed to inspire reverence. If she ignored that first hint, she'd get nudged again.

I will not cry.

Silas Thomasohn beamed as the congregation stood. Well-wishers surged forward. Zack touched Samantha's elbow, meaning to usher her up front. Always the brother to make sure appearances were met, Zack usually had the shovel ready before the snow flurried. Shrugging off his hand, Samantha tried to turn down the middle aisle.

Zack's fingers gripped her elbow. "Papa is expecting you."

She'd sensed Jacob's presence before she saw him. Was it a scent? A feeling?

He easily removed her from Zack's grip. "Samantha, Mrs.

Crabtree was hoping you'd open up the store so she can get a few staples before heading out to your brother's."

The slight beard and mustache were new. Samantha didn't like facial hair, much. And, she certainly hadn't liked the wink. Still, Jacob was offering her an opportunity to escape. "That can wait—" Zack began.

With a jerk, Samantha freed her elbow and clutched at Jacob's sleeve, noticing for the first time how he towered over her. At five feet, three inches, everyone towered over her—just not with Jacob's bearing. Oh, pshaw, the wedding had befuddled her. "I'll go right away. Thanks for fetching me."

The sting of winter greeted her at the church's door. Samantha breathed deeply till it almost hurt.

"I'll help you." Jacob's voice came, right at her ear.

He took her cape from the peg and handed it to her. How he knew the correct one, Samantha had no idea. His fingers brushed hers, and she shivered. The cape dropped to the floor. Samantha bent to pick it up and finally scratched at the spot just above her ankle. So what if Jacob Stahl thought her unladylike. Truly this day could get no worse. Her father remarried, and she acting clumsy in front of Jacob Stahl. As if he mattered. He shouldn't have winked. He was her brother's friend, not hers.

She felt so removed from everything. As if her world tilted and suddenly she no longer stood on firm ground. Taking a deep breath, and holding her chin steady, she marched toward the mercantile.

Jacob watched Samantha. He'd never seen her so tense. Looked like the little princess really disliked having Cecilia

James as a stepmother. That Samantha had managed to stay single nigh until age eighteen was an answered prayer. He'd wait a bit longer, to let her get over the misgivings she had with her stepmother. When he took her hand in marriage, he'd know that she was leaving home *to be* with him and not leaving home to *get away* from Cecilia Thomasohn.

God would show him when the time was right.

Jacob believed in prayer.

So did Olivia Crabtree, who marched with Samantha toward the mercantile. She had Samantha all picked out for her son. Martin Crabtree graduated from college last semester and was apprenticing with a lawyer in Capital City. To Jacob's notice, Martin had no designs on Samantha.

Only God knew Jacob's feelings. Samantha was sunshine and elegance, and Jacob was nothing more than an oversized bear. He admired her high-spiritedness and the way she so easily shone during the town's spelling bees. He liked to see a woman add a sum in her head and challenge the town miser.

Jacob had fallen in love with Samantha the day she'd tricked Oskar Bedloe into paying his mercantile bill. She'd been fifteen, with blond hair pulled back in a knot that showed the graceful curve of her neck. Her cheeks had been flushed.

Jacob liked the thought that he could bring a blush to her cheeks. He'd make the wedding celebration at Trevor's an opportunity. The cocoon of Samantha's family was hatching open, exposing her to the world, and maybe he'd be the one to help her spread her wings.

But, first, he needed to get there. Jacob walked to the barbershop. The red-and-white striped pole symboled haircuts and surgery. The curtains were drawn. Doc's hands could no more manage the scissors than they could the knife. So far, no one seemed interested in trusting their hair to Jacob. Pushing open the door, he took the stairs two at a time until he got to Doc's rooms. For years, Doc had lived in one room while using the other for patients. Now both rooms were for patients, Doc being one.

"How was the wedding?" Doc's deep voice belied his condition. A person might expect the man to jump out of bed and do a jig, so strong was the sound. Only when the listener saw his glassy eyes and gnarled fingers did the truth dawn.

Covering Doc's feet with a blanket, Jacob answered, "Seemed like most weddings. It was too long."

"I stood up with Silas when he married Rachel."

"Really? I wasn't aware of that." Jacob adjusted Doc's pillow and grasped the frail man by the arms. He pulled him to a sitting position and placed a water glass on the bedside table.

"Silas wasn't a rich man then. No, his family came from New York. They were craftsmen. The money was Rachel's."

"The Gustefans are good people."

"They are, and Silas was the peddler."

Jacob blinked. "He was?"

"Yes, he'd come through twice a year. He always had a treat for Rachel. Got so she looked forward to his comings. Then, she looked forward to him."

"I didn't know that."

"It caused a stir for awhile, then they built the store and started nesting."

"He has such bearing."

"Sometimes confidence comes from inside, not from your surroundings."

"And is that my piece of advice for today?" Jacob smiled

as he held the water glass up to Doc's mouth. Doc often dispensed medical wisdom; today the topic had turned to something a bit more personal.

"Go after what you want."

"Oh, I intend to."

"She's worth it."

Jacob blinked. "And you'd be talking about?"

"Miss Samantha."

"And how—"

"You talk in your sleep, Boy. Don't think you're ever going to be able to keep many secrets from a wife."

Chapter 2

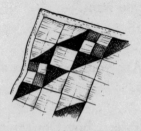

If March intended to go out like a lamb, it had better hurry, Samantha decided. She propped herself up on one elbow and peeped out the window while still cocooned in the warmth of her bed. She let the curtain go and lay back down. It was time to get up, but she didn't want to.

The comfort of the green and yellow quilt wrapped her in a momentary peace. She'd been seven years old when Mama put the quilting needle in her hand. Her feet hadn't even touched the floor as she sat beside Rachel Thomasohn. Hunched over the quilting frame, Samantha learned about the family and how the girls were always slight of build. She'd learned how to behave around boys, and about her mother falling in love with her father. It seemed like the past was sewn right into the threads of the Shoo Fly, their first quilt. Samantha stroked a ragged corner. Some of the stitches, probably hers, were breaking loose.

Outside, a plop of snow fell from the roof and hit the ground. The sound reminded Samantha of other March mornings and snowball fights with her brothers. She wished Raymond still lived at home. The three rooms above the mercantile echoed with the footsteps of three people tiptoeing around each other. Raymond would joke the rooms back into being a home. No matter how Samantha tried, she couldn't muster the effort, and it had been over four weeks.

She shivered as her bare feet touched the cold, wooden floor. Hurrying, she found her slippers. She rid her hair of the rags she'd slept in. Since Mama died, she'd rarely managed a decent curl. She took her day dress from the peg, slipped it on, and picked up her brush. Instead of brushing twenty-five strokes, as Mama had suggested, she did ten before heading downstairs. She wanted to help Cecilia open the store, and then be off to the sewing circle. Lately, it had been her only source of comfort. Not that she dared share her unhappiness with her friends. Mrs. Tidewell would quote a scripture about selfishness and remind Samantha that her father was lonely.

No, Father wasn't lonely, but Samantha was, and she didn't know how to rid herself of the feeling. For the first time in eighteen years, Samantha's prayers were full of muttering what-ifs instead of heartfelt thanks. She never felt better after "amen."

Hurrying through the main room, Samantha stopped to bury her face in Mouse's fur. The cat slept—without complaint—in the box Cecilia made for it, right next to the Franklin stove. He meowed now, annoyed at his nap's interruption. The sound perked Samantha up, taking away a bit of the silence. Father must be at the docks supervising a load. Cecilia would either be downstairs in the store or over at Virginia's dress shop. Checking the weather out the back door, Samantha saw it was cold enough for snow but not cold enough to beg off fetching the water. She changed from her slippers to her boots. Grabbing her cloak and the water bucket, Samantha headed outside to the community well. In the summer, the green grass and the daffodils encouraged her steps. In the winter, the wind pushed against her, warning her away. Fetching water was her least favorite chore. Cecilia's too which was why the job now daily fell to Samantha. When Mama was alive, they'd taken turns.

Old snow, streaked with gray and footprints, crunched underfoot. Samantha shivered and hurried. The well waited behind Oskar Bedloe's shop. Perhaps because of her mood, it seemed to regress into the distance as she hurried closer.

Only one other person fought the winter wind. Samantha knew better than to offer help to Charlotte Warner, who drew on the rope to the well. The gray-haired widow pooh-poohed the assistance of others. She claimed the day she couldn't take care of herself, was the day she wanted to go meet her maker.

"Surprised to see you here," Mrs. Warner said.

"Why?" Samantha sat down on a stone bench to wait her turn.

"You been by to see Betsy?"

Samantha fidgeted with a hole forming in the mitten of her right hand. She needed to mend it, but had forgotten. Like she'd completely forgotten that Betsy's little sister, Greta, was sick. And that Betsy was torn between caring for her new husband and taking care of a little sister who grew weaker every day.

Like Mama had.

Sickness Samantha could deal with; death had her running scared.

"Has something new happened?" Samantha asked slowly. Betsy was an elbow cousin and almost like a sister at times.

"I saw Doc Stahl's sleigh go by last night. Didn't see it return, couldn't stay awake that long. I hoped you had news."

"No." Samantha clutched her bucket tighter, almost wishing the cold would seep through her mittens so she'd have something to jar her into action. So, Jacob was at Betsy's again. Since returning to town last month, he'd been away just as often as when he'd been at school. Only once had she seen him at church. The townspeople buzzed about all the good he was doing. It bothered Samantha that she felt the urge to know his whereabouts. It also bothered her how little she'd done to help out Betsy. She'd change that today. "Thanks for letting me know what's going on. I'll let you know when I find out."

"You do that, Girl." The look Charlotte Warner gave Samantha sent chills down her spine. Samantha had seen that look before. Master Jarrod had used it when he'd caught her letting one of the younger students copy sums from her slate. Mrs. Tidewell had used it when Samantha was nine years old and threw a doll in the baptismal to see if it would float or sink. Father used it last night, when Samantha had sassed Cecilia.

The bucket seemed weighted down by more than water as Samantha trudged back to the store. Little Greta had been bedridden for weeks, ever since Silas and Cecilia's wedding. Both the Walkers and Jacob Stahl had been called away from the wedding reception almost as they walked in the door. Betsy had missed three sewing circles because of Greta. Clara and Elsa missed too, when they were helping Betsy. Samantha tried to quell the shame that spread through her. In a town the size of Hickory Corners, Samantha was one of the few too busy drowning in her own sorrows to lend a helping hand with Greta.

Twenty-seven steps it took to get to the upstairs dwelling

of the Thomasohns'. In summer weather, Samantha could make it without spilling a drop. In winter, it took more effort. Today she didn't lose any. And the bucket just got heavier.

"Good morning." Cecilia's words were cordial. The hem of her new pink linen dress barely missed brushing the floor. The smell of frying bacon lingered in the air.

"Good morning." It sounded like a croak to Samantha's ears. The kitchen table, which had for so long dominated the middle of the room, now resided against one wall. Cecilia's doing. It looked so small. When the three of them sat there, Samantha felt cramped. Her feet curled in fear of contacting Cecilia's. Samantha often thought she'd not manage to swallow.

"Your father is still at the dock. I thought we'd eat breakfast then clean up the store a little." Cecilia dumped the water into the pitcher. She poured two glasses and motioned toward the table.

Mouse curled on Samantha's chair. Picking him up, Samantha cleared her throat. "If you don't mind, I'd like to go over to the Larkins' and help. Charlotte said that Greta took a turn for the worse. I'll imagine Betsy is beside herself."

Cecilia nodded. "I can start in the store."

Thirty minutes later, as Samantha marched up the front walk to Betsy's old house the thought occurred, *The store isn't dirty and just what is Cecilia starting?*

Jacob closed his hands around Greta's fingers. They were cold and limp. He'd been there for over four hours and couldn't think of a thing he'd done to improve Greta's health. *Father, this is one of Your precious ones. She is much beloved. I fear that I*

am too unskilled to help her. Guide me, Lord. She is in Your hands.

"Well," Betsy encouraged, "what are you going to try now?"

He'd been doctoring Hickory Corners and the neighboring towns for all of a month and already knew that worriers came in all shapes and sizes. There were the weepers: they weren't much good as they huddled in the corner and gasped out answers to his questions. There were the gripers: they thought he took too long to get to them. Why they could have died! They spent their time scolding him as he tried to help them and their families. There were also the misers. How dare he act like they owed him something for his visit. Indeed, they'd begun to feel better minutes before he arrived, but since he was there, it would do for him to give an opinion. And there were the helpers: Betsy Walker rated as queen of that list. He figured if he asked her to climb on the roof and sing a ditty, she'd do it if she thought it would help Greta.

"I think you ought to let me take her to Doc's."

Betsy's eyebrows raised. "I can put on another quilt, if you think that will help. You trying to bring on a sweat?"

"No, I just think she'd be more comfortable."

"Kids, go outside." Betsy ordered.

The other Larkin children bundled into their winter clothes and were out the door in minutes, too subdued to argue.

"Tell me the truth," Betsy ordered.

"She's not getting any better. I want to keep a closer eye on her."

"What do you think is wrong?"

"I'm thinking it is pneumonia, but it could be typhoid fever."

Betsy collapsed against the wall, her face as pale as Greta's. Jacob knew why. He'd already lost a little girl up toward Wabash Springs, the same symptoms, just last week.

Jacob didn't intend to lose Greta, but unless he got her temperature down, inflammation of the kidneys or an ear infection would follow.

Betsy didn't look convinced, and Jacob wished he had more of a way with words. He needed a wife to advise him on how to speak to the women. Doc always said that the ladies often wouldn't tell doctors what was ailing them due to embarrassment. Now was not the time to be thinking about wives— and that meant Samantha—Greta needed his attention.

Betsy took a drawer from the dresser and started packing. "She can come home with me. I should of thought of it earlier. It will be much easier?"

Jacob started to move toward Betsy. Poor woman had enough on her plate. Just as he let go of Greta's hand, he heard a thump upon the door and then a hesitant knocking.

"It's Pa," Betsy said. "He's not going to like this."

But it was Samantha Thomasohn, opening the door against the cold and looking like she'd faint dead away. Still, Jacob had to admire her. She stood shivering from the cold, with her chin in the air, clutching her reticule like it was her only hold on sanity. Behind her stood the other Larkin children. The look on their faces said it all. Sickness was no stranger to this clan.

"What can I do to help?" Samantha herded the children to the kitchen table. Everyone looked at Betsy. She held onto a nightgown of Greta's and frowned. Jacob started to stand, but stayed crouched. The little girl, if possible, had grown even hotter to the touch.

As if realizing she was the center of attention, Greta woke up and whined.

"I'm so glad you're here," Betsy said.

Jacob wasn't sure if the words were directed to her siblings or to Samantha. Giving Greta a quick pat on the shoulder, he moved over to Samantha. "Take the drawer and put it in the sleigh. Betsy, you need to talk to the little ones. It will frighten them that Greta is gone."

Betsy lay the last nightgown in the drawer and nodded.

"I'll get Greta settled over at your place," Samantha said. "I want to."

A few minutes later, Jacob stopped the sleigh in front of Betsy and Ty's place. He tethered the horses before reaching for Greta. He wanted to help Samantha down, but she followed too quickly. He heard her behind him. Even taking careful steps, her shoes were slippery. Silly female whim. Her feet might look small and dainty in the pretty, black leather boots, but the hard, flat sole acted much like an ice skate. If he weren't already carrying Greta, he'd sweep Samantha off her feet to keep her from falling.

"Jacob, you feeling all right?" Samantha stared at him.

He'd gone right to their door and stopped. Greta stared at him, awake, not coughing, and curious.

"Come on, then." Jacob pushed open the front door and carried Greta the few steps to Betsy's bed. Soon the little girl snuggled into the sheets. She probably smelled Betsy and felt secure. Jacob checked her pulse and tongue. No change since he'd done that the first time an hour earlier. "Greta, does it hurt when you breathe?"

"Um dra hgum now." Greta closed her eyes and went to sleep.

Jacob pulled the blanket up to the child's shoulders. "What did she say?"

Samantha settled on the edge of the bed. "She said it doesn't hurt now."

Chapter 3

At six foot, Jacob was the runt of the Stahl litter and had an easygoing manner that his family lacked. He'd helped Raymond with pranks, mimicked Zack's seriousness at times, and always listened closely when Trevor read aloud to the family. When he'd played at Samantha's house, he'd bossed her as bad as her brothers had.

At the schoolhouse, and even the few times she'd seen him at her home, she'd considered Jacob clumsy, inept. But now his fingers worked magic as he bathed Greta's forehead. The little girl went to sleep, soothed by the gentle touch of a man who couldn't roll a decent snowball. Only the child's labored breathing broke the silence in the room.

Samantha was suddenly very aware that she was practically alone with Jacob. Stepping back, she tried to focus on something—anything—else. Betsy's home smelled of gingerbread and peppermint. No, Betsy's home smelled of gingerbread. Jacob Stahl smelled of peppermint.

Pushing herself off the bed, Samantha stepped closer to him. "What can I do to help?"

"Boil some water. Steam will help her breathing."

Glad for something to do, Samantha hauled the black

cast-iron pot from the fireplace and went outside. The slim piles of snow still holding their own at the Walker place were a tad cleaner than in town. Samantha scooped handfuls into the pot and hustled back toward the house. Since March hadn't turned, the wicked wind sent tendrils of frost inside Samantha's cape.

Betsy came running up the road, caught up with Samantha, and hurried to the front door. Samantha struggled to follow. Her bonnet blew back and blond hair streamed behind her, caught in the wind that strained to keep her outside.

Samantha shivered then, not from the cold, but from the realization that Betsy was hurting and no matter how much help was offered, hers was a pain to be borne alone. They'd tried steam on Mama too. And Samantha had made countless trips to the well to keep the water supplied.

The door closed behind them. Samantha took the pot to the fire and hung it on the spit. Jacob left Greta's side, opened his doctor's bag, and withdrew a bag. Samantha recognized pulverized Peruvian bark. Her father carried it at the store.

"What do we do now?" Betsy asked her favorite question.

Jacob's lips formed a thin line as he gave a slight shrug and pulled the blanket tighter about the child's shoulders.

The seconds ticked by, and the room grew smaller. Jacob's attention focused on Greta. Betsy put away Greta's belongings and all but collapsed on the kitchen table.

Ten minutes later, with a bundle of laundry—the least she could do—Samantha headed home. Her boots clamored on the slick, frozen ground. Struggling to keep her balance, she passed the sheriff's office and the cold wrapped around her. She told herself the sharp, prickling sensations were penance for being selfish—for leaving Betsy alone; but in the pit of her stomach and even in the back of her mind, she knew herself a coward.

Once home, she climbed the stairs and dumped the clothes in the hamper. Usually, home was the place Samantha Thomasohn most wanted to be. She hadn't appreciated the security of her family enough. She wanted to be involved in a family Bible reading, with Raymond tickling the back of her feet, trying to make her laugh so she'd get in trouble. She wanted to watch the face of Zack, as he nodded in agreement to everything Father said. She missed the homey feeling that settled in her stomach when Trevor took his turn reading the Scriptures.

Thumps, from downstairs, echoed through the room and jarred Samantha from her melancholy. Father never unloaded during business hours. He insisted that stocking should take place either early morning or late at night. And Father hadn't returned yet with the wagon.

The door leading down to the store stood open. Samantha took a few hesitant steps and stopped. Even from there she could see the changes. Bolts of material now took up space on the top shelf of the east wall. Coffee grinders were arranged artistically on the high shelf behind the counter.

"What do you think?" Cecilia grinned. A streak of dirt across her nose made her look even younger.

"I think you've put much of our stock out of my reach."

"What do you mean?"

"I mean that if someone comes in wanting to buy a sausage gun or meat chopper, I won't be able to sell it to them, unless of course the customer happens to be six-foot tall and can reach it themselves."

"Why—"

"Who told you you could do this?" Samantha's stomach hurt. She put one hand on the wall to help her stand straight. No way did she want to hunch over and show weakness.

It didn't look like Cecilia felt any stress. The woman's eyes blazed. "Nobody told me. I thought—"

"You're changing everything!"

"I'm just trying to help."

"You call this help? I can't reach anything. I wish you'd just go—"

"Samantha, that's enough." Father stood at the top of the stairs. His hair, once dark brown and thick, now mimicked the picture of a monk Samantha had seen in one of Master Jarrod's many books. At the moment, what was left of Father's hair stuck out in jagged lines, half frozen from the Ohio winter and anger.

"But—"

"You will apologize to Cecilia."

Samantha's lips went dry. Her tongue snaked out, back in, and her mouth went as dry as her lips.

"Now."

"I'm not sorry." Her voice betrayed her, becoming an embarrassing squeak.

Father moved closer. Even the echo from his boots sounded fierce. The back of Samantha's throat tightened. Those stupid tears; they were trying to surface.

"I'm sorry."

Before her father could say another word, before Cecilia could open her mouth and really bring tears to Samantha's eyes, she sailed out of Thomasohn's Mercantile. She only managed the boardwalk and a few steps toward Oskar's before bumping into a solid form. Anybody sensible would have moved.

"Whoa, whoa. And what sends a comely gal fleeing without a coat?"

The funny thing was. . .anger had a warmth to it, and Samantha didn't feel a single chill, although she noted the difference when a black frock went around her shoulders.

"When did you get back in town, Martin?" If possible, Samantha noted, he had grown handsomer. Yet, the observance didn't pool in the pit of Samantha's stomach like it usually did.

"This morning. Now what vexation has you knocking me over in the street?"

"If I was knocking you over in the street, Martin Crabtree, I'd certainly have waited until a cart was going by!" The words came easily, slipping from her tongue like the hot butter on Elsa Gerhard's sourdough rolls.

"You wound my heart, Samantha. Now, who wounded yours?"

Tossing back her head, and glad that she could blame her tearing eyes on the weather, Samantha forced a grin. "Ah, but you have to have a heart in order for it to be wounded. I've probably given mine away while you've been gone."

Martin laughed. He plucked off his Cumberland top hat and set it on her head. It was too big and quickly blinded her. The buoyancy of her curls made the hat lopsided. He tucked her hand in his elbow. "Walk with me over to Elsa's."

Samantha pushed the hat up. Martin didn't deserve her wrath. He was an innocent bystander in the path of her anger.

"Come on, Mantha, you know you can't stay vexed long."

He tickled her under the chin and forced a smile from her. Martin was considered a prize by all of the eligible young ladies in Hickory Corners. Her *oma*, Rosie Gustefan, said he could charm the starch out of fresh laundry. Samantha began to calm down and even forgave him for calling her Mantha.

"Come with me while I call on Elsa." Without any further encouragement, Martin tugged Samantha across the street. Each step took her farther away from the mercantile and the ugly memory of what had just happened inside.

The Hickory Corners Boardinghouse offered warmth, not just from the roaring fireplace. Elsa and Shane had created a real showplace. The dining room, once outfitted with hand-hewn benches and uneven tables, now sported a set of furniture unequaled in Hickory Corners. It was the rocker in the corner of the room that caught Samantha's eye. Working in the store had given her an eye for craftsmanship, and this piece didn't come from the hands of Nate Harmon, the cabinet maker. Harmon was good, but this was exquisite.

"Where did you get this?"

"Jacob Stahl."

Samantha rubbed the fine-grained hickory wood with the tips of her fingers and remembered the sounds of Raymond and Jacob whistling as they sat on the side stairs whittling. It had been over a month since he'd had the audacity to wink at her. Oh, what was Jacob Stahl doing on her mind! And especially when Martin, in his double-breasted tailcoat and tight-fitting trousers, still had his hand on her arm long past the time he should have let go.

Jacob rubbed the sleep from his eyes as he exited Betsy's home. Little Greta had finally fallen into a healing sleep, at least he hoped it was a healing sleep. At college, many of the professors held fast to the ideas of Benjamin Rush. Steaming was one of the great man's favorite cures. So far, Jacob could not add any names under the list of those cured by steam. If Greta didn't show some improvement soon, Jacob intended to try a treatment of calomel.

The horses stamped their impatience. They wanted the livery and food. Normally, Jacob would have walked to the Larkins', but he'd started his morning with two distant house calls before settling down with Greta. Jacob clucked and drove them the mile into town. After turning the reins over to the livery owner, Leonard Melvin, Jacob headed for Doc's place. In the irony of fate, Doc was improving while Greta sagged. Doc's aged body daily grew stronger, not from steam or purging, but from sheer will to survive.

The ancient clock above Doc's mantel showed ten o'clock. Jacob picked up the key and wound it. Doc was sleeping, not an unreasonable pastime for a man of his age and health. His forehead was cool and his breathing even. Without waking Doc, Jacob rubbed Professor Low's liniment on the old man's hands, paying special attention to the joints. No matter how many times Jacob reminded Doc to lubricate his hands, he didn't do it.

When there wasn't a patient in the other room, Jacob used it. Since he hadn't made the bed, he took the time to do it, then glanced at the cradle on the floor near the window. Elsa Gerhard was turning into a regular customer. The cradle was a prize. He was tempted to keep it and make Elsa another. A Stahl child would look fine in the contraption.

The thought of a babe turned into a vision of Samantha seated in a rocking chair like the one he'd made Elsa and Shane. He could see her Madonna-like features soften as she looked at a babe in her arms, their babe.

All thoughts of sleep vanished. Jacob went to the basin and splashed cold water on his face. Samantha had surprised him this morning. First, she'd shown up to help. Second, she'd looked at him as a man, rather than as her brother's annoying friend. Well, maybe she'd given him a similar expression when he'd winked at her during church.

Since her mother's death, Samantha had avoided illness with a determination unequaled. Was a bit of healing finally coming along? Jacob figured if that was true, then maybe the time had come to act. So far the only hint he'd given Samantha that he was interested was that wink at church. Winking might have gotten her attention, but was not all that fulfilling.

He changed his shirt, stuck a peppermint in his mouth, and picked up the cradle. Might as well deliver it before Elsa headed to the sewing group she so loved on Tuesdays. Besides, Samantha and Elsa always walked together. If he timed delivery just right, he might get to wink—or something more —with the girl he intended sparking.

Chapter 4

J acob adjusted the cradle under his arm and took a deep breath of the March crispness. Most of the people who scurried along Main Street were bundled up against the cold. They held the neck of their cloaks together and wrapped their chins with brightly colored scarves. Not him! He relished the brisk breeze that reminded him how good it was to be alive.

His jubilation waned as his thoughts returned to Greta. Somehow it didn't seem right for him to be in high spirits when at Miss Betsy's a small child struggled to breathe. He'd pore over Doc's medical books again when he got back to the barbershop. Surely there was something he'd missed, some remedy yet to try.

Just as he turned the corner, Olivia Crabtree came out of the dress shop. Her black mourning dress, worn since he was knee high to a grasshopper, knew better than to brush the ground. She didn't clutch her coat or wear a scarf. Weather didn't seem to affect her. She tipped her head to the side, an inquisitive gesture by anyone else but from her more a demand, eyed the cradle, and asked, "Is that for Elsa?"

Jacob didn't know how she did it, but Mrs. Crabtree was

the only woman in town who had her dark and graying hair drawn so tightly into its bun, it didn't dare move. He'd soon make some extra money from prescribing headache powders. Forcing a pleasant smile, he responded, "Yes, what do you think?"

She pressed her thin lips together and stepped closer, clearly hoping to find a flaw. Begrudgingly she admitted, "I'm thinking someday you'll be making one for my boy and his wife."

Jacob's fingers grasped the cradle harder. To his knowledge, Martin had yet to act on his mother's advice, but then, being a dandy took up a lot of his time. With the ink on his law degree still drying, Martin just might be thinking it was time to settle down. Mrs. Crabtree would be talking up Samantha.

Jacob studied the cradle. Yes, he should have kept this one, but if he knew Samantha, she'd be pleased he chose to give it to her friend.

Samantha was free, done mourning, and much too gentle to deserve a mother-in-law like Mrs. Crabtree. The woman didn't know how to smile. It was unnatural.

He hoisted the cradle onto his shoulder, uttered a terse excuse, and hurried to the boardinghouse. It was well past noon, yet as he opened the door and stepped inside he heard voices coming from the dining room. Jacob followed the sound. Samantha sat in his rocking chair. Next to her, with his hand on her arm, stood Martin. She was wearing his coat and hat.

They looked good together.

Samantha's gaze met Jacob's. She reached up and took Martin's hat off. Handing it back, she shrugged his hand off her arm and started to slip out of his coat. Martin silently helped her.

Once, years ago, Jacob watched as a fox grabbed his mother's prize chicken. An uncanny grin graced the carnivore's face as it made off with its booty. Smug was too polite a word.

Martin Crabtree looked a bit like a fox.

Jacob Stahl had often been compared to a bear.

No way was the fox getting the prize this time.

"Jacob." Elsa rushed toward him. "Are you finished with my cradle already? I figured it would be at least another week."

He carefully set it on the floor. "I've had some sleepless nights."

Samantha's eyes turned misty. Were the tears still from this morning? From watching little Greta suffer? Jacob wished he were standing next to Samantha. He'd do more than touch her shoulder. He'd sweep her into his arms and promise her the moon. Well, he'd promise her undying love anyway, which was all he, a struggling doctor, had to offer.

Shane helped his wife to her feet and picked up the cradle. "Where do you want it, Wife?" His jovial tone and dancing hazel eyes were aimed at Elsa.

Envy took hold of Jacob, not a comfortable or familiar feeling. Martin was standing too close to the woman Jacob wanted. Jacob didn't like it one bit. "I saw your mother, Martin. She said she'd someday order one for you."

"Did she now? I say a cradle's a fine place for storing fire kindling. Don't you agree, Samantha?"

"Hush," Elsa said. "Such nonsense. Come on, Samantha, let's go to my room and you can help me decide where to put it."

Before Jacob had time to catch his breath, the Gerhards

and Samantha were gone. Martin remained behind the rocking chair, fingering his hat and grinning.

A good general always prepared for battle. Jacob hadn't realized how close to camp the enemy had maneuvered. With fierce determination, he forced himself to study Martin Crabtree as a possible adversary.

Martin eyed him with a gleam. "It would bother you to make a cradle for me, wouldn't it?"

"No, not a bit."

"Good, then maybe you should see about assembling the piece. I mean, no sense waiting for the last minute. You never know what might happen."

"I'll wait a bit."

"Really, you think there might be surprises in store?"

"No, I don't think. I know."

Elsa barely gave Shane time to place the cradle on the floor of their bedroom. Nudging him past the oak vanity and out the door, she whirled to face her friend.

Samantha protested, "Really, Elsa, Shane probably wants to help decide—"

"Oh, pooh, he'll rearrange it the way he wants later. Now he's talking about ordering me one of those fancy bathtubs. He read that half of Pittsburgh owns one. Imagine," Elsa patted her swollen abdomen, "as if I could even fit into one." Perching on the edge of the bed, Elsa pulled Samantha down with her, folded her hands in her lap, and with an amused expression asked, "So, do tell."

"Do tell what?"

"I mean, when you walked in with Martin, I wasn't a bit

surprised. You've swooned over him since first primer, then in walks Jacob Stahl, of all people, and suddenly I saw two men sizing up the territory."

"They didn't," Samantha insisted. Her stomach lurched. Maybe they had.

"You've taken off the black. You're beautiful and of marrying age. It makes sense the men will come courting."

"It's too soon," Samantha whispered.

"That's not the problem." Elsa's foot tapped on the floor, a steady *trip, trap, trip,* of reproach.

"Things keep changing." Samantha knew her friend only meant to give comfort, but the walls were closing in. Elsa was married, with a babe on the way. Betsy had a ring on her finger. Not only did Samantha feel alone within her family, but her friends were growing up and away faster than she could count to ten.

"Jacob's a good man," Elsa said.

"So is Martin."

"Martin has his moments, I'll agree. But think, you know Martin will never stay here. We've no need of a lawyer, and he'll chafe under the dictatorship of that mother of his."

Samantha stood up and offered Elsa a hand, changing the subject as she did. "That reminds me. Martin brought news from your sister."

It worked. Elsa put a hand to her heart and scurried from the room amazingly fast for a woman in her condition.

Samantha followed slowly. Elsa was right, Martin would never stay in Hickory Corners. Moving would be good, Samantha decided. She wouldn't have to watch Cecilia contrive to change the look of Mama's home. Moving would be bad, Samantha changed her mind. Everything that had ever spelled comfort was right here in Hickory Corners.

"Samantha, we're late! Mrs. T will wonder what's keeping us." Elsa's voice dragged Samantha from her musings. Looking at the grandfather clock Shane had shipped in as a wedding present for Elsa, Samantha quickened her step.

"Keep the coat," Martin suggested, handing it to her. "I'll fetch it tonight when I come calling."

Before she knew what she was doing, Samantha looked at Jacob. His chin jerked to one side and back, a minute indication of *no*.

Samantha blinked. What was she thinking? Looking to Jacob Stahl for permission! "That would be fine, Mr. Crabtree. I'll tell Papa to expect you at seven." Grabbing Elsa's hand, she barely gave her friend time to grab a cloak before pushing her out the front door.

"Don't say it," Samantha warned as they hustled up the street toward Mrs. T's.

"Don't say it? You've got to be joshing. I can hardly wait to tell Betsy. Do you think she'll be there?"

"No, Greta's taken a turn for the worse. Jacob and I—"

"Jacob and you?"

"No, not us together. He was already at Betsy's house when I went to help this morning."

Elsa gave Samantha a hug as they turned onto Birch Street. "And to think I was worrying this winter would be dull. I do believe Hickory Corners is due for a high time."

Mrs. T opened the door and hustled the girls in. The minister's wife always kept the stove hot and the sweets ready on quilting day. "Samantha, I'm sending Brady to your father's store. He stopped by earlier. Seemed right concerned about your whereabouts." Squinting, Mrs. T stepped closer. "Did you get a new coat?"

Clara jumped in. "Is that a man's frock?"

"I'm wearing it for a bit," Samantha defended. "It means nothing."

"Martin Crabtree's," Elsa piped in.

"He happened along, and I was cold."

"Where were you? When did Martin get back in town? Why—"

"Girls." Mrs. T expertly stalled Clara's questions. "Let's settle down and perhaps Samantha will fill us in. . . ."

Samantha shook her head.

"And perhaps not." Mrs. T left the room and soon the girls heard her calling Brady's name.

Samantha slipped from the room and caught hold of Brady's shoulder before he headed for the store. The Tidewells' nephew was pretty easygoing. He wouldn't mind traipsing through town with a flowered basket.

"Brady, will you ask for my sewing basket, please?"

Deep blue eyes twinkled. "Why, Miz Samantha, if you can walk through town in a man's frock, I'll surely get by with your sewing basket." He laughed all the way out the front door.

The girls busied themselves at the quilting frame. Elsa saved Samantha from more questions by chattering about the upcoming baby. Although, from the looks Elsa cast Samantha, the subject was not dropped.

Mrs. T delved into her Bible, not bothering to join the girls at the frame. She left the Scriptures to accept Samantha's basket, then delved back in, a troubled look on her face. Samantha knew the minister's wife looked forward to the sewing circle as much as the girls did. Betsy's absence left a void. Mrs. T probably hunted for Scriptures of comfort.

Glancing over at Clara Bucey, Samantha noted that she'd already turned the point of the Pieced Star. Not one stitch had Samantha managed. Running her finger along the silver dimples of her mother's thimble, she remembered the first time she'd tried it on. She'd been five, and it had slipped right off her finger.

Mama's thimble. Samantha blinked back tears and tried to shake the sadness. Instead, she shivered.

"I'm going to read today from the Book of Ephesians," Mrs. T said softly. "Chapter six, the first few verses: 'Children, obey your parents in the Lord: for this is right. Honour thy father and mother; which is the first commandment with promise; That it may be well with thee, and thou mayest live long on the earth.'"

Strange, Samantha considered, the verse had nothing to lessen the pall of Betsy's absence.

The thimble slipped from Samantha's finger and fell to the floor.

"Oh." Clara immediately pushed back her chair and went to her knees. "I don't see it."

Samantha gently rubbed her left middle finger. It felt warm and tender, much like her heart.

Elsa peered under the quilt's edge. Mrs. T started to stand up. The frame trembled as Clara crawled through to the other side.

"It's lost," Clara announced.

So am I, Samantha thought.

Chapter 5

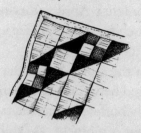

Samantha couldn't remember the schoolroom being more crowded for a Friday Night Social. Enterprising men had moved some of the benches from the church so families would have a place to sit. Older children stood against the wall. Master Jarrod sat at his desk. Usually the schoolhouse was as tidy as Mrs. T's house, *except for Master Jarrod's desk*. Slates, primers, a giant hourglass, and all kinds of homemade gifts called the top of his desk home. Today only the bell occupied space. In contrast, the mud from the towns-folks' boots marred the floor. Reticules, baby blankets, and even a few dried beef droppings decorated the floor. The Bunks occupied the dried beef corner. They tended to leave a trail wherever they ate. More than once, Samantha had swept the mercantile floor after the Bunk brothers vacated. She figured Master Jarrod would rather not cross the river-rat brothers, otherwise the two men would have already seen the ruler rap their knuckles and the dried beef would be long gone.

Master Jarrod reminded Samantha of a stork. She felt a bit guilty about the comparison, especially since the only reason she knew what a stork looked like was from a quick peek at one of the teacher's personal books.

Mrs. T darted from one end of the schoolhouse to the other. She whispered in Charlotte Warner's ear, glanced out the window, and nervously fingered the teacher's bell. She had put together tonight's April gathering. During the winter months, the church tried to organize a few social events to break up the monotony.

A fire roared in the stove. Samantha was warm, but not from the fire. Wedged between Millie Sanderson and Martin, Samantha felt firmly buffeted from the faint chill sent by the early April wind. For a moment, as Millie scooted closer to make room for another latecomer, Samantha wondered where Clara was. Surely not at home sewing? Clara would leave for New York in two weeks, and for the last few days all she talked about were relatives and the excitement of visiting.

The cuff of Martin's sleeve brushed Samantha's wrist. Startled, she looked up. Martin smiled and took her hand. This wasn't the first time she'd attended a social with Martin. Before Mama's illness, and when he was in town, he'd often squired her around town. This wasn't the first time he'd taken her hand either.

It was the first time the gesture made her start. It used to make her tingle.

Looking around the schoolroom, she noticed that only Roy Schmidt, the banker, wore clothes of the same quality as Martin. Pride? Is that what she felt when regarding Martin's ruffled shirts? He'd taken off his frock. He sported the only silk damask vest in the room.

Samantha straightened the skirt of her blue cotton dress. It fit perfectly when Mama tailored it, but after putting on the mourning black, Samantha lost weight. She wondered if Martin noticed that her sleeves had the fullness a bit too high. Fashion changed quickly, or so Cecilia had reminded her as they dressed for the evening's event.

Leaning forward, Samantha searched for her father. There he was, sitting near the front, with his arm protectively around his new wife. Clothes didn't matter to Silas Thomasohn; family did, Cecilia did.

"Stop letting her bother you," Martin whispered.

Samantha took her hand out from under his. Was she that obvious? "I'm not."

"I've listened to you recite that 'obey your parents' Scripture at least ten times during the last week."

"It's helping."

"You know what comes after verse one, don't you?"

Samantha's brow wrinkled. She should know it.

Martin didn't give her a chance to think. "Fathers, provoke not your children."

It did give her pause, but she shook her head. "Oh, Martin, that has nothing to do with what's bothering me."

"Used to be, you stared at me during our evenings. I don't think you've looked at me even once this evening."

"That's not true."

Master Jarrod chose that moment to ring the bell.

Once everyone had quieted down, Reverend Tidewell started the evening with a prayer. Mrs. T nodded from her perch by the window. The school door burst open and an outrageously tall man ducked in. He was padded with what looked like, Samantha squinted, quilt stuffing. As he scuffled up the aisle she noticed the coffee cans tied to his shoes. They must be made of rock, she thought, to hold Tyson Walker up. The blacksmith easily outweighed and outstood every man in town, including the Stahl brothers who'd towered over everyone until Ty moved to town. Briefly, she wondered why he wasn't home with Betsy helping take care of Greta.

He turned once he reached the front of the room and boomed, "I hear tell this town is tired of winter. Is that true? I said, IS THAT TRUE? Well, the same thing happened over in Michigan in '26. So I let out a hot breath, melted that snow quicker than you could say Jehoshaphat. The townspeople were mighty obliged, especially when they realized that the melting water formed one of the Great Lakes."

The school door opened again. After being surprised by such a "tall" entrance, Samantha expected to see something big enter. Big was correct, but blue was a better description. Unless she missed her guess, the blanket the mystery guest wore came straight from Mrs. T's bed. The horns were made from two of Doc's hearing aides. Children laughed and scrambled out of the way. Samantha noticed the Larkin children, minus Greta, in the corner. That explained why Ty was there. Betsy probably told him it was important for the young ones to have some fun.

As the unconvincing ox clumsily moved up the aisle, its head swung right and left. Samantha's eyes caught sight of Ole Babe, and she felt tingles go down her arm.

Jacob Stahl.

He'd taken to dropping by the store regularly and not just to purchase dry goods. Yet, he didn't ask her father for permission to court as Martin had. No, instead he told her what nursing he wanted her to do over at Betsy's. And because Samantha loved Betsy, she obeyed. And she pretended she didn't want him to wink again.

Martin leaned over and whispered in Samantha's ear. "An improvement in the sawbones' wardrobe, wouldn't you say?"

"Ah," cried Paul Bunyan, saving Samantha from having to answer. "My trusted friend, Babe."

Jacob snorted and pawed at the ground. His ragged boots, a Stahl brothers' hand-me-down, did not make oxenlike noises. Children giggled and parents smiled indulgently. Checking the schoolroom for Jacob's parents, Samantha located them in the back row. They didn't usually come to town for socials, thinking them frivolous. Jacob's mother had a smile on her face. The first Samantha had seen.

"He looks a bit ridiculous," Martin whispered in her ear.

"Hush," she whispered back. She wasn't about to tell Martin that betwixt the two men, Jacob came out the winner in more ways than one.

The blanket added more heat than Jacob needed. Sweat pooled at the back of his neck and ran down his spine. Perhaps he should dress Greta up in the getup and see if it helped. Before coming to the social, they'd practiced their act in front of Betsy, Mr. Larkin, and Greta.

Not even a smile came from the child.

It was easier dealing with Mrs. Cullen over in Taylorville. During his first visit, she'd been in denial over her illness. Now she was angry. Anger sometimes cured people, to Jacob's way of thinking. They decided to get better by sheer will power, and it worked. Jacob knew prayer had a lot to do with it. Greta had prayer, but it surely looked like God was calling her home.

Jacob had no speaking lines, unless snorting counted. From beneath Mrs. T's blanket, he could watch as the audience *oohed* and *aahed* at Ty's monolog. As Ole Babe, Jacob pretended to move a mountain—Brady Forbes in disguise; danced with a hurricane—Shane Gerhard in disguise; and gave the sheriff's young son a ride. Just as Tyson ordered a tornado—Benjamin Melvin's role—the schoolhouse door burst open and Mr. Larkin rushed in. One look said it all. Without missing a beat, Brady ducked under the blanket and took over Jacob's role. Jacob moved down the crowded aisle, grabbed his doctor bag and coat, and followed Greta's father to the wagon.

"Are you sure you want to come?" Mr. Larkin's face had a gray cast to it. His eyes were bloodshot and his hands shook.

Jacob started to answer what he considered a silly question, but then a soft voice came from behind him.

"I might be able to help."

Samantha clutched her coat to her neck. Jacob helped her into the wagon and scooted in beside her. Reaching behind the bench, he grabbed the blanket to tuck around them, although he didn't feel the cold.

"Tell me what's changed," Jacob ordered.

"Her lips turned blue, as blue as that blanket you were wearing."

"Go faster," Jacob urged.

Chapter 6

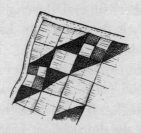

The sun shone broadly in Samantha's eyes as it reflected off one of the few remaining patches of snow at the cemetery behind the church. She shivered, but not from the cold. Father slipped his arm in hers and hugged her. Cecilia stood a few feet away looking decidedly forlorn.

Reverend Tidewell cleared his throat as he paused beside the newly erected headstone. "Greta Larkin wasn't but four. She was a special child, full of God's love. She often sought comfort in my wife's lap."

Samantha looked over at Mrs. T Her cheeks were moist and not even the constant dabbing of the handkerchief hid the sorrow. Mama's words came back: *They have no children of their own, so you girls and Brady are their family.*

There were not many dry eyes, that Samantha could tell. Neither Crabtree showed emotion, nor did Oskar Bedloe, although he did seem to have a never before seen bothersome twitch.

Blinking, Samantha tried to make the tears come. Greta, who had often called Samantha, "Tha" because she couldn't manage the whole word, had left this world. Then, Samantha noticed Greta's father. Matthew Larkin stood as close to the coffin as possible, as if determined to retain contact with his youngest child. He wasn't crying. Not a drop. His head was bowed, but there was a peace to the expression. He'd fallen apart at Greta's mother's funeral. Reverend Tidewell had tried to offer comfort back then, but Mr. Larkin cursed at the preacher and at God.

Samantha moved closer to her father and wished she was anywhere save there. Unable to stop herself, she peered over at her mother's grave. Jacob stepped in front of it.

Did Jacob think she didn't know what her mother's grave looked like? Even with him standing in the way, she could see it clear as— But she couldn't see it, nor could she see the headstones for Mama's two babies who'd gone to Heaven before her. All Samantha could see was Jacob.

He rolled his hat in his hands. Samantha noted the pain in his eyes and felt it. He'd tried everything! The onion poultice drove Samantha, eyes and nose running, from the room. Betsy heated stones in the fire to put at Greta's feet. For three hours the girl lingered, caught somewhere between life and death. Yet, despite Jacob's best effort, death won. And why did Matthew Larkin have a peaceful look on his face and Jacob look so torn?

The Reverend droned on, his face red from the cold. A few tufts of white hair escaped from under his hat. Samantha shifted from one foot to the other. Greta's wake was on its second day and would be ending soon. They'd moved to the cemetery less than an hour ago, and the mourners were all stamping their feet trying to ward off the cold that paid no attention to the bright, shining, April sun. Bright and shining like Greta's smile.

Samantha turned her attention back to the coffin, closed

now and looking hauntingly insignificant among so many mourners. People came from as far away as Wabash Springs. Funerals always garnished a crowd. They brought food, comfort, and other things as well. This morning, Samantha had brushed away the salt and earth that the Bunk brothers had placed on Greta's stomach. They were superstitious men claiming that salt was a symbol of the spirit and earth represented the flesh. All Betsy wanted was for Greta's dress to stay clean. The coffin was lined with the Pieced Star quilt the sewing circle had been working on. Mrs. T left it incomplete, saying that like Greta, more time was needed.

Everyone bowed in final prayer. Samantha mimicked the others and tried to concentrate. From the corner of her eye, she could see Martin inching closer. He'd stayed away the last three days, partly in respect, partly in anger. He hadn't liked it a bit when she left with Jacob Stahl, no matter the reason.

With a start, Samantha realized that Martin wasn't sad, because Martin didn't *know* Greta, indeed didn't *know* most of the townspeople. Oh, he knew their names, what they did, where they lived, and possibly a family background, but he didn't *know* them. He'd always been with the crowd but never in it. Why hadn't she noticed that before? He'd be the perfect lawyer—detached.

Betsy leaned against Tyson. He'd come to the store yesterday for crape. Samantha had refused to charge him for the material and visually dared Cecilia to interfere. To her surprise, Cecilia had added some black muslin after Samantha hurried upstairs to fetch the mourning attire she no longer wore.

Today, Betsy wore the black Samantha had so unwillingly

shed only a few months ago. *Did I look that forlorn?* Samantha wondered. Looking at her father, she noted his eyes on Mama's grave. Rachel was gone but not forgotten. For the first time, Samantha felt an inkling of relief that she'd taken off the mourning. *Yes, God,* Samantha thought, *You knew that Betsy would need it more than I do.*

Reverend Tidewell ended his eulogy. Samantha took a step toward her father and Cecilia but before she could catch up with them, Martin stopped beside her. "Sap's rising. Mother wants to know if you'd like to go with us tomorrow for a gathering."

"This is hardly the time to be talking about having fun."

"This is exactly the time. Greta is gone, and you were barely an elbow cousin. Don't start grieving again, Samantha. This time I might not wait."

Samantha felt her mouth fall open, very unladylike, and she hurriedly closed it. Looking around, she noticed that everyone had moved in the direction of the Larkin farm. Most women would be stopping by home to gather up more food to take. Her father and Cecilia tarried by the school-house keeping Samantha in sight.

"Wait for me, indeed, Martin Crabtree. You were not even here while I was mourning. Besides, you're waiting in vain."

He blinked, and unreasonably, Samantha felt a bit smug. Then, she caught sight of Jacob beside the Stahl clan. He looked back at her, and Samantha knew that at the slightest provocation, he'd leave his family and stand beside her.

That's what it was about: God, family—

Family? When had she started thinking about Jacob and the word family as a combination. The dreaded blush rose to her cheeks. Jacob Stahl made her uncomfortable. No, not uncomfortable. Jacob made her feel like she'd never felt before. No, she couldn't deal with it now. She hurried to catch up with her father and Cecilia.

Everyone knew the Stahls had the best maple trees. Jacob jumped off his wagon and started unloading the sap buckets and yokes. He'd spent six days without a crisis. Greta's death weighed heavy on his mind. What could he have done differently?

Master Jarrod drove up in a hay wagon. He'd wedged in almost fifteen schoolchildren. Laughing and singing songs, they served as a good reminder that life went on. Behind them came at least four more wagons from town.

Jacob's heart lightened when he saw Samantha scramble down from the Gerhards' wagon. Not wanting to appear too eager, Jacob slowly walked over as Elsa handed down the troughs and paddles. "Let me take that for you." Jacob reached over Samantha's head. Her bonnet had slipped and blond curls beckoned his fingers. He wanted to touch her. He wanted to bury his face in the fine strands of her hair and tell her he loved her.

She'd made some huge steps in recovering from her mother's death and accepting Cecilia. Jacob knew Greta's death set things back some. It only made him want to grasp life and love with both hands before it was too late.

"Thought things would have been started by now," Shane remarked.

"It's still early." Jacob put a hand to Samantha's back and liked the way she moved in the direction he guided. It was the first time he'd touched her without it being a tease as a boy, or a doctor giving comfort. It felt better than he'd dreamed.

Then she sent him a smile meant just for him, and he experienced a taste of heaven.

Not counting the schoolchildren, over ten adults came to the Stahls' land to gather sap. Jacob set the men to boring holes in each maple. Jacob had whittled out the insides of ash branches to form the tubes, which the older schoolboys now bored into the holes. When that was done, the men drove nails under the tube. The women came behind and hung buckets on the nails.

As children screamed with delight to watch the sap drip, Jacob watched Samantha. He noted the way her hair swayed in the wind and how it blew against her cheeks. He fought the urge to brush her hair back. She'd not like it if he touched her so intimately in public. Not when he hadn't bothered to ask her father permission to call. He needed to get his affairs in order, garnish a nest egg, and prepare for family life. Right now his pay had more in common with the barter system than the monetary one.

The noise from the children putting their tongues at the end of the spouts to taste thin, icy cold sap drew him from his meanderings. The afternoon, spent with Samantha, proved what he already knew. He was in love.

"I saw you at the sap running," Clara said, settling into a chair at Mrs. T's house, and pulling out her piecework. "You certainly looked all cozy with Jacob Stahl."

The blush started at Samantha's cheeks and spread clear to her ears.

"Oh." Clara clasped a hand over her mouth. "I was just

teasing, but there is something to tell, isn't there?"

Samantha started to say no. The word wouldn't surface.

"Are you throwing over Martin?" Clara's piecework dropped in her lap. "Did something happen? What?"

"Clara, leave Samantha alone. You're making her uncomfortable." Mrs. T's scissors cut a perfect square for her new pattern.

"Jacob's a good man." Betsy spoke her first words. She'd arrived late to the sewing circle, somberly nodded a greeting to her friends, and sat down to sew without talking. They'd left her to her thoughts. Two weeks had passed since Greta's funeral. Betsy's needle shook as it wove in and out of the fabric with such determination that, left up to her, the quilt pieces would soon be finished.

"Of course he is," Elsa agreed.

Surely there was a comment to be made, Samantha thought. *And by me.* The words stuck in her throat. It felt so strange to be thinking these thoughts about Jacob. He was nothing like Martin. Martin was excitement, adventure, and mystery. Jacob was more like an old shoe. One that fit comfortably but had been in the family forever.

"Jacob is a good man," Samantha finally said.

Betsy's head stayed bowed. Elsa nodded with a knowing gleam in her eye. Clara frowned, clearly aware that somehow she'd missed a major upheaval in the midst.

Mrs. T changed the subject. "Girls, I have today's Scriptures. I think Ecclesiastes, the third chapter, will do: 'To every thing there is a season, and a time to every purpose under heaven: a time to be born, and a time to die.' " Mrs. T paused, as did every thimble.

Betsy's piecework lay in her lap, the needle carefully

threaded into the edge. For a moment, Samantha thought Betsy would make a move, but she didn't.

Elsa rubbed her stomach, almost an unconscious movement. Looking at her friends, Samantha was struck by her love for them.

Mrs. T continued, " 'A time to plant, and a time to pluck up that which is planted.' "

Clara gave a little gasp. Her needle flashed in and out of the handkerchief she hemmed. At least six times this afternoon, she'd mentioned her trip and the importance of having enough toiletries. She would leave tomorrow morning. Samantha tried to drive the thought from her mind but Mrs. T, with her infinite wisdom, reminded the girls to cherish the remaining time.

" 'A time to love, and a time to hate.' "

This time Samantha's flush had nothing to do with Jacob Stahl. Hate? Did she hate Cecilia? No, not possible. Samantha had been taught better than to hate. Dislike maybe. Resent probably. But hate?

" 'God shall judge the righteous and the wicked: for there is a time there for every purpose and for every work.' " Mrs. T closed her Bible and bowed her head in silent prayer. The other three girls did the same.

Yes, thought Samantha, changes were coming. Not only in the lives of her friends, but in her own life as well.

And there was nowhere to hide.

Chapter 7

The docks were busy and cold. Everything was brown. April swept a warm hand over Hickory Corners but never touched the ground. Through her black boots, Samantha felt a chill stealing steadily upward. Her toes almost curled from the force of it.

Clara couldn't manage to stand still. Her light brown curls bobbed with excitement. Her Aunt Charlotte didn't even reprimand her. For over ten years, Charlotte Warner had been more mother than aunt to Clara. Watching her ward leave couldn't be easy. Noticing how eager she was to go surely made it harder.

Eager to go, that described Raymond as well, and Samantha worried that once he finished medical school he'd not return. The worry had intensified after Jacob took over Doc's practice.

He was with his brothers today, she figured. She'd seen him load up his wagon and head in that direction. And she was at the docks saying good-bye to Clara.

The Ohio River moved like a herd of schoolchildren late for school. The river men seemed filled with the same anticipation.

"I'll take these, Ma'am." Horace Bunk pretended not to recognize Clara, as he reached for her valise.

"It's me," Clara exclaimed. "Clara Bucey."

Horace winked at the girls. "Ah, all growed up and off to play in the big city. You know, folks often get a taste of the *wanderjahr* and never return to the place of their birth."

Clara's eyes brightened.

What was this? *Never return?* Samantha hadn't realized Clara's dreams were so vastly different. Had she? Truth? She had realized, just pretended not. Clara always had her nose in a geography book. She and Master Jarrod had played Spin the Globe many a school day morning. Clara had willingly written essays on the places her finger landed.

A time to pluck up that which is planted.

Too soon, Clara's luggage was taken aboard. A too quick good-bye, then Clara's steps faltered a bit as she walked up the loading plank of the *A. M. Phillips*. Yet, she didn't look back.

No, wait! Samantha wanted to cry.

Horace must have noted Samantha's distress. He stepped off the loading plank. "Don't worry, Miss Samantha, we ain't got no preachers or white horses aboard. It will be smooth sailing."

"Thank you, Horace," Samantha managed, resisting the urge to push him into the water. White horses, indeed!

A violin started playing from somewhere on deck. Ropes left their moorings, river men scurried to their posts, and the mighty steamship pulled away from the dock.

Samantha expected to cry—wanted to—but Elsa wept instead.

"I cry all the time," she excused. "Last night, Shane

remarked that his potatoes were cold, and I broke down right there. Poor man, when I fed him potato cakes this morning, he looked at them in fear."

The bugle blew as the *A. M. Phillips* sailed out of sight.

"I'll miss her," Betsy said, bringing a black handkerchief to her nose.

"Me too," Elsa echoed.

Samantha was the first to leave the group as they returned to town. As she entered the store to see Cecilia waiting on a customer, she had to admit her stepmother had been good lately about allowing her time away from the store and chores.

A few people lingered inside. Victoria Alexander fondled a French silk that had arrived just yesterday. Sheriff Abner had Pa off to one corner questioning him about the recent purchases of two Ottawa Indians who now resided in the town jail. Jacob Stahl leaned against the counter chatting with Cecilia.

Samantha took a breath. She hadn't sassed, snapped, or even scoffed at her father's wife for weeks. The Thomasohn home was a bit quieter since the effort sorely limited the words that popped out of Samantha's mouth.

"'*A time to love, and a time to hate.*'"

Samantha bit down until a coppery taste filled her mouth.

"Here she is, Jacob. I told you she'd be right back." Cecilia positively glowed.

What had they been speaking about? Samantha felt it again! The flush that betrayed her emotions. Never had anyone looked at her so appreciatively, so admiringly. It nigh took her breath away.

"Go ahead. Show her," Cecilia urged.

She hadn't noticed his smile before, not really. It started

at the corners of his mouth and spread until his whole face was a mass of approval.

He approved of her. She didn't deserve it, not lately.

"I knew you'd be feeling down some," he said, "what with Clara leaving. Elsa told me how much you liked her rocking chair, so I made you this."

He'd made her a rocking chair? Oh, dear. Rocking chairs made her think of Elsa and babies. It was much too forward a gift, just like that wink in chur—

She'd seen ladders before, only not quite so short and squat. Cecilia pushed while Jacob tugged, and soon his creation sat in the center of the store.

"It's so you can reach the top shelf. I'm going to lean it against the wall here. It's really rather light. Just push it where you want, and you'll be able to reach anything."

"And in a ladylike stance too," Cecilia added.

"That's quite a ladder, Jacob." Victoria bent down and fingered the smooth sanding. "I'd like to order one for my shop."

Samantha stared down at Jacob's ladder. There were no elegant lines; this was made to be sturdy. He'd painted it brown, and like Olivia Crabtree, the ladder didn't cotton to elegance. Three steps up, a platform, and three steps down, the ladder looked a little like the giant wooden blocks her brothers had played with as a child.

Elsa got a rocking chair and a cradle. Samantha got chunks of wood stuck together.

For a moment, she felt disgruntled. Then, she remembered Martin whispering to her the verse, *"Fathers, provoke not your children."* She looked around the mercantile, at the shelves of dry goods, at the barrels of beans on the floor. She thought back to helping Mama arrange the window display. Samantha knew that as much as upstairs was her home, this store held just as many cherished memories.

Jacob had made something that felt all wrong—the store not looking the way her mother arranged it—into something that felt almost right. How wise he was. What a wonderful father, husband, he would make.

"Thank you, Jacob. It's the nicest gift anyone's ever given me."

And she kissed him on the cheek.

"Come on, you can do it." Sheriff Abner sat in the old barber chair Doc had inherited from his father.

Jacob much preferred getting a haircut to giving one. Just what was up with the sheriff's hair anyway? A man his age should be thinning some.

"You been using Professor Low's hair tonic?" Jacob asked.

Abner laughed. "No, I figure chasing bad men must stimulate growth or something. Fact is, my wife gets plumb annoyed at this mop of mine."

Jacob used the strop attached to the barber chair to sharpen the scissors.

"You sharpen those scissors much more, Son, and you won't have nothing but a file." Abner chuckled. "Don't know as I want a young pup in love messing with my hair."

"Keep talking, Sheriff, and I'll tell your wife what Low puts in that medicinal elixir you prescribe to."

Abner kept chuckling, and Jacob slowly circled the man. The sheriff wore his blond hair a bit longer than most of the Hickory Corners men. Dime novels, combined with pride, no doubt.

Trying to remember what Doc had done, Jacob gently gathered a hank of hair between his fingers. The scissors sliced through the strands as easily as his mother's paring knife cut through husks of corn. But corn husks neither yelped if they didn't like their shape nor carried handcuffs.

A beetle scurried across the floor and Jacob wished it needed a haircut so he could get the practice.

The door opened and Silas Thomasohn entered. He headed for one of the three-legged chairs by the front door. Paying no attention to the dust lining its seat, Silas sat down.

The sheriff and Jacob both stared. The man didn't have enough hair to cut. Surely he didn't want a shave, Jacob hoped.

Pulling out a piece of ash wood, Silas took to whittling.

"Are you here for a haircut?" Abner asked, saving Jacob the words.

"Nope."

Jacob finished Abner's trim and grabbed the bar of soap still on the shelf. It took some doing, but finally he managed a lather and soaped the back of Abner's neck. Doc kept three straight edge razors. Jacob chose what looked like the sturdiest. He flicked it open and grabbed the strop again. After sharpening it, he scraped an inch of soap off the sheriff's neck.

Now that Abner had shown faith in testing the new barber's abilities, others would follow suit. At one time, the barbershop had garnished quite a gathering of men wanting to jaw the time away. It was good for Mr. Thomasohn to see a reliable business. Jacob guessed he'd have to check behind the back curtain where two tubs waited for filthy customers to bathe.

It was a part of Doc's profession that Jacob hadn't considered taking over. Yet, it would be an income. Doc had already hinted that he'd move out of the upstairs room if Jacob wanted to move Samantha in.

Eyeing Mr. Thomasohn, Jacob wondered why the man was here. This morning, Jacob had intended to pull Samantha's father aside, ask permission to court, and lay out his intentions. Instead, Silas had been huddled in the corner with Abner, and Cecilia had beckoned to Jacob. Once she'd seen the little ladder he'd made for Samantha, any hope of talking with Silas disappeared.

A bit headstrong was the new Mrs. Thomasohn. Jacob could see why Samantha, who was fully capable of caring for a home, might feel stifled.

"Doc never took this long," Abner complained.

Jacob stared at the back of the man's neck. As smooth as a baby's behind, there wasn't a single nick. Jacob dropped the razor into the mug.

What next? A hot towel? Doc always cleaned the back of the customer's neck with a clean, hot towel. Jacob looked down at the stove. Since the weather had warmed, he'd not even thought to fire it up. If he intended to make a side living at barbering, he'd need to keep the thing going during trade hours.

Even the towel was a bit dusty. Jacob whacked it against his knee a few times before applying it to the sheriff's neck. "Sorry, Sheriff, you're my first haircut, and you're going to have to make due with a dry towel. I'll do better next time."

Abner stood and stared into the broken mirror. He ran a hand across the back of his neck, as if to assure himself that it was still there. "You did fine."

A nickel richer, Jacob set the shaving mug on the table beside the barber chair. "A shave?" he questioned Silas.

"No, I can get that at home. I came by to ask about your intentions toward my Samantha." Silas carefully put away his whittling. He brushed his hands as he stood.

Jacob was a tall man, but looking down at Samantha's father, Jacob realized that height offered no advantage when dealing with a doting father.

"I intend to marry her, Sir. I came to your mercantile this morning to ask permission to court."

Silas nodded, "I figured as much. I'm sorry, Jacob. You're a good man, but I cannot give you my blessing. The answer is no."

Chapter 8

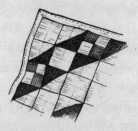

Jacob couldn't remember the last time he'd sat at his parents' kitchen without a whole herd of siblings traipsing through. Arlene Stahl expertly pinched the ends off a handful of beans and broke them in two while his father sat looking guilty for leaving the fields during daylight hours. His eyes were on the window and the flax outside waiting to be harvested.

"What I want to do," explained Jacob, "is take the plot of land you've allotted me and sell it back to you."

"Why," Gunther said, "that land—"

"Let him finish," Arlene interrupted.

"I've asked for permission to court Samantha."

"I knew it." The beans in his mother's hands became a blur as she doubled her speed. "When's the wedding?"

"Her father didn't give me permission to court."

Gunther sat straighter. "Why? Is he thinking there's something wrong with her marrying a Stahl?"

"No, Pa, that's not it. He says a doctor is married to his profession, and that I'll be gone more than I'll stay put. He doesn't think the two rooms above the barbershop constitute a home."

"Marrying a Gustefan certainly gave the man airs." Gunther slammed a fist down on the table.

The bowl of beans shuddered. Arlene put out one hand to steady it. "So, what are you thinking, Son?"

He'd prepared for the question, knowing his practical mother. Opening his doctor's bag, he drew out a plan he'd worked on for three weeks. Three agonizing weeks. He'd spent part of the time over in Wabash Springs amputating the arm of a farmer who'd gotten too close to an ax. He'd delivered a baby out at the docks. Mother, father, and child were staying at the inn for a few days.

Jacob had spent some of the time conferring with Reverend Tidewell, praying, and figuring his next course of action. He lay that action in front of his parents now. "Doc says he'll sell me the building, barbershop and all. I'm going to tear it down and build a combination doctor's office, barbershop, and home. I want to order bricks from the kiln over in Wabash Springs. Once Silas sees that Samantha will live in town, instead of out here, I think he'll reconsider. Then, there's also the fact that Raymond still intends to practice here. With two doctors, we can share the out-of-county calls. What do you think, Pa?"

"I think you're going to a lot of trouble for a man too blind to see how much you love his daughter."

"In all honesty, Silas only voiced concerns I already had. I owe him thanks. He made me take action."

"Does Samantha know how you feel?"

For three weeks, Samantha had watched him with curious eyes. During week one, he'd imagined those eyes longing for him to say something. During the second week, she withdrew, a slight frown on her face as if something puzzled her. This week, her chin jutted in the air as she carefully avoided him.

"She does, and she returns the feeling. But," Jacob carefully folded the plan, "I don't think she knows her father refused me permission to call."

Fifteen minutes later, Jacob Stahl headed for the bank.

Samantha cut through a yard of muslin.

"Martin left for New York this morning. Oh, what a job offer he has." Olivia Crabtree narrowed her eyes into slits. "He'll be back in a month. He'll be wanting to pack up the last of his things. Why, he might ask me along. He'll need someone to take care of the big house he'll be able to afford. Some people don't know what's good."

It had been three weeks since Jacob stopped by with the sole intent of seeing Samantha. Oh, he'd been by to purchase goods. He'd also attended church and sat with his family. From her pew, sitting next to Father, she'd longed for a wink.

"New York's far away," Silas said. "You think he'll stay there forever? Hickory Corners is growing. Two new families this last month. Soon we'll be needing a lawyer."

To Samantha's chagrin, Father looked at her. Lately, he'd been bringing up Martin just as often as Olivia.

" 'Tis possible," Olivia agreed. "Let's hope the future works itself out." The look she sent Samantha said it all: Samantha was upsetting Olivia Crabtree's carefully constructed plans.

Folding the material into a neat square, Samantha gathered matching thread and a few buttons. Olivia moved over next to Father.

One thing Samantha knew, Martin Crabtree wasn't husband material. She'd recognized that at Greta's funeral. Oh, to be honest, she'd figured it out at the Friday Social.

After Olivia left the store, peace returned. Samantha returned the sewing paraphernalia to its shelf. Cecilia was upstairs, and Samantha enjoyed the time spent with Father alone. For a moment, she pretended that nothing had changed. In all honesty, the Thomasohn home seemed a bit more tolerable. Less and less, Samantha felt resentment taking hold. Lately, Cecilia spent more time piecing together a quilt than she did interfering.

The afternoon toiled on. Samantha sold a seventeen-cent broom and a handful of lamp wickings. Father whistled over his ledger as he tallied profits and losses.

A feeling of happiness overtook Samantha and lasted until five o'clock when Father closed the door and Samantha finished pricing the beeswax she'd taken in exchange for a yard of bleached sheeting.

Cecilia had supper on the table but instead of hustling to serve Father, she struggled in the corner of the living room next to where Samantha used to sleep.

She'd lowered Rachel's quilting frame from the ceiling. It swayed gently under the pressure of Cecilia valiantly trying to fasten the quilt to the tacks stuck in the edges for just that purpose. Samantha couldn't remember Mama ever trying to set up the quilting frame on her own.

Father quickly tugged on the opposite end and pulled it taut. "Samantha, get the other end."

Cecilia chuckled as they set the frame together. "My mama always said when you finish a quilt what you need to do is put a cat in the center. Then, everyone tugs on the sides. When the cat runs off, whichever girl he passes by, that will be the girl to get married next. Perhaps when I finish this quilt, Samantha, we can try that."

The quilting frame swayed under Samantha's hands. Weeks ago Samantha would have figured the words were Cecilia's way of hinting that Samantha should leave, but now she didn't know. She didn't know anything except that feeling the soft fabric under her hands made her remember crawling underneath this very frame with Raymond and watching Mama's needle dipping in and out, a silver blur. They'd felt so safe with the quilt over their heads and Mama's feet tapping to thoughts they couldn't hear.

Samantha climbed the ladder to the loft, dropped to her knees, and leaned against the bed to pray. The resentment hadn't left, but what she'd learned from the scene below told her the problems lay with her and her alone.

"I want to go visit Opa and Oma for awhile." Samantha tried to eat a piece of toast. Her stomach rolled, and she set the bread back on her plate. She'd thought long and hard about it. Visiting her grandparents would give her time to work through all the turmoil.

"Are you feeling okay? Shall I call Doc Stahl?" Father felt her forehead, as he'd done hundreds of times before.

"Let her go, Silas." Cecilia looked pale today.

For the first time Samantha wondered how acutely her stepmother felt the animosity. Cecilia probably thought Samantha's leaving a good idea.

"Why? I don't understand. I thought things were better." Father looked confused. He stared at Cecilia for a long time, then turned a stern gaze at Samantha. "Are you sure that's what you want?"

She thought of the quilting frame in the corner. She saw Cecilia hunched over it every night. Cecilia's foot tapped in the same way Mama's used to. "Very sure."

"Well, then, Zack is heading out there with some supplies later today. Pack your things. You may go."

For a moment, Samantha had it in mind to give her father a hug. But she didn't feel happy. She'd expected him to put up a bit more fuss.

It didn't take long to pack a valise. It had been years since she'd spent time at Opa and Oma's. The Gustefans lived a good eight hours from town. Zack would be spending the night before returning to his farm. It would be different staying there now that she was older. Maybe Opa would let her help milk the cows. She'd loved that as a child. Then, there were the banty hens. One summer, because Oma wanted fryers, Samantha and Oma stuck Barred Rock chicken eggs under the banty hens to set. Samantha always wondered if the banty hens marveled at the size of their much larger offspring, or if the hens had any clue about the switch. Samantha closed her eyes. The last time she'd stayed with Oma, she'd been so small she had to stand on a chair to see out the window.

Zack didn't waste any words when he pulled in front of the store at noon and found Samantha waiting. "Pa needs you."

"Cecilia's here to help him."

"You're running away. It's time you faced whatever it is that has your lips looking like you sucked on a lemon."

"Leave me alone, Zackery Gus Thomasohn, you only come to see Father once a month when you deliver these supplies. You have no right to tell me what to do."

"You're a spoilt brat, that's what you are."

Eight hours she'd have to spend with him in the wagon.

Of all her brothers, she understood him the least. Trevor was the silent one, only offering words when he deemed it important. Raymond would have scolded her too, no doubt. But first he'd have mussed up her hair and given her a peck on the cheek. Zack must have been dropped as a baby, that's the only thing Samantha could figure. "I'm going to walk over and say good-bye to Mrs. T I need you to do me one favor."

He shot her a look of disbelief.

"I want to take Mama's old cedar chest."

"You need to get over this, Mantha." He surprised her by using the nickname that no longer echoed through the upstairs of Thomasohn's Mercantile.

"I know. I'm trying." Her feet grew heavier each step she took. The town looked brighter, and Samantha wondered if that was because she didn't know how long it would be before she saw it again. She crossed to the other side so she wouldn't have to walk in front of Doc's place. Her feet dragged as she slowed a bit. All the Stahl brothers were busy loading Doc's belongings into farm wagons. To the side, Samantha could see at least a thousand bricks stacked taller than Jacob. The man didn't deserve a good-bye. He'd winked at church, prayed with her at Greta's side, made her a ladder, flirted with her over maple sap, then backed away so fast that if Samantha didn't know better, she'd think maybe a giant wart had appeared on the tip of her nose. What was he up to now?

She forced herself not to walk backward. She didn't care what Jacob did.

"Everybody is talking," Mrs. T said from her front step, "except Jacob."

Samantha stared back at the sight of chaos on the corner of the street. "You'll have to write and tell me what's going on."

"Write? Oh, Darling, not you too?"

"Just to Opa and Oma's and just for awhile."

Mrs. T insisted on packing up a hefty lunch. Samantha hadn't given thought to that, although Zack's wife probably had.

"I'll tell the girls," Mrs. T promised. She hugged Samantha close. "Oh, now you don't stay away too long. Our little sewing circle is dwindling down. We need you."

Zack knocked at the door. A moment later, he took the box of food from Mrs. T "Not too late to change your mind," he said out of the corner of his mouth.

"I need to go."

Zack looked down the street. "Doc's staying at the inn, and I think Jacob's lost his mind. I wonder where he got the money?"

As the town of Hickory Corners disappeared from sight, Samantha wondered if she'd been wrong about Jacob's reasons for leaving medical school.

Rosie Gustefan didn't bat an eye at Samantha's arrival. She opened up the extra bedroom and set about enjoying her granddaughter.

Living on the farm was vastly different than visiting. Milking the cows lost its appeal after four days. At the mercantile, they'd never needed livestock. They took everything in trade. The third time Old Bess slapped Samantha in the face with her tail, leaving a residue Samantha would rather not think about, she wished she had a tail to slap back with.

The chickens were another matter. There existed something called a pecking order. The dominant chickens actually cornered a cowering Rhode Island Red and pecked it half bald. Samantha removed it from the brood and stuck it in a pen all by itself. Instead of saying thanks, the chicken pecked her! Of course, the daring rescue of the Rhode Island Red gave the rooster an opportunity to escape. The silly thing frantically stayed near the pen wanting back in but was too stupid to take advantage as Samantha held open the door. Five hours Samantha spent chasing Wilber the rooster. Oma didn't name the farm animals, but Samantha named the ones she scolded. She also named what she fell in love with, like the collie puppies in the barn. Opa grumbled that her favorite, Ike, would not learn how to walk if she didn't put him down.

While there was more work at Oma and Opa's, there was more time for solitude too. Samantha sat in the living room in the evening and read the Bible aloud to Opa.

On Sunday, they met in the home of a cousin. The men took turns preaching. It was very different than the church in town. Not the words or the feeling of reverence, but the absence of friends who were more family than anything else. Samantha wondered if Elsa had delivered the baby. She wondered if Betsy still visited Greta's grave every day. She wondered if Father missed her. And, she wondered what in the world Jacob Stahl was doing with all those bricks.

They rested on the Sabbath but made up for it on Monday. Samantha knelt in the dirt beside Oma and patiently listened to the lecture on how to tell a weed from a tomato plant.

Oma said, "The leaves on the tomato plant have tiny little hairs. Oh, there he is."

Samantha leaned closer to stare at the leaves. Just which "he" was Oma referring to?

Oma's knees popped as she stood. Samantha looked down the road. It wasn't Zack's wagon, although he was due any day now. This was a buggy.

"Who is it?" Samantha asked.

"Why, he's finally come for you. I knew he would."

Jacob pulled up in front of the house. Samantha looked down at her blue cotton dress. Sweat stained under her arms. Dirt smeared near her knees. She was pretty sure dirt streaked her face too.

"Jacob Stahl," Oma greeted. "About time you got here. The cobbler said you were building a house for your bride. Can't figure why you let her stay here a month. You don't have second thoughts, do you?"

"Oma," Samantha whispered frantically. "He's not building a house for me."

"Sure he is. Cobbler said so."

Jacob never looked more handsome. He wore a brown vest over a white shirt. Brown homespun pants hugged his thighs. His chestnut hair danced in the wind; it was longer than she would have liked. . .on anyone else.

Oma brushed the dirt from her hands. "Close your mouth, Samantha, and let's pack you up."

"I'm not going."

Jacob somehow had grown taller. His voice held that same commanding tone he so often tried to use with her. "Yes, you are. Morning, Mrs. Gustefan."

Samantha gazed up, intending to argue, and instead felt her breath quicken.

"You can call me Oma. Might as well start getting used to it. She never completely unpacked, so it shouldn't take long. Sure you don't want to spend the night? You look spent."

"Can't," Jacob said. "Cecilia is sick. I need to get Samantha back there as soon as possible. Silas needs help."

Numbness washed over Samantha. He hadn't come for *her*, after all. He'd come because of Cecilia.

Jacob took it easy on the way back. The horse looked as weary as Jacob felt. Samantha sat silently by his side, her posture as straight as the ironing board his mother propped against the kitchen wall. It made him tongue-tied to watch her grip the side of the seat to keep from bumping into him.

She'd changed out of the blue dress and now wore a simple, yellow cotton. A white petticoat peeked out near the same silly boots that often had her accidentally ice-skating in winter. They made her feet look dainty and small. He liked having her beside him in the buggy. He'd have gone another seven hours to retrieve her. "You might as well tell me what's bothering you. We can't fix it until I know what's broken."

"Nothing's broken. I just didn't want to come back to town, that's all."

No, that wasn't all. He knew that much. Her eyes had lit up at the sight of him, but they'd dimmed just as easily. He replayed his words, but couldn't think of anything he'd said amiss. Surely, Samantha didn't feel such ire at Cecilia as to consider not pitching in.

"I missed you," Jacob said softly.

"I didn't miss you." She stared straight ahead.

Jacob smiled. For someone who didn't miss him, she sure seemed bent on pointedly ignoring him. He grinned. "I think your pa missed you too."

"Why didn't he send for me sooner?"

"He didn't send for you at all. I took it upon myself to come get you."

She forgot to hold herself erect. She let out her breath and slumped against the back of the seat. "That doesn't make sense. I always help out."

"I think he was worried about how you would take it."

"Take what?"

"Cecilia's in the family way."

Chapter 9

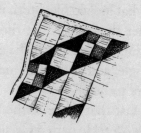

The sound of Hickory Corners carried over the trees. People's voices raised in conversation. She'd gotten used to the silence of the farm. The *rat-a-tat* of Ty Walker's hammer welcomed her home.

They passed the Larkin farm. Matthew waved from atop a pile of hay. His oldest boy, Karl, immediately took off in the direction of Betsy's house.

The corner where Doc lived looked completely different. The clapboard building no longer stood. In its place, bricks formed what would someday be a grand building.

"There is a lot to say for having ten brothers." Jacob grinned.

Samantha smiled weakly. It indeed looked like it could be a home for a bride. Glass windows, leaning against a wagon, glittered in the sun. A porch, that only needed a swing, waited for a family to move in. The cobbler claimed the bride was her. If that was true, why hadn't Jacob come calling?

Oh, she had more to worry about than Jacob's wishy-washiness. Too soon, Jacob pulled up in front of the mercantile. Samantha hopped down, again forgetting to let Jacob help her, and scurried up the steps.

Trevor stood behind the counter. Shane Gerhard counted out money for a pound of sugar. Taking the steps two at a time, Samantha hurried up the stairs. Father set in a chair by the bed, spooning what looked like broth into Cecilia's mouth.

"She's a bit older than most first time mothers." Jacob's voice was so near Samantha's ear that she could feel his breath. There came that tingle, and at such an inopportune time too.

"Father, I'm here to help."

Silas turned so fast that some of the broth spilled out of the bowl. Jacob took over. He patted Cecilia's arm and cleaned up Silas's mess with a towel.

It was only for a moment, but the look in Father's eyes said it all. He touched her on the chin, nodded, and took off down the stairs.

"He's a little choked up," Cecilia said. "He's prayed every night, even before I took sick, that you'd come back."

Jacob set down Samantha's valise and felt Cecilia's forehead. "Keep her still. She keeps asking to get up, and the answer's no. Read to her, she can do some piecework if you prop her up, and she stays in bed."

"Thank you, Jacob."

"I'll talk to you later." His eyes made promises his words didn't encourage.

She nodded and took his place next to Cecilia. "First, let's change you out of this damp nightgown. It can't be comfortable to lie with broth seeping down your neck."

"I can manage on my own." Cecilia sat up, grimaced, and tried to swing her legs over the edge of the bed.

"Don't be silly. I'm here to help."

"Did it ever occur to you, Samantha, that I'm as uncomfortable around you as you are around me?"

Mouse chose that moment to skid to a stop at Samantha's feet. Glad for something to do with her hands, she picked the cat up.

Cecilia's brown hair was flat on the side. She'd always kept it so carefully coiled, Samantha knew her stepmother must feel truly terrible.

"It's my little brother or sister you're carrying. Seems we can make a truce until you feel better." Samantha set Mouse down and took a clean gown from the armoire. Cecilia didn't look pregnant, but she did look vulnerable. Samantha took the woman's hand. "Maybe truce is the wrong word. You make my father happy, and that should make me happy. I really want to help. Will you let me?"

Cecilia gripped the edge of the mattress in much the same way that Samantha had earlier gripped the buggy's edge. It took a bit of bullying, but Samantha managed to slip off Cecilia's gown, give the woman a sponge bath, and tuck her into bed. Sleeping, Cecilia looked young enough to be part of the sewing circle. Well, once Cecilia got better, Samantha would go again. It would be fine to see Elsa's shining eyes and hear Betsy's dour humor.

Samantha looked around the room. The place needed cleaning. First, Samantha tidied up the kitchen, then she started on the main room. It felt good to be needed. The quilting frame acted as a magnet, drawing her attention, until she gave in and went to look at Cecilia's work.

Jacob's Ladder.

"She's making it for you, you know." Silas silently crossed the room and sat in the chair meant for the quilter.

"Really?"

"She's a smart woman, and strong. I knew that when she

went to work for Virginia. Cecilia still hurt as bad as I did from the loss of a spouse, yet she dug in her heels and kept living."

"I understand, Father."

"Do you?" Silas looked over at his sleeping wife. "I wish you'd give her as much of a chance as she keeps giving you."

Samantha's teeth hurt and she unclenched them. Of its own volition, her head shook. "I am trying."

"You call running away trying?"

"I call coming back trying."

Father ran his fingers over a section of stitching. "I didn't even know the name of this quilt until she told me. Jacob's Ladder. Then she had to tell me why she chose the pattern. Seems she recognized something I missed. I always knew Jacob had feelings for you, but I didn't realize you returned them."

"He doesn't—"

"He asked permission to call, you know."

"Jacob did? When?" Her cheeks flamed, and this time her stomach didn't hurt because of Cecilia.

"A few weeks before you left for your grandparents'."

"He didn't call."

"I told him no."

"Father!"

"Don't go scolding me. Cecilia's done nothing but. Then, that crazy doctor starting building nothing less than a brick house."

"For me." Samantha whispered.

"That's what the cobbler says." Silas reached down into the sewing basket by his chair. "Is Jacob Stahl what you want?"

"Yes."

"Then, I'll give him my blessing."

Samantha flew across the room. It had been months since

she'd felt his arms around her in love.

"You did good, Husband," Cecilia said from the bed.

"One more thing," Silas said. He pushed something in Samantha's hand. "The reverend's wife thinks you'll be happy to see this. Seems it had somehow landed in the hem of her skirt."

Mama's thimble.

No longer lost.

Dust drifted with the wind as the town settled down for the evening. Samantha adjusted the bodice of her favorite dress and took a deep breath. Down the way she could see Jacob sitting on the front step of his building. The boardwalk echoed under the soles of her boots. She and her brothers had often gotten in trouble for making too much noise when they played in the shade under the awning.

Jacob looked tired, but then the trip to her grandparents' farm had cost him fifteen hours.

All her life Samantha had striven to be the perfect lady but always she'd failed. Walking toward the man she loved felt like the scariest and bravest step she'd ever taken. To know Jacob had asked her father for her hand weeks ago made her the happiest girl in Hickory Corners. To know that her own stubbornness put that precious love in jeopardy made her a fool.

"Hello, Jacob."

He stood so fast, whatever he'd been whittling fell.

Samantha picked it up. The wood felt smooth and strong in her hand. "What are you making? Something for the business?"

A lantern sat on one of the porch rails. Its light flickered across Jacob's face. "Do you really want to know?" He wrapped his fingers around the piece of wood and her hand.

Feeling bold, Samantha stepped closer. "Yes."

"I'm making another cradle. I've decided not to wait for the last minute. In many ways, I've let too much time pass by."

"I agree."

"Do you?"

"Yes. Did my father come by to see you tonight?" Samantha stepped back as Jacob moved closer.

His hand traveled up to cup her chin. "He did."

"And?"

"And what?"

"Did you ask him any questions?"

"No."

She would have stumbled and fallen had not his hands gripped her shoulders. Was she mistaken about—

He tugged her even closer, the grip on her shoulders turning into a caress. "I do have a question to ask you, though."

"Yes," she whispered.

"You need to hear the question before you say yes."

"Yes."

He kissed her then, right on Main Street. Samantha quickly glanced right and left. Why, anyone could have seen! Fresh!

And just in case somebody was looking, Samantha kissed him back.

PAMELA KAYE TRACY

Living in Glendale, Arizona, where by day she teaches first grade at Southwest Christian School and by night she teaches Freshman Reading at Glendale Community College, Pamela had her first novel of inspirational fiction published in 1999 by Barbour Publishing's **Heartsong Presents** line. She has been a cook, waitress, drafter, Kelly girl, insurance filer, and secretary, but through it all, in the back of her mind, she knew she wanted to be a writer. "I believe in happy endings," says Pamela. "My parents lived the white picket fence life." Writing Christian romance gives her the opportunity to let her imagination roam.

four Hearts

Sally Laity

Chapter 1

The *Blue Hummingbird*'s engines shut down, and the wakes behind her paddle wheel smoothed out as the ornate white steamship coasted over the swift indigo current of the Ohio River to the broad, wooden wharf. Dock workers seized the stout ropes tossed from the vessel and secured them to the stationary landing posts, while at the wheel, silver-haired Captain John Sebastian hollered orders to his bustling crew.

Diana Montclair, her lace-gloved hands grasping the iron railing, blew wisps of honey-blond hair from her eyes while she watched the familiar activity; a mixture of resignation and anticipation flowing through her. Home again. . .at this place that had never truly been home.

Filling her lungs, she glanced around at the tiny hamlet nestled against a rolling scape of forest just donning the variegated greens of late spring. Changes were slight in Hickory Corners. A new doctor's office of the same red brick as the bank now complemented the quaint white clapboard church, but the rest of the town was made of plain or rough-hewn log dwellings. The dirt streets often blew with dust, or worse yet, lay ankle deep in mud from frequent rains. Yet she had to admit the town had a certain warmth and charm. A surprising array of shops and enterprises provided just about any service needed. Even the smallest home appeared tidy and inviting, and the local inhabitants seemed cheerful and content. What a pity she had so little in common with any of them.

She would never understand why her father insisted upon maintaining a house in this rural outpost in southwestern Ohio, with Cincinnati but a few hours west. Surely prestigious Montclair Shipping Line would fare much better with the larger city as its headquarters. Not that her mother and father ever deigned to spend any more time than necessary in this provincial settlement they had helped found. "And I shan't, either," she declared under her breath. "There is nothing for me here. Nothing at all."

"Diana! Over here!" a voice called from ashore.

Diana shifted her attention to the older woman waving so enthusiastically from the quay, and she smiled. Mildred Sanderson, the family's faithful housekeeper for what seemed like forever, had been the single mainstay in Diana's nineteen years. At least Millie always seemed happy to have her around. Drawing comfort from that, she lifted her arm and returned the welcoming gesture.

"Looks like somebody's glad to see ya, Miss Montclair," Ozzie Mallory teased from a few yards away.

Diana hiked her chin at the curly-haired "rooster," as the roustabouts were commonly called. He stacked cartons of supplies brought up from the hold to be delivered to the various business establishments in town. Barely older than herself, the sandy-haired sailor had known better than to make unwelcome advances to the boss's daughter. He had kept his distance, making only polite conversation in her presence.

Nevertheless, she hadn't missed the admiring glances the ruddy-cheeked young man and other crew members cast her way from time to time.

"Mrs. Sanderson always meets me when I come home," Diana answered, subtly correcting her posture to that of a proper young lady.

"Guess we won't be havin' ya aboard much, now your schoolin's over. I wish ya the best, Miss. Good day." With that, the sturdily built seaman hefted a bulky crate to his muscled shoulder and headed for the gangway being lowered.

Watching after him from the shade of her bonnet's brim, Diana drew her woolen shawl snugly about herself and tried not to think about how her travels to Hickory Corners for Christmases and summers had come to an end. There might be some things about growing up in Boston's best boarding schools and finishing schools that she hadn't particularly liked, but free trips on her father's numerous ships and other sailing lines had pleasured her. Thanks to his reputation and influence, she always enjoyed the best accommodations and service. She knew the captains so well, they were almost like uncles, and every one of them took exceptional care of her.

Gathering the skirts of her stylish plum linen ensemble, Diana went to see if Mrs. Woodwright, the assistant teacher-chaperon provided by Prentiss Finishing Academy For Young Ladies, had finished repacking the trunks Diana would take ashore.

The broomstick-thin widow stood within the close confines of the tiny cabin they'd shared during this leg of the journey. The somber navy traveling suit on her slight figure only accented the darkness of the bunk-lined room as her nimble fingers fastened the buckles on the second piece of

Diana's luggage. "All set," she announced a little too brightly. "It's been a singular pleasure accompanying you, Diana. I trust you'll enjoy being home with your family now."

"Thank you." Diana saw no point in elaborating on how little she really knew her parents. "Will you be taking tea at the boardinghouse before returning to Boston?"

The chaperon raised a pale hand to knead temples framed by tight brunette curls. "No, I think not. I'm fighting a bit of a headache just now. At times prolonged sailing does not agree with my constitution."

"I'm sorry. Shall I request a tray for you, then, before the ship weighs anchor?"

"Thank you, no. I'll just lie down for awhile and have something brought in later. Remember all the things you learned at the academy, Dear. You were one of our finest students, and I have every confidence you will find success in all your domestic ventures."

For a split second, Diana expected the dark-haired woman to hug her, but the awkward moment passed without an embrace. Diana moistened her lips and smiled. "Thank you. . .for everything."

The bun atop Mrs. Woodwright's head bobbed with her nod. "God be with you, Dear."

"And with you," Diana whispered. Plucking her mulberry satin reticule from the built-in cabinet separating the two narrow bunks, she cast one more smile over her shoulder, then took her leave.

In moments she descended the gangway, one of a scant few arrivals. But then, who would come to Hickory Corners on purpose, she wondered caustically.

Diana's black kid traveling boots scarcely touched the

dock's wooden planks before Millie Sanderson hastened over and enveloped her in loving arms. The housekeeper's plump frame and braided gray coronet emitted the spicy smell of apples and cinnamon, evidence that today was baking day. How strange to see her without her ever present bib apron.

"Oh, my little darling," the older woman gushed, leaning back, her creased face absolutely beaming, her smile adding even more squinty lines at the corners of her small blue eyes. "So lovely to have you home. Did you have a good trip?"

"Oh, yes. Very. Except for two rainy days, the weather was ever so mild and lovely."

"Well, even so, I expect you're tired. We'll let the menfolk deal with your trunks. I'll draw you a hot bath, and you can have a nice soak while I whip up some supper." Sliding an arm around Diana, she waved to the brawny Bunk brothers working at the wharf as usual. "Tote her belongings up to the house, when you've a minute, and I thank you kindly."

"Will do, Ma'am," the stringy-haired pair chorused, then jabbed one another in the ribs and grinned before resuming their duties.

"I've been counting the days, little one, till you got here," Millie confessed, her button nose as rosy as her cheeks. She escorted Diana along the nearly straight route up Main Street toward the big two-story Montclair house occupying a sizable chunk of Birch Street.

"Will Mother and Daddy be coming to visit soon?" Diana hadn't meant to ask, but the words popped out seemingly of their own accord.

"Well, now, they know you were expected to arrive today, so mayhap they'll arrange their travels in a way that'll bring them our way one of these days."

I won't hold my breath waiting, Diana affirmed inwardly. Her unwelcome birth late in life to parents still grieving the loss of the son who'd been the light of their world had never quite been forgiven.

Catching a glimpse of Elsa Gerhard sweeping down the front steps of her father's newly renovated hotel, Diana ventured a small smile at the buxom brunette she knew from the stitchery group which gathered weekly at Edna Tidewell's home.

"Good afternoon, Diana," the blue-eyed girl said, resting a hand on the top of the broom handle. "Home to stay now?"

"So it would seem," she answered casually.

"Well, perhaps we'll be seeing you at the sewing circle, then. Oh, I think I hear little Georg waking up. I'd better run." And with that, she turned in a swirl of tan calico and dashed inside.

"Such a sweet new mama Elsa makes," Millie said.

Diana nodded politely, keeping pace with the older woman's slower stride.

"And doesn't the old boardinghouse look grand, now that all the improvements are completed?" Millie went on. "Elsa's husband worked night and day to turn the place into a real hotel, with Brady Forbes lending a hand whenever needed." She paused. "You remember Brady, don't you? The Tidewells' nephew."

"Quite," Diana muttered. Recollections of the bold young man who possessed an uncanny ability to rankle her on every visit home filled her with chagrin. Whenever she left to return to school, it would take weeks to dismiss him from her thoughts. . .which also vexed her to no end.

"Good day, ladies." As if hearing his name being mentioned, the person in question hailed them cheerily on his way out of the mercantile across the street.

Diana gave the lanky, square-jawed carpenter a casual nod as they went by. With that glossy brown-black hair and deep blue eyes, he was far too handsome for his own good. She sensed his gaze following them as they continued walking, but resisted the impulse to glance back and find out for certain. No sense in giving him the idea she was interested. Besides, this was the last place on earth she'd look for a mate, handsome or not. He probably had his cap set for some local girl himself.

Her gaze flitted over the simple but stylish dress displayed in the single window of the dress shop as they strolled by. Suitable for the town's special occasions, it was considerably less elegant than even the simplest frock Diana owned. Most of her wardrobe arrived at school in parcels shipped from New York, Philadelphia, or Paris, compliments of her mother. In truth, however, though always lovely and the latest fashion, not one of them had been Diana's personal choice.

By the time they passed the bank and her father's shipping office and crossed Birch Street, the peacefulness contrasted pleasantly with the noise and bustle so prevalent at the docks. Diana felt a measure of pride at the sight of the neatly kept grounds surrounding her parents' stately residence. She loved the fresh dove gray paint and black shutters, the broad front door in gleaming federal blue, the wrought iron eagle weather vane atop the cupola. This was one of the few buildings in town sporting anything other than a weathered log or whitewashed exterior.

Millie had even made new cushions for the settees on the front porch, Diana noticed. Mounting the steps, she easily imagined herself curled up in the pillowy softness on sunny afternoons, reading James Fenimore Cooper or Keats or Shelley. Thank heaven, her father had a decent library of books here.

When the door latched behind them, Diana inhaled deeply, smiling with pleasure. The interior of the house bore sweet scents of baking. When had she last eaten? Before she finished calculating, her stomach growled audibly.

"Oh, you poor dear," the housekeeper crooned, taking their shawls and bonnets and draping them over a hook on the hall tree in the wide entry. "Let me fix you a bite to eat while the water heats for your bath."

"You're too kind," Diana said, a touch embarrassed. "I know you've been busy this whole day, then that long walk down to the wharf. . ."

"Nonsense. What's a body to do, if not keep busy? You go have a seat in the parlor, and I'll holler when the food's ready."

The offer was far too tempting to resist. Still smiling, Diana crossed the gleaming wood floor and entered the arched doorway to her right, where matching settees in striped silver damask caught the light pouring through white lace undercurtains and satiny burgundy drapes. Choosing an upholstered wing chair near the fireplace, she set her reticule on a marble-topped side table and kicked off her boots to rest her feet on the padded footstool. Home. She leaned her head back and closed her eyelids.

In what seemed the briefest of moments, Millie's light touch on her shoulder awakened Diana. Much to her surprise, she'd dozed off.

Upon entering the cheery kitchen with its shiny walls and yellow curtains, she took the proffered seat at the pine trestle table where a dainty feast of coddled eggs, raisin scones, cinnamon applesauce, and hot tea awaited her. "It looks delicious."

The housekeeper glowed. "Well, you just take your time and eat, little one. I'll start filling the tub. And after your bath, you just go on up to your room and have a snooze. There's church tonight, if you've a mind to go anyplace after you've rested up a bit. If not, there's always Sunday."

"I'll think about it," Diana promised as the older woman carried the first kettle to the round wooden tub kept in a small side room off the kitchen.

Later, however, bathed and changed and snuggled in the comfort of the feather bed in her rose-and-white room, Diana didn't know if she could bring herself to appear in public just yet. She'd only been in Hickory Corners in snatches and bits since she was old enough to be sent off to live with her Aunt Eunice, then to school. Everybody in town knew everybody else, and all of them lifelong friends.

And at nineteen, she didn't have the slightest notion how to make friends. . .with anybody. Never had. None of the girls at school had cared a whit about her. Only the teachers. And Millie. The dear, sweet housekeeper whom Diana wished for the thousandth time had been her mother.

At least in Boston there were theaters and museums, social soirees and activities to keep herself occupied, to say nothing of her studies. She hadn't counted on her school years coming to end just yet, before she'd decided what she wanted to do with the rest of her life. A sigh of depression came from deep inside at the bleak future now looming ahead. Her teachers expected the domestic skills they'd taught her at school would be put to use in a fine marriage, but Diana saw no hope of finding a suitable mate in this tiny place. How in the world was she supposed to endure being stuck here. . .perhaps for good?

That does it, Brady Forbes thought, pounding the last nail into the steps he'd replaced on the porch of his aunt and uncle's parsonage. He picked up the tools scattered about him and placed them inside the toolbox he'd borrowed from his employer, Nathaniel Harmon, the cabinetmaker. The man had taught him more than he'd imagined there was to know about working with wood. Thanks to the skills he'd picked up through Nate's tutelage, these new steps would probably outlast the rest of the house, no matter how many feet traipsed up and down them in their comings and goings.

For a hamlet small as Hickory Corners, the parsonage saw much more than its share of visitors, Brady conceded, heading back to the shop. Aunt Edna's gracious spirit seemed to blossom when surrounded by ladies. Older ones attended a new prayer circle every Thursday, the younger ones made up a sewing circle on Tuesdays. But far be it from him to find fault with those weekly gatherings. Truth be told, he held parsonage repairs in reserve for those very occasions. That way he could get in on all the delicious goodies served to the guests.

Brady's mouth watered as he recalled the peach tarts the banker's wife provided for today's prayer circle. Fit for a king, they were, and the ladies had persuaded him to have more than one. . .not that he'd put up much of a fight.

The sewing circle, though, was where the really good stuff was. Sometimes one of the gals would whip up some fudge or bake gingersnap cookies, two of his favorites. Those and the melt-in-the-mouth currant scones of Mildred Sanderson's.

Now that his thoughts had meandered in that direction, he wondered if little Miss Montclair ever deigned to soil her soft pink hands with floury dough. The golden-haired beauty dressed like a plate in a fashion catalog at Thomasohn's Mercantile. He chuckled, envisioning her in the voluminous apron she'd have to don to protect those fancy gowns of hers.

Then Brady's smile flattened. Of course, a guy would have to be blind not to recognize true beauty when he saw it. Glorious curls the color of warm honey—and likely as silky. Eyes of misty gray. The first time he'd lost himself in those silvery depths, his ability to speak coherently vanished. Took considerable joking around before he regained strength in his knees. To this day he didn't even remember all the asinine remarks he made to that ever so proper girl. But a few too many must have hit their mark, because she scarcely gave him the time of day now.

Funny thing, but he didn't see her as snobbish or haughty, the way some of the other young women in town did. He never had. Yet he did view Diana Montclair on an entirely different plane from the rest. . .and not merely because of her money and grand house. Not even because of her outward beauty. Something else about her called to his spirit, made him want to find out who she truly was inside. That intense loneliness in her eyes, maybe. Or the droop of those fragile shoulders when she neglected that rigid posture. The sad wilt to the corners of her rosy, upturned lips.

Whatever the elusive quality, he would try harder to be her friend, now that she'd come home to stay. Perhaps this time he'd get it right.

Chapter 2

A tantalizing blend of cooking smells from downstairs prompted a smile as Diana exited her bedroom late the next morning. More of her favorites, no doubt. Millie, bless her heart, always made sure that whenever her charge came home, there'd be a steady supply of dishes and baked goods Diana especially liked. But since this was no mere visit, a bit of discretion might be prudent. Too much indulgence, and soon enough, none of her gowns would fit.

Passing the older woman's bedroom, next door to hers, Diana couldn't help but note the homey quality. So different from the cloudlike rose-and-white frills which made up her own domain, the bright warm colors in Millie's room invited a person to come in, sit down, linger. She admired the reds, yellows, and blues of a Log Cabin quilt draped over the walnut sleigh bed, the complementing hues in the shirred curtain. The coziest cushioned rocker occupied the corner. A last wistful glance, and she continued toward the staircase a few yards away.

But instead of going down, an impulse took Diana beyond them, to her parents' quarters at the end of the hallway. She stopped respectfully in the open doorway, as if visiting a museum or the bed chamber of one of America's founding fathers, feeling like an intruder.

Immaculate, as always, the room appeared ready for occupancy at a moment's notice, with hand-crafted furniture proof of Nathaniel Harmon's incredible talents. Sunshine glinted across the emerald and ivory satin coverlet on the four-poster bed, lighting upon the cut glass trinket dish on the carved wooden bureau and scattering miniature rainbows about the pristine walls. A plush Oriental carpet's intricate pattern graced the floor. Such splendor, Diana thought sadly, and no one here to see or enjoy the beauty. She would never understand why. Hiking her chin, she turned and retreated to the stairs, clutching her lavender-striped dimity skirts in both hands as she descended.

"Mmm. Something smells delicious," she said, upon reaching the kitchen, where fat cinnamon rolls cooled on the sideboard, creamy icing trailing down their puffy edges.

Stirring a pot of porridge at the hearth, Millie turned. "Good morning, Dear. Sleep well?"

"Like a dream." She took the spot awaiting her at the table.

"Good. Perhaps you'd like to run a few errands with me, then." Ladling out some oatmeal, she carried the bowl to Diana, then brought over a pitcher of milk.

"Thank you, Millie. I doubt I'll ever be the cook you are."

"Stuff and nonsense, Child. All a body needs is practice." She replaced the lid over the pot.

Spreading the linen napkin across her lap, Diana bowed her head for grace, knowing the housekeeper would expect that much. Even the school kept up that ritual, though it didn't carry much significance for Diana. She had difficulty with the concept of a *loving* Father. "What sort of errands?"

she finally asked, pouring milk over the hot cereal.

"Oh, I wanted to take some baked goods to Charlotte Warner."

"The widow down the street?"

Millie's gray head nodded. "The old dear sprained her ankle a few days ago. Of course, she's much too self-reliant to allow anybody to do things for her, whether she's hobbling around or not. But she's so good about fixing meals for others, even making sure if there's a prisoner at the sheriff's place the fellow has a decent supper. About time somebody does her a kind turn. She shouldn't find fault with a couple cinnamon buns."

Chewing thoughtfully, Diana had to agree. "I'd be more than happy to tag along."

"Splendid. And since I made so many, I'll take a few to the Tidewells while I'm at it. That nephew of theirs about eats them out of house and home when he comes in from working at Nate Harmon's."

The oatmeal suddenly tasted like straw. Brady Forbes, with that quick wit and smart mouth of his, had embarrassed her to no end on her last visit. Just as she arrived at the sewing circle, she caught the cad doing an exaggerated impression of her. She could still hear the stifled giggles and snickers from the other girls at Mrs. Tidewell's gathering, and she didn't relish being the butt of his jokes again any time soon.

Not picking up on Diana's discomfort, Millie whipped off her big apron without missing a beat. "Edna promised to let me borrow a new crochet pattern that came all the way from Philadelphia too. While you finish eating, I'll just run upstairs for my bonnet, make sure I don't have flour on my nose. Shouldn't be more than a minute."

"Take your time," Diana mumbled in the housekeeper's talkative wake.

But Millie turned out to be amazingly spry for someone of her age and returned to the kitchen before a single minute had gone by. She removed two baskets from the cupboard and filled them with baked goodies, spreading a checked cloth over top of each. "There. All ready. We'd best hurry. My old bones feel a storm coming."

"Yes, Ma'am." No longer hungry since Millie mentioned visiting the home of Brady Forbes, Diana left the remains of her breakfast and rose. She washed her hands on a damp rag and hastened after the housekeeper.

"The shawl you wore yesterday should do nicely," Millie suggested, plucking it and Diana's straw bonnet from a hook in the entry and handing them over. With no further ceremony, the two of them stepped out into the crisp morning, baskets looped over their forearms.

The Widow Warner's small dwelling, a few houses down Birch Street, sported an uncustomary light coat of dust on the porch, evidence that the woman's mishap had slowed her down. But greenery in the flowerbeds on either side promised a bounty of geraniums to come, now that winter was but a memory and summer just around the corner. Millie rapped softly.

"Come in," came the labored reply.

"It's Mildred," the housekeeper announced as they entered the dimly lit cabin, "and our Diana, come to visit. How are you getting along, Charlotte?"

"Oh, fair to middlin'," the slight widow responded from the padded rocking chair where she sat tatting lace, her brownish hair askew, the heavily splinted ankle propped on a pillowed footstool. A thin fire crackled in the hearth, casting a golden glow over plain, but serviceable furnishings. "Set a spell." She gestured to the faded settee and smiled as they sat down. "Don't mind sayin', it's been kinda lonesome around here lately. Seems odd not to be up and about the way I'm used to. My backside is purely tired of stayin' in one spot."

"I'd imagine. You are a person who keeps hopping." Millie paused. "I thought you might enjoy some sweets. You know me, always making too much."

"Yes, and I do appreciate your kindness, Millie." She switched her attention to Diana. "Home for the summer again, Child?"

"No, to stay, this time," she answered. "I've finished my schooling, and my aunt back East has passed on."

"Well, the town can always do with another young face," Mrs. Warner said kindly. " 'Specially one pretty as your'n."

"My sentiments exactly," Millie affirmed, precluding Diana's response.

Diana averted her attention to some samplers and embroidered proverbs on the walls while the two older women chatted for a time about local happenings.

"Can I fix you some tea while I'm here?" the housekeeper eventually asked.

"Thank you, no. Just finished a pot. Thought it might help keep me awake, since settin' around makes a body sleepy."

"Well, then, we shan't keep you from your rest." Standing, Millie moved to put the basket within the widow's reach. "We've a few more errands to run before the sky completely clouds over. We'll come by again real soon."

"God bless you, Mildred, little Diana. Many thanks."

Neither spoke for several moments after taking their leave.

Then Diana broke the silence. "I wonder if Mrs. Warner would like one of us to drop in and read to her now and then, while she's laid up, I mean. Since she can't get out at all, her days must seem overlong."

Millie beamed at her. "Why that's a splendid idea. Wouldn't seem so much like we were keeping a close eye on her that way. I do worry about the old gal, seeing as how she's by herself so much."

"Then let's look through Daddy's library when we get home and see what we can find." Though she had never done anything of that nature before, Diana actually found herself anticipating the possibility of reading to a shut-in. She'd always gotten along with older people. Somehow they didn't seem so critical and judgmental as people nearer her own age.

But as she and Millie neared the parsonage, the elation faded. Would *he* be around?

"New steps," the housekeeper remarked with an appreciative eye when they started up to the porch. "No one can accuse young Mr. Forbes of not being handy. Those old ones were starting to sag in the middle."

The front door opened before they knocked. "Saw you two comin', I did," short Mrs. Tidewell informed them. "Come in. Come in." The woman's little round face had a glow about it which Diana always found endearing.

"We can't stay long," Millie said. "Just brought over some cinnamon buns from this morning's baking. Thought perhaps that nephew of yours might appreciate them when he comes home at noon."

Brady's dark-haired head peeked around the kitchen door at the opposite end of the room. "Is that what I'm smelling? Let me at 'em."

Diana's pulse thudded to a stop when, grinning broadly and rubbing his hands together in anticipation, he crossed the expanse between him and his aunt in a few long strides. His presence somehow made the air around them seem charged, as if a thunderstorm were directly overhead, though why he had that effect on her was a mystery. After all, it wasn't as if she was interested. Anything but.

Mrs. Tidewell bestowed a proud smile on him and slipped an arm about his trim waist. "Brady came home a little early today, since he's in the middle of some project or other that needs long, involved work this afternoon." A light dawned over her sweet features. "In fact, the two of us were just about to sit down to dinner. Noah's visiting some of our sick folk in the outlying areas. We'd love to have you join us."

No! Diana pleaded silently, her gaze studiously avoiding his. She'd only just had breakfast a short while ago, even if she hadn't consumed all of it.

"Well," Millie hedged, "I did have a few more things to do before we head home, but the sky doesn't look too threatening just yet. We'd be glad to stay." With that, she shrugged out of her shawl, then waited for Diana to do the same.

Moments later, they gathered around the long, linen-covered table in the dining room, Mrs. Tidewell and Millie occupying the end chairs. Diana and Brady sat opposite one another on the sides. A hearty beef vegetable soup and crusty hot buns with butter lay before them. Diana tried to focus on that and the tidy familiarity of the parsonage in general, while she picked at the food.

"We're so happy you've come back to us, Diana," the minister's wife gushed. "All finished with school now?"

Diana swallowed the bite of roll she'd been chewing. "Yes,

Ma'am. I won't be returning to Boston."

"Splendid. The girls will love having you at the sewing circle again."

"Should make for a livelier group," Brady said.

Having caught the teasing glint in his eyes, Diana lowered her lashes and concentrated on her meal.

"Well, it certainly is much livelier at home," Millie admitted. "Not so many echoes, and I don't feel I'm rattling around in all that empty space anymore."

"You know? Noah and I felt the same when our Brady came to us," Mrs. Tidewell said wistfully. "Just having him here made us feel young again. I can barely remember what our life was like before that. And he's so good about repairs. This old house has never been in better shape. All one has to do is mention something needing attention, and he does it."

Detecting a slight puffing out of the manly chest across from her, Diana gave intent consideration to repositioning the napkin on her lap.

"I'd imagine Nate Harmon keeps you pretty busy, then, Brady," Millie said, offering the plate of rolls to her friend's nephew.

"Thanks." He helped himself. "Yes, he keeps me hopping."

Relief flickered through Diana. Perhaps his job would keep him too occupied to pop in during sewing sessions. Even diminish the chance of running into him elsewhere. If so, living at Hickory Corners probably wouldn't be so tiresome after all.

"I still have a little time for other projects, though," he said. "Something in particular you need done?"

"Now that you mention it, yes. But there's no real hurry. Perhaps sometime when you have a spare minute or two you might stop by and check the roof. I noticed a damp spot on the ceiling after the last rainstorm."

Diana's gaze shot to him just in time to see a broad grin spread across his face.

"Sure thing. Be glad to."

"Oh, good. When you come by, I'll take you right to it. In the upstairs bedroom. The one on the left."

But that's my *room!* Diana's heart gave a lurch. Even if she wasn't likely to endure his presence at the sewing circle, or chance meeting him in public, the clod was coming to her own private domain. She felt warmth rise over her cheekbones.

"I'll try to come over one day this week, Miz Sanderson," he promised. "Of course, I don't have much experience with roofing, but I should be able to figure out the problem."

"I'd appreciate that. And so will Diana, since the problem concerns her room."

"Ah. In that case, I'll make it a top priority." The man had the audacity to flash a wink at Diana.

Suddenly devoid of even the hint of an appetite, she sank back against the chair's spindles, no longer caring whether her spine had the proper arch.

"Might I offer everyone some apple tarts?" Mrs. Tidewell asked, rising to clear the dishes. "Made fresh just this morning."

"They do sound tempting," Millie confessed. "You know the weakness I've always had for those little pies of yours."

"Good. I'll be just a second." With that, she toted away the soiled things.

"I'll help, Aunt Edna." Brady carted to the kitchen what she couldn't carry. He returned with a stack of plates, which he set out with a flourish one by one, his unrelenting gaze lingering a touch overlong when he placed Diana's.

His aunt brought in a platter of folded, golden-brown pastries and passed them around before pouring tea into everyone's cups.

"Excellent, as always," the housekeeper commented shortly, smacking her lips. "Just excellent. I must try this recipe sometime."

"There's none easier," the minister's wife told her. "Oh, and don't forget, I promised to let you borrow the new pattern I received the other day. You can adjust the stitch count to make either doilies or scarves." She tilted her head at Diana. "You crochet as well, I believe?"

"Yes, but it's not my favorite pastime."

"What is, Miss Montclair?" Brady challenged, obviously endeavoring to maintain a straight face. "If you don't mind my asking."

She met those taunting indigo eyes evenly. "I particularly enjoy going to the symphony or visiting museums. . .neither of which is available at Hickory Corners, of course."

"Of course. Well, we'll have to come up with something to provide you with a few *pleasant diversions* then."

Diana opened her mouth to issue a crisp retort, but Millie rose at that instant. "I do thank you, Edna, for your hospitality. We had a delightful visit."

The minister's wife smiled. "Always a pleasure to be in your company. And Diana. So nice to have you back home again. Please don't be a stranger. We hope to see much more of you at church. And don't forget the sewing circle."

Blotting her lips on the napkin, Diana stood to her feet and smiled sweetly as she and Millie went to put on their wraps and take their leave. "Thank you, Mrs. Tidewell. I'll definitely make time to visit with the other girls."

"My little group is changing so quickly," the older woman mused. "Three of the dear girls married already, one with a baby, another in the family way. But we still relish our sewing sessions. Of course, we don't always labor over quilts or items for hope chests these days. Nowadays it can be a wedding dress, a baby blanket, what have you."

"Well, I'll look forward to being part of the circle again."

"And I'll look forward to more of that fudge you used to bring," Brady called from the dining room.

With a disbelieving roll of her eyes, Diana followed the housekeeper outside. The man was worse than the mosquitoes of summer. There was just no getting rid of him.

Chapter 3

O ff to a brilliant start, Dunderhead," Brady muttered, striding purposefully back to Nathaniel Harmon's place of business. All those gallant plans, and what's the first thing he does in Diana Montclair's presence, but act the village idiot? Maybe he should borrow one of Nate's wood clamps. . .that ought to keep a big, overgrown mouth shut.

What quality about the gently bred gal made him act like a clod or blurt out the first thing that popped into his mind? Shaking his head in a futile attempt to slough off his frustration, Brady glanced toward the well-kept mansion positioned halfway between the parsonage and Nate's place. So the front bedroom belonged to her. . . .

A barely discernable movement behind the ruffled pink curtains stirred the gauzy panels. He didn't immediately avert his gaze, but merely adjusted it slightly, as if trying to spot a missing shingle above the chamber. Nothing seemed amiss, at least from this vantage point.

At the *clop* of approaching horse hooves, Brady redirected his attention to the wagon turning from Main Street onto Birch. He waved when he recognized Betsy Walker at the reins.

The brown-eyed blond tipped her bonneted head and smiled a greeting while the rig clattered past him, its bed laden with supplies to be divided between her own home and her father's farm. Though married, she still did the marketing for both households. Aunt Edna had mentioned that Betsy's father and siblings managed breakfast on their own, but they ate dinner and supper with Betsy and Ty each day.

Once the dust cloud settled, Brady angled across the street to the carpentry shop, where spring's sweet freshness gave way to the more pungent smells of cut wood, resin, and glues emanating from the squat building. He'd grown to appreciate those distinctive odors.

The front door stood open, amplifying the high-pitched whine of the lathe as he went inside.

"Oh. You're back." The master carpenter looked up from the foot-powered machine now slowing to a stop. The warmth of Nate's smile and a merry twinkle in his eyes kept him from being downright homely. The twitch of a grin widened his graying handlebar mustache, curled on either end to the size of a two-bit piece. Somehow, the waxed perfection detracted from the man's underbite, lessening the prominence it might otherwise have. "Edna feed ya good, did she?"

"Yep," Brady replied, patting his stomach. "To the gills." He navigated the clutter of partially completed projects scattered about the remaining floor space. Even in a town the size of Hickory Corners, Nate found a ready market for the excellent cornices, cabinets, and finely crafted furniture produced in his shop. What didn't sell locally he transported to settlements in the outlying areas, so the livelihood generated a steady income.

Brady went to check the joinings on the mahogany desk he'd been working on before noon.

"Lookin' good, don't ya think?" Nate prodded, his faded blue eyes making a slow perusal from where he sat. "Right fine job on the carvin' and joints. You'll soon be puttin' me outta business, Lad."

"That'll be the day. You've taught me everything I know. If not for you, I wouldn't be able to tell a chisel from a keyhole saw."

The older man gave a nod. "Well, holler if ya need any help. I'm almost finished with these table legs."

"Will do." Brady returned to measuring lengths of the woods he'd use to construct drawers. Then he began sawing, taking care to keep the angle of the cuts straight, the way he'd been taught. He smiled to himself, picturing the piece finished and in Uncle Noah's office at the church. The unassuming minister had made do with a dilapidated relic long enough. His upcoming birthday would provide the perfect excuse for a well-deserved surprise. Little enough thanks, Brady mused, after he and Aunt Edna took him in, showed him what love is. The two of them turned him around. Saved his wayward life from ruin.

Now, if only he could learn to corral his mouth. A golden-haired vision stole into his thoughts, adorned in translucent colors as delicate as the hues of a rainbow. Would she ever forgive him for embarrassing her last summer?

"Whatcha stewin' over?" His employer set down the table leg he'd finished shaping. "Considerin' the season, must be gal trouble."

Brady shot him a droll grin. "What makes you say that?"

"A man don't get to be nigh onto two-score years without

learnin' a thing or two."

"Reckon not."

They both resumed working, the whirring of the lathe and the sharp grating of the saw's teeth echoing off the hard planes of cabinets and shelves. Then Brady stopped mid-stroke, waiting until Nate did the same. "I don't suppose—" he began, feeling uncomfortably warm in the vicinity of his neck. "Aw, shucks. Ever get yourself on some young lady's wrong side?"

"Whoo-ee." The man's guffaw accompanied a smart whack on his sturdy knee. "Ain't nobody on this earth done that more'n me. In case ya never noticed, I don't have myself a little wife t'home, greetin' me of an evenin'."

Brady shrugged. "I figured you just weren't interested."

Running stubby fingers through his graying hair, the carpenter grew thoughtful. "I was interested enough, all right, in my younger days. Just seemed to have this talent for puttin' my foot in my mouth. All the way up to my belt buckle."

"Somehow, I know what you mean." Brady wagged his head.

"Well, time helps more often than not. Eventually a gal forgets what the problem was." With a decisive nod, Nate fingered a section of smooth, turned wood on the machine and began pumping the treadle with his booted feet once more.

Brady tried to draw comfort from his employer's words, but couldn't quite believe things could work so smoothly in this case. A goodly number of months had gone by since he'd humiliated her in front of the other girls, unintentional or not. And before he had a chance to apologize she'd been on her way back East. He had his work laid out, all right, trying to redeem himself in Diana Montclair's eyes.

Sunday dawned surprisingly clear after a day and a half of steady rains. Glancing up at the damp circle on the ceiling above the maple chest-on-chest which contained her frilly "sit-upons," as the teachers from the academy so delicately termed "underthings," Diana wondered how long it would be before a chunk of wet plaster would come crashing down on her head, shingles and all.

Much as she cringed at the thought of Brady Forbes stepping foot in her private boudoir, she knew Millie had been right in seeking help. Expelling a breath of resignation, she looped a fresh chemise and some drawers over one arm and moved to the matching wardrobe to choose a gown for church. The russet silk, perhaps, so as not to show the inevitable mud she and the rest of the congregation would track in.

An hour later, after a delay caused by a loose button on the housekeeper's dress, Diana and Millie arrived at Hickory Corners Church mere moments before the start of the service. They took seats in their customary pew. Although the rustic meetinghouse could not compare to some of the loftier houses of worship Diana had attended in Philadelphia and Boston, she found the atmosphere here noticeably friendlier and more welcoming.

Even with most of the churchgoers facing forward in anticipation of the opening prayer, Diana realized how many of the townsfolk had become familiar to her during her many visits. She tried not to be obvious in picking out the ones easiest to recognize.

In their Sunday finery and seated with their respective husbands now, rather than being clustered shoulder to shoulder the way they used to, Elsa Gerhard, Samantha Stahl, and Betsy Walker offered tentative smiles of greeting. So did the Widow Warner, whose makeshift crutches lay propped against the wall alongside the pew she occupied. Diana returned their smiles with a polite one of her own, wondering if any of the girls would approach her afterward to visit.

Her meandering gaze idly drifted across the aisle. . .and met Brady's lopsided grin. Even before she could lower her lashes, she noticed how tall and splendid he looked in a chocolate frock coat and matching trousers, every strand of his nearly ebony hair in place. She couldn't suppress a tiny smile, but assured herself it was only proper to return his, after all.

Interrupting her musings, Reverend Tidewell, in his best black suit, his tuft of white hair slicked back, stepped to the lectern. He raised a bony white hand to signify silence, then bowed his head. "Our most gracious Father and Lord, we ask Thy blessing on this Sabbath service. May all that is said and done in Thy name be honoring and glorifying to Thy precious Son, in whose name we pray.

"Now," he continued, "let us begin by standing and singing 'A Mighty Fortress Is Our God,' page twenty-seven in the hymnal."

The pump organ wheezed out a few chords in introduction, and Millie edged closer to share the open book in her hands. The older woman's contralto blended pleasantly with Diana's clear soprano through every verse, yet the lovely lilt of Elsa's sweet voice stood out ever so slightly above the rest. Brady, she noted, only held a hymnal and followed the words in silence.

But directly behind Diana a rich tenor belted out the lyrics. Recognizing the particular range, she surmised that successful attorney Martin Crabtree must also be visiting from Capital City. The handsome bachelor possessed considerable charms, and with his fine education seemed somehow out of his element in rustic Hickory Corners whenever he came to visit his gossipy mother.

"Please be seated," the minister said, his expression gentle as ever as he assessed his flock. "I must say, it's gratifying to see such a goodly number of folk present this morning, after yesterday's rain."

Nods and smiles made the rounds.

After a slight pause, he cleared his throat, removed reading glasses from a breast pocket, and put them on. His kindly eyes scanned the congregation over the gold wire frames. "The title of my sermon this morning is, 'Ye Are the Salt of the Earth.' Turn with me if you will to the Gospel of Matthew, chapter five."

In the ensuing shuffle of pages, Diana stifled a yawn and sought a more comfortable position on the hard pew, bolstering herself for a long half hour's tedious dronings. She didn't exactly see any connection between living people and the common substance, salt. Besides, she had other things to occupy her mind, such as ignoring the surreptitious glances from a certain bachelor across the aisle. And the occasional brushings of a man's booted foot against her heel—which occurred a touch too often for it to be merely accidental. No one ever accused Martin Crabtree of being subtle. Straightening in her seat, Diana moved her feet safely out of his reach. She stared unseeing toward the minister, while her fingers toyed with the lace-edged handkerchief from her reticule, folding it a dozen ways, then rolling impossibly narrow rolls.

Eventually she heard the good reverend announce the

closing prayer. Revitalized at having endured the Sunday service, she smiled with satisfaction and stood for the benediction.

A noticeable rustle of skirts and scuffle of feet immediately followed the minister's final "amen," and Millie moved a few steps away to chat with her lady friends.

"My, my." Fair-haired Martin stepped in front of Diana, his most dazzling smile focused on her as he gave a somewhat formal bow. His expertly tailored suit enhanced his manly form to perfection. "If it isn't the lovely Miss Montclair, gracing our little hamlet with her glorious presence. Home for another summer?"

The rust-colored plume on Diana's bonnet fluttered as she tilted her head with cool reserve, first at him, then at his sharp-nosed mother. Obviously the young man had inherited his marvelous features from his late father's side. "Mr. Crabtree. Mrs. Crabtree. How nice to see you both."

"You've not answered my question," Martin prompted. "How long will we mere mortals be treated with the benefit of your angelic face?"

From across the aisle, Brady snickered, then shook his head and blended into the departing crowd waiting to shake his uncle's hand.

"Actually, I've come home to stay this time," she admitted, a little miffed at the departing carpenter's attitude.

Martin's golden eyebrows rose high. "Do tell. That is splendid news, is it not, Mother? Just splendid." A smugly serene look passed between the pair.

At that moment Elsa stepped nearer, her sleeping cherub in her arms. She looked every inch the doting mother. "So glad to see you at service, Diana. I do hope you'll be coming to Mrs. T's on Tuesday."

"I'm considering it, yes," Diana said.

"See?" Martin Crabtree said, adding a knowing smile. "You're in great demand with the locals."

In the distance, Diana caught Samantha's and Betsy's decidedly frosty glares in the attorney's direction and furtive glances in her own as the two took their leave. Her confusion gave way to doubt. Even if she attended the sewing circle every week from now until doomsday, would she ever truly be part of their close-knit group?

Chapter 4

Tuesday. The dreaded day had come.

Even as she dressed for breakfast, Diana still debated whether to go to the sewing circle. Conflicting thoughts warred in her mind. The other town girls shared the memories and experiences of a lifetime in Hickory Corners. She did not know how to relate to them. Surely they would believe she was trying to elbow her way into that close-knit group.

"All ready for your special day?" Millie asked with a cheery smile when Diana entered the kitchen. The housekeeper dished up a generous serving of scrambled eggs and feather-light biscuits and brought them to the table.

Diana forced a smile. "I. . .thought perhaps you might need me here at home. To. . .help with. . . ," she fluttered a hand, trying to think of a word, "something."

Millie tucked her chin, a baffled expression scrunching her features. "Nonsense. I haven't a thing pressing, and even if I did, what couldn't wait a few hours? Now that you're home to stay, you need to spend time with the other girls again. Rekindle those friendships."

Diana heaved a sigh. Millie had no idea, no idea at all.

Only one thing would make her understand. Honesty. "But that's just it, Millie," she confessed at last. "They're not my friends. They've never been." Maddening tears came dangerously near the surface, their presence stinging the back of Diana's eyes, causing moisture she couldn't quite suppress. She swallowed hard. "If my own mother and father don't consider me worth being around, why should anyone else?"

The older woman's mouth fell open with a gasp. She dropped the dish towel she'd been using and flew to Diana's side, wrapping comforting arms around her. "Don't think such things. I have a hard time myself, understanding your parents' actions, but I know they love you. They truly do. Your brother's sudden death hit them real hard, and the only way they could get through that sorrow was to throw themselves into that shipping business. Things were just coming together for them when you came along. It just wasn't the best time for them to let up."

"What about now?" Diana asked miserably. "Everyone knows Montclair Shipping Line is one of the biggest enterprises on the Ohio and Mississippi Rivers. When will there be enough success and enough money for them to make room for me?"

"I don't know that," the housekeeper crooned. "Only the Good Lord can see into the future. But I pray every day that He'll open their eyes to see the treasure they have right here." She hugged harder.

Diana didn't know if she should set any hopes on that or not. Even if her parents did decide to come here and make a life with her, the house would be filled with inhabitants who barely knew one another.

"In the meantime," Millie went on, straightening and

returning to her chore, "there are people in town who'll accept you, if you'll only let them. You have to remember, though, in order to make friends, you must *be* a friend."

Be a friend.

A simple concept, yet profound. Diana pondered it throughout the remainder of the morning and during dinner.

Afterward, with the housekeeper's admonishment still ringing in her ears, Diana couldn't help but take her time walking the short distance to the minister's home. What sort of reception would she have? Did the others truly want her to come, or had the invitation at church merely been a pretense, a polite gesture one might make to any regular visitor in town?

Happy chatter wafted out of the parsonage's open window, along with the hem of a lacy curtain fluttering on the breeze. Her reservations intensified. Gazing idly at her feet, she did notice the new steps sported a coat of paint since her and Millie's visit, a gray reminiscent of the decks on her father's steamships. Grasping the skirt of her pale green lawn gown in her hands, she drew a strengthening breath, approached the door and rapped.

"Oh, Diana," Mrs. Tidewell said, her gracious smile more than welcoming. "Come in, my dear." Disposing of Diana's shawl and bonnet, she ushered her inside to the comfortable sitting room, where the other girls from town were positioned around a quilt frame. The older woman raised her voice slightly. "Everyone, our little group is complete once again."

Elsa, Betsy, and Samantha, looking fresh in crisp muslin and calico dresses, paused in their stitching and glanced up, their smiles pleasant, their demeanors expectant.

"What did you bring to work on?" Mrs. T asked, guiding

Diana to the padded rocker in the corner which she'd always preferred.

"Nothing, really." Venturing a step into the unknown, Diana cast caution to the wind. "I. . .was wondering if I might learn to stitch on the quilt, if it isn't too much trouble to teach me. I must confess, sewing has always been my weakness. I've only ever done well with embroidery." She held her breath, expecting a rebuff.

"Sure, we'd love to have you." Elsa scooted her chair to one side, making room between her and Betsy.

Diana, greatly relieved, pulled up a seat for herself, while across from her, Betsy's cousin Samantha offered a tentative smile. Perhaps this wouldn't be so bad after all, Diana decided.

The pastor's wife brought a quilting needle, a thimble, and a spool of thread to her from the sideboard. "Let me show you how to get started."

She threaded the eye expertly and sat down, one hand above the quilt, the other below while she rocked the needle, collecting a series of ten stitches on that minuscule length. Watching her, Diana immediately lost heart. Her best efforts at sewing had been miserable failures. How could this one be any different?

Mrs. Tidewell's conspiratorial smile put her at ease. "That's how you'll quilt once you've had some practice. But for now, merely poking the needle straight down, like this, then up again from below, will do nicely. Down, up. Down, up. Here, you try." Mrs. Tidewell relinquished the chair and handed her the needle and thimble.

Diana drew an uneasy breath, took the seat, and set to work, not even daring to imagine attempting two stitches in a row on the needle, even with these lightweight layers of fabric. She gave all her concentration to laboring over the simpler method.

"You should have seen me trying to master this process," Elsa said kindly, an understanding sparkle in her blue eyes as she worked on her section. "Poor Mrs. T must have sat for hours after we'd all gone home, ripping out every pathetic stitch I'd done and redoing them."

An astonished gasp issued from the little woman. "I did no such thing." Coming to peek over Diana's shoulder, she perused the crooked stitches and nodded her encouragement. "On the contrary, I shall always treasure those first sweet projects completed by my fledgling seamstresses. One of my greatest joys has been witnessing your progress over the years. None of us is born with any ready-made skills. We learn things by practice. Including quilting."

Somewhat more optimistic, but still feeling all thumbs, Diana jabbed the needle into the bright material. She stopped now and then to give a critical eye to her work while the other girls chattered in the easy way she'd always envied, sharing special memories of events unknown to her. Perhaps it was her own fault she had virtually no pleasant memories of classmates from her school years.

Diana contemplated the unique design of the quilt, each block of which held four hearts in different patterns, but complementing colors, with the points meeting at the center. To her, the theme seemed symbolic of the sewing circle. . .at least how it might have been, had she not lived away from town. Four girls, growing up together, forever friends.

Yet, part of her still felt like an intruder. Perhaps always would.

Just then, the grandfather clock across the room chimed

the hour, then Elsa yawned and stretched, a sheepish grin widening her rosy cheeks.

"Sounds like somebody had another long night with baby Georg," Betsy said. "I'm learning what to expect when my own little one makes his entrance into the world." She patted her blossoming tummy and blushed becomingly.

Elsa ceased stitching momentarily. "After being wakeful much of the night, I expect he'll sleep the afternoon away. Of course, that should make it easier for Shane to look after him. Now that our little angel is toddling around, he finds some rather interesting things to get into when our backs are turned."

Diana's curiosity got the best of her. "He wakes you up in the night?"

Elsa nodded. "He must be cutting new teeth again."

"I should think that's why people hire nannies," Diana blurted without thinking. "How can one function during the daytime if deprived of sleep?"

A peculiar look passed between the others.

"I really don't mind tending to Georg," Elsa said, her tone gentle. "I consider the responsibility a joy and a blessing. He's growing so quickly, he'll soon be out of this stage. Then I'll get more sleep."

Mrs. Tidewell took advantage of the awkward moment to cross the room for her Bible. "I believe we'll read the Twenty-third Psalm today, pertaining to the way our Lord looks after His own."

Listening to her soothing voice while continuing to sew, Diana paid close attention to the words being read. On Sunday, the Reverend suggested that God's children were salt. Now it seemed they were also considered sheep. How very strange, those two mental images.

After the Scripture reading, the girls took a break for refreshments, serving themselves from the sideboard, where the minister's wife had just poured cups of tea.

"These gingersnaps," Samantha said dreamily, munching a cookie, "are truly delicious, Betsy."

"Thank you. Ty especially likes them, so I bake them pretty often. Of course, with little brothers and a sister popping over to gobble every batch warm from the oven, I have to hide some, or he'd never get any."

"It's much the same at the hotel," Elsa confessed, "trying to keep up with boarders and guests."

Diana almost injected something about the benefits of having Millie around, but caught herself just in time. It seemed difficult to relate to people who did things for themselves, when she'd been waited on practically her whole life. In reality, however, the very fact the other girls were so self-reliant only made her envy them all the more.

"Would you care for more tea, Dear?" Mrs. Tidewell asked, making the rounds with the china pot.

Diana peered into her cup, amazed to see the bottom. She'd been so absorbed in her thoughts, she couldn't recall drinking a drop. "Yes, please."

"Are you glad to be home for good now?" Elsa asked, coming to sit beside her on the settee.

In all Diana's years, she could remember no one ever asking her opinion on anything, only an endless string of *go here, do this, do that*, to which she'd submitted with no other recourse. Now, however, she dared another step into this strange new life. "I'm. . .trying to adjust. Everything's so different."

"I would imagine. I've often wondered how it must have

been for you, going far away to the big city, living in boarding schools, taking excursions to see wonderful sights, traveling all that way home again. You must miss those benefits."

"I did enjoy sailing on the steamships," Diana confessed, some favorite memories surfacing. "Watching the lovely countryside passing by."

"Mind if we listen in?" Betsy asked. "I haven't traveled any-where." She and Samantha, obviously having overheard at least part of the conversation, drew up chairs and perched on them.

Having an audience who actually appeared interested in what she might say gave Diana a heady feeling she'd never before experienced. She felt some of her guard melting away as a yearning for the other girls to like her came to the fore. Was this what it was like to make friends? She looked from one face to the next, their sincere interest enabling her to relax and smile. "The schools I attended were quite lovely, with sprawling grounds one could stroll across between class hours. I most enjoyed visiting museums and going to the symphony."

"I'll probably never see anything beyond Hickory Corners," Elsa mused, "though my family did travel some when I was a youngster. Shane has been all over, of course. He tells me lots of stories."

Mrs. Tidewell, restoring order to the sideboard, smiled their way. "Perhaps we could continue sharing our recollections as we get back to work."

"Yes, Mrs. T," they singsonged.

Scarcely had they settled back into their places, when lively footsteps sounded from outside. The door opened, admitting Brady, unrolling the sleeves of his blue homespun shirt while he craned his neck in the direction of the baked treats. "Any good stuff left?" His unabashed grin made the rounds.

At least, Diana surmised, it included more than just her. She'd looked down so quickly, she could only guess. She had quite enough to focus on, remembering how the stitches were supposed to go.

"Oh, pshaw," his aunt said. "As if we'd let a grown man starve. I've a plate already fixed for you out in the kitchen. Then if you're still hankering for sweets, you can help yourself to the cookies."

His not-so-quiet steps clumped across the plank floorboards, diminishing only a little as he disappeared into the other room.

"So what's it like, going to an actual symphony?" Samantha asked Diana, her eyes aglow as she held her needle poised to sew. "To be in some huge hall, with music filling all the nooks and crannies. I should think that would be heaven."

"Much better than having only a string quartet providing the entertainment," Diana said with a smile. "Although, they too can be quite. . .entrancing."

"I hope to go to a grand music hall one day," Samantha said. "We don't have much entertainment here in town."

"What's this about entertainment?" Brady echoed, carrying his dinner in one hand on his return. He plopped down onto a side chair next to the wall. One with a direct line of vision to Diana as he ate. "You saying you don't like Nate's fiddlin' at socials?"

"We like it fine," Betsy said. "But I'm sure we'd also enjoy some more refined music now and then."

"*Refined.* Ah, yes. You're hearing about the advantages of city life, as opposed to the more lowly lifestyle of country bumpkins." A smirk took up residence on his face as his gaze slid to Diana.

Diana felt her cheeks burning. "I merely answered their questions," she said in her own defense, miffed that he'd butted in.

"I reckon. But quiet towns have some benefits of their own. I wouldn't discount country life altogether."

"I wasn't doing that." Aware of her mounting emotions, Diana clamped her lips together, lest she really speak her mind. Here she'd been, on the verge of relating to the young women who'd been practically strangers to her over the years, and *he* had to come in and ruin everything. "Oh, would you look at the time," she said in a rush. "I really must be going." Knotting her thread, she clipped it off and rose. "Splendid visiting with you all," she told the others, then smiled at her hostess. "Thank you for the refreshments and the sewing lesson. I had a lovely time." She marched right past Brady Forbes without so much as a glance, her clipped steps beating a staccato tempo on her way to the door.

"Actually," Elsa remarked, "I need to get back to the hotel myself. We're expecting a ship around the supper hour." Dropping her sewing supplies in Mrs. T's basket, she snatched up her belongings and followed after Diana.

Outside, Elsa placed a hand on Diana's forearm. "Thank you for coming to the circle this week. Don't mind Brady, though. He's far from being the town rake. He's really quite the wit and takes singular pleasure in teasing us all, as you'll discover week by week. Please don't let him get to you."

"What makes you think he gets to me?" Diana asked through gritted teeth.

The dark-haired girl merely smiled. "Oh, I don't know. Intuition, perhaps."

Despite herself, Diana calmed a little. But reliving the

humiliation she'd suffered last summer thanks to the Tide-wells' nephew, it was pointless to correct the new mom. "Thank you, Elsa."

"For what?"

"For helping me to feel less a stranger today. I appreciate it."

"You're most welcome. The other girls and I, well, we've always wondered what you were really like. Now you're home to stay, we'll finally have a chance to get to know you. So you'll keep coming every week then?"

"I'll try. I really will."

"Good. I'm glad. See you at church on Sunday." Swiveling on her heel, she crossed Birch Street, heading for the hotel.

Diana watched after her, amazed at how truly *friendly* Elsa Gerhard seemed now that she was married. Samantha and Betsy had made an effort to make her feel at ease today too. If those girls were willing to accept her presence in Hickory Corners, perhaps it was time she accepted her fate and did the same.

At least *some* of her new life would be easier to endure. With a scathing glance over her shoulder at the parsonage, Diana headed for the nearby sanctity of her parents' big house.

Where *that man* would appear soon enough, to fix the roof.

Chapter 5

Considerably lighter at heart after the gathering at the parsonage, Diana would have skipped home, except for the conviction that such childish behavior hardly befit a proper young lady. Nevertheless, she hurried, eager to tell Millie about how the town girls had welcomed her into their group and made her feel a part of the sewing circle.

The only dark cloud had been Brady's appearance. The very sight of him dredged up the memory of the incident when he'd embarrassed her in front of those same girls. Did they remember too? Hoping not, Diana ignored thoughts of him and focused on her new friends as she traipsed up the porch steps and went inside.

"That you, Honey?" Millie called from the kitchen.

"It is, indeed." Not even attempting to control her smile, Diana followed the housekeeper's voice to the room that seemed the woman's personal haven.

"Well, well. Look at that face." Millie paused in rolling a batch of biscuits and propped floury knuckles on one hip. "Methinks you had a pleasant time at Edna's this afternoon."

"I did. And you were right. The other girls, they—"

A knock rattled the front door.

"I'll run my bonnet upstairs while you see who's come," Diana said. "I'll tell you all about the sewing circle later." Upon reaching her room, she flung the straw hat gleefully toward her wardrobe and flopped across her bed to relive every minute of her experience at the parsonage. Or rather, almost every minute of it. Part of her couldn't help wondering if Elsa's parting comments about Brady Forbes were true. If so. . .

Those musings hung in suspension when footsteps approached her door and stopped.

"Diana?" Millie rapped lightly.

"Come in." She eased to an upright position as the housekeeper entered.

He strolled in behind her.

Diana blanched and sprang to her feet, her pulse beating in her throat.

"Miss Montclair," Brady said, with a polite nod, the brim of his everyday hat clutched in those long fingers, while midnight blue eyes made a sweeping circuit of her private boudoir.

"There's the problem," Millie told him, pointing to the discoloration bordering the crown molding on the ceiling. "And it's getting worse every time it rains. Or even sprinkles, as it did last night."

"Hmm." He tipped his dark-haired head back and assessed the spot from where he stood. "Don't suppose you have a ladder."

"Matter of fact, I do, out back. Not the sturdiest one around, but it's handy. I'll take you to the shed."

"Great. Much obliged, Ma'am."

As the two took their leave, Diana exhaled a nervous breath. She gave fleeting thought to making herself scarce, but before she figured how to do so without being obvious, Brady came clomping up the stairs again. Alone this time. Cutting off any hope of an exit. . .but was she really certain she wanted one?

He seemed so much. . .taller. . .up close. How could his presence fill up so much of the room's space?

A knowing grin softened those angular features. "Miz Sanderson had to tend to some biscuits, then said something about reading to Miz Warner later."

Diana gave a mute nod and fidgeted with a fold of her skirt, watching him survey the feminine trappings surrounding them both. Realizing she was gawking at his strong, noble profile, she quickly averted her gaze.

"Nice place you've got here. Real pretty." He carried the ladder over below the water stain and propped it against the wall, adjusting the footing a time or two. Then he swung her a sidelong glance. "Suppose you could hold onto this while I climb up? Looks like the thing's seen better days."

"I. . .of course." Even with the little experience she'd had around workmen, and the tools of their trade, Diana knew a rickety contraption when she saw one. She put aside her reservations and went to help. So far he didn't seem threatening in the least. "What should I do?"

He shrugged. "Hold the sides. If the thing collapses, cushion my fall, okay?"

Eyes widening, she took a step backward. "You can't be serious!"

His grin broadened as he chuckled and shook his head. "I'm sorry. Really. I don't know what there is about you, Diana Montclair, that makes me act the fool. But I really would appreciate your help here. Just take a firm grip on the sides. I'll only be a second. Promise."

Be a friend. With Millie's encouragement ringing in her ears, Diana chose to give him the benefit of the doubt and moved to do his bidding. As Brady ascended the few rungs required to reach the ceiling, she tried not to be brazen enough to stare at that masculine form while her fingers absorbed the vibrations of his movements. But when he stopped, she couldn't help checking to see what he was doing.

Brady pressed his fingertips against the darkened spot. "Soft, all right." He climbed down again, more confidently, then brushed his hands on his trousers. "This place have an attic?"

She nodded. "The door leads off the hall."

"Let's go see what we can find up there, shall we?"

Inside, Diana knew he spoke in generalities. He might need to be guided to the attic door, but he didn't need her tagging along up into those dark recesses after him.

Still, she went anyway. . .the *friendly* thing to do.

Reaching the dusty top landing, Brady stood aside so she could join him. Then he glanced around. "Let's see. If my calculations are correct, over there's about where your room is." He strode toward where he'd pointed, and knelt down. "Sure 'nuf. It's damp here too."

Diana swung her gaze upward the same instant he did, and saw the tiny gap where some skylight shone through.

"Well, would you look at that," Brady said with a quirk of his mouth. He cut her a glance. "How are you at climbing roofs?"

Despite herself, Diana had to laugh. "I'm afraid that wasn't one of the subjects covered at the Prentiss Academy."

"Pity," he quipped. "Well, looks like I'll have to get me a

real ladder over at Nate's and see what needs done up top. Thanks for the help, Miss Montclair."

"You're quite welcome. . .and Diana will do." She hadn't meant to add that last part, but the words popped out all by themselves. More than that, she was glad they had.

His slow smile did amazing things to her insides. Perhaps Elsa was right in assuming he wasn't really so horrid. Maybe the time had come to forget the hurtful past. After all, both of them were older now. Perhaps they too could become true friends. The delightful possibility tickled her heart.

Somehow she refrained from watching out the window while Brady strode over to the carpentry shop. But after he left, Diana headed back downstairs where the aroma of Millie's biscuits permeated the air. Turning at the bottom to go to the kitchen, she noticed that the small rag rug the house-keeper kept on the porch had caught in the door. She stepped outside to straighten it.

"Associating with the riffraff, are we?" a woman's nasal voice called from the next house.

Diana moved farther out on the porch, where she could see acid-tongued Olivia Crabtree's insinuating sneer. The widow knew everyone's business and didn't hesitate to express her opinion about it. "I beg your pardon?"

Making a pretense of sweeping the always immaculate stoop, the gaunt woman stood rigid, gnarly fingers still grasp-ing the broom handle as her close-set eyes peered over her hook nose. "There's not a soul in town who doesn't know that one's sorry background. I'm sure your parents would prefer you to keep company with someone more. . .suitable. My Martin, for example. Any young woman would be fortunate to have his attentions."

"I'm sure they would."

Her jaw gaped, but she recovered quickly. "Splendid. He'll be happy to hear of your high opinion of him." With that, she turned and strutted back inside.

The woman's movements reminded Diana of a black crow she'd once been fascinated by as a child. Moistening her lips, she frowned and shook her head, wondering what in the world that was about. This truly had been the most surprising day. She had a lot to relate to Millie. . .and something to ask about Brady Forbes, as well.

Brady whistled all the way to the shop.

Practically a castle, that Montclair house, he conceded. Little wonder the shipping magnate's daughter dressed like royalty. She didn't act regal, though, at least while he'd been there. On the contrary, she'd been rather ordinary. Not ordinary enough to give a guy like him a second look, then he wasn't exactly in the market for a significant relationship. What did he have to offer a gal—especially one like her? What started him thinking along those ridiculous lines anyway?

"Hey, Nate," he hollered, entering the shop. "Where's that big ladder of yours?"

The cabinetmaker peered around the door he'd been attaching to a large walnut wardrobe. "Leaning against the outside of the shop, like always. Find that leak at the Montclair place?"

"Yep. Must be some roofing blew off when we had that windstorm last month. Thought I'd climb up and see for sure."

"Give a yell if you need help, Lad. I've patched a roof or two in my day."

"Thanks, I'll do that."

Nothing to offer a gal. The grim reality bounced around in Brady's head while he toted his ungainly burden back to the Montclair mansion. He'd never given much thought to fortunes or worldly goods before. He had his hands plenty full enough working at Nate's and keeping the parsonage and church in good repair. The only thing he'd ever considered important was repaying his aunt and uncle for their faith in him. Along with all his free labor, he turned over every cent he earned. Figured they'd put it to better use than he ever would.

Funny, though. There'd been a lot of changes in town the last couple years. The guys he used to joke around with had moved on with their lives. Married. Started families of their own. First Shane Gerhard, then Tyler Walker, and not long ago, Jacob Stahl. Maybe it was time to give some thought to his own future. Or did he want to spend the rest of his days going to work and coming home to pore over his uncle's theology books till he was as old and snowy-haired as Uncle Noah?

That unsettling possibility fit like a square peg in a round hole. Perhaps the time had come to start looking for some nice gal to settle down with. He wasn't dense enough to daydream that one as classy as Diana would give him a tumble, of course. Still, it beat everything the way she stuck in a guy's mind. Maybe the reason he didn't already have a girl of his own was because he'd been comparing them all to her in the first place. Drawing an unsteady breath at that realization, Brady crossed the street to the Montclair house.

There on the front porch, Diana chatted with that foppish Martin Crabtree.

The sight of that dandy, spruced up as always in his fine,

city-bought suit knotted Brady's stomach. Diana's musical laugh over some ever so clever remark hardened his jaw. What more proof did he need that his earlier convictions were right? Compressing his lips, he tromped right on by to the side of the house. He had a job to do. Best he get on with it.

Even with the unexpected guest seated between her and the opposite end of the porch, Diana caught the blur of Brady's movements as the handyman went around the far side of the house, a long ladder tucked under his arm. Surely that sour expression on his normally jovial face was a product of her own imagination.

"...So, with this being a particularly fine day," Martin was saying, "I thought to myself, perhaps Diana might enjoy going for a stroll along the river." He arched his brows suggestively. "The birds are singing, the flowers are coming into bloom...certainly too nice an afternoon to go to waste. What do you say?"

This did seem to be her day for making friends, but she'd had virtually no experience with young men her age and had no idea how to conduct herself. "Well, I. . ." She hesitated a fraction too long.

"See?" He stood in his shiny shoes and gave an exaggerated bow. "I knew you'd have no reason to refuse." He held out a soft, pale hand, waiting.

Gratified at being the recipient of her good-looking neighbor's attention, Diana politely acquiesced. "I'll just get my bonnet," she said, returning in moments.

She managed not to glance in Brady's direction as she hooked her fingertips in the crook of Martin Crabtree's arm and accompanied him across the street. Nevertheless, she sensed the carpenter's gaze on their backs. Perhaps even his displeasure, though she could find no reasonable explanation for that. After all, this making friends was getting more enjoyable by the hour.

"Millie tells me you've earned your law degree from Capital City and apprenticed with a barrister there," Diana began, her tone casual.

"Quite true." Beneath his crisp bowler, her sandy-haired companion's chin rose a notch.

"Then what brings you back to Hickory Corners? I should think you'd prefer living someplace where your education might be put to better use."

Martin nodded and gazed down at her. "You speak my own mind. Mother, however, had some legal matters that required my assistance, so I'm here to take care of them. But I also have a few personal decisions to make. Regarding my future." His intense gaze lingered a touch overlong.

"I see." Purposely diverting her attention to the dress shop as they went by, Diana observed the new ensemble displayed in the window. She also noticed the lady who owned the business eyeing them. . .along with a few other individuals on Main Street. No doubt by tomorrow news of this innocent stroll would be broadcast from one end of town to the other, yet she could see no cause for worry.

The spring breeze gathered a little more strength in the open expanse near the Ohio, stirring the trees and ruffling the long grasses. As she and Martin slowly walked along the bank overlooking the fast-moving river, a playful draft tugged at her bonnet's brim, and she reached up to hold her hat in place until the gust passed.

A large side-wheeler from her father's line sat at anchor, the flawless white paint stark against the blues of sky and water. The vessel Elsa had mentioned, no doubt. It appeared deserted, and Diana imagined the crew partaking of the delicious supper at the hotel. She couldn't help feeling a twinge of disappointment that she wouldn't be setting sail with them as she had so many times before.

"Do you ever give thought to leaving this hamlet?" Martin asked. "Making a life in some big city?"

"Yes, I do, actually," she confessed in all honesty. "After spending most of my life in Philadelphia and Boston, there are many things I miss, being here."

A satisfied smile spread across his patrician face. "Doesn't that strike you as fortuitous? Both of us preferring the advantages of civilization to the rustic style of life in this tiny town?"

"It is rather funny, isn't it?" Diana mulled over the amazing coincidence that in this rural hamlet, of all places, was a handsome bachelor who shared some of the same deep longings as she did. To think she expected never to meet a young man with whom she had anything in common as long as she lived here.

"Well, perhaps we can do something about that. . .you and I."

Meeting Martin's speculative gaze, a niggle of uncertainty crept up Diana's spine, bringing a shiver. "I–I'm a little cold just now. Perhaps we should go back."

"As you wish." He turned and guided her toward the homeward route.

Chancing an oblique glance at her companion, Diana detected a hint of smugness in his expression. The same one she'd seen at church. It had made her a little nervous then, and still did, even though she had no idea why.

For some reason, she had misgivings about rushing into a relationship with Widow Crabtree's pride and joy. Friendship was one thing, but perhaps her son's expectations exceeded those bounds.

Diana couldn't help feeling it was simply too soon to encourage him—or anyone else—along that line. Not that there *was* anyone else to encourage.

Yet a certain lopsided smile drifted across her memory, one as playful as the spring breeze itself, and the recollection of the twinkling dark blue eyes that went with it warmed her like summer sunshine.

Chapter 6

When Diana returned home from her stroll with Martin Crabtree, a sweeping glance alongside the house revealed no sign of Brady. An unexpected wave of disappointment coursed through her. Could he have discerned and repaired the roof problem in just the short time she'd been gone? Even as she chided herself for feeling let down, her companion's voice derailed her train of thought.

"I'm so pleased you accompanied me, Diana." Coming to a halt at her porch steps, Martin removed his bowler, took her hand, and gave a slight bow. "No doubt I was the envy of all the locals, keeping company with the most beautiful belle in town." The slanting rays of late afternoon sunshine glistened over golden highlights in his hair, lending added richness to his clear complexion.

Martin certainly knew how to charm a lady. A flush rose over Diana's cheeks. She'd always wondered how it would feel when a young man sought her company. The fact that the individual was as learned and sophisticated as he, made it even more enjoyable than she imagined. "Why, thank you, Martin. I had a lovely time. Thank you for inviting me."

"I'll be staying at Mother's awhile longer before I leave

Hickory Corners again. Perhaps we might go for a stroll another time." His fair brows acquired a hopeful arch.

Diana saw no reason to discourage him. "I would like that."

His eyes probed hers, and he gave a satisfied nod. "Then I shall call again. Perhaps we might discuss a decision I'm facing. For now, I bid you good day."

"And to you, Martin. Thank you for the pleasant time." She watched him straighten to his full height and turn on his heel. A tip of the head, and he replaced his hat and strode away, his bearing cheerful and confident. Any woman's dream.

Smiling after him, Diana gathered her skirts and started up the steps, but her wayward gaze darted alongside the house once more. When Brady didn't materialize after all, her smile wilted.

Diana dawdled over supper, savoring Millie's succulent roast chicken and light, flaky biscuits. She'd already related the day's happenings to the older woman, including the sewing session and the walk with her neighbor. Odd, how the housekeeper made so few comments about Martin during the discourse. Diana tried not to make too much of that. She had other things on her mind, like mustering nerve to bring up a different subject.

Millie stood and took her own plate to the sideboard before returning with the teapot to refill their cups. "Methinks the sewing group will be the high point of your week now. That's a real answer to prayer." She set the pot on a trivet on the table and reclaimed her chair.

"You pray about such trivial matters?" Astonished, Diana forked a slice of chicken breast to her mouth.

The housekeeper smiled gently. "Believe me, my dear, nothing that affects His children's dear ones is a trivial matter to the Lord. He's concerned about every part of our lives."

To Diana, the notion sounded far-fetched, yet it struck a tender note in her heart. Did God truly care so much about her? Did He even remember her? Years ago, she'd heard the accounts of various Bible heroes and martyrs of the faith. Once as a child she'd even prayed and asked Jesus to come into her heart and be her Savior. But on her own at boarding schools, those sweet childhood memories faded, gradually losing importance. Most of her teachers had more modern ideals, the sophisticated sort that fit well with city life.

Here in the country, however, surrounded by His handiwork, a person perceived the Creator in a whole different way. Perhaps the time had come to revive some of her former beliefs. Surely her father had a Bible amid all those leather-covered books in his library. She had plenty of time now to read and get reacquainted with the once familiar contents.

Millie's voice cut across her musings. "Edna and I prayed often for you, especially when we knew you'd be coming back for good. We wanted you to fit in and feel at home."

"I'm hoping not to miss a single sewing session," Diana assured her. "There's so much to learn—about stitching and my new friends." Pausing in thought, she drew her lips inward momentarily, then released them. "Millie?"

"Hm?" Squinty blue eyes blinked, then focused on her.

"What has Mrs. Crabtree got against Brady Forbes?"

The housekeeper gave a wry huff. "That old biddy? There's hardly a person in town she doesn't have something against, except for that *faultless* son of hers, of course. Seems her lot in life to aggravate decent folks. She's like a toothache. Some of us hope Martin will yank her off to Capital City for good, to live with him."

Hoping the attractive young man wouldn't be too hasty along those lines, Diana squelched a smile. His sudden interest in her was quite intriguing. "But why would she consider Brady riffraff?"

"She said that?" Stray hairs from the older woman's coronet of braids stirred as she slowly shook her head. "There's not a finer young man in town, in my opinion—and that includes her beloved Martin."

Recalling how polite and attentive Widow Crabtree's son had been on their walk earlier, the end of Millie's statement baffled Diana. He'd been the perfect gentleman. How could one ask for more? She took another sip of tea.

"Young Brady did have a bit of a questionable past, and that's the truth," the housekeeper went on. "After his folks died, he got mixed up with some bad company in Cincinnati. Older ruffian troublemakers who were headed for jail and finally ended up there."

Diana raised her eyebrows, and her lips parted in surprise. With an understanding nod, Millie continued. "Seems the judge at the trial took Brady's youth into consideration and decided discipline and guidance could still salvage him. That's how he came to live with his aunt and uncle. Been here a good four or five years already, and is turning out fine as can be, if you ask an old lady like me. Edna and Noah just love him to death. He'll do anything for them—and for anybody else who needs help. He's more than proved himself."

"I'm. . .astounded," Diana said, though the word scarcely expressed her shock. "I have to admit, he does strike me as having a few rough edges." *He's not half as polished as Martin,* she nearly added. At twenty-four, three years older than Brady, her neighbor's attributes made her opinion of him take a decided turn in his favor.

"Well, once you get to know him better you'll see those as the facets that reflect God's love and grace the brightest." Millie's cheeks plumped into a smile. "He's quite the wit too, in case you haven't noticed. He has a unique gift. He can imitate anybody around town. Plays each one to the hilt too. You should see him portray old Olivia herself!" The housekeeper laughed until she had to dab at tears with her apron.

"He imitates everyone?"

"Oh, yes. He makes merciless sport of all the girls in the sewing group. But they're all so used to it, they pay him no mind."

Diana frowned. Elsa had alluded to the same thing. Could it be that Brady hadn't set out purposely to embarrass her at all last summer? She'd arrived at the gathering awhile after it was under way, only to walk in on his portrayal of her. In retrospect, it had been rather comical too. She shouldn't have stomped off in a dither.

Still, she couldn't ignore how much more at ease she felt in Martin's presence. He seemed so worldly-wise and treated her like a real lady.

Brady, on the other hand, had a teasing way about him which made her feel self-conscious and tongue-tied. Much less sure of herself. Thoughts of him were as hard to shake as a summer cold.

Diana stifled a smile. Scarcely a week ago she'd expected she'd languish away in this little hamlet with no hope of attention from any respectable bachelors, and already she found herself comparing two completely opposite men. . .both of whom fascinated her in entirely different ways. The summer was turning out far more interesting than she ever imagined. Who knew what lay ahead?

"That's it, Dear Heart. I can't eat another bite." Uncle Noah leaned back in his chair and patted the vest straining over his slight frame.

Aunt Edna feigned indignation as she rose to clear the table. "Not even a slice of your birthday cake?"

"It's your favorite," Brady added, enjoying the interplay between the two. He truly admired their loving relationship —as constant in the privacy of the house as it was at church. One day he hoped to emulate the godly example they'd set for him. . .assuming he ever found a woman with whom he'd consider a lifetime commitment. Presently that hope seemed quite slim. Or had, until recently.

"Well," the white-haired minister drawled, "mayhap a smidgen wouldn't hurt. Never could resist that chocolate cake of yours."

"I figured that's what you'd say." With a conspiratorial wink at Brady, she carted the remaining food to the kitchen.

He sprang to his feet, stacking soiled plates and gathering utensils. From the day he finally rid himself of the chip on his shoulder, he'd made a habit of helping out in as many ways as possible. Another of their examples he liked to follow.

"I hear you've taken on another sideline of late," Uncle Noah said, blue eyes twinkling when Brady and his aunt returned with the dessert. "Roofing, is it?"

"Just another of my many talents," he quipped, accepting the slice of cake passed his way. "Miz Sanderson's roof had a leak she needed fixed."

"I'm surprised you found the time." The older man sampled his own chunk of the rich sweet. "Seems Nate's been working you night and day for awhile now."

Brady swapped furtive glances with his aunt, but maintained a relaxed expression as he contemplated the newly finished desk now gracing the minister's study. "The project's done now, Uncle Noah. I'll take you to see it as soon as you are through."

"Can't say as I'm up to hoofing down the street just now," he returned with a pained look. "Not after tramping about the countryside calling on sick folks all day. My rheumatism's kicking up again. Must be a storm on the way."

"It's not at the shop," Brady assured him. "Just next door."

"Next door? At the church?"

"Yes, so hurry and finish," Aunt Edna coaxed, her own pride on the verge of popping her apron strings. "You've really got to see this."

He looked from one to the other and back. "With both of you set on getting me over there, I'm getting a mite curious. Remember, though, it takes a lot to surprise a man my age." Taking a last gulp of coffee, he brushed crumbs from his hands and stood. "Lead the way."

Shortly thereafter, standing before the gleaming example of Brady's finest workmanship, the normally eloquent man stood speechless for the first time in his life. "I. . .don't know what to say." He blinked wetness from his eyes, then grabbed Brady in a back-thumping hug, while his wife stood on the sidelines, mopping tears with her apron.

It took Brady a few seconds to speak past the lump in his own throat. "Happy birthday, Uncle Noah. This is only a fraction of what you deserve. I owe you and Aunt Edna my life. Likely it'll take that long to repay you both."

The older man held him at arm's length and shook his head. "Love doesn't charge for its services, Lad. Your aunt and I couldn't be more proud of what you've become since allowing God to direct your life. And as sure as this magnificent desk will outlast the three of us put together, I know He has some wonderful plans for you ahead. You're going to make some fortunate young woman a good husband one day soon."

"A good husband, indeed," Aunt Edna echoed. Moving closer, a secret smile on her guileless face, she hugged the two of them.

The older woman emitted faint scents of lavender and roses, and Brady inhaled deeply. His aunt kept sachets of dried flowers in her armoire. . .lacy, frippery things made by Diana Montclair. Now that he thought about it, those enticingly feminine fragrances seemed to fill up a room, whenever Diana was present.

He liked them. A whole lot. In fact, a guy could get used to such fripperies, if he set his mind to it.

Even as he smiled inwardly, Brady felt his spirit plummet like a broken kite. The problem was what a gal like her would have to give up, if she chose a guy with so little to his name. He ought to back off and let that foppish Martin have her.

Diana set the Bible on the bedside table and lay back on her pillow. The Psalms were pleasant enough reading, but her active mind kept drifting to the events of the day. Had it been only this afternoon Brady Forbes had been right here in her bedroom? His presence had so filled the air around them, it left very little air for breathing. She could still see the mischievous sparkle in those blue eyes, still envision his playful grin.

Considering the poor start he'd had in life, did any of the rough character of his youth remain hidden to surface again? Was that the mysterious quality about him which she found so disconcerting? So. . .utterly fascinating?

Diana shifted to a more comfortable position, propping an arm beneath her head. Better to direct her thoughts toward a safer, more predictable route. Martin Crabtree. Now there was a fine example of manhood, a person of means and culture, who would make something of himself. Diana had seen him only a few times in her life, yet she could never imagine Martin doing anything one might find scandalous. She chuckled. More than likely, he'd be so predictable and practical he'd be an absolute bore.

What had gotten into her anyway, with so much of her time suddenly claimed by thoughts of those two bachelors? Her teachers affirmed that the domestic skills she'd learned at school would enable her to make someone a worthy bride, but Diana didn't really know if that was what she wanted for her life. There had to be more to one's existence than courtship and marriage and raising babies. Many intellectuals alleged that women would eventually enter fields once forbidden, fields other than domestic ventures and teaching. Soon there would be women doctors, women lawyers, and who knew what else? With all her father's resources behind her, Diana knew she could get the required training for whatever she wanted. All she had to do was figure out what that was.

But in the meantime. . .

A smile tickled the edges of her lips.

Chapter 7

"There. Good as new, almost." Avoiding Diana's eyes, Brady climbed down the ladder in her bedroom, a white-tipped paintbrush still in his hand.

Diana watched him from the padded rocking chair where she'd sat embroidering, a few feet away, aware that her presence made him uncomfortable. Tiny dots of white speckled the strands of his dark brown hair and the bridge of his nose, adding even more appeal to his square-jawed face. He made quite a sight in that faded cambric shirt and trim-fitting trousers. Despite herself, she couldn't help gawking at him or enjoying it. The very thought warmed her cheeks. "You do excellent work, Brady. Thank you."

With nothing but a lackluster grin, he bent over and began rolling up the oilcloth protecting the floor beneath the work area. "I'd keep the windows open the rest of the day so the fumes don't give you a headache."

Diana already had a headache, and it had nothing to do with the smell of new paint. Aside from a few wordless glances in her direction while he worked, Brady had studiously ignored her since her first stroll with Martin Crabtree last week. He hadn't even dropped in on the sewing circle for baked treats.

The uncharacteristic silence bewildered her. She missed his easy smile, his funny remarks. More than that, she missed the new friend she thought she'd found in him. Had someone told him to mind his place around her? Had it been Martin?

While Brady had been occupied covering the water stain on her ceiling, she'd tried to picture Martin doing something enterprising like repairing a leaky roof or repainting a ceiling. But the widow's son had hands even whiter and softer than Diana's. Most likely if the young attorney were to be faced with such needs around the home, he'd have to hire the work done for him, as her father did.

That had been her own mind set, until coming home to stay. How different things were here. Everyone appeared self-reliant and competent enough to handle most tasks. Not only would folks in town not pay someone to do common repairs, they would help each other out, when possible, with no charge for the service. *Being neighborly,* they called it, a term Diana appreciated more each day.

The roll of oilcloth under his arm, paint supplies in hand, Brady gave a tight-lipped smile on his way to the hall. "Stay dry, Diana."

"You too. Don't fall off any ladders." But her attempt at levity drew no response whatever. "Thank you," she repeated lamely as he clomped downstairs.

Diana gave a resigned sigh and put down the bookmark she was embroidering for Elsa, the last of three she'd made to surprise her sewing circle partners. She couldn't let it pass, this —whatever it was—between her and Brady. She had to learn what was amiss.

She found the kitchen deserted on her way through, but the scent of Millie's scones lingered. No doubt the housekeeper had taken some over to Charlotte Warner. Though the widow's sprained ankle had healed well enough, she'd caught a chill a few nights past and was abed once again.

Exiting the house through the kitchen, Diana spied Brady in the backyard, putting away the paint things. His none too quiet movements and the closing of the squeaky shed door masked the sound of her footsteps as she approached. Just what she'd hoped, since she hadn't an inkling what to say.

Brady secured the latch and turned. Indigo eyes focused on her, and his dark brows flared high. "Did I forget something upstairs?"

Why did he seem so much taller up close? Diana swallowed. She shook her head.

A frown etched a pair of grooves above his nose. "Then what is it?"

"That's what I've been wondering." Feigning bravado to conceal her quivering insides, she schooled her expression to remain calm.

With a grimace, Brady ran spattered fingers through his hair. "Look, Diana, I'm kinda busy right now. If there's something you need me to do, spit it out. Otherwise, I gotta get back to work." He shot a sidelong glance toward the Crabtrees' house. "Besides, you wouldn't want to keep His Loftiness waiting. It's probably time for your little stroll."

Her jaw gaped. "You've been keeping tabs on me?" she asked incredulously.

The tips of Brady's ears reddened. With an offhanded shrug, he shifted his stance. "Well, it's not exactly a secret, you know. The whole town watches the two of you strolling the riverbanks together every day."

"We are not together every day." But even as she defended

herself, Diana fought to temper the offense caused by his remark. She placed her hands on her hips. "And I've only gone walking with Martin twice. . .not that it's any of your concern."

He raised a hand in concession. "Forgive me. You're right. It's none of my business who you spend time with. Now, if you'll excuse me, Miss Montclair, I have to get back to the shop. Some of us common folk must work for our living."

Diana elevated her chin and arched an eyebrow. "Well, far be it from me to detain you," she flung back in her haughtiest tone. "I've neglected my needlework too long as it is. I. . .I just—" Her shoulders sagged, and she softened her voice. "I just missed the friendship I thought we shared. Excuse me." Snatching her skirts in both hands, she bolted for the house before completely humiliating herself by bursting into tears in front of him.

Inside, she sagged against the door. What made her think she needed Brady Forbes anyway? Widow Crabtree was probably right. If Diana ever wanted to be accepted in her parents' world, she'd be wiser to cultivate a relationship with a man they'd approve.

"My, but you're quiet today, Diana," Mrs. Tidewell remarked the next afternoon. Reading silently in the rocking chair, she closed the Bible, but kept a finger in place.

"Most likely has her head in the clouds," Elsa said on a teasing note. "Strolls along the river, drinking in the beauties of approaching summer. . .I remember when I first fell in love." A dreamy smile curved her lips.

Diana stopped stitching. The whole town *did* know of her walks with Martin. But just what was everyone saying about the two of them? "I assure you, I am not in love," she insisted.

Directly across from her, Samantha regarded her but did not speak as she exchanged significant glances with her cousin Betsy. It never ceased to puzzle Diana the way those two always had their heads together. . .especially whenever Martin Crabtree's name cropped up in conversation. Frowning inwardly, she worked harder at her stitches.

She'd spoken the truth about not being in love. Nevertheless, Martin gave the distinct impression he was concocting some sort of scheme. He'd dropped hints on their last walk, regarding the possibility of a future for the two of them. As tempting as the idea appeared on the surface, Diana wasn't completely convinced she wanted to deepen their relationship. She certainly didn't know the man well enough to consider marriage, if that's what he had in mind. She hadn't even written to her parents to let them know she was interested in anyone. Likely they'd be relieved if she were no longer their responsibility.

On the other hand, if she did marry Martin, it would effectively get her out of Hickory Corners, back to civilization. Away from disturbing thoughts of Brady Forbes. Wasn't that what she'd been hoping for?

Gradually, from the background, Mrs. Tidewell's voice overpowered Diana's contemplations. ". . .So I thought I'd pass on some verses I've been reading about wisdom," she said, opening her old Bible once again. "In the fourth chapter of Proverbs, Solomon refers to wisdom as the 'principal thing.' I'll begin at the first verse."

Listening to the Biblical admonishment to seek after wisdom, Diana became even more perplexed. How could one be sure if a particular choice would be considered wise? She remembered that Millie often prayed about things. Perhaps therein lay the secret. Tonight at bedtime, Diana would ask God for wisdom. Somehow even the thought itself comforted her, and her spirit breathed a wordless petition on the spot.

After the gathering, Elsa hurried away to tend her son, and Betsy drove off in her wagon. Diana and Samantha took a turn helping Mrs. Tidewell restore order to the parsonage. Exiting when they'd finished, Samantha started toward the mercantile, but halted abruptly and turned back. "Diana? Wait."

Diana stopped until the fair-haired girl came to join her. "What is it?"

Samantha released a troubled breath. "I wasn't going to say anything. Betsy says you'll think I'm prying into your personal affairs. But I wouldn't be your friend if I didn't tell you."

"Tell me what?"

"About Martin."

Diana stiffened. Samantha had once kept company with the young attorney herself. But she was married now. Was she actually *jealous* that Martin was lavishing attention on someone else?

"I got a letter from Clara a few days ago," Samantha said, her words tumbling out of her like water over a fall. "You remember her, don't you? Clara Bucey? She used to be part of the sewing circle, only she left Hickory Corners to visit some out-of-state relatives. Now she's decided to stay and live in New York."

"Yes," Diana said, trying to make some sense out of the one-sided conversation.

Samantha caught her lower lip in her teeth as if struggling over how to go on. "Well, it seems Martin's going to relocate in New York City, did you know that?"

"I thought his practice was in Capital City."

"Yes, it is. Or was. He's gotten a new position, in a rather prestigious law firm back East. That's why he's here. To settle his affairs, sell his mother's house, and pack up. He'll be taking her along, of course."

Diana shook her head. "I don't understand. He's mentioned nothing of that to me. Nothing at all. Well, he did hint of some change coming up, and how I might be a part of it. . . ."

"Don't trust him, Diana. He's a real bounder. He gives all the girls in town the eye when you're not around. He's always been like that. Take it from someone who knows."

"But. . .but he seems the perfect gentleman when he's with me," Diana insisted. "So sincere."

Samantha grimaced. "Martin Crabtree hasn't a sincere bone in his body. I might as well tell you the rest. Clara says he'll be working for her uncle. . .and that one of the stipulations for securing that lofty position is marriage to her spinster cousin."

"So, I'm what one might call a 'last fling,' " Diana said in a flat tone.

"More like a way out, I'd venture to say. He's told Clara's uncle he's practically engaged to someone 'back home.' "

"Me."

Samantha nodded. "But believe me, the only person Martin loves is himself. He's positive all women find him irresistible, so he uses that. He always has. I just thought you needed to be told, in case. . ." She bit her lip again, letting the unfinished thought dangle.

Searching her friend's eyes, Diana sensed she'd spoken

from her heart. There was no reason not to trust her. Stepping nearer, she gave Samantha a hug. "Thank you. I appreciate your telling me that. I know it couldn't have been easy."

"I just couldn't bear having him hurt one more of my friends," she returned, blinking against gathering tears.

Diana couldn't speak. She smiled instead, and with a nod, turned and walked home.

To her dismay, her handsome neighbor waited on the porch. Diana's stomach lurched.

"Ah," he said smoothly. "The fair mistress of the house returns at last. Would you care to come strolling? I've something of import to ask you."

Forcing a smile, Diana effected her most refined posture. "Thank you, no, Martin. I'm afraid I've promised not to see you again."

His features fell flat. "Promised whom?"

"Why, Brady Forbes, of course," she blurted, then decided a fabrication ought to be elaborate enough to be believed. "Just last evening he asked me to marry him, and I accepted."

"Forbes!" Martin spat. "You can't be serious."

"Oh, but I am." Smiling gaily, she pranced up the steps and took hold of the door handle, opening it as she spoke. "Good day, Martin. All the best in your new life. . .in New York." With that she sailed inside.

Right into a grinning Brady Forbes.

Chapter 8

W ell, now. That was interesting. Very interesting, indeed." His tongue in his cheek, Brady rocked back on his heels, arms crossed over his chest.

Diana wished the floor would open up and swallow her, scarlet face and all. She'd never been more mortified in her life. Surely she could provide a reasonable explanation for her *faux pas*. Gathering her dignity as best she could, she squared her shoulders and raised her chin. "I. . .needed a way to put Martin off for good," she said breathlessly, hating the unnatural high pitch of her voice. "I figured that if I told him you and I. . . ," she fluttered a hand in exaggerated nonchalance, "were *involved*. . ."

"I believe the term was *engaged*," he corrected, his face maddeningly straight.

Diana swallowed the huge lump in her throat and dipped into the fragile remains of her fortitude to continue. "And I surmised that, *friend that you are*, you wouldn't mind if I. . ." Wincing, she shrugged.

"Bandied my good name about?" he finished. "So freely?"

The last of Diana's composure evaporated, and her knees gave out. She sank to the floor in a puddle of skirts and covered her still burning face in her hands. "I must ask you to leave now," she moaned, her fingers muffling her words. "Just let me die in peace."

"No need for you to go to that extreme," Brady said gently. He dropped down beside her. "Anyway, he's gone now. That's what you wanted, right?"

She nodded.

"That makes two of us."

Diana uncovered her face and ventured a look at him. "You're not mad, then?"

"Naw. I've been wanting to punch the stiff out. You saved me the trouble. Nothing worse than sore knuckles when you're trying to build things."

The beginnings of a smile trembled on her lips.

The kitchen door banged shut, and Millie came into the entry hall, her arms full of folded linens. "What's happened? Someone get hurt?"

Diana swapped a conspiratorial grin with Brady. "No one who matters."

The housekeeper eyed him. "You checked that repair in the ceiling?"

"Yes, Ma'am. Seems to be holding fine."

"Well, then, I'll just go put these away." With a curious look encompassing both of them, Millie carted the clean sheets upstairs.

The carpenter stood and offered Diana a hand.

She placed her fingers in his, and he assisted her effortlessly to her feet, sending delicious shivers through her being.

"Guess I'll be off. I need to see Uncle Noah," he said with a wink. "Takes awhile to plan a wedding."

"Oh, you. . ." Diana had the strange feeling she'd never be

able to stay mad at Brady for long.

Partway out the door, he stopped in his tracks and looked over his shoulder, his expression incredibly vulnerable, for once. The sight stopped her heart. "So, does this mean you would consider keeping company with a poor workingman, if he asked?"

"Why doesn't he ask and find out?" she murmured.

"He might. Soon. Very soon." With a lopsided grin, he left.

Suddenly aware of the hall's emptiness, Diana hugged herself and smiled. "I'll be waiting, Brady Forbes."

A gentle autumn breeze rippled across water as blue as Brady's eyes. Diana watched the fascinating movement of his muscles as he rowed the boat to the picturesque grove they'd found some months ago. It had become their favorite picnic spot, a place where they could talk and pray and watch the steamships chugging to and from town. A place where they could share their dreams and their hearts.

She'd found him to be thoughtful and considerate, and she reveled in the respectful way he treated her. He allowed her the freedom to be herself. For that, she loved him more than she'd dreamed possible.

Reaching their haven, Brady veered toward the shallows and beached the rowboat, then, as always, got out and carried Diana to dry ground. "What would you do if I never put you down?" he challenged.

Arms looped about him, she rested her head on his shoulder. "I guess I would just die happy."

Diana felt a chuckle rumble through his chest as he swung her around, then set her on her feet without releasing his hold.

"You'd leave me all alone, huh?"

Her gaze rose to meet his. "No. Never. I couldn't bear being without you."

"Funny, I feel the same way," he said huskily, all levity vanishing from his expression. "I want to be with you all the time. To come home to you at night, take care of you through good times and bad, raise a family with you. Diana. . .would you honor me by becoming my wife?"

"Oh, my sweet Brady." She snuggled closer, trying to quiet her throbbing pulse enough to speak around it.

"I'm willing to wait until your parents can come and check me out," he added.

She gave a small huff and eased away slightly. "By that time, we'd both be old and toothless and doddering about on canes. They've never cared about anything else in my life, why should this be different?"

Disbelief clouded his eyes as Brady stroked gentle fingers through her hair. "They don't know the treasure they've wasted. If God blesses us with a daughter someday, she'll never doubt that her parents love her every bit as much as they love each other." Drawing her close again, he kissed her tenderly.

When the kiss ended, a hopeful light shone in Brady's eyes, and his expression held the vulnerable quality Diana always found endearing. She hesitated only a heartbeat. "My answer is yes, Brady," she whispered. "I was only waiting for you to ask."

His arms tightened around her as he crushed her to himself. . .and even the birds sang out with joy.

Epilogue

O ctober is such a perfect time for a wedding," Elsa said on a sigh. She handed Diana the final gift from the stack of presents surrounding her. "Yours and Brady's was the loveliest Hickory Corners has ever seen."

Samantha and Betsy nodded in agreement

"I'm so glad you were all part of our special day." Diana grinned at the trio of attendants who over the past several months had become her best friends in the world. How lovely they'd looked during the ceremony, in gowns of crushed gold satin, and carrying bouquets of yellow and white roses. Mother and Father sent funds enough to cover the best, plus deeded the house to Diana. . .an excess they assumed would make up for never sparing time in their lives for their only daughter, she surmised. Sadly, they were still off on a tour of Europe.

Diana had long ago accepted their disregard. She sat straighter and looked around at her new family, the one God had given her. . .Millie, the Tidewells, and the threesome from the sewing circle. People who truly cared about her and Brady.

Her fingers toying with the ribbon on the gift Elsa had placed in her lap, she glanced across the room to her new husband. Tall and respectable in his new suit, he chatted with some well-wishers who'd waylaid him at the refreshment table. She dragged her gaze away to finish unwrapping the big present.

Raising a fold of the paper, Diana looked closer at the contents, and her eyes grew misty. "Why, it's the quilt we worked on together!"

"Four Hearts," Samantha supplied. "We each signed our name in a corner. Mrs. T embroidered yours, so you'd always remember this past summer."

"How sweet. This will make the memory even more special. My forever friends. Thank you all so much."

Diana's heart felt full to bursting. The Tidewells had presented the newlyweds with a bank account containing every cent Brady had earned over the years. That, along with the big Montclair house and a housekeeper who doted on them, would give them a much better start in their married life than most people had. But Diana had grown enough to appreciate the value of things more precious than money. She knew now that happiness lay in friends and neighbors all striving to help each other, and in honoring the Lord. That true contentment was found in giving, in sharing.

She and Brady had a lot of love to share. He'd make a good life for her and, hopefully, for the little ones to come. In time, the big house would boast four hearts of its own, possibly more. Its walls would ring with joyful laughter. What more could she ask?

Brady crossed to her side once more and held out his hand. Tugging her gently to her feet, he wrapped his arms around her. "I'm the luckiest guy in the world," he murmured, his warm breath feathering tiny hairs on her neck. "I plan to spend the rest of my life making you glad you chose a poor workingman for your husband."

Diana looked up at the features that had grown so dear, at the dark blue eyes that could see into her soul. "Poor, my dearest Brady, is being surrounded by wealth, without love. Having you and knowing how you feel about me, has given me more riches than I've ever had."

He smiled that heart-stopping smile and lowered his lips to hers with a kiss that fulfilled all her dreams. "Then let's go home, my love."

To Diana, there seemed to be no one else in the room as she placed her hand in her husband's and strolled with him toward the door.

SALLY LAITY

Sally spent the first twenty years of her life in Dallas, Pennsylvania, and calls herself a small-town girl at heart. She and her husband Don have lived in New York, Pennsylvania, Illinois, Alberta (Canada), and now reside in Bakersfield, CA. They are active in a large Baptist church, where Don teaches Sunday school and Sally sings in the choir. They have four children and twelve grandchildren.

Sally always loved to write, and after her children were grown, she took college writing courses and attended Christian writing conferences. She has written both historical and contemporary romances and considers it a joy to know that the Lord can touch other hearts through her stories.

Having successfully written several novels, including a co-authored series for Tyndale, three Barbour novellas, and six **Heartsong Presents** titles, one of this author's favorite things these days is counseling new authors via the Internet.

A Letter to Our Readers

Dear Readers:

In order that we might better contribute to your reading enjoyment, we would appreciate your taking a few minutes to respond to the following questions. When completed, please return to the following: Fiction Editor, Barbour Publishing, Inc., PO Box 719, Uhrichsville, OH 44683.

1. Did you enjoy reading *The Sewing Circle?*
   ❏ Very much. I would like to see more books like this.
   ❏ Moderately—I would have enjoyed it more if _____
   _____
   _____

2. What influenced your decision to purchase this book?
   (Check those that apply.)
   ❏ Cover   ❏ Back cover copy   ❏ Title   ❏ Price
   ❏ Friends   ❏ Publicity   ❏ Other

3. Which story was your favorite?
   ❏ *Tumbling Blocks*   ❏ *Jacob's Ladder*
   ❏ *Old Maid's Choice*   ❏ *Four Hearts*

4. Please check your age range:
   ❏ Under 18   ❏ 18–24   ❏ 25–34
   ❏ 35–45   ❏ 46–55   ❏ Over 55

5. How many hours per week do you read? _____

Name _____

Occupation _____

Address _____

City _____ State _____ ZIP _____

E-mail _____